the
OATH OF THE
VAYUPUTRAS

Also by Amish

The Immortals of Meluha
The Secret of the Nagas

THE
OATH OF THE
VAYUPUTRAS

AMISH

Jo Fletcher
BOOKS

First published by Westland Ltd. 2013
First published in Great Britain in 2014 by

Jo Fletcher Books
an imprint of Quercus
55 Baker Street
7th Floor, South Block
London
W1U 8EW

Cover Design by Rashmi Pusalkar.
Photo of Lord Shiva by Chandan Kowli
Artwork within text by Nicola Budd

A CIP catalogue record for this book is available
from the British Library

ISBN 978 1 78087 408 1 (PBO)
ISBN 978 1 78087 410 4 (EBOOK)

10 9 8 7 6 5 4 3 2 1

Typeset by Ellipsis Digital Limited, Glasgow

Printed and bound in Great Britain by
Clays Ltd, St Ives plc

To the late Dr Manoj Vyas, my father-in-law.

Great men never die.

They live on in the hearts of their followers.

Har Har Mahadev

All of us are Mahadevs, all of us are Gods.
For His most magnificent temple, finest mosque
and greatest church exist within our souls.

The Shiva Trilogy

Shiva! The Mahadev. The God of Gods. Destroyer of Evil. Passionate lover. Fierce warrior. Consummate dancer. Charismatic leader. All-powerful, yet incorruptible. Quick of wit – and of temper.

No foreigner who came to India – be they conqueror, merchant, scholar, ruler, traveller – believed that such a great man could ever have existed in reality. They assumed he must have been a mythical god, a fantasy conjured within the realms of human imagination. And over time, sadly, this belief became our received wisdom.

But what if we're wrong? What if Lord Shiva wasn't simply a figment of a rich imagination but a person of flesh and blood like you and me? A man who rose to become godlike as a result of his *karma*. That is the premise of *The Shiva Trilogy*, which attempts to interpret the rich mythological heritage of ancient India, blending fiction with historical fact.

The journey of this extraordinary hero began in *The Immortals of Meluha* and continued in *The Secret of the Nagas*. It will conclude in the book you are holding in your hands: *The Oath of the Vayuputras*.

This fictional series is a tribute to my God; I found Him after spending many years in the wilderness of atheism. I hope you find your God as well. It doesn't matter in what form we find Him, so long as we find Him eventually. Whether He comes to us as Shiva, or Vishnu, or Shakti Maa, or Allah, or Jesus Christ, or Buddha or any other of His myriad forms, He wants to help us. Let us allow Him to do so.

Yadyatkarma karomi tattadakhilam shambho tavaaraadhanam.
My Lord Shambo, My Lord Shiva,
every act of mine is a prayer in Your honour.

CONTENTS

CHAPTER 1

The Return of a Friend

Blood dribbled into the water, and Shiva watched the unhurried ripples distort his reflection as they expanded slowly to the edges of the cistern. He dipped his hands in and splashed water on his face, washing off the blood and gore. Recently appointed Chief of the Gunas, he was in a mountain village far from the comforts of Mansarovar Lake. It had taken his tribe three weeks to get there despite the punishing pace he'd set. The frigid water was bone-chilling, but Shiva didn't even notice — not because of the heat emanating from the Pakrati huts behind him being gutted by gigantic flames but because of the fire that burned within him.

Shiva wiped his eyes and stared at his reflection in the water. Raw fury gripped him. Yakhya, the Pakrati chieftain, had escaped. Still recovering from the exhaustion of combat, he inhaled and exhaled slowly, trying to steady his breathing.

He thought he saw his Uncle Manobhu's bloodied body in the water and thrust his hand beneath the surface with a startled cry. 'Uncle!'

The mirage vanished. Shiva squeezed his eyes shut.

The macabre moment when he found his uncle's body replayed in his mind. Manobhu had gone to discuss a peace treaty with Yakhya, hoping the Pakratis and Gunas could end their incessant warmongering. When he didn't return at the appointed time, Shiva sent out a search party. Manobhu's mutilated body, together with those of his bodyguards, was found next to a goat trail on the way to the Pakrati village.

A message had been written in blood on a rock next to where Manobhu had breathed his last: Shiva. Forgive them. Forget them. Your only true enemy is Evil.

All his uncle had wanted was peace, and this was how they'd repaid him.

'*Where's Yakhya?*' *Bhadra's angry voice broke Shiva's chain of thoughts and he turned. Fierce Bhadra, bloodied sword in hand, had led twenty Guna guards in pursuit of the fleeing Pakratis and now some thirty dead bodies lay strewn across the clearing, brutally hacked to death by the enraged Gunas seeking vengeance for their former chief's murder. Five Pakrati men knelt on the ground, bound together by a single length of rope looped around their wrists and ankles; both ends had been hammered into the ground. The entire Pakrati village was going up in flames and, a little way off, another contingent of Guna warriors was guarding the shackled Pakrati women and children. The Gunas never killed or hurt women and children.* Never.

'*Where's Yakhya?*' *repeated Bhadra, pointing his sword menacingly at a Pakrati.*

'*We don't know,*' *the Pakrati answered.* '*I swear, we don't know.*'

Bhadra dug his sword-point into the man's chest, drawing blood.

'Answer and you shall have mercy. All we want is Yakhya. He will pay for killing Manobhu.'

'We didn't kill Manobhu — I swear on all the mountain gods, we didn't kill him.'

Bhadra kicked the Pakrati hard. 'Don't lie to me, you stinking arse-hole of a yak!'

Shiva turned away and scanned the forest beyond the clearing. He closed his eyes. He could still hear his Uncle Manobhu's words echoing in his ears: 'Anger is your enemy. Control it! Control it!'

He took more deep breaths as he tried to slow down his furiously pounding heart.

'If you kill us, Yakhya will come back and kill all of you,' shouted the Pakrati at one end of the rope line. 'You will never know peace — and we shall have the final vengeance!'

'Shut up, Kayna,' hissed another Pakrati. Turning to Bhadra, he said, 'Release us. We had nothing to do with the death of your chief.'

Undeterred — or perhaps unhinged by fear — Kayna shouted, 'Shiva!'

Shiva turned.

'You should be ashamed to call Manobhu your uncle,' Kayna taunted.

The other captive Pakratis tried to shut him up, but Kayna was beyond caring. His intense loathing for the Gunas had overwhelmed any instinct for self-preservation. 'Manobhu was a coward,' he spat. 'He bleated like a goat while we shoved his intestines and his peace treaty down his throat!'

Shiva's eyes widened as the rage he'd been trying to control finally burst forth. Screaming at the top of his lungs, he drew his sword and charged. Without breaking step, he swung viciously as he neared the line

of Pakratis and beheaded Kayna with one mighty blow. The severed head
thumped into the Pakrati beside him, then bounced across the clearing.

'Shiva!' Bhadra cried, aghast. They needed the Pakratis alive if they
were to find Yakhya, but Bhadra was too disciplined a tribesman to state
the obvious to his chief.

Besides, at that moment, Shiva didn't care. He spun smoothly,
swinging his sword again and again, decapitating the next Pakrati in line,
and the next, until, in a matter of moments, five headless Pakrati bodies
lay in the mud, their dying hearts still pumping blood from their gaping
necks to pool around their bodies until they were lying in a lake of blood.

Shiva breathed heavily as he stared at the dead, his uncle's voice still
ringing loudly in his head; 'Anger is your enemy. Control it! Control it!'

— 𓏤 𓂀 𓍯𓍯𓎡 𓂝 ✺ —

'I have been waiting for you, my friend,' said the teacher. He
was smiling, though his eyes were moist with welling tears. 'I
told you I'd go anywhere for you — even into *Patallok* itself, if
it would help you.'

Shiva had replayed these words in his mind a thousand times
since they had first been uttered by the man who stood before
him, but until this moment he'd never fully understood the
reference to 'the land of the demons'. Now everything fell
into place.

The man was clean-shaven except for a pencil-thin moustache. His broad shoulders and well-defined muscles suggested
he was getting regular exercise. A *janau*, the holy thread declaring
his Brahmin identity, was loosely draped across his shoulder

and chest. His head remained shaven, but the tuft of hair at the back of his skull looked longer and more neatly dressed than Shiva remembered. The deep-set eyes were filled with the same serenity that had drawn Shiva to him in the first place. It was truly his long-lost friend, his comrade-in-arms: his brother.

'Brahaspati!'

'You took your time finding me,' said Brahaspati as he stepped close and embraced Shiva. 'I've been waiting for you.'

Shiva hesitated for a moment before allowing his emotions to take over and joyously embracing Brahaspati, but as he regained his composure, doubts began to creep into his mind.

Brahaspati created the illusion of his death. He allied with the Nagas. He destroyed his life's purpose, the great Mount Mandar. He was the Suryavanshi mole!

My brother lied to me!

Shiva stepped back silently and felt Sati's hand on his shoulder, offering silent commiseration.

Brahaspati turned to his students. 'Children, could you please excuse us?'

The students immediately rose and filed out, leaving Shiva and Brahaspati in the classroom, with Shiva's wife, Sati, his son, Ganesh, and his sister-in-law, Kali.

Brahaspati stared at his friend, waiting for the questions he knew were coming. He could see the hurt and anger in Shiva's eyes.

'Why?' Shiva asked at last.

'I thought I'd spare you the dreadful personal fate that is the

Mahadevs' inheritance. One cannot fight Evil without its claws leaving terrible scars upon one's soul, and I wanted to protect you. I tried to do your task for you.'

Shiva's eyes narrowed. 'Were you fighting Evil all by yourself? For more than five years?'

'Evil is patient,' said Brahaspati. 'It creeps up slowly. It doesn't hide but confronts you in broad daylight. It gives decades of warnings – centuries sometimes. Time is never the problem when you battle Evil; the problem is having the will to fight it.'

'You say you've been waiting for me, but you hid every last trace of yourself. Why?'

'I've always trusted you, Shiva,' said Brahaspati, 'but I couldn't trust all those who were around you. They'd have prevented me from accomplishing my mission – they might even have assassinated me had they discovered my plans. My mission, I admit, prevailed over my love for you. I couldn't meet you safely until you had parted ways with them.'

'That's a lie: you're only meeting with me now because you *need* me – because you now know you can't accomplish your mission by yourself.'

Brahaspati smiled wanly. 'It was never meant to be *my* mission, great Neelkanth. It was always yours.'

Shiva stared at Brahaspati, his face expressionless.

'You're partially right,' said Brahaspati after a few moments of awkward silence. 'It's true that I wanted to meet you – no, I *needed* to meet you – now because I've failed. The coin of Good and Evil is flipping over and India needs the Neelkanth. It *needs* you, Shiva. Without you, Evil will destroy this beautiful land of ours.'

Shiva, his face still impassive, asked, 'The coin is flipping over, you say?'

Brahaspati nodded.

Shiva remembered Lord Manu's words: *Good and Evil are two sides of the same coin* and his eyes widened. *The key question isn't, 'What is Evil?' The key question is, 'When does Good become Evil? When does the coin flip?'*

Brahaspati watched Shiva keenly. Lord Manu's rules were explicit: he couldn't suggest anything. The Mahadev had to discover the truth and decide for himself whether he would act – or not.

Shiva inhaled deeply and ran his hand over his blue throat, which still felt intolerably cold. It looked as if his journey would have to end where it had begun.

What is the greatest Good – the Good that created this age? thought Shiva. *The answer's obvious. And exactly the same thing became the greatest Evil when its power began to disturb the balance.*

'Tell me why this happened,' he said.

But Brahaspati remained silent, waiting. The question had to be more specific.

'Tell me why you think the *Somras* has tipped over from being the greatest Good to the greatest Evil.'

Parvateshwar and Bhagirath were busy examining the wreckage. Shiva had asked the Meluhan general and the Ayodhyan prince to determine who had sent the men to attack their convoy on the way to Panchavati. A hundred soldiers remained with them, while the rest of Shiva's convoy had carried on to Panchavati.

Parvateshwar glanced at Bhagirath, then returned his attention to the wooden planks lying on the ground before him. Slowly but surely his worst fears were coming true. He glanced at the Suryavanshi soldiers and was relieved to see them standing at a respectful distance, as instructed. It was best if they didn't hear what Parvateshwar was about to say. The rivets on the planks were clearly Meluhan.

'I hope Lord Ram has mercy on your soul, Emperor Daksha.' He sighed.

Bhagirath frowned at Parvateshwar. 'What have you learned?'

Parvateshwar's angry eyes met Bhagirath's. 'Meluha has been betrayed, its fair name tarnished forever – tarnished by the very one sworn to protect it.' He swallowed, and then finished, 'These ships were sent by Emperor Daksha.'

Bhagirath's eyes widened with disbelief. 'What—? Why do you say that?'

'These rivets are Meluhan. These ships were built in my land.'

Bhagirath looked at the planks again. He'd noticed something completely different; he was stunned by the general's statement. 'Parvateshwar, look at the wood, at the casing around the edges.'

Parvateshwar frowned: the casing was indeed of an unfamiliar design, now that he looked more closely.

'It improves waterproofing in the joints,' said Bhagirath. 'This technology is *Ayodhyan*.'

'Lord Ram, be merciful!' the general whispered.

'Indeed! It looks like Emperor Daksha and my weakling father have formed an alliance against the Neelkanth.'

Bhrigu and Daksha joined Dilipa in the Meluhan emperor's private chambers in Devagiri, where the maharishi and the Emperor of Swadweep had arrived the previous day.

'Do you think they've succeeded in their mission, my Lord?' asked Dilipa.

Daksha looked remote and uninterested, lost in the intense pain of separation from his beloved daughter, Sati. A year had passed since the terrible event in Kashi, when he'd lost his child, and with that loss, all the love he'd ever felt in his heart. The memory still haunted him.

A few months earlier, Bhrigu had hatched a plan to assassinate the Neelkanth and his entire convoy en route to Panchavati, and Daksha and Dilipa had sent five ships up the Godavari River to attack Shiva's convoy. After that, they were to destroy Panchavati, leaving no survivors to bear witness to these events. There was nothing unethical in attacking an enemy, even one unprepared, and if this worked, all their foes would be destroyed in one fell swoop. But it would be possible only if Daksha and Dilipa joined forces, for only together would they have the means and the technology to carry out the attacks.

The people of India would be told that the ghastly Nagas had lured the naïve and trusting Neelkanth to their city and assassinated him. Bhrigu understood the importance of simplicity in manufacturing convincing propaganda and had come up with a new title for Shiva: *Bholenath* – 'the simple one' or 'the one who is easily misled'. By laying the blame on the Nagas' treachery *and* the Neelkanth's simple-mindedness, Daksha and Dilipa would be spared any backlash – and even better, the general population's hatred for the Nagas would be strengthened even more.

Bhrigu glanced at Daksha briefly, then turned his attention back to Dilipa. He had begun to favour Dilipa over the Meluhan. 'They should have succeeded,' he said. 'We'll soon receive reports from the commander.'

Dilipa's face twitched and he took a deep breath to calm his nerves. 'I hope no one ever finds out that we did this. The wrath of my people would be terrible. Killing the Neelkanth with this subterfuge—'

The *Saptrishi Uttradhikari* interrupted Dilipa, his voice calm. 'He wasn't the Neelkanth. He was an imposter. The Vayuputra Council didn't create him – or even recognise him.'

Dilipa frowned at Bhrigu's words. He'd heard the rumours about the legendary tribe left behind by Lord Rudra, the previous Mahadev, but he'd never really believed that the Vayuputras actually existed. 'Then how did his throat turn blue?' he asked.

Bhrigu glanced at Daksha, then said, 'I don't know. It's a mystery. The Vayuputra Council are still debating whether Evil has risen or not and they won't create a Neelkanth until they've reached a consensus. Consequently, I raised no objection to the Emperor of Meluha persisting with his search for the Neelkanth as I knew there was no possibility of a Neelkanth actually being discovered.'

Dilipa looked stunned.

'Imagine my surprise,' continued Bhrigu, not bothering to hide his exasperation, 'when this endeavour actually led them to an apparent Neelkanth. But a blue throat doesn't make a saviour. He'd not been trained. He'd not been educated for this task. He'd not been appointed by the Vayuputra Council. But Emperor Daksha thought he could control this simple tribesman from Tibet and fulfil his ambitions for Meluha. My trust in his Majesty was misplaced.'

Dilipa looked at Daksha, but when he made no response to the barb, the Swadweepan emperor returned his attention to the great sage. 'Regardless, Evil will be destroyed when the Nagas are destroyed.'

Bhrigu frowned. 'Who said the Nagas are evil?'

Dilipa stared at Bhrigu, nonplussed. 'What are you saying, my Lord? That the Nagas can be our allies?'

Bhrigu smiled enigmatically. 'The distance between Evil and Good is a vast expanse in which many can exist without being either, your Majesty.'

Dilipa nodded politely, though he did not understand Bhrigu's intellectual abstractions. Wisely, though, he kept his own counsel.

'But the Nagas are on the wrong side,' continued Bhrigu. 'Do you know why?'

Dilipa shook his head, now thoroughly confused.

'Because they are against the great Good. They are against Lord Brahma's finest invention, the source of our country's greatness. This invention must be protected at all costs.'

Dilipa still didn't understand Bhrigu's words, but he knew better than to argue with the formidable maharishi – he needed the medicines Bhrigu provided to keep him alive and healthy.

'We will continue to fight for India,' said Bhrigu. 'I won't let anyone destroy the Good at the heart of our land's greatness.'

CHAPTER 2

What is Evil?

'It's obvious that the *Somras* has been the greatest Good of our age,' said Brahaspati. 'It's literally shaped our world. Hence it's equally obvious that someday it will become the greatest Evil. The key question is when that transformation will occur.'

Shiva, Sati, Kali and Ganesh were still sitting in Brahaspati's classroom in Panchavati. The teacher had declared a holiday for the rest of the day so that their conversation could continue uninterrupted. The legendary five banyan trees after which Panchavati had been named were clearly visible through the classroom window.

'As far as I'm concerned, the *Somras* was evil the moment it was invented,' spat Kali.

Shiva frowned at her, then turned back to Brahaspati. 'Please, go on.'

'Any great invention has both positive and negative effects, and as long as the positive sides outweigh the negative, one can safely continue to use it. The *Somras* created our way of life: it has allowed us to live longer in healthier bodies, and this in turn has enabled great men to continue contributing towards the welfare of society for much longer than was ever possible in the past. At first the *Somras* was restricted to the Brahmins, who were expected to use their extended healthier years – almost a second life – for the benefit of the whole of society.'

Shiva had heard this story from Daksha many years ago, but still he listened carefully.

'Later,' continued Brahaspati, 'when Lord Ram decreed that the benefits of the *Somras* should be available to all, that the Brahmins should no longer have special privileges, the *Somras* was administered to the entire populace, resulting in huge progress in society as a whole.'

'I know all this,' said Shiva. 'When did the negative effects start becoming obvious?'

'The first sign was the Nagas,' said Brahaspati. 'There have always been Nagas in India, but they were usually Brahmins. Ravan, for example – Lord Ram's greatest foe – was a Naga and a Brahmin.'

'Ravan was a *Brahmin*?' asked Sati, shocked by this unexpected revelation.

'Yes, he was,' Kali interrupted. Every Naga knew his story. 'He was the son of the great sage, Vishrava, a benevolent ruler, a brilliant scholar, a fierce warrior and a staunch devotee of Lord Rudra. He had some faults, no doubt, but he wasn't Evil personified as the people of the Sapt Sindhu would have us believe.'

'Does that belief make your people think less of Lord Ram?' Sati wondered.

'Of course not,' Kali snorted. 'Lord Ram was one of the greatest emperors who ever lived, and we worship him as the seventh Vishnu. His ideas, his philosophies and laws, are the foundation of the Naga way of life. His reign, Ram Rajya, will always be celebrated across India as the perfect way to run an empire. But you should know that some believe even Lord Ram didn't see Ravan as pure evil. He respected his enemy. Sometimes there can be good people on both sides of a war.'

Shiva raised his hand to silence them and turned his attention back to the Meluhan chief scientist. 'Brahaspati, please continue.'

'As I said, the Nagas, though initially small in number, were usually Brahmins. But the *Somras* had only been used by the Brahmins until then. Today, the connection's obvious, but no one saw it at the time.'

'The *Somras* created the Nagas?' asked Shiva.

'Yes. The Nagas discovered this only a few centuries ago, and I learned it from them.'

'*We* didn't discover it,' Kali corrected him. 'The Vayuputra Council told us.'

'What's the Vayuputra Council?' asked Shiva.

'The previous Mahadev, Lord Rudra, left behind a tribe called the Vayuputras,' Kali replied. 'They live beyond the western borders in a land called Pariha, the "land of fairies".'

'I know about the Vayuputras,' said Shiva, recalling a conversation with one of the Vasudev pandits, 'but I've never heard of this council.'

'The Vayuputras are ruled by their council, which is headed by their chief, the Mithra. He's the earthly representative of the Vayuputra god Ahura Mazda – he's a formless god, much like the Hindu Parmatma. Lord Rudra commanded that the Chief Vayuputra should always be called Mithra, which translates literally as "friend", and once a man becomes the Mithra he renounces all his previous identities and associations. He's advised by a council of six wise people, collectively called the Amartya Shpand. The council controls the twin missions of the Vayuputras: to help the next Vishnu, whenever he appears, and to train one of the Vayuputras to become the next Mahadev, when the time comes.'

Shiva raised his eyebrows in surprise.

'I'm sure your appearance must have given the Vayuputra Council quite a shock,' said Kali, 'because, quite clearly, they didn't create you.'

'You mean this is a *controlled* process?'

'I've told you all I know,' said Kali, 'but I'm sure your friends will be able to tell you a lot more.'

'Do you mean the Vasudevs?'

At her nod he frowned and reached for Sati's hand, then asked Kali, 'So how did you find out about the *Somras* creating the Nagas? Did the Vayuputras approach you, or did you find them?'

'They approached the Naga King Vasuki a few centuries ago – they suddenly appeared out of nowhere, lugging a huge hoard of gold, and offered to pay us an annual "compensation". King Vasuki, quite rightly, refused to accept the money without an explanation. That's when the Vayuputras told him that the *Somras* was causing the deformities – they'd discovered Naga births were a random side effect to parents who had been using the *Somras* for a long time.'

'So not all babies are affected?'

'No, not at all – in fact, the vast majority are born without any defect or deformity. But a few unfortunates, like me and Ganesh, are born Naga.'

'Why?'

'I call it dumb luck,' said Kali, 'but King Vasuki believed that the deformities caused by the *Somras* were the Almighty's way of punishing those souls who had committed sins in their previous births, and so he accepted the Vayuputra Council's explanation along with their compensation.'

'*Mausi* rejected the terms of the agreement with the Vayuputras the moment she ascended the throne,' said Ganesh, smiling at Kali.

'Why?' exclaimed Shiva. 'I'm sure the gold could have been put to good use by your people.'

Kali's laugh was humourless. 'That gold was nothing but a palliative – not for us, but for the Vayuputras. Its only purpose was to make them feel less guilty for the carnage being wrought upon us by the "great invention" they were protecting.'

Shiva could understand her anger. He turned to Brahaspati. 'So how exactly is the *Somras* responsible for this?'

'We used to believe the *Somras* blessed us with a long life by removing poisonous oxidants from our bodies,' replied Brahaspati, 'but it turns out that's not the only way it works. It also operates at a more fundamental level. Our bodies are made up of millions of tiny living units called "cells": the building blocks of life.'

'One of your scientists in Meluha described this notion to me.'

'Then you'll know that these cells are the tiniest of living beings, and they have the ability to divide and grow and combine together to form organs, limbs – the entire body. Each division is like a fresh birth: one old, unhealthy cell magically transforms into two new healthy cells, and as long as they keep dividing, they remain healthy. So a child's journey begins in the mother's womb: a single cell that keeps dividing and growing until it eventually forms an entire body.'

'That's just how they explained it to us in the Meluha *gurukul*,' Sati said.

'Obviously, this division and growth has to end sometime,' Brahaspati continued, 'otherwise a body would just keep growing continuously, with pretty disastrous consequences. So the Almighty put a limit on the number of times a cell can divide, and after that, the cell simply stops: in effect, it becomes old and unhealthy.'

Shiva contemplated Brahaspati's words for a moment, then said, 'That's what makes one's body age and die? And the *Somras* removes this limit on division?'

The teacher smiled. 'That's it: with the *Somras* your cells keep dividing while still remaining healthy. In most people, this continued division is regulated by natural body processes. But in a few, some cells lose control and keep growing at an increased pace.'

'This is cancer, isn't it?' asked Sati, who'd been listening with interest.

'Yes,' said Brahaspati, 'and this cancer can lead to a painful death. But sometimes when these cells continue to divide, the results appear in a different way: as physical deformities or out-growths – like extra arms, say, or a very long nose.'

'How polite and scientific your description is!' said Kali, sounding furious. 'You can't even begin to imagine the physical pain and torture we suffer as children when these "outgrowths" occur—'

Sati reached out and held her sister's hand as she continued, 'Nagas may be born with small outgrowths that don't look like much initially, but they're harbingers of *years* of torture. It feels as if a demon has taken over your body and he's bursting out from within, slowly, over many years, causing soul-crushing pain that becomes your constant companion. Our bodies are twisted beyond recognition, and, by adolescence, when these "outgrowths" – what a polite word! – finally stop, we're stuck with what Brahaspati so politely calls "deformities".' She was almost spitting with rage as she turned to the teacher. '*I* call them the wages of sins we didn't even commit! We pay for the sins others committed by consuming the *Somras*.' She looked around the room, and Shiva noticed her eyes were filled with tears of anger.

Shiva met the Naga queen's fierce gaze. Her anger was entirely justified. 'And the Nagas have suffered this for centuries?' he asked quietly.

'Unfortunately, yes,' said Brahaspati. 'As the number of people consuming the *Somras* grew, so did the number of Nagas. Most of them are from Meluha, where the *Somras* is used most extensively.'

'And what's the Vayuputra Council's view on this?' asked Shiva.

'From the little I've been able to find out, the council believes that the use of the *Somras* continues to be more good than bad. They regard the Nagas' suffering as "collateral damage" that has to be tolerated for the greater good.'

'Nonsense!' snorted Kali.

Shiva completely understood Kali's rage, but he could not instantly dismiss the enormous benefits the *Somras* had brought over several millennia. *On balance, does the good still outweigh the bad?* he asked himself.

He turned to Brahaspati. 'Are there any other reasons to believe that the *Somras* is evil?'

He looked down at his hands, then admitted, 'We Meluhans choose to believe that the Saraswati is dying because of some devious Chandravanshi conspiracy, but we're actually killing our mother river all by ourselves. We use vast quantities of Saraswati water to manufacture the *Somras* – it helps to stabilise the mixture during processing, and it's also used to churn the crushed branches of the sanjeevani tree. I'm not the only scientist to have conducted many experiments to see if water from any other source can be used, but nothing else works.'

'Could you reduce the amount of water used in these processes?'

'Unfortunately not: when the *Somras* was being made for only a few thousand Brahmins, the amount of Saraswati water used was negligible. But once we started mass-producing *Somras* for eight million people, the dynamics changed completely, and the giant manufacturing facility at Mount Mandar started seriously affecting the Saraswati. It no longer flows into the Western Sea but ends its journey in an inland delta south of Rajasthan – and the land to the south of this delta has become a desert. It's only a matter of time before the entire river dries up. Can you imagine the impact that will have on Meluha? On *India*?'

'The Saraswati is the mother of our entire Sapt Sindhu civilisation,' said Sati, shocked. 'It's why it's called the land of the seven rivers!'

'Indeed,' said Brahaspati. 'Even the Rig Veda – our oldest and most sacred scripture – sings paeans to the Saraswati. It's not only the cradle but also the lifeblood of our civilisation. What will happen to our future generations without this great river? The Vedic way of life itself is at risk. We're stealing the lifeblood of our future progeny so that our present generation can revel in the luxury of living for two hundred years or more. Would it be so terrible if we lived for only a hundred years instead?'

Shiva considered the terrible side effects and the ecological destruction caused by the *Somras*, but he still couldn't see it as a great Evil that left only one option: a *dharmayudh* – a holy war – to destroy it. So what was he missing? Why didn't Brahaspati just come right out and say it?

'What else don't I know about the *Somras*?' he asked.

'The destruction of the Saraswati is truly bad, but it is nothing compared to another even more insidious impact of the *Somras*. You know of the plague of Branga? It's killed innumerable people – children are especially vulnerable – and there are only two real remedies, both hard to get. The only alternative to the Naga medicine is an even harder to source exotic substance derived from peacocks – and it's the killing of our sacred birds that has led to the Brangas being ostracised, even in peace-loving cities like Kashi.'

Shiva looked surprised. 'What does that have to do with the *Somras*?'

'It has *everything* to do with the *Somras*!' said Brahaspati. 'It's not just difficult to manufacture; it also generates huge amounts of toxic waste, and that's a problem we've never truly tackled. It can't be disposed of on land because it would contaminate the groundwater and poison entire districts. And it can't be dumped in the sea either, because the *Somras* waste explodes when it comes into contact with salt water.'

Shiva's eyes widened as a sudden thought hit him. *I wonder, did Brahaspati accompany me to Karachapa that first time to pick up sea-water? Was that what he used to destroy Mount Mandar?*

'Our experiments at Mount Mandar proved that cold fresh water reduced the toxicity of the *Somras* waste products, and ice worked even better. Obviously, we couldn't use the rivers of India to filter large quantities of *Somras* waste – we'd have ended up poisoning our own people. So we decided to use the high mountain rivers in Tibet, which flowed through uninhabited lands: their waters are almost ice-cold, which was perfect for filtering the *Somras* waste. So many decades ago, Meluha set up a gigantic waste treatment facility high in the Himalayas on the Tsangpo River.'

'Are you telling me that the Meluhans have visited my land before?'

'Yes – in secret.'

'But how could such large consignments of waste possibly be kept hidden?'

'You've seen how much *Somras* powder is needed to feed an entire city for a year: ten small pouches are sufficient. Then it's mixed with water and other ingredients to convert it into the *Somras* drink at designated temples across Meluha.'

'So are the waste products similarly small?'

'Yes – but even that small quantity packs a huge dose of poison.'

'So, this waste facility that was set up in Tibet—'

'It was built in a completely desolate area along the Tsangpo. We chose that site because the river flows east, through relatively unpopulated lands, away from India, so our land wouldn't suffer from the harmful waste.'

Shiva frowned. 'But what about the lands beyond Swad-weep the Tsangpo flows through? What about the Tibetan land around Tsangpo itself? Wouldn't they have suffered due to the toxic waste?'

'They may have,' said Brahaspati, 'but that was considered acceptable collateral damage. The Meluhans monitored the people living along the Tsangpo very carefully: there were no outbreaks of disease, no sudden increase in deformities. The icy river waters appeared to be working successfully to render the toxins inactive. These reports were given to the Vayuputra Council, which also sent scientists into the sparsely populated land of Burma, east of Swadweep. They believed the Tsangpo flowed into those lands, where it became Burma's main river, the Irrawaddy. But once again there was no evidence of a sudden increase in diseases or deformities, so the scientists concluded that we'd found a way to rid ourselves of the *Somras* waste without harming anyone. When the Meluhans learned that Tsangpo means "purifier" in the local Tibetan tongue, it was considered divine confirmation that a solution had been found. This was the received wisdom passed down to the scientists of Mount Mandar.'

Shiva had been following Brahaspati's revelations closely, but now he looked bemused. 'I'm still not sure what this has to do with the Brangas,' he said.

The teacher sighed. 'Unbeknownst to the Meluhans, the upper regions of the Brahmaputra had never been properly mapped. They assumed that the river came from the east because it flows west into Branga. The Nagas, with Parshuram's help, finally mapped the upper course of the Brahmaputra and found that in fact it flows from the great heights of the Himalayas to the plains of Branga through gorges with sheer walls almost six thousand feet high.'

'Six thousand feet!' gasped Shiva.

'As you can imagine, navigating the Brahmaputra's perilous course was a great challenge, but Parshuram succeeded and led the Nagas along that path. Parshuram didn't realise the significance of the discovery of the river's course, but Queen Kali and Lord Ganesh did.'

'Did you travel up the Brahmaputra yourself?' asked Shiva. 'Where does the river come from? Is it connected to the Tsangpo?'

Brahaspati said sadly, 'It *is* the Tsangpo.'

'*What?*'

'The Tsangpo flows east only while it's running through Tibet. In the eastern foothills of the Himalayas it takes a sharp turn, almost reversing its course, and begins to flow south-west, crashing through massive gorges before emerging near Branga as the Brahmaputra.'

'By the Holy Lake!' said Shiva as he realised the full extent of the problem. 'The Brangas are being poisoned by the *Somras* waste!'

'Exactly. The cold waters of the Tsangpo dilute some of the toxic impact, but as the river turns into the Brahmaputra and enters India, so the rising temperature reactivates the dormant toxins in the water. The Branga children suffer from the same body-wracking pain as the Nagas, but they're free from deformities. And Branga also has a much higher incidence of cancer. The death toll on their population is simply unacceptable.'

Shiva had already begun to connect the dots. 'Divodas told me the Branga plague always peaks during the summer – that's when ice melts faster in the Himalayas, so less of the poison is deactivated.'

'That's exactly what happens.'

'Obviously, since both the Nagas and Brangas are being poisoned by the same toxins, our medicines work on the Brangas as well,' said Kali, 'so we can help to ameliorate their suffering a little. But even though we told King Chandraketu the truth about how his people were being poisoned, some Brangas still prefer to believe that the plague strikes every year because of a curse the Nagas have cast upon them. If only we were that powerful! But Chandraketu believes us, which is why he regularly sends us men and gold to stealthily attack the *Somras* manufacturing facilities which are the root cause of all our problems.'

'Evil should never be fought with subterfuge, Kali,' said Shiva. 'It must be attacked openly.'

Kali opened her mouth to retort, but Shiva had turned back to Brahaspati. 'Why didn't you say something – raise the issue in Meluha or with the Vayuputras?'

'I did,' said Brahaspati. 'Of course I did! I spoke to Emperor Daksha himself, but he doesn't understand scientific things, nor does he involve himself with technical details. He turned to the one intellectual he trusts, the venerable royal priest, Bhrigu. Lord Bhrigu appeared to be genuinely interested. He took me to the Vayuputra Council so I could present my case before them – but they wouldn't believe me. They laughed when they heard I was listening to the Nagas. According to the Vayuputra Council, the Nagas were now ruled by an extremist harridan whose frustration with her own *karma* made everyone else the object of her ire.'

'I'll take that as a compliment!' said Kali.

Shiva flashed Kali a brief grin. 'But how did the Vayuputras rationalise what's happening in Branga?'

'According to them,' said Brahaspati, 'the Brangas were a rich but uncivilised lot with strange eating habits and disgusting customs, so the plague was most likely caused by their own bad practices and *karma* rather than the *Somras* – you have to remember, the Vayuputras have little sympathy for the Brangas because they drink the blood of peacocks. The birds are sacred to the followers of the previous Mahadev, Lord Rudra.'

'So you just gave up?' retorted Shiva. 'Emperor Daksha's weak and easily influenced – surely you could have persuaded him to change the way things are done in Meluha. The Vayuputra Council doesn't govern your country.'

Brahaspati looked ashamed as he said, 'I was given a good reason for not persisting with the argument. Tara, the woman I intended to marry, suddenly went missing. The last time I saw her was in Pariha. When I returned to Meluha, I received a letter from her telling me that she hated my tirades against the

Somras. I asked Lord Bhrigu to check with his friends in Pariha and he told me that she'd disappeared.' Seeing Shiva's frown, Brahaspati said, 'I know it sounds like I'm making excuses, but I believe Tara was taken hostage to send me a message: keep quiet, or else—'

'I still don't understand why you gave up when you believed you were right.'

'I didn't,' continued Brahaspati defensively, 'but by then I was losing credibility amongst the senior scientists of other countries. If I'd made more of the issue in Meluha, I'd have lost what little standing I still retained amongst the Suryavanshis too – I'd have lost the ability to do anything at all. I knew I had to do something, of course, but I had come to the conclusion that open lobbying and trying to encourage debate had become counterproductive. Too many vested interests were tied to the *Somras*. Only the Vayuputra Council had the moral strength to stop it openly, through the institution of the Neelkanth, but they refused point-blank to believe that the *Somras* had turned evil.'

'So what happened then?' asked Shiva, though he thought he knew the answer.

'I opted for silence,' said Brahaspati, 'at least on the surface, but I had to do *something*. Maharishi Bhrigu was convinced there was nothing to fear from the *Somras* waste, so they continued manufacturing it at the same frantic pace, which meant the depletion of the Saraswati continued and huge quantities of *Somras* waste were being generated. The emperor, having been told that cold river-water successfully dissipated the toxic waste, ordered new plans drawn up to use other rivers – this time the upper reaches of either the Indus or the Ganga.'

'Lord Ram, be merciful,' whispered Shiva.

'Millions of lives were at risk: we would be sending toxic waste right through the *heart* of India. Then Lord Ganesh approached me, just at that moment, and I took it as a message from the Parmatma, the ultimate soul. There was only one possible solution: the destruction of Mount Mandar – without Mount Mandar, there would be no *Somras*, and with the *Somras* gone, all these other problems would disappear, too. And Ganesh had formulated a plan that made eminent sense to me.'

Shiva cast a quick look towards Ganesh.

'Whatever doubts remained,' said Brahaspati, 'disappeared when I was confronted with something unexpected – something that convinced me the time really had come to take my stand against Evil.'

'What "something"?' asked Shiva.

'*You*. Even without the Vayuputra Council's permission – perhaps even without their knowledge – the Neelkanth appeared. That was the final sign for me that the time to destroy Evil was upon us.'

— ⚶ ⫛ ⫚ ⚶ —

Vishwadyumna made the hand signals and his Branga hunting party went down on their knees.

Kartik, right behind Vishwadyumna, whistled softly and his eyes lit up. 'Magnificent!'

While most of Shiva's convoy was settling in at the visitors' camp outside Panchavati, soldiers had been despatched to gather meat for the large entourage. Kartik, who had proved himself an accomplished hunter throughout the journey to Panchavati, took one of the parties. Vishwadyumna accompanied the son of the Neelkanth, whose fierce warrior skills he greatly admired.

'It's a rhinoceros, my Lord,' he whispered.

The rhinoceros was a massive animal, nearly twelve feet in length. The bumpy brownish skin which hung over its body in multiple layers looked like tough armour. Its most distinctive feature was its fearsome nasal horn, which was almost two feet long.

'I know,' replied Kartik. 'These beasts live around Kashi, too. They have terrible eyesight, but their fantastic sense of smell and hearing more than make up for it.'

'So what do you propose, my Lord?'

The rhinoceros was a tricky beast to hunt: they might be quiet animals who kept to themselves, but if threatened they could charge wildly. A direct blow from that massive body and terrifying horn was usually fatal.

Kartik reached over his shoulders and drew the two swords sheathed crossways on his back. In his left hand was a short double-blade like the one his elder brother, Ganesh, favoured, which was good for thrusting. In his right, the heavier curved blade was perfect for swinging and slashing, a style of fighting in which Kartik excelled.

The young man said, 'Shoot arrows at its back and make as much noise as you can – I want you to drive it towards me.'

Vishwadyumna's eyes filled with fear at the thought of the danger to the Neelkanth's son. 'That's not wise, my Lord—'

'Too many soldiers charging in at the same time will hinder us – one swing of its mighty horn could wound several men.'

'But we can kill it from a distance with arrows.'

Kartik raised his eyebrows. 'Vishwadyumna, you should know better! Do you really think our arrows could penetrate that thick hide deeply enough to cause serious damage? It's not the arrows but the noise your men will make that'll provoke it to charge. Also, it's standing upwind, so the stench of your soldiers combined with the noise will also drive the animal forward. It's a good thing they haven't bathed in two days,' said Kartik, straight faced.

Like all warriors, Vishwadyumna admired humour in the face of danger, but he checked his smile, not sure whether Kartik was joking. 'What will you do, my Lord?'

Kartik whispered, 'I'll kill the beast.' And with that, he slowly began to edge forwards, directly into the path the bull would take when Vishwadyumna's soldiers attacked. At the same time, the soldiers moved upwind, behind the rhinoceros.

Once Kartik was in position, he whistled softly and Vishwadyumna shouted, '*Now!*'

A volley of arrows flew towards the animal as the soldiers

began to scream loudly. The rhinoceros raised its head, ears twitching as the arrows bounced harmlessly off its skin, but as the soldiers drew closer, some of the missiles managed to penetrate enough to agitate the beast and it snorted mightily and stomped the dirt, radiating strength and power as light gleamed off its tiny black eyes. It lowered its head and charged, its feet thundering against the ground.

The beast only had side vision and couldn't see straight ahead, so Kartik wasn't surprised when it crashed straight into an overhanging branch in its path. It changed direction slightly, then, seeing Kartik standing there, the furious rhinoceros bellowed loudly, changed course back to its original path and charged straight towards Shiva's diminutive son.

Kartik remained still, his eyes calmly focused on the beast, his breathing regular and deep. He knew the rhinoceros couldn't see him, not now that he was directly in its path again; the animal's charge was guided by the memory of where it had seen Kartik last.

Vishwadyumna continued rapidly firing arrows into the animal, hoping to slow it down, but the beast's thick hide deflected most of them. It was still running straight towards Kartik, but the boy didn't move; he didn't even flinch in the face of this terrifying beast. Vishwadyumna saw the boy warrior was holding his swords lightly – that was completely wrong for a stabbing action, for which the blade needed to be firmly held. The weapons would fall out of his hands the moment he thrust with them.

Just when it looked like Kartik was about to be trampled underfoot, he bent low and rolled to the left, moving with lightning speed. As the rhinoceros ran past him, he slashed out, left sword first, pressing a lever on the hilt as he swung, and one of the double-blades extended and sliced through the beast's front right thigh, cutting through the flesh like butter. As blood spurted, the animal's injured leg collapsed beneath it and it grunted, confused, still trying to put weight on the appendage now flopping uselessly against its belly. But it continued its charge, its three good legs heaving against its bulk as it struggled to turn and face its attacker. Kartik ran forwards and circled in from behind the beast. He hacked brutally with the curved blade in his right hand and sliced through the thigh of the rhinoceros' right hind leg, cutting down to the bone. With both its right legs incapacitated, the rhinoceros collapsed to the ground, writhing in pain, then rolled sideways as it tried in vain to stand on its two good legs. Its blood mixed with the dusty earth to make a dark red-brown mud that smeared across its body as it flailed against the ground, panting in fear.

Kartik stood quietly a short distance away, watching the animal in its final death throes.

Vishwadyumna's mouth was agape. He'd never seen an animal brought down with such skill and speed.

The boy warrior approached the rhinoceros calmly. In spite of its injuries, the beast reared its head menacingly at him, grunting and whining in a high-pitched squeal. Kartik maintained a safe distance as the other soldiers joined him.

The Neelkanth's son bowed low to the animal. 'Forgive me, magnificent beast. I'm only doing my duty. I will finish this soon.'

Suddenly, he darted forwards and stabbed hard, his blade piercing the folds of the rhinoceros' skin to plunge deep into its heart. He held the sword there, feeling the beast's final shudders run through its body, until at last it was still.

— ⅄ ⓄⓊ⚕✳ —

'Your Majesty, a bird-courier has just arrived with a message for your eyes only,' said Kanakhala, the Meluhan prime minister. 'I thought I should deliver it to you personally.'

Daksha was in his private chambers, a worried Veerini seated beside him. He took the letter from Kanakhala and dismissed her.

With a polite namaste towards her emperor and empress, Kanakhala turned to leave. Glancing back, she glimpsed a rare intimate moment between them as they held each other's hands. The last few months had inured her to the strange goings-on in Meluha, she thought. The emperor's past betrayal of his daughter during Sati's first pregnancy had shocked Kanakhala enormously, and she'd lost all respect for him. She continued performing her duties as prime minister only out of loyalty to Meluha, and no longer bothered questioning his strange orders, like the one he'd given the previous day, to make arrangements for Maharishi Bhrigu and Emperor Dilipa to travel to the ruins of Mount Mandar. She could understand Bhrigu's interest in

Mount Mandar, but what earthly reason could there be for the Swadweepan emperor to accompany him?

As she shut the door quietly behind her, Kanakhala saw Daksha release Veerini's hand and break the letter's seal.

Daksha began to cry and Veerini immediately reached over and snatched the letter from him. As she quickly scanned it she let out a deep sigh of relief, and tears began to fall from her eyes too. 'She's safe. They're *all* safe . . .'

The plan to assassinate the Neelkanth had been in the interests of all three main conspirators. Maharishi Bhrigu wanted to prevent the Neelkanth from targeting the *Somras* – the people's faith in the legend of the Neelkanth was strong, and if the so-called Neelkanth sided with the Nagas and declared that the *Somras* was evil, his followers would do the same. For Daksha, the Swadweepan emperor, it would kill two birds with a single stone: not only would he continue to receive the elixir from Bhrigu to keep him alive, he'd also do away with Bhagirath, his heir and greatest threat. And Emperor Daksha would be rid of the troublesome Neelkanth and be able to blame all ills on the Nagas once again. The plan had been perfect – except for the fact that, when it came down to it, Daksha couldn't countenance the killing of his daughter; he'd been willing to put everything on the line to ensure that Sati was left unharmed. Bhrigu and Dilipa had hoped the rupture of the relationship between Daksha and his daughter would restore the Meluhan emperor's wholehearted support for this mission, but they had been wrong: Daksha's love for Sati was deeper even than his hatred for Shiva.

Acting on Veerini's advice, Daksha had sent the Arishtanemi brigadier, Mayashrenik, known for his blind loyalty to Meluha and his deep devotion to the Neelkanth, on a secret mission: Mayashrenik had accompanied the five ships sent to attack the Neelkanth's convoy. Veerini had secretly kept in touch with her daughter, Kali, through all these years of strife, and she knew of the Nagas' river warning and defence system. Mayashrenik's mission had been to ensure that the alarms were triggered, after which he was to escape and return to Meluha. The message the emperor and his wife were now reading was from the Arishtanemi brigadier, delivering news of the subsequent battle. The happy message for the Meluhan emperor was that Sati and Kartik were alive and safe.

Veerini looked at her husband. 'If only you'd listen to me a bit more.'

Daksha inhaled deeply. 'If Lord Bhrigu ever finds out—'

'Would you rather your children were dead?'

Daksha sighed and shook his head. He would do anything to ensure Sati's safety.

'Then thank the Parmatma that our plan worked. And we will never breathe a word of this to anyone. *Ever!*'

Daksha took the note from Veerini and set it aflame, holding it by the edge to ensure that every part of it was charred beyond recognition.

CHAPTER 3

The Kings Have Chosen

'Do you believe Brahaspati?' asked Shiva.

Night had fallen on the Panchavati guest colony just outside the main city. Shiva's entourage, most of them exhausted and many injured, had retired to their quarters for some well-deserved rest.

Sati and Shiva had gone straight to their chambers after returning from the city. They hadn't spoken to a soul about what they'd learned at the Panchavati school – they hadn't even told the Suryavanshis that their beloved chief scientist was still alive. They had arranged to meet Brahaspati again the next day.

'Yes,' said Sati slowly. 'I don't think Brahaspatiji's lying. I remember that Lord Bhrigu once spent many months in Devagiri – it was more than two decades ago – which was highly unusual for the Raj guru. He's a rare sight in Meluha – he prefers to spend his time meditating in his Himalayan cave.'

'Aren't Raj gurus supposed to reside in the royal palace and guide the emperor?'

'Not someone like Lord Bhrigu. He helped my father get elected as emperor because he believed he would be good for Meluha. Beyond that, he's taken no interest in the day-to-day governance of the country. He's a simple man, rarely seen in the so-called powerful circles.'

'So he spent a lot of time in Devagiri: that might have been unusual, but what about the other things Brahaspati said?'

'Well, Lord Bhrigu, my father and Brahaspatiji were also away for many months. Their absence was announced as an important trade trip, but I can't imagine Lord Bhrigu or Brahaspatiji being at all interested in trade. Perhaps they were in Pariha at that time. And yes, the talented and lovely Taraji, who worked at Mount Mandar and had been sent to Pariha for a project, *did* disappear suddenly. I remember being told that she'd taken *sanyas* – renouncing public life is very common in Meluha, so I didn't really think much of it. But what Brahaspatiji revealed today was another side of the story altogether.'

'So you believe Brahaspati speaks the truth?'

'All I'm saying is that Brahaspatiji may believe this to be the truth – but is it actually so, or is he mistaken? Whatever decision you make, Shiva, you will change the course of history. Your actions will have repercussions for generations to come. A big battle is a momentous decision: you have to be completely sure.'

'I must speak with the Vasudevs.'

'Yes, you must.'

'You have something else to say to me, don't you?'

'I think there's another aspect to be considered. What made Brahaspatiji disappear for more than five years? What was he doing in Panchavati all that time? I feel this is an important question. Perhaps his absence was linked to the back-up manufacturing facility for the *Somras* that Father told me about.'

'I didn't think it that important before, but if the *Somras* is evil, that facility is going to be the key to destroying it.'

'Actually, the Saraswati is the key,' Sati pointed out. 'A manufacturing facility can always be rebuilt, but, wherever it's put, it'll always need the Saraswati's waters. When we were at Icchawar, Kali told me that her people attacked Meluhan temples and Brahmins only if they were directly harming the Nagas. Maybe those temples were making the *Somras* drink for the locals? She also said that a final solution would emerge from the Saraswati – that the Nagas were working on it. I don't know what she meant – it's a pretty cryptic statement – but I think we need to find out.'

'You've never mentioned this conversation with Kali before—' Shiva started, but Sati stopped him.

'Shiva, this is the first honest conversation we've had about Kali and Ganesh since you met my son at Kashi. I'm not blaming you,' she continued, 'because I understood your anger – you thought Ganesh had killed Brahaspatiji. Now that the truth has emerged, perhaps you're finally willing to listen to me.'

'Are you sure?' asked Shiva, looking at the Meluhan general and the Ayodhyan prince as Parvateshwar and Bhagirath held out a plank for him to examine. It was late the next morning, four hours into the second *prahar*, and the pair had just returned from surveying the destroyed battleships.

'Yes, my Lord,' said Bhagirath. 'The evidence is indisputable.' He drew Shiva's and Sati's attention to various points along the plank. 'Look – the rivets are clearly Meluhan, can you see? Lord Parvateshwar has identified them' – he glanced at the general, who nodded his agreement – 'and the casing, which improves the waterproofing, is clearly Ayodhyan.'

'Are you suggesting that Emperor Daksha and Emperor Dilipa have formed an alliance against us?' Shiva whispered softly.

'These ships had navigated through a lot of seawater, judging by the molluscs on them. They'd have needed the best technologies from both our lands to be able to make that journey quickly enough.'

Shiva breathed deeply, lost in thought.

'My Lord,' said Bhagirath, 'for all his faults, I can't imagine that my father could have led such a conspiracy – he simply doesn't have the capability. He's just a follower. You have to target him, of course, but don't mistake him for the main conspirator. That's someone else.'

Sati leaned towards Shiva. 'Do you think my father planned this?'

Shiva shook his head. 'No. Emperor Daksha's no more capable of leading this conspiracy than Dilipa.'

Parvateshwar, still shamed by the dishonour brought upon his empire, said quietly, 'The Meluhan code calls upon us to follow the rules, my Lord, and our rules bid us to carry out our emperor's orders. In the hands of a lesser man, this can lead to a lot of wrongdoing.'

'Emperor Daksha may have issued the orders, Parvateshwar,' said Shiva, 'but he didn't dream them up. Some other master has brought the royal heads of Meluha and Swadweep together – the same someone who also managed to procure the *daivi astras*, and heaven alone knows if he has any more of those fearful divine weapons. It was a brilliant plan, but, by Lord Ram's grace, we were saved by the skin of our teeth. This master can't be Emperor Daksha or Emperor Dilipa; this is someone of far greater importance, intelligence and resources – and someone who's clever enough to conceal his identity.'

— ⁀ 𖼷 𝕎𝕌 𖼹 ✦ —

'Return to Meluha?' Veerbhadra asked, surprised. He looked around at the others in the Neelkanth's private chambers.

Sati nodded.

'Yes, Bhadra,' said Shiva. 'It's clear the Meluhans and the Ayodhyans joined forces to attack us.'

'Are you sure Meluha's involved?' asked Veerbhadra.

'Parvateshwar himself confirmed it.'

'And now you're worried about our people.' He couldn't help but look at his wife, Krittika, as he said the words.

'Of course,' said Shiva. 'I'm concerned the Gunas we left

behind will be arrested and held hostage as leverage over us. So, before that happens, I want you to slip into Meluha quietly and take our people to Kashi. I'll meet you there.'

'My scouts will guide you and Krittika along a secret route,' said Kali. 'If we use our fastest horses and speediest boats, my people can get you close to Maika in two weeks. After that, you're on your own.'

'Meluha's a safe country to travel in,' said Krittika. 'We can hire fast horses to take us to the mouth of the Saraswati. After that we can buy passage on one of the boats that trade up and down the river. It's an easy route – with luck, we'll reach Devagiri in another two weeks. The Gunas are in a small village not far from there.'

'Perfect,' said Shiva. 'Time is of the essence, so it's best you go now. And Bhadra,' he added as Veerbhadra and Krittika turned to leave, 'don't try to be brave! If the Gunas have already been arrested, leave Meluha quickly and wait for me at Kashi.'

Veerbhadra's mother was with the Gunas and Shiva knew he wouldn't abandon her to her fate so easily. He stood and grasped Veerbhadra's shoulder. 'Bhadra, you must promise me.'

Veerbhadra clenched his jaw and remained quiet.

'If you try to release them by yourself, you'll be killed,' Shiva said quietly. 'You'll be of no use to your mother if you're dead, Bhadra.' As Veerbhadra still didn't respond, he added, 'I promise you, nothing will happen to the Gunas. If you can't get them out, I will. But don't do anything rash: you must promise me.'

Veerbhadra placed his hand on Shiva's shoulder and stared

into his friend's eyes. 'There's something you're not telling me
– what is it? What have you discovered here? Why are you so
afraid suddenly? Is there going to be a war? Will Meluha become
our enemy?'

'I'm not sure, Bhadra. I haven't made up my mind yet.'

'Then tell me what you *do* know.'

It was Shiva's turn to remain silent, and Veerbhadra's to speak.
'I'm going back to Meluha for you, Shiva. Had you asked me a
month ago, I'd have said it'd be the safest journey imaginable,
but a lot's changed since then. You have to tell me the truth. I
deserve that much.'

Shiva sighed. His friend was right, of course.

Everyone sat back down again and he revealed everything
he'd discovered over the last few days.

'And you killed the rhino all by yourself?' Anandmayi was
impressed.

'Yes, your Highness,' said Kartik, stoic and expressionless as
usual, even in the face of the princess' broad smile.

Anandmayi, Ayurvati and Kartik were settled comfortably
on soft cushions in the dining room of the main Panchavati
guest house. Anandmayi and Kartik, both Kshatriya to the core,
partook of the delicious rhinoceros meat, while Ayurvati, a
Brahmin, restricted herself to *roti*, *dal* and vegetables.

'Have you decided never to smile again?' asked Anandmayi,
'or is this just temporary?'

Kartik looked up at Anandmayi with the barest hint of a smile on his face. 'Smiling takes more effort than it's worth, your Highness.'

The doctor shook her head. 'You're just a child, Kartik. Don't trouble yourself so much. You need to enjoy your childhood.'

'My brother, Ganesh, is a great man, Ayurvatiji. He has so much to contribute to society – to the country – and yet he was almost eaten alive by dumb beasts because he was trying to save me.'

Ayurvati reached across and patted Kartik's shoulder comfortingly, but he refused to be comforted. 'I will never be so helpless again,' he swore. 'I refuse to be the cause of my family's misery.'

The door swung open and Parvateshwar and Bhagirath walked in, and Anandmayi could tell just by their faces that they'd discovered what she'd feared. 'Was it Meluha?'

Ayurvati winced. She couldn't imagine her great country's name being dragged into a vile conspiracy like the attack on the Neelkanth's convoy at the outskirts of Panchavati. And yet, after what she'd learned of Emperor Daksha's perfidy during Sati's pregnancy at Maika, perhaps it wasn't so difficult to believe that Meluhan ships had carried out this dastardly act.

'It's worse than that,' said Bhagirath with a sigh as he sat down opposite his sister.

Parvateshwar sat next to Anandmayi and held her hand. He looked at Ayurvati, his misery clear on his face. The general prized his country, his Meluha, as Lord Ram's ultimate legacy, for Meluha was the custodian of Ram Rajya, the rule of Ram, the perfect way for any empire to be run. How could this emperor of this great country have committed such a terrible crime?

'Worse how?' prompted Anandmayi.

'It appears Swadweep's in on the conspiracy as well,' said Bhagirath.

The princess was stunned. 'What?'

'I don't know how many Swadweepan kingdoms are following Ayodhya's lead, but Ayodhya's certainly involved.'

Anandmayi glanced at Parvateshwar, who nodded confirmation.

'Lord Rudra, be merciful,' she whispered. 'What's *wrong* with Father?'

'I'm not surprised,' said Bhagirath, barely able to conceal his contempt. 'He's weak and easily exploited. It doesn't take much for him to succumb to pressure.'

For once, Anandmayi didn't rebuke her brother for denigrating their father. She glanced at Parvateshwar, who looked lost and uncertain. Change was always hard for the masculine Suryavanshis, so accustomed to fixed rules and stark predictability. Anandmayi turned her husband's face towards her and kissed him gently, reassuringly. She smiled warmly at him and after a moment he half-smiled back.

Kartik quietly put his plate down and walked out of the room.

It was early afternoon and Kartik and Ganesh, walking around Panchavati, found themselves at the banyan trees. Non-Nagas did not enter the inner city, for fear of a superstition that promised misfortune would befall any who came too close to the Nagas. But the Neelkanth's family didn't believe in superstition – and nobody wanted to enforce an entry ban on them, regardless.

'Why is Lord Ram the only person depicted on these trees, *dada*?' Kartik asked his elder brother as they admired the beautiful idols of Lord Ram carved into the main trunk of each of the five banyans. 'It's not just Lady Sita, and his brother, Lord Lakshman, not included, but even his great devotee, Lord Hanuman, is missing,' he pointed out.

The ancient king, respected as the seventh Vishnu, was depicted in the five different roles of his life: son, husband, brother, father and godly king, a different one on each tree. The sculptors had made the idols look towards the temple of Lord Rudra and Lady Mohini, on the opposite corner of the square, and, as their idols were, unusually, placed in the front section of the temple rather than towards the back, it looked like the two deities were looking at all five tree idols. It was as if the architects and sculptors always intended to show the great Mahadev and the noble seventh Vishnu being respectful to each other.

'It's in keeping with our founding goddess' instructions,' Ganesh told his little brother. 'I know in his traditional depiction in the Sapt Sindhu, Lord Ram's always accompanied by his three favourite people in the world – his wife, Lady Sita, Lord

Lakshman and Lord Hanuman. But Bhoomidevi ordered that Lord Ram always be shown alone in Panchavati, especially at the five banyans.'

Kartik looked confused. 'Why?'

'I don't know. Perhaps she wanted us to always remember that great leaders, like the Vishnus and the Mahadevs, may have millions of followers, but in the end they carry the burden of their mission alone.'

'Like *baba*?' asked Kartik.

'Yes, like *baba*: your father alone stands between Evil and India. If he fails, life in the subcontinent will be destroyed by Evil.'

'*Baba* will not fail.'

Ganesh smiled at Kartik's response, but the young man had not finished. 'Do you know why?' And when Ganesh shook his head, he clasped his brother's right hand and held it against his chest, like the brother-warriors of old. 'Because he's not alone.'

Ganesh smiled and embraced Kartik, then they walked silently through the banyan trees, doing the holy parikrama, the circumambulation, of Lord Ram's idols.

'What's going on, *dada*?' asked Kartik after a few moments. 'Why have both emperors allied against *baba*?'

Ganesh took a few deep breaths before replying. He never lied to Kartik – he considered his brother an adult, and treated him as such – so he would not start now. 'Because *baba* threatens them, Kartik. They're the elite: they're addicted to the benefits they derive from Evil. *Baba*'s mission is to fight for the oppressed, to be the voice of the voiceless. Surely it's obvious that the elite will want to stop him.'

'What's this Evil that *baba*'s fighting? How has it sunk its claws in so deeply?'

Ganesh took Kartik by the hand and made him sit at the foot of one of the banyans. 'This information is for you alone, Kartik. You mustn't tell anyone else – it's up to *baba* to decide when and how others are to be told.'

Kartik looked very serious as Ganesh sat next to him and started the story.

'So what have you been doing these past five years?' asked Shiva soon after he and Sati joined the chief scientist in the Naga queen's chambers.

Brahaspati was beginning to feel like he was being interrogated, but he could understand Shiva's need to get to the bottom of the issue. 'I've been trying to find a permanent solution to the *Somras* problem,' answered Brahaspati.

'What do you mean by "permanent"?'

'Destroying Mount Mandar is a temporary solution – we know it'll be rebuilt. The Nagas tell me the reconstruction has been surprisingly slow – it shouldn't have taken five years, not with Meluhan efficiency – but it's still only a matter of time before it's done.'

Shiva glanced at Sati, but she remained silent.

'Once Mandar is back to full manufacturing capacity, the

destruction of the Saraswati and production of the toxic waste will begin again, so we need to find a way to stop it once and for all. The best way to do that is to study the *Somras'* ingredients. If we could somehow reduce the efficacy of those ingredients, we could control the poisonous impact of the *Somras* waste – even if it made the *Somras* itself much less effective. Many of the ingredients can be easily replaced, but two sources cannot: the bark and branches of the sanjeevani tree, and the water of the Saraswati. We can't destroy the trees – Meluha has large plantations of them right across its northern reaches, and how many plantations can one destroy? Besides, trees can always be replanted. So that brings us to the Saraswati, and we're asking ourselves if there is a way to control its waters.'

Shiva suddenly remembered parts of a conversation with Sati's father when he'd first arrived in Devagiri. 'Emperor Daksha told me that the Chandravanshis did try to destroy the Saraswati more than a hundred years ago by diverting one of its main tributaries, the Yamuna, to flow towards the Ganga instead. It didn't really make much sense to me, but the Meluhans appear to believe it was true.'

Brahaspati sniggered. 'The Chandravanshi ruling class can't even build roads in their own empire – how could anyone believe they have the ability to change the course of a *river*? An earthquake changed the Yamuna's course. The Meluhans subsequently defeated the Chandravanshis and the resultant treaty mandated that the early course of the Yamuna would become a no-man's-land. Meluhans, on the other hand, do have the technology to change the course of rivers. They built giant embankments to block the Yamuna and make it flow back into the Saraswati.'

'So what was your plan: destroy the Yamuna's embankments?'

'No. I considered it, but it's impossible – they have too many fail-safes. It'd take five brigades and months of work in the open to destroy those embankments. A small number of people working in secret would never have got it done.'

'So what was your back-up plan?'

'We can't take the Saraswati away, but I was wondering if there was something we could add to the Yamuna's waters at its source which would then flow into the Saraswati and, control the amount of waste being produced. I thought we'd found one such ingredient – a bacterium which reacts with the sanjeevani tree and makes it decay almost instantly.'

'Ayurvati told me that the Naga medicine is created by mixing the crushed branches of another tree with the sanjeevani bark to stabilise it. If the sanjeevani's already unstable, why would you need bacteria to aid the decay? Wouldn't it just decay anyway?'

'The sanjeevani bark becomes unstable once it's stripped off the branch, but the branch itself isn't. The bark's easier to use for small-scale production, but to manufacture the *Somras* in large quantities, we have to use crushed branches – that's what we did at Mount Mandar, but it's a method known only to my scientists.'

'So you hoped to make the entire sanjeevani branch as unstable as the bark.'

'Exactly – and I discovered that this bacterium does the trick. But there's a problem: it's only available in Mesopotamia.'

'Is that what you picked up from Karachapa when you accompanied me on my first travels through Meluha? You said you were expecting a shipment from Mesopotamia.'

'Indeed it was,' said Brahaspati, 'you have a good memory. And it would have worked perfectly. The *Somras* can't be made without both the sanjeevani tree and the Saraswati water, and the presence of the bacteria in the water would render the tree useless at the beginning of the process itself, and, as a result, the *Somras* wouldn't be as potent: it won't triple or quadruple one's lifespan, just increase it by twenty or thirty years. However, there'd be practically no waste products. So by sacrificing some of the *Somras*' power, we'd eliminate the toxic waste. Even better, these bacteria multiply prodigiously when added to water, so we'd only have to release a single batch into the Yamuna and the rest would follow.'

'Sounds perfect. So what stopped you?'

'There's no such thing as a perfect solution,' said Brahaspati. 'The bacteria comes with its own problems: it's mildly toxic, and in large quantities we discovered it would inflict a whole new set of diseases on all the living beings dependent on the water of the Saraswati and Yamuna Rivers. In the end, all we'd be doing is replacing one problem with another.'

'So you were trying to find out if the poisonous effect of the bacteria could be reduced or neutralised without affecting its ability to destroy the sanjeevani tree?'

'Correct – and so great secrecy was required. If those who support the *Somras* knew about this bacteria, they'd try to destroy it at its source – and if they'd found out I was working on an experiment like this, they'd have had me assassinated.'

'Aren't you afraid of being killed now?' asked Shiva. 'A lot of Meluhans will be angry with you when they discover you weren't the victim but rather the perpetrator of the attack on Mount Mandar.'

Brahaspati breathed deeply. 'It was important for me to remain alive until now because I was the only one who could have done this research. But I've failed and the burden of solving the *Somras* problem rests with you now, not me. It no longer matters if I live or die. Mount Mandar will be reconstructed and *Somras* production will begin once again. You have to stop it, Shiva. For the sake of India, you have to stop the *Somras*.'

'The reconstruction's a charade, Brahaspatiji,' said Sati. 'It's to mislead our enemies into thinking that Meluha must be sur- viving on lower quantities of *Somras* until the Mount Mandar factory's functional again.'

'What? Are you telling me there's another facility?' asked Brahaspati. He looked at Kali. 'But that can't be true—'

'It is,' answered Sati. 'Father told me himself. It was built years ago as a back-up to Mount Mandar, just in case—'

'Where is it?' asked Kali urgently, but when Sati shrugged, she swore and, scowling darkly, turned back to Brahaspati. 'You said this wasn't possible! The churners can only be built with materials from Egypt and our allies are constantly monitoring those Egyptian mines — nothing excavated there has gone to Meluha!'

Brahaspati's face turned white as the implications dawned on him. He held his head and muttered, 'Lord Ram, be merciful . . . How could they resort to this?'

'Resort to what?' asked Shiva.

'There is another way to mix the Saraswati waters with the crushed sanjeevani branches, but we have always considered it wasteful — and repugnant.' He shuddered, and then explained: 'Firstly, it uses much larger quantities of water — but it's worse than that: this process requires animal or human skin cells.'

'By the Holy Lake!' cried Shiva.

'We don't have to skin a live animal — or human,' Brahaspati admitted, though that obviously didn't reassure him. 'The process requires the old dead skin cells that we shed every minute we're alive: they help the water to break down the branches at the molecular level. It's quite simple: dead skin cells are mixed with the water and simply poured over crushed branches — this method doesn't even require churning. But it wastes *a lot* of water — and it needs animals and human volunteers to bathe in a pool of Saraswati water above the chamber that contains the crushed Sanjeevani branches, which is risky in itself. The usual method is inherently unstable, but producing *Somras* the skin-cell way is even more dangerous. You don't want large populations anywhere near a *Somras* facility — if something goes wrong, the resultant explosion could kill hundreds of thousands of people. That's why we've never built *Somras* production centres close to cities: can you imagine what would happen if the more dangerous skin-cell process was being conducted within a city, in a *Somras* production centre beneath a pool in which large numbers of humans ritually bathe?'

Shiva's face suddenly turned white. 'The public baths,' he whispered.

'Exactly,' said Brahaspati. 'Build the facility within a Meluhan city, beneath a public bath, and you'd have all the dead skin cells you'd ever need.'

'And if something goes wrong . . . If there's an explosion—'

'They'll blame the *daivi astras* or the Nagas – even the Chandravanshis, if you like,' fumed Brahaspati. 'We've created so many evil spectres – just take your pick!'

'Something's wrong,' Bhrigu told Dilipa as they surveyed the destroyed remains of Mount Mandar. Reconstruction had been going on for some time now, but the facility looked nowhere near completion.

'I agree, Maharishiji,' said Dilipa. 'It's been more than five years since the Nagas destroyed Mandar; it should have been rebuilt by now.'

Bhrigu waved a hand dismissively at Dilipa. 'Mount Mandar isn't important any more. It's nothing but a symbol. I'm talking about the attack on Panchavati.'

Dilipa stared wide-eyed at the sage. *Mount Mandar isn't important? This means the rumours are true: there is another Somras manufacturing facility!*

'I gave the attackers crates of homing pigeons,' continued Bhrigu, ignoring Dilipa's incredulous expression. 'All of them were trained to return to this site. The last pigeon arrived two weeks ago.'

Dilipa frowned. 'You can trust my man, my Lord. He will not fail.'

Bhrigu had appointed an officer from Dilipa's army to lead the attack on Shiva's convoy at Panchavati – he hadn't trusted Daksha to be able to detach himself from his love for his daughter. 'Of that I'm sure,' he agreed. 'He's proven himself trustworthy by strictly complying with my instructions to send back a message every week. The fact that the updates have suddenly stopped means that he's either been captured or killed.'

'I'm sure a message is on its way. We needn't worry.'

Bhrigu rounded on Dilipa. 'Is this how you govern your empire, great King? Is it any wonder that your son's claim to the throne appears legitimate?'

Dilipa's silence was telling.

Bhrigu sighed. 'When you prepare for war, you should always hope for the best but be prepared for the worst. The last despatch clearly stated that they were six days' sail from Panchavati. Having received no word after that, I'm compelled to assume the worst: the attack must have failed. Also, I must assume Shiva now knows the identity of his attackers.'

Dilipa held his tongue. He still thought the sage was over-reacting.

'I'm not overreacting, your Majesty,' said Bhrigu.

Dilipa was stunned. He hadn't uttered a word.

'Do not underestimate the issue,' said Bhrigu. 'This isn't about you or me: this is about the future of India. This is about protecting the greatest Good. We can't afford to fail! It's our duty to Lord Brahma, our duty to this great land of ours.'

Dilipa remained silent, though one thought kept reverberating in his mind: *I'm way out of my depth here. I've entangled myself with powers that are beyond mere emperors.*

CHAPTER 4

A Frog Homily

The aroma of freshly cooked food wafted from Shiva's chambers as his family assembled for their evening meal. Sati's culinary skill was bountifully displayed in the feast she'd prepared for what was in effect their first meal together as a family. Shiva, Ganesh and Kartik waited for her to take her seat before they began to eat.

In keeping with custom, the Mahadev's family sprinkled water from their glasses around their plates, symbolically thanking Goddess Annapurna for her blessings in the form of food and nourishment. Traditionally, the first morsel of food was offered to the gods, but Shiva always offered his first morsel to his wife: to him, she was divine. Sati reciprocated by offering her first morsel to Shiva.

And thus the meal began.

'Ganesh has brought some mangoes for you today,' said Sati, smiling indulgently at her younger son.

Kartik grinned. 'Yummy! Thanks, *dada*!'

As Ganesh smiled and patted Kartik's back, Shiva said, 'You should smile a little more, son. Life's not so grim.'

'I'll try, *baba*.'

Then Shiva inhaled sharply. Brahaspati had told him that he'd made Ganesh take an oath of secrecy regarding his fate; other than the Naga queen and her nephew he trusted no one else, and he needed his experiments to remain secret. Ganesh had kept his word, at the cost of almost losing his beloved mother and grievously damaging his new relationship with Shiva.

Now Shiva said, 'Ganesh?'

'Yes . . . *baba*?' Ganesh added that last hesitantly, unsure of the response he'd receive for calling Shiva *father*.

'My son,' whispered Shiva, 'I misjudged you.' And as Ganesh's eyes moistened, he begged, 'Please forgive me—'

'No, *baba*,' exclaimed Ganesh, embarrassed, 'how can you ask me for forgiveness? You're my father.'

'You're a man of your word,' said Shiva. 'You honoured your promise to Brahaspati without sparing a thought for the price you'd be paying. I'm proud of you, my son,' said Shiva.

Ganesh remained quiet, unable to speak, but, as he smiled at Shiva, Sati looked around the table, gazing at her husband and then her sons. Her world had come full circle and life was as perfect as it could possibly be. She could happily live out the rest of her days in Panchavati — but she knew this wasn't to be. A war was coming, a great battle that would require major sacrifices. She had to savour these happy moments for as long as they lasted.

'What now, *baba*?' asked Kartik, his expression serious once more.

'We're going to eat!' said Shiva, laughing. 'And then, hopefully, we'll get some sleep.'

'No, no,' replied Kartik, 'you know what I mean. Are we going to proclaim the *Somras* the ultimate Evil? Are we going to declare war against all those who continue to use or protect it?'

Shiva looked at Kartik thoughtfully. 'There's already been a lot of fighting, Kartik. We won't rush into anything.' He looked at Ganesh. 'I'm sorry, my son, but I need to know more. I *have* to know more.'

'I understand, *baba*. There are only two groups of people who know all there is to know about this matter.'

'The Vasudevs and the Vayuputras?' At his son's nod, he said wryly, 'I'm not sure whether the Vayuputra Council will help me, but I know the Vasudevs will.'

'Then I'll take you to Ujjain, *baba*. You can speak to their chief directly.'

'Where's Ujjain?'

'It's up north, beyond the Narmada.'

Shiva thought for a moment. 'That would be along the shorter route to Swadweep and Meluha, right?'

Kali had had the security of the hidden Naga city uppermost in her mind when she had led Shiva and his entourage on an elaborate year-long route from Kashi to Panchavati. The party had first headed east through Swadweep, then south from Branga before travelling west from Kalinga through the dangerous Dandak Forest, eventually reaching the headwaters of the Godavari and the Naga city of Panchavati. Shiva realised there must be a shorter northern route to Meluha and Swadweep, though it would still need a Naga guide to lead them through the impregnable forests.

'Yes, *baba*. *Mausi*'s very secretive, but I know she'd be happy to tell you.'

'I understand her caution,' said Sati. 'The Nagas have many powerful enemies.'

'Yes, *maa*,' said Ganesh. 'But that's not the only reason, let's be honest. Although the war hasn't yet begun, we already know that the most powerful emperors in the land are against us. Over the next few months, everyone else will choose sides, including those waiting in the Panchavati guest-house colony. Panchavati's a safe haven. It wouldn't be wise to give away all its secrets just yet.'

Shiva nodded. 'Let me figure out what I should do with my convoy. There aren't too many kings in the Sapt Sindhu I can trust right now. Once I've made up my mind, we can make plans to leave for Ujjain.'

Kartik turned to Ganesh. '*Dada*, there's one thing I simply don't understand: the Vayuputras are the tribe left behind by Lord Rudra. They helped the great seventh Vishnu, Lord Ram, complete his mission. So how is it that these good people don't see the Evil that the *Somras* has become?'

'I have a theory about that,' said Ganesh.

Shiva and Sati looked up with interest, but continued to eat.

'You've seen a frog, right?' asked Ganesh.

'Yes,' said Kartik, 'interesting creatures – especially their tongues!'

'A long time ago, an unknown Brahmin scientist conducted some experiments on frogs. He dropped a frog in a pot of boiling water and the frog immediately jumped out. He then placed a frog in a pot full of cold water and it settled down comfortably. The Brahmin then began raising the temperature of the water gradually, over many hours. The frog kept adapting to the increasingly warm water until it finally died, without making any attempt to escape. Naga students learn this story as a life lesson,' he added, noticing Kartik was not the only one listening with rapt attention. 'Often it's our immediate reaction to a sudden crisis that helps us save ourselves. Our response to gradual crises that creep up on us, on the other hand, may be so adaptive that they ultimately lead to self-destruction.'

'Are you suggesting that the Vayuputras keep adapting to the incremental ill-effects of the *Somras*?' asked Kartik. 'That the bad news is trickling in rather than coming all at once, so it's not big enough for them to really notice?'

'Perhaps,' said Ganesh, 'for I refuse to believe that the Vayuputras, Lord Rudra's chosen people, would consciously choose to let Evil live. The only explanation must be that they genuinely believe the *Somras* isn't evil.'

'Interesting,' said Shiva. 'Perhaps you're right.'

'But do you really believe the frog experiment story?' said Sati playfully, in an attempt to lighten the atmosphere.

'It's such a popular story around here that I actually tried it when I was a child.'

'Did you really boil a frog slowly to death? And it sat still all the while?'

Ganesh laughed. '*Maaaaa!* Frogs don't sit still no matter what you do! Boiling water, cold water or lukewarm water, a frog always leaps out!'

And the Mahadev's family laughed heartily.

— 𑀣 ꧑ U ⚹ ꙮ —

After meeting with the Naga nobility, Shiva and Sati left the Panchavati *Rajya Sabha*. Many of the nobles were in agreement with Queen Kali and wanted to attack Meluha immediately, to destroy the evil *Somras*. But some, like Vasuki and Astik, powerful Naga nobles, wanted to avoid war.

'Vasuki and Astik genuinely want peace, but for the wrong reasons,' said Shiva. 'They may be Naga nobility, but they still believe their own people deserve their cruel fate because they're being punished for their past-life sins. This is such nonsense!'

Sati did believe in the concept of *karma* extending over many births and couldn't hold back her objection. 'Just because we don't understand something doesn't necessarily mean it's rubbish, Shiva.'

'Come on, Sati: there's only this life, this moment. That's the only thing we can be sure of. Everything else is just theory.'

'Then why were the Nagas born deformed? Why did I live as

a *vikarma* for so long? Surely we deserved it on some level – we were paying for our past-life sins—'

'That's ridiculous!' he burst out. 'Sati, how can *anyone* know *anything* about past-life sins? The *vikarma* system – just like every other system that governs human lives – was created by *us*. You fought the *vikarma* system and freed yourself.'

'But I didn't free myself, Shiva: you did. All the *vikarmas*, me included, were set free because that was your *karma*.'

'So how does that work?' he asked incredulously. 'Are you saying that, when I struck down this stupid law, many life-times' worth of sins were washed away? A day of divine pardon, indeed!'

'Shiva, are you mocking me?'

'Would I ever do that, dear?' But his smile gave him away. 'Don't you see how illogical this entire concept is? How can one believe that an innocent child is born with sin? It's clear as daylight: a newborn child has done no wrong – he's done no right, either; he's just been born. He can't have done anything yet; it simply isn't possible!'

'Perhaps not in this life, Shiva, but it's possible that the child committed a sin in a previous life. Or perhaps the child's ancestors committed sins for which the child must be held accountable.'

Shiva was not convinced. 'Don't you get it? It's a system designed to *control* people. It makes those who suffer or are oppressed blame themselves for their misery. You believe you're paying for sins committed in your own previous lives – or by your ancestors, or by your entire community – perhaps even the sins of the first man ever born! The system propagates suffering as a form of atonement, but at the same time it doesn't allow a person to question the wrongs being done to them in *this* life.'

'Then why do some people suffer?' she cried. 'Why do some get far *less* than they deserve?'

'For the same reason others get far *more* than what they deserve,' he said quietly. 'It's completely random. Life isn't fair.' He gallantly reached out to help Sati mount her steed, but she declined and gracefully vaulted onto the stallion's back. He had to smile – he loved nothing more than her intense sense of self-sufficiency and pride.

He leapt onto his own horse and spurred it on to match Sati's pace.

She looked at him as their horses drew level. 'Do you really believe that the Parmatma plays dice with the universe? That we're all handed our fate randomly?'

The Nagas they passed on the road bowed low in respect as they recognised the Neelkanth. They didn't believe in the legend, but clearly their queen respected the Mahadev and that made most Nagas believe in Shiva, too. He politely acknowledged every person as he replied to Sati's question. 'I don't think the Parmatma interferes in our lives. He sets the rules by which the universe exists, and then He does something very difficult.'

'What's that?'

'He leaves us alone. He lets things play out naturally. He lets His creations make their own decisions about their own lives. It's not easy being a witness when one has the power to rule.

It takes a Supreme God to be able to do that. He knows this is our world: the land of our *karma*, our *karmabhoomi*,' said Shiva, gesturing all around.

'Don't you find this notion difficult to accept?' Sati asked. 'If people truly believed their fate was completely random, surely they would have no sense of understanding, no real purpose or motivation – they wouldn't have any reason for or understanding of why they are where they are.'

'On the contrary, I find it an empowering thought. When you know your fate is completely random, you have the freedom to follow any theory that *you* believe will empower you. If you've been blessed with good fate, you can choose to be humble and believe it's God's kindness, but if you've had bad luck – if you feel you've been cursed with bad fate – you know that no Great Power is seeking to punish you. Your situation's just a result of completely random circumstances, an indiscriminate turn of the universe; so, if you decide to challenge your destiny, your opponent won't be some judgemental Lord Almighty who's seeking to punish you for some reason; your opponent will only be the limitations of your own mind. It's this knowledge that will empower you to fight your fate. Bad luck is not set in stone.'

Sati shook her head. 'Sometimes you're too revolutionary for me.'

Shiva's eyes crinkled as he smiled at his wife. 'Maybe that in itself is a result of my past-life sins!'

Laughing together, they cantered out through the city gates. When the Panchavati guest-house colony became visible in the distance, Shiva whispered gravely, 'But there is one man who'll have to account to his friends for his *karma* in this life.'

'Brahaspatiji?'

Shiva nodded.

'What do you have in mind?'

'I asked Brahaspati if he'd like to meet Parvateshwar and Ayurvati, to explain to them how come he's still alive.'

'And?'

'He agreed without hesitation.'

'I'd have expected nothing less from him.'

— 🜊 —

'Are you all right?' Anandmayi asked her husband.

Parvateshwar looked around their private room in the Panchavati guest-house colony as if searching for answers before admitting, 'I'm thoroughly confused. The ruler of Meluha should embody the very best qualities of our way of life – truth, duty and honour. So what does it say about us if our emperor's a habitual lawbreaker? He broke the law when Sati's child was born.'

'What Emperor Daksha did was patently wrong,' she agreed, 'but one could argue that he was just a father trying to protect his child, albeit in an exceptionally stupid way.'

'The fact that what he did was wrong is enough! He broke *Meluha*'s law – and now he's broken one of *Lord Rudra*'s laws by using the *daivi astras*. How can Meluha, the finest land in the world, have an emperor like him? Something must be wrong somewhere.'

Anandmayi held her husband's hand. 'Your emperor was never any good. I could have told you that years ago. But you don't need to blame all of Meluha for his misdeeds.'

'But that's not how it works.' The general tried to explain his thoughts. 'A leader isn't just a person who gives orders: he also symbolises the society he leads. If the leader's corrupt, then the society must be corrupt, too.'

'Who feeds you this nonsense, my love? A leader's just a human being, like everyone else. He doesn't *symbolise* anything.'

Parvateshwar shook his head. 'Some truths can't be challenged. A leader's *karma* impacts his entire land. He's supposed to be his people's icon. That's a universal truth.'

Anandmayi leaned towards him, her eyes twinkling. 'Parvateshwar, there's your truth and there's my truth. *Universal* truth doesn't exist.'

Parvateshwar smiled as he brushed a stray strand of hair away from her face. 'You Chandravanshis are very good with words.'

'Words can only be as good or as bad as the thoughts they convey.'

'So what are your thoughts on what I should do? My emperor's actions have put me in a situation where the Neelkanth – my god – may declare war on my country. What do I do then? How do I know which side to pick?'

'You should stick with your god,' said Anandmayi, without

hesitation. 'But it's a hypothetical question, so don't worry too much about it.'

'My Lord, you sent for me?' said Ayurvati.

The doctor and Parvateshwar had been summoned to Shiva's chambers. Since their arrival in Panchavati, Shiva had spent most of his time with the Nagas, and Ayurvati, convinced that the Nagas were somehow complicit in the attack on Shiva's convoy, believed the Neelkanth was investigating the roots of the Naga treachery.

'Parvateshwar, Ayurvati, welcome,' said Shiva. 'I called you here because it's time you knew the secret of the Nagas.'

'But why only the two of us, my Lord?' Parvateshwar asked.

'Because both of you are Meluhans. I have reason to suspect that the attack on us at the Godavari is linked to many things: the plague in Branga, the plight of the Nagas and the drying up of the Saraswati,' Shiva began. 'But there is one thing of which I am certain: the attack is connected to the destruction of Mount Mandar.'

'What——? How——?' exclaimed Parvateshwar, looking shocked at Shiva's words.

'Only one man can explain it: a man you believe to be dead.'

Ayurvati and Parvateshwar spun around as they heard the door open.

Brahaspati walked in quietly.

'The *Somras* is evil?' asked Anandmayi incredulously, looking at Parvateshwar and Bhagirath, who had just joined them. 'Is that what the Lord Neelkanth thinks?'

'I'm not sure what he thinks,' said Parvateshwar, 'but that's what Brahaspati appears to believe.'

'But Evil is supposed to be Evil for everybody,' said Bhagirath. 'Why should a Suryavanshi turncoat decide what Evil is? Why should we listen to him? Why should the Neelkanth listen to him?'

'Bhagirath, do you expect me to defend Brahaspati, the man who destroyed the soul of our empire?' asked Parvateshwar.

'Just a minute,' said Anandmayi, raising her hand. 'Let's think this through . . . If the plague in Branga is linked to the *Somras*, if the slow depletion of the River Saraswati is linked to the *Somras*, if the birth of the Nagas is linked to the *Somras* – then isn't it fair to consider that maybe it *is* evil?'

'So what's the Neelkanth planning to do?' asked Bhagirath. 'Does he want to ban the *Somras*?'

'I don't know, Bhagirath!' Parvateshwar snapped. His world had been turned upside down, first by Emperor Daksha and now again by Chief Scientist Brahaspati. 'You keep asking me questions for which I have no answers!'

Anandmayi placed her hand on her husband's shoulder. 'Perhaps the Neelkanth's just as shocked as we are. He'll need to think things over – he can't afford to make any hasty decisions.'

'He's made one decision already,' said Parvateshwar. 'We're to leave for Swadweep as soon as everyone's recovered from their injuries. The Lord has asked us to wait for him at Kashi until he has decided his next move. He doesn't believe King Athithigva sold out to Ayodhya. He doesn't think he was in on the conspiracy to assassinate us on the Godavari.'

'But if we go to Kashi, my father will find out that we're alive,' said Bhagirath. 'He'll know his attack has failed.'

'We have to keep quiet about that – we have to pretend that nothing happened, that we were never attacked. That we had an uneventful journey to Panchavati and back.'

'Won't they wonder about their ships?'

'The Lord says we don't need to worry about that. Many things can happen during long voyages – their ships might have met with an accident before they could attack us.'

Bhagirath raised his eyebrows. 'My father might be stupid enough to believe that story but he's not the leader. Whoever put this conspiracy together will certainly investigate what went wrong.'

'But investigations take time, which will allow the Neelkanth to check whatever he needs to check.'

'Where is the Lord going?' asked Anandmayi.

Parvateshwar shook his head. 'I don't know. And he said we should let it be known that neither he nor his family are with us at Kashi; we're to say that he remains in Panchavati – that should keep us safe, since the attack was aimed at him.'

Bhagirath looked thoughtful. 'It looks to me like he's taking Brahaspati's claims at face value but wants to gather some more information before he makes up his mind once and for all.'

Anandmayi looked at her husband with concern in her eyes. She knew that a war was approaching – perhaps the biggest war India had ever seen. And in all probability, Meluha and Shiva would be on opposite sides. Which side would her husband choose?

'Whatever happens,' said Anandmayi, holding Parvateshwar's gaze, 'we must have faith in the Neelkanth.'

Parvateshwar nodded silently.

Shiva, lost in thought, took a deep drag from the chillum as he stared towards the Godavari River. He let out a sigh as he turned to Parshuram and Nandi. 'Are you sure, my friend?' he asked Parshuram.

'Yes, my Lord,' replied Parshuram. 'I can even take you to the uppermost point of the mighty Brahmaputra where it's still the Tsangpo. But I wouldn't recommend it – that treacherous route is very dangerous.'

Shiva's silence provoked Parshuram to probe further. 'What is it about that particular river, my Lord? First the Nagas and now you – why is everyone so interested in it?'

Shiva looked round and said seriously, 'It may be the carrier of Evil.'

Nandi, surprised, asked, 'Doesn't the Tsangpo rise close to your own home in Tibet?'

'Yes,' said Shiva, 'and it would appear that Evil has been closer than we first thought.'

Nandi remained quiet. He was one of the few who knew the ships that had attacked their convoy were from Meluha. If it came to a choice between Shiva and his country, he'd choose Shiva, of course, but knowing he might have to be part of an army attacking his beloved motherland was a dreadful thought. Having to make such a choice would hurt him immensely and he hated his fate for having put him in such an invidious position.

— ⫟ ⬯Ü⫟ ✹ —

Bhagirath sought an appointment with Shiva as soon as he left Parvateshwar's chambers. If his father had decided to oppose the Neelkanth, it made sense for him to prove his own loyalty to Shiva immediately. He didn't expect Shiva to lose; regardless of their emperor's opinions, the people would side with the Neelkanth when the time came.

'I think I know how to find the mastermind, My Lord,' he said, and at Shiva's request, explained: 'You agree that my father doesn't have the wherewithal to come up with such an elaborate plan. I'd say his selfish needs have made him succumb to the evil designs of another.'

Shiva looked intrigued. 'You think he's been bribed? Surely your father's in no need of money?'

'What can be a better bribe than life itself, my Lord? Had you seen my father a few years ago you'd have thought he was but a small step away from the cremation pyre. A life of debauchery and drink had wreaked havoc within his body. But today he looks younger than I've ever known him.'

'Has he been taking the *Somras*?'

'I don't think so. He tried the *Somras* in the past, but it didn't work for him. I suspect somebody's supplying him with medicines that would otherwise be unavailable, even to an emperor.'

Shiva's eyes widened. *Who could be more powerful, more knowledgeable than an emperor?* 'Do you think a maharishi's helping him?'

Bhagirath shook his head. 'No, my Lord. I think a maharishi's *leading* him.'

'But who can that maharishi be?'

'I don't know. But when I return to Ayodhya—'

'Ayodhya?'

'If we're to maintain the illusion that no ships attacked us on the Godavari, then what reason can there be for me not to go back to Ayodhya? If I don't return, it'll arouse suspicion. More importantly, I can only uncover the true identity of the master in Ayodhya. Despite my father's best efforts, I still have eyes and ears in that impregnable city.'

Shiva considered this for a moment, then said, 'Yes, all right. Go to Ayodhya.'

'But, my Lord,' Bhagirath added, 'when the time comes, I hope Ayodhya and Swadweep will be shown some kindness.'

'Kindness?'

'We haven't used the *Somras* excessively, my Lord – only a few Chandravanshi nobles use it, and then sparingly. It's the Meluhans' abuse of it that's caused Evil to rise, so surely it's only fair that, when the *Somras* is banned, this ban be imposed only on Meluha. Swadweep hasn't benefited from the drink of the gods, so I hope we'll be allowed to use it now.'

'You didn't *choose* to use less *Somras*, Bhagirath,' said Shiva. 'You just didn't have the opportunity to do so. If you had, the situation would be very different. You know that as well as I do.'

'But Meluha—'

'Yes, Meluha's used more, so naturally, they'll suffer more. But let me make one thing clear: if I decide the *Somras* is evil, then no one will use it. *No one*. Is that clear?'

Bhagirath kept silent for a moment, then said, 'Of course, my Lord.'

CHAPTER 5

The Shorter Route

A caravan of five hundred people moved up the northern path from Panchavati towards the Vasudev city of Ujjain. Shiva and his family, in the centre, were surrounded by half a brigade of Naga and Branga soldiers in standard defensive formations. Kali hadn't wanted to reveal this route to anyone from Shiva's original convoy, so only Nandi and Parshuram were there. Brahaspati was with Shiva too, in case the Neelkanth needed his insight to interpret whatever the Vasudevs might have to say about the *Somras* – but, although Shiva had many questions for him, the brotherly love they'd once shared was still missing.

Parvateshwar, Anandmayi, Ayurvati and Bhagirath had remained in Panchavati along with the original convoy. They were to leave for Kashi in a few weeks, and their eastern route would take them through Dandak Forest and onwards through Branga. Vishwadyumna was going to guide them as far as Branga.

'Ganesh, is Ujjain on the way from Panchavati to Meluha, or do we have to take a detour?' asked Shiva, urging his horse along the forest path, which was fenced by two protective hedges, an inner layer of harmless Nagavalli creepers and an outer of poisonous vines, to prevent wild animals from straying onto the path.

'Ujjain's to the north-east, on the way to Swadweep, *baba*,' replied Ganesh. 'Meluha's north-west.'

When the convoy paused for rest, Sati tried to get her bearings. She knew that Maika, the Meluhan city of births, was not too far from the mouth of the Narmada. 'Does the Narmada serve as your waterway, Ganesh? One can sail west along it for Meluha and east for Ujjain and Swadweep.'

'Yes, *maa*,' answered Ganesh.

'Have you ever been to Maika as an adult?' Shiva asked. 'How do abandoned Naga children get adopted?'

'Maika's the one place where there's no bias against the Nagas, *baba*. Perhaps the sight of helpless Naga babies shrieking in pain as cancerous growths burst through their bodies melts the authorities' hearts. The Maika governor tries to save as many Naga babies as he can in that crucial first month after their birth. We send a ship down the Narmada every month for them. We dock at Maika late at night and all the Naga babies born in that month are handed over to us by the Maika record-keeper. Some non-Naga parents choose to move to Panchavati with their children.'

'Don't the Maika authorities stop them?'

'Actually, it's the other way round: by law, parents *should*

accompany their Naga children to Panchavati, and some do –
but others break the law and refuse, abandoning their children so
they can return to their comfortable life in Meluha. The Maika
governor turns a blind eye to these transgressions.'

Sati had lived in Meluha for more than a hundred years, but
Ganesh's revelations were making her see her upright nation in
an entirely new light. Her father hadn't been the only parent
who'd broken the law; many Meluhans apparently valued the
comforts of their homeland above their duty to their children
or observing Lord Ram's laws.

Looking ahead, Shiva could see a large ship anchored in a massive lagoon surrounded by a dense grove of trees. He recalled the
grove of floating sundari trees he'd seen in Branga and assumed
these trees were the same, with free-floating roots that allowed
them to move apart to allow the ship through into open water.
'I guess we've reached your secret lagoon,' he commented. 'I
assume the Narmada's beyond that grove?'

'There is a massive river beyond that grove, *baba*,' said Ganesh,
'but it's not the Narmada – it's the Tapi. The Narmada's a few
days' journey beyond the Tapi.'

Shiva smiled. 'The Lord Almighty has blessed this land with
so many rivers – India can never run short of water!'

'We might, if we continue to abuse our rivers the way we're
abusing the Saraswati,' Ganesh pointed out, and Shiva nodded
ruefully, silently conceding Ganesh's point.

Bhrigu tore open the letter. It was exactly what he'd expected: the Vayuputras had excommunicated him.

Lord Bhrigu,

It has been brought to our attention that daivi astras were loaded aboard a fleet of ships in Karachapa. Investigations have led us to the regrettable conclusion that you manufactured them, using materials given to you strictly for research purposes. While we assume you would never misuse the weapons expressly banned by our god, Lord Rudra, we cannot allow the unauthorised transport of these weapons to go unpunished. You are therefore prohibited from ever entering Pariha or interacting with a Vayuputra again. We hope you will honour the greater promise that every friend of a Vayuputra makes to Lord Rudra: that of never using the daivi astras. It is the expectation of the council that you will surrender the weapons at once to Vayuputra Security.

What did surprise Bhrigu was that the letter had been signed by the Mithra himself. It was rare for the leader of the Vayuputra Council to sign orders personally; that task usually fell to one of the six deputies of the Amartya Shpand. The Vayuputras were clearly taking this very seriously indeed.

But Bhrigu didn't believe he'd broken the law. He'd already written to warn the Vayuputras that they were making a mockery of the institution of the Neelkanth by not acting against this self-appointed imposter. Alas, the Vayuputras had done nothing, which had forced Bhrigu to act alone. He could see how they might think he'd misused their research materials, but ironically, he hadn't: the small quantities of ingredients supplied by the council had been inadequate for his purposes, so he'd used materials he himself had collected over the years. Of course, that might explain why the *daivi astras* he'd manufactured hadn't had the full destructive potency of those made from Vayuputra materials. They had whole laboratories at their disposal, while Bhrigu had been forced to work alone.

He sighed. He'd used all the weapons he'd made, but he still had no idea if they'd actually achieved their purpose and killed the Neelkanth. Daksha had been in a state of shock since the breakdown in his relations with his daughter, so trying to talk to him was an exercise in futility. He'd had no choice but to send another ship to the mouth of the Godavari to investigate the matter, this one manned by sailors drawn from Dilipa's army, but it would be months before they learned what had happened.

'Anything else, my Lord?' asked the attendant.

Bhrigu dismissed her with an absent-minded wave. Perhaps the job was done; maybe the false Neelkanth was no more. But it was also possible that Bhrigu's ships had failed – or, even worse, the Neelkanth might have been persuaded by the Nagas and even now be plotting with them to turn the people against the *Somras*. For now, much as he disliked living in Devagiri, he had no choice but to wait until he received news one way or the other. India's very future was at stake: he could do nothing until he knew whether the *Somras* was safe or not.

Bhrigu took a deep breath and slipped back into a meditative trance.

— ⚊ 𝖠 ꙮ∪꙰ ⚛ —

Shiva's caravan had covered ground quickly after crossing the Tapi and was soon waiting at the edge of another secret lagoon to board more Naga vessels. Beyond this floating grove was the mighty Narmada, which Lord Manu had declared the southern border of the Sapt Sindhu.

'How much further, *dada*?'

'Not too far, Kartik. Just a few more weeks,' Ganesh said. 'We'll sail east up the Narmada for a few days, then march on foot through the passes of the great Vindhya Mountains until we reach the Chambal River. A few days' sailing down the Chambal will bring us to Ujjain.'

Sati watched the sailors pull the gangway towards the rudimentary dock and prepare the ship for boarding. She wished her sister, Kali, had accompanied them on this journey, but she knew the Naga queen had many responsibilities back in Panchavati.

Her thoughts were interrupted by the loud thud as the ship's gangway landed on the dock, and she turned her attention to the next leg of their journey.

— ⚊ 𝖠 ꙮ∪꙰ ⚛ —

Parvateshwar, Anandmayi, Bhagirath and Ayurvati led their convoy, the sixteen hundred soldiers who'd originally accompanied Shiva more than a year ago, into the first of five clearings along the Dandakaranya Road, which led from Panchavati to the hidden lagoon on the Madhumati River in Branga.

Bhagirath looked at the five paths that branched off from the clearing in wonder. Only one led to Kashi. The others were decoys that would lead trespassers to their doom. 'These Nagas are obsessive about security,' he observed.

Anandmayi laughed a little. 'Can you blame them? And don't forget that their security-conscious attitude saved our lives when those ships attacked us on the Godavari.'

'True,' he said. 'The Nagas will no doubt prove to be good allies. Their loyalty to the Neelkanth isn't suspect – though their reasons might well be. When the moment of truth is upon us, everyone will have to answer one simple question: *Will I fight the world for the Neelkanth?*' He smiled. 'I know I will.'

Seeing Parvatashwar's pained reaction to the prince's words, Anandmayi's eyes flashed a warning at Bhagirath. 'Calm down, little brother.'

Parvateshwar's own eyes were tortured when they met his wife's. 'I don't think the Parmatma will be so cruel to me,' he said, though his words sounded like a prayer rather than a statement. 'Surely he hasn't made me wait for more than a century to find my living god, only to force me to choose between my country and him. I pray that the Almighty will find a way to ensure that Meluha and the Lord Neelkanth are not on opposite sides.'

But Parvateshwar's sad smile told Anandmayi he didn't believe his own words, and she touched her husband's shoulder gently.

Bhagirath played with his *roti* absentmindedly. He was beginning to believe they couldn't count on Parvateshwar, which would be a huge loss for the Neelkanth's army. He was certain the general's strategic abilities could turn the tide in any war.

Ayurvati had sympathy for Parvateshwar's dilemma; she could identify with his inner conflict. But she'd found a solution that sat comfortably in her own heart: her emperor had committed heinous acts which had dishonoured Meluha. It was no longer the country she'd loved and admired all her life. She knew in her heart that Lord Ram wouldn't have condoned the immorality into which Meluha had descended under Daksha's leadership, and so her path was clear: in a fight between Meluha and Shiva, she would choose the Neelkanth, for he would set things right in Meluha as well.

The Naga ship anchored close to the Chambal shore and Shiva, Sati, Ganesh and Kartik climbed down the rope ladders into a boat ready to ferry them ashore. Brahaspati, Nandi, Parshuram and ten Naga soldiers followed them.

Shiva studied the bank as they approached, though the Vasudevs were even more secretive than the Nagas so he didn't expect to find any signs of habitation close to the river. A dense wall of foliage blocked the view inland and the weeds that had spread over the gentle Chambal waters were making rowing a back-breaking task.

Ganesh navigated the boat towards a narrow clearing between

two immense palm trees. There was something unnatural about the clearing, but Shiva couldn't put his finger on it. He noticed that Kartik was also staring in the same direction.

'*Baba*, look at the trees beyond the clearing,' said Kartik. 'You'll have to bend down to my level.'

Couching down beside his son, the image became clearer: the trees behind the clearing were growing in a very orderly formation, getting taller as they receded, quite unlike the dense, uncontrolled growth surrounding them. Shiva realised that the optical illusion was caused by the ground sloping upwards in a gentle gradient – and the hillock was obviously not natural. Most of the trees behind the clearing were gulmohur, with their fiery flame-orange flowers. Then he suddenly stood up, rocking the boat, and Sati and Ganesh quickly reached out to hold him steady.

'What is it?' Sati asked, trying to work out what Shiva had seen, but the gulmohur trees had been placed in a specific pattern that was only visible from a certain position directly in front of the small clearing between the twin palms.

Shiva had spotted that they formed the shape of a flame – a very specific symbol that he recognised. '*Fravashi*,' he whispered.

Surprised, Ganesh asked, 'How do you know that word, *baba*?'

Shiva glanced at Ganesh, then back at the gulmohur trees. The pattern had disappeared. Shiva sat down and said, 'I'd ask you the same question.'

'It's a Vayuputra term – it's the feminine spirit of Lord Rudra, which has the power to assist us to do the right thing. We're free to either accept it or reject it, but the spirit never refuses to help. Never.'

Shiva smiled as he suddenly began to understand his ancient memories.

'Who told you about *Fravashi*, *baba*?' asked Ganesh again.

'My Uncle Manobhu,' said Shiva. 'It was one of the many things he made me learn. He said it would help me when the time came.'

'Where did he learn such things?'

'I have no idea,' said Shiva. 'I thought I knew him, but I'm beginning to wonder if I knew him at all.'

Their conversation came to a halt as the boat hit the bank. Two Naga soldiers jumped out and held the boat steady while everyone else got out, then they moored the craft to a conveniently located tree stump.

Kartik glanced at the palms surrounding the clearing as Ganesh walked to its centre and said loudly, 'Can everyone stand behind me, please. I don't want anybody standing between me and the palm trees.'

The others did as he requested and Ganesh closed his eyes to drown out possible distractions and focused his concentration. He breathed deeply and began to clap hard in an irregular rhythm, transmitting a message in the Vasudev code to the gatekeeper of Ujjain: *This is Ganesh, the Naga Lord of the People, requesting permission to enter your great city with our entourage.*

The soft sounds of claps reverberated back as Ujjain's gatekeeper answered. Ganesh heard: *Welcome, Lord Ganesh. This is an unexpected honour. Are you on your way to Swadweep?*

No — we've come to meet with Lord Gopal, the great Chief Vasudev. Is there something specific you need to discuss?

Clearly, the Vasudevs still weren't comfortable with the Nagas, despite the fact that they'd reached out to Ganesh for the Naga medicines to help with Kartik's birth. The Ujjain gatekeeper was trying to deny Ganesh's request without insulting him.

Ganesh continued to clap rhythmically. *It is not I who seeks Lord Gopal, honoured gatekeeper. It is the Lord Neelkanth.*

A few moments' silence ensued, followed by a series of claps in quick succession. *Is the Lord Neelkanth at the palm clearing with you?*

He's standing right next to me. He can hear you clapping.

Silence again, then the gatekeeper responded: *Lord Ganesh, Lord Gopal himself is coming to the clearing. We will be honoured to host your convoy. It'll take us a day to get there — please remain in or near the clearing until we arrive.*

Ganesh rubbed his hands together and looked at Shiva. 'It'll take a day for them to get here, *baba*. We can wait aboard the ship until they arrive.'

'Have you ever been to Ujjain?' asked Shiva.

'No, *baba*. I've met the Vasudevs just once before, in this very clearing.'

'You're right: we might as well be comfortable while we're waiting. Back to the ship it is.'

— ⚹ ◉∪✛◈ —

'Are you telling me Lord Bhrigu visited Ayodhya *eight times* in the last year?' Surapadman, Crown Prince of Magadh, sounded surprised. He maintained his own espionage network, independent of the notoriously inefficient Royal Magadh spy service, for just this reason: this was the first he'd heard of the goings-on in the Ayodhyan royal household.

'Yes, your Highness,' answered the spy. 'Furthermore, Emperor Dilipa himself has visited Meluha twice during the same period.'

'That, I'm aware of,' said Surapadman, 'but your news throws new light on things. Perhaps Dilipa wasn't going to meet that fool Daksha after all – maybe he was going to meet Lord Bhrigu. But why would the great sage be interested in Dilipa?'

'That I do not know, your Highness. But I'm sure you've heard about Emperor Dilipa's new youthful appearance. Perhaps Lord Bhrigu has been giving him the *Somras*?'

Surapadman waved his hand dismissively. 'The *Somras* is easily available to Swadweepan royalty – Dilipa's been using the *Somras* for years; he certainly wouldn't need to plead with a maharishi for it. But when one has abused the body as much as he has, even the *Somras* would find it difficult to delay his ageing. I suspect Lord Bhrigu must be giving him medicines even more potent than the *Somras*.'

'But why would Lord Bhrigu do that?'

'That's the mystery, isn't it? Try to find out – oh, and any news of the Neelkanth?'

'No, your Highness. He remains in Naga territory.'

Surapadman rubbed his chin and looked out of the window at the Ganga. The gaze of his mind's eye stretched beyond the river into the jungle to the south, into the forests where his brother, Ugrasen, had been killed by the Nagas. He silently cursed Ugrasen, for he knew the truth of his brother's murder. Ugrasen had become addicted to bull-racing; he'd been indulging in increasingly reckless bets. Desperate to obtain good child-riders for his bulls, he'd started scouring the tribal forests, kidnapping children at will. On one such expedition, he'd been killed by a Naga who was trying to protect a helpless mother and her young boy. What Surapadman still couldn't understand was why a Naga would risk his life to save a forest woman and her child.

But Ugrasen's death had narrowed Surapadman's options. The Neelkanth would lead his followers against whomever he decided was evil, and there would be those who'd oppose him. Surapadman didn't care much about this war against Evil. All he wanted was to ensure that Magadh would fight on the opposite side to Ayodhya. He intended to use the chaos of the coming war to establish Magadh as the ruling kingdom of Swadweep, with himself as emperor. But Ugrasen's death had deepened their father King Mahendra's distrust of the Nagas into unadulterated hatred, and he knew Mahendra would force him to fight *against* whichever side the Nagas allied with. His only hope lay in the Nagas and the Emperor of Ayodhya choosing the same side.

Kanakhala waited patiently in Maharishi Bhrigu's chambers at Emperor Daksha's palace. The maharishi was in deep meditation. Although his chamber was inside a palace, it was as simple and severe as his real cave home in the Himalayas. Bhrigu was sitting on the stone bed, the only piece of furniture in the room, so Kanakhala had no choice but to stand. Icy water had been sprinkled on the floor and the walls, and the resultant clammy cold was making her shiver. She looked at the bowl of fruit on a small stand in the far corner of the room. The maharishi appeared to have eaten just one apple over the last three days. She made a mental note to order fresh fruit to be brought in. An idol of Lord Brahma had been installed in an alcove in the wall and now Kanakhala stared fixedly at the idol as she repeated Bhrigu's soft chanting.

Om Brahmaye Namah. Om Brahmaye Namah.

Bhrigu opened his eyes and gazed at Kanakhala for a moment before saying, 'Yes, my child?'

'My Lord, a sealed letter has been delivered for you by bird-courier. It's marked *strictly confidential*, so I thought I should bring it to you personally.'

Bhrigu nodded politely and took the letter from Kanakhala without saying a word.

'As instructed, we've also kept the pigeon with us so it can take a reply to wherever it came from. Of course, this won't be possible if the ship's moved. Please let me know if you'd like to send a message back with the bird.'

Bhrigu continued to stare at her contemplatively, but said nothing.

'Will that be all, my Lord?' asked Kanakhala at last, and he nodded.

As the prime minister shut the door behind her, Bhrigu broke the seal and opened the letter. Its contents were disappointing.

My Lord, we've found some wreckage from our ships at the mouth of the Godavari – they've obviously been blown up. It's difficult to judge whether they were destroyed as a result of sabotage or an accident owing to the goods they carried. It's also difficult to say if all the ships were destroyed or if there are any survivors. We await further instructions.

The words gave Bhrigu information without adding anything to his understanding of the situation. Not one of the five ships he'd despatched to assassinate the Neelkanth and destroy Panchavati had returned or sent a message. The wreckage of at least some of the ships had been discovered, having drifted down the Godavari. Both possible conclusions were disturbing: either the ships had all been destroyed, or some of them had been captured. Bhrigu couldn't afford to send another ship up the Godavari to try and investigate further; he might end up gifting another well-built warship to the enemy just before the final war. Of course, there was also the possibility that the ships had succeeded in their mission and been destroyed subsequently – but he simply couldn't be sure.

He would have to wait. Maybe an angry Neelkanth would emerge from the jungles of Dandak to rally his followers and attack those allied against him – if that didn't happen, then he would assume that the Neelkanth threat had passed.

Bhrigu rang the bell to summon the guard outside. He would order the ship at the mouth of the Godavari to return, and he would have Meluha and Ayodhya prepare their armies for battle. Just in case.

CHAPTER 6

The City That Conquers Pride

Shiva stood at the anchored ship's balustrade and stared into the dark expanse of forest on the Chambal's banks. Deep in the distance, silvered by a full moon, was a massive hill made of pure black stone. Shiva had been observing that hill all evening. It was too smooth to be natural, and at its summit was a domed cupola coloured an even deeper hue of black.

'It's man-made, *baba*,' said Kartik, who was crouching next to Shiva, Ganesh and Brahaspati, looking at the riverbank from a lower height. Shiva squatted down until he was at the same level as Kartik and scanned the area beyond the clearing. He could plainly see the pattern of the ancient Vayuputra *Fravashi* image. As his eyes traced the slope, he realised that, had the incline continued, it would have ended at the very top of the black hill in the distance, at the cupola.

Brahaspati said, 'The slope's probably the remnant of a very long ramp that was used to carry that stone cupola to the top of the hill.'

Shiva smiled at the Vasudevs' precise engineering skills. He'd been speaking with his mysterious advisors for years; now he was looking forward to finally meeting their leader.

Daksha gazed at the full moon reflected in the shimmering waters of the Saraswati. He was standing by the large window of his private palace chamber. He had isolated himself more and more in the past few months, avoiding people as much as possible. He was especially terrified of meeting Maharishi Bhrigu, convinced as he was that the maharishi would read his mind and realise it was Daksha himself who had foiled the attack on Panchavati in an attempt to save his beloved daughter.

But this period of isolation had done wonders for Daksha and Veerini's relationship. They were conversing, even confiding in each other once again, almost like they had during the first few years of their marriage – before Daksha had developed ambitions to become the ruler of the whole of Meluha.

Veerini walked up to her husband and placed her hand on his shoulder. 'What are you thinking?'

Daksha pulled back from his wife and she frowned, then noticed his hands. He was holding the amulet of his chosen-tribe, the self-declared ranking within the caste hierarchy adopted by every young man and woman. His was a subordinate rank, a humble goat. Many Kshatriyas felt the goat chosen-tribe was so lowly that its members shouldn't be considered full Kshatriyas. Brahmanayak, Daksha's father, had selected the goat as his son's chosen-tribe, clearly reflecting his contempt for the boy.

'What's the matter, Daksha?' Veerini asked again.

'Why does she think I'm a monster? I got rid of her son for her own good – and we didn't *abandon* Ganesh – he was well taken care of in Panchavati. And how can she imagine that I'd even *think* of having her husband killed? It wasn't me.'

Veerini remained silent. Now was not the time to confront her husband with the truth. He could have saved Sati's first husband, Chandandhwaj, had he wanted to – he might not have given the order for Chandandhwaj to be killed, but he was complicit in the man's death by not preventing it. But Veerini knew that weak people never admit their responsibility for their own situation. They always blame circumstances, or the actions of others.

'I'm asking you again, Daksha: let's forget everything that's happened,' she said. 'You've achieved your greatest ambition. You're Emperor of India. We can't live in Panchavati any longer – we lost that opportunity long ago. Kali and Ganesh despise us, and I don't blame them for it. Let's take *sanyas*, retreat to the Himalayas and live out the rest of our lives in peace and meditation. We'll die with the name of the Lord on our lips.'

'I will *not* run away!'

'Daksha—'

'Everything's clear to me now. I needed the Neelkanth to conquer Swadweep, and now he's served his purpose. Sati will be back once he's gone, and then we'll all be happy again.'

Veerini stared at her husband, horrified. 'Daksha, what in Lord Ram's name are you thinking?'

'I can set everything right by—'

'Trust me, the best thing you can do is to leave all this alone. You should never have tried to become emperor. You can still be happy if—'

'Never tried to become emperor? What nonsense! I *am* the emperor – not just of Meluha, but of all India. You think some barbarian with a blue throat can defeat me? That a chillum-smoking, uncouth ingrate is going to take my family away from me?'

Veerini held her head in despair.

'I made him,' said Daksha, 'and I will finish him.'

— ⵊ ⵕⵓⵉⵛ —

'My Lord,' exclaimed Parshuram, 'look!'

Shiva turned towards the dense forests beyond the palm tree clearing. In the distance, a flock of birds flew into the sky, obviously disturbed by whatever was forging its way through the forest below.

'They're here,' said Nandi.

'Ganesh,' said Shiva, 'lower the boats.'

— ⵊ ⵕⵓⵉⵛ —

Shiva was waiting in the clearing with an entourage of two hundred men when the enormous elephants burst through the jungle. Their foreheads were adorned with ceremonial gear of intricately carved gold. Their *mahouts*, seated just behind the beasts' heads, were secured in position with ropes. The beasts were covered from head to toe in cane armour, which protected them from the whiplash of the branches they pushed aside so effortlessly. The *mahouts* expertly guided the elephants into the clearing using their feet and some gentle prodding with hook-like tools Ganesh told Shiva were called *ankush*. Sturdy wooden *howdahs*, fashioned to extend horizontally from the animals' sides, were firmly secured to the elephants' backs. They were completely covered on all sides, protecting the passengers travelling within. There was a door on one side, and angled slats allowed in light and air.

Shiva's eyes were fixed on the first elephant in the line. As it halted, its *howdah*'s door was flung open and a rope ladder rolled down to the ground. A tall, lanky pandit, clad in a saffron *dhoti* and *angvastram*, descended. As soon as the pandit's feet touched the ground, he turned towards Shiva with his hands folded in a respectful namaste. He had a flowing white beard and a long silvery mane, and his wizened face, calm eyes and gentle smile showed a deep understanding of true wisdom: the wisdom of *sat-chit-anand*, of *truth-consciousness-bliss*, the eternal bliss of having one's mind and consciousness drowned in truth.

'Namaste, Panditji,' said Shiva. 'It's an honour to finally meet the Chief Vasudev.'

'Namaste, great Mahadev,' said Gopal politely. 'Believe me, the honour's all mine. I have lived for this moment.'

Shiva stepped forward and embraced Gopal. The surprised

Chief Vasudev responded tentatively at first, then he returned the embrace as the Neelkanth's open-heartedness made him smile.

Shiva stepped back and looked at the large number of men and elephants waiting patiently. 'That's quite the crowd you've brought.'

Gopal smiled. 'This is a small clearing, great Mahadev. We don't meet many people.'

'I can't wait to see Ujjain. May we travel aboard your elephants?'

'Certainly,' said Gopal as he gestured towards his men to help Shiva and his entourage.

The *howdahs* were surprisingly spacious; each could seat eight people in relative comfort. Shiva and Sati rode with Gopal, along with Ganesh, Kartik, Brahaspati, Nandi and Parshuram.

'I hope your journey was comfortable,' said Gopal.

'It was,' said Shiva, and smiled at Ganesh. 'My son guided us well.'

'The Lord of the People has the reputation of a wise man,' agreed Gopal, 'and stories of your other son Kartik's warrior spirit have already reached our ears.'

Kartik acknowledged the compliment by folding his hands into a respectful namaste.

'Panditji,' asked Shiva, 'does the journey to Ujjain take a day because of the distance, or because of the density of the forest?'

'A bit of both, great Neelkanth. We haven't built any roads from the clearing on the Chambal into the city of Ujjain – as

I said, we don't meet many people. But when we do need to travel, our well-trained elephants don't need roads to take us where we need to go.'

— ☩ ⑩Ủ☩⊛ —

The passengers soon became used to the sounds of branches scraping against the outside of the *howdahs*, and they noticed the silence as soon as the sounds stopped.

'We're here,' said Gopal, and pressed a lever on his left. Hydraulic action made the sides and back of the *howdah* slowly collapse outwards, and Shiva realised the *howdah*'s roof was supported by strong pillars, with horizontal metal railings running between them. But no one else was paying attention to the *howdah*'s design. They were all transfixed by Ujjain, the 'city that conquers pride'.

The circular city had been laid out within a giant, perfectly square clearing cut into in the dense forest and encircled by a sturdy stone wall almost ten feet wide and thirty feet high. The Shipra River, a tributary of the Chambal, had been channelled to run around the walls, and the moat was infested with crocodiles.

As the elephants ambled slowly towards the moat, Shiva kept expecting the beasts to stop and wait for a drawbridge to be lowered. But the elephants kept moving, and there was no sign of any bridge. As the convoy approached, he counted twenty armed men standing guard on the raised embankment. Then two of the men stepped onto an area paved with slabs of stone next to the moat. As he watched, one of the slabs depressed into the embankment and a section of ground slid sideways to reveal broad, shallow steps descending deep into the earth.

As the elephants walked down the steps and entered a well-lit tunnel beneath the moat, the Vasudev guards went down on their knees in obeisance to the Neelkanth.

Kartik smiled at Ganesh. 'What a brilliant idea! The paved ground camouflages the entrance completely – and look – the slabs run all around the moat, so there won't be any tracks left around the entrance to the tunnel.'

'So unless an enemy knows exactly where the entrance is, he won't be able to cross the moat and enter the city.'

Nandi looked at Gopal with awe. 'Your tribe's brilliant, Panditji.'

Gopal smiled politely.

As the elephants moved towards the city gates, the passengers noticed large geometric patterns decorating the walls: a series of concentric circles, each circle boxed within a single perfect square, which appeared to symbolise the layout of Ujjain as seen from above. The city's circular fort wall was no accident, but rather what the Vasudevs believed was the perfect geometric design.

'We've built the entire city in the form of a *mandal*,' said Gopal.

'What's a *mandal*, Panditji?' asked Shiva.

'It's a symbolic representation of an approach to spirituality.'

'How so?'

'The square boundary of the moat symbolises *Prithvi*, the land we live on. It's represented by a square bounded on four sides, just as our land is bounded by the four directions. The space within the square represents *Prakriti*, or nature, just as the land we live on is uncultivated, wild jungle. Within it, the path of consciousness is the path of the Parmatma, which is represented by the circle.'

'Why a circle?'

'The Parmatma is the supreme soul. It's infinite, so if you want to represent infinity through a geometric pattern, you can't do better than a circle. It has no beginning and no end. You can't add another side to it or remove a side from it. It's perfect. It's infinity.'

Shiva smiled as Gopal went on to explain that a bird's-eye view of Ujjain would reveal five tree-lined ring roads within the circular fort wall, which divided the city into five zones. The outermost road skirted the inside of the wall with the rest, decreasing concentric circles, ending with the smallest encircling the massive Vishnu Temple at the centre of the city. Twenty paved radial roads extended in straight lines from the outermost ring road to the innermost.

The outermost zone, between the fourth and fifth ring roads, contained massive wooden stables housing the city's cows and horses and other domestic beasts, including the thousands of well-trained elephants. The next zone, between the third and fourth ring roads, was where the novices and trainees resided; it also housed their schools and markets, as well as places of entertainment. The zone between the second and third ring roads housed the Kshatriyas, Vaishyas and Shudras, while the zone between the first and second housed the Brahmins, the community which administered to the tribe of Vasudevs. And within the first ring road, in the heart of the city, was the central temple, the holiest place in Ujjain.

Shiva realised the temple, constructed from black bricks, was the hill-like structure he had seen from the banks of the Chambal. It was shaped like a perfect inverted cone, with a thousand pillars running around its circumference to support the base, then six hundred feet to the peak. A central pillar of hard granite had been erected within to support the massive weight of the ceiling, which included a forty-ton giant cupola at the apex of the temple. The cupola had been rolled up to the top of the temple by elephants along a ten-mile-long gradual incline, Shiva was told; he had seen the remnants of that slope at the Chambal.

As the elephants emerged from the tunnel onto the ring road next to the fort's inner wall, all eyes fell upon the Vishnu Temple at the heart of the city, a vision that was impossible to miss from any part of Ujjain. The entire entourage stared in wonder at the awe-inspiring sight.

Brahaspati finally voiced what everyone felt within when he sighed, 'Wow!'

CHAPTER 7

An Eternal Partnership

Shiva's entourage was housed in Ujjain's Brahmin zone, abutting the Vishnu Temple. Shiva had just finished breakfast with his family when a Vasudev pandit arrived to escort him to the temple for a meeting with Gopal.

The simple grandeur of the massive temple became even more apparent as Shiva approached it. The circular base platform was built of polished granite stones fixed together using an ingenious method Shiva hadn't seen before. Holes and channels had been drilled into the stones and filled with molten metal; as it solified, so it bound the stones together. It was no doubt expensive, but the bond was far stronger than traditional mortar. There were no carvings on the platform; Shiva was not alone in thinking that statues and carvings would have been an unnecessary distraction from this architectural marvel. Steps had been chiselled all around the circular platform, enabling visitors to approach the great seventh Vishnu, Lord Ram, from every direction.

The pandit told Shiva that elephant-powered lathes had been used to carve the thousand pillars into perfect evenness and uniform solidity. The massive black-stone spire looked as smooth up close as it had from a distance. Each stone block fitted together perfectly, and was polished smooth. The giant cupola of black limestone had been placed on top of the spire. The Vasudev pandit was silent as he watched Shiva climb the steps of the temple, gazing around in wonder.

As he entered the main temple, Shiva noticed that the spire was completely hollow inside, giving a magnificent view of the giant conical ceiling that enveloped the cavernous hall. Unlike those Shiva had seen in India, this temple didn't have a separate *sanctum sanctorum*; instead, the interior was an open communal place of worship. The ceiling was ablaze with brightly coloured paintings depicting scenes from the life of Lord Ram: his birth, education, exile and eventual triumphant return. Large frescoes on a prominent surface were devoted to the lord's life after he ascended the throne of Ayodhya: his real enemies and the wars he waged against them; his intense relationship with his inspirational wife, Lady Sita; and his founding of Meluha.

A giant white pillar stood in the centre of the hall, reaching six hundred feet to the apex of the conical spire. Shiva was amazed to see the detailed carvings on the granite pillar, one of the hardest stones known to man. They were giant images of Lord Ram and Lady Sita. Unadorned by royal ornaments or crowns, they wore plain hand-spun cotton, the garments of the poorest of the poor. The divine couple had worn such clothing during their fourteen-year exile, most of it spent in dense jungles. Even more intriguing were the absences of Lord Lakshman and Lord Hanuman, who were normally included in all depictions of the seventh Vishnu. Lady Sita held his right hand from below, as if showing support.

'Why has the worst phase of their life been chosen for depiction?' asked Shiva. 'This was after they'd been banished from Ayodhya, before Lady Sita was kidnapped by the demonic King Ravan and Lord Ram fought a fierce battle to rescue her.'

The Vasudev pandit smiled. 'Lord Ram said that even if the rest of his life was forgotten, the part he spent in exile along with his wife, brother and follower Hanuman should be remembered by all, for he believed this to be the period that made him who he was.'

Gopal was standing close to the base of the central pillar. Next to him were two ceremonial chairs, one at the feet of the statue of Lady Sita and the other at the feet of Lord Ram. A small ritual fire burned between the two chairs. The presence of the purifying Lord Agni, the God of Fire, signified that no lies could pass between those who sat on either side. Many Vasudev pandits stood patiently behind Gopal.

Gopal bowed to Shiva and joined his hands in a respectful namaste. 'A Vasudev exists to serve but two purposes. The next Vishnu must arise from amongst us, and we must serve the Mahadev, whenever he should choose to come.'

Shiva bowed low to Gopal in reciprocation.

Gopal continued, 'Every single one of us present here is

honoured that one of our missions will be fulfilled within our lifetime. We are yours to command, Lord Neelkanth.'

'You're not my follower, Lord Gopal,' said Shiva. 'You're my friend. I've come here to seek your advice, for I am not able to come to a decision.'

Gopal smiled and gestured towards the chairs.

Shiva and Gopal took their seats as the other Vasudev pandits sat around them on the floor, in neat rows.

Ganesh, Kartik and Brahaspati had set off on a short tour of Ujjain, accompanied by a Vasudev Kshatriya. Ganesh was deeply interested in the animal enclosures in the outermost zone, most specifically the stables.

Guiding his horse alongside Ganesh's mount, the Vasudev Kshatriya asked, 'Why are you so interested in the elephants, my Lord?'

'They're going to be very important in the impending war. They'll play a big role if they're as well-trained as I hope they are.'

The Vasudev smiled and prodded his horse forward, leading the way to the enclosures. He was happy to see the son of the Neelkanth interested in their war elephants. The Kshatriyas amongst the Vasudevs had revived the art of training them, against the advice of the ruling Vasudev pandits. These magnificent beasts had once formed the dominant corps in Indian armies, though countermeasures had been developed that offset their fearsome power, foremost amongst them the use of specific drums which disturbed the elephants and made them run amok, resulting in high casualties within their own ranks. Most armies had stopped using them, but well-trained elephants could still be devastating on a battlefield. Ganesh had heard about the elephants of the Vasudev army, but their famous reticence made it difficult to know for sure whether the stories were true or nothing but rumours.

Kartik leaned close to his brother. '*Dada*, we already saw how exceptionally well trained their elephants were when we rode them here from the Chambal.'

'Indeed,' answered Ganesh, 'but those were female elephants, used for domestic work like ferrying people or materials. Male elephants are needed in times of war.'

'Is that because they're more aggressive than the females?'

'All elephants can be provoked – even trained – to be aggressive, but it's more difficult to train a female elephant, for she'll kill only with good reason – for example when her offspring is threatened. It's easier to train a male elephant to be belligerent.'

'Why is that?' asked Kartik. 'Are they less intelligent than the females?'

'I've heard that the female of the species is smarter, but it's a little more complicated than that. Elephant herds are matriarchal; in the wild, it's usually the oldest female who makes all the decisions: when they'll move, where they'll feed, who remains in the herd and who gets kicked out—'

'Kicked out?'

'Male elephants are made to leave the herd when they reach adolescence. They either learn to fend for themselves or join nomadic male elephant herds.'

'That's not fair!'

'Nature isn't concerned with fairness, Kartik. It's only interested in efficiency. A male elephant isn't much use to the herd. The females are quite capable of defending themselves and taking care of each other's calves. The male is only needed when a female wants to reproduce.'

'So how do they—? You know . . .'

'During the mating season, the female herd accepts the presence of a few nomadic male elephants amongst them so that the females can be impregnated. Then the males are abandoned once again.'

Kartik shook his head. 'That's so cold.'

'That's just the way it is. The female wild elephants have well-defined social behaviour and group dynamics enforced by the matriarch. The male elephant, on the other hand, is a nomad with no ties to any of his kind. Since he's usually a loner, he has to be much more aggressive to survive – that means he's more difficult to break, so one needs to catch him young. But once he's broken in, he's much easier to handle, and he remains loyal to the *mahout*, his rider. More importantly, unlike a female elephant, he'll kill just because his *mahout* orders him to do so.'

'My Lords,' said the Vasudev Kshatriya, interrupting the conversation as he pointed, 'the elephant stables.'

'I guess you already know what I suspect is evil,' Shiva started.

'I wouldn't be much of a mind-reader if I didn't,' said Gopal with a smile. 'I imagine you're more interested in knowing whether I agree with you or not.'

'Yes – and if you do, why?'

'First things first: of course I agree with you. Every single Vasudev agrees with you.'

'Why?'

'Because we're faithful followers of the institution of the Mahadev. We *have* to agree with you once you have the right answer.'

Shiva's quick mind latched onto the pandit's strange phrasing. 'Once I have the *right* answer?'

'Yes; despite many challenges, you've arrived at the correct answer to the question posed to every Mahadev: *What is Evil?*'

'Does that mean you already knew the right answer?'

'Of course! What I didn't know were the answers to the questions posed to the institution of Vishnu. The Mahadev and the Vishnu are asked very different questions. The Mahadev's key question is: What is Evil? For the Vishnu, there are *two* key questions: What's the next great Good? And, *When* does Good become Evil? A Mahadev is an outsider; a Vishnu has to be an insider. His job is to use a great Good to create a new way of life and then lead men to that path. The great Good could be anything: a new technology like the *daivi astras* or a substance like the *Somras*; it could even be a philosophy. Most leaders simply follow what's been ordained by a previous Vishnu. But once in a while a Vishnu emerges who uses a great Good to create a new way of life. Lord Ram used more than one, such as the idea that we can choose our own community rather than being stuck with the community we're born into. He also allowed for the widespread use of the *Somras* so that everyone, not just the elite, could benefit from its powers. But remember, great Good will, more often than not, lead to great Evil.'

'I understood that from Lord Manu's teaching,' Shiva said, 'but I'd like to hear your explanation.'

'We have a philosophical book in our community that answers this question beautifully. It contains the teachings of great philosophers we've revered over the centuries, such as Lord Hari and Lord Mohan. It also contains the teachings of the chiefs of the Vasudev tribe, beginning with our founder, Lord Vasudev. The book is called the *Song of our Lord*, or *Bhagavad Gita* in Sanskrit. The *Gita* has a beautiful line that encapsulates what I want to convey: "*Ati sarvatra varjayet*", or "Excess should be avoided". Excess of anything is bad. Some of us are attracted to Good, but the universe tries to maintain balance, so what is good for some may end up being bad for others. Agriculture's good for us humans because it gives us an assured supply of food, but it's bad for the animals that lose their forest and grazing land to our farms. Oxygen's good for us because it keeps us alive, but it was toxic for the anaerobic creatures that lived billions of years ago, and it destroyed them. Therefore, if the universe is trying to maintain balance, we must assist this process by ensuring that Good isn't enjoyed to excess, or the universe will rebalance itself by creating Evil to counteract Good. That's the purpose of Evil: it balances Good.'

'Why can't there be a Good that doesn't need to create Evil? Why can't we establish a way of life that doesn't imbalance the universe?'

'That's impossible, I'm afraid. We create imbalances simply by existing. In order to live, we breathe, and when we breathe, we take in oxygen and exhale carbon dioxide. Aren't we creating an imbalance by doing so? Isn't carbon dioxide evil for some? The only way we can stop creating Evil is if we also stop doing Good – or, to put it another way, if we stop living altogether. But if we've been born, then it's our duty to live. Let's look at it from the perspective of the universe: the only time the universe was in perfect balance was at the moment of its creation. And the moment before that, it had just been destroyed, for that was when it was in perfect *im*balance. Creation and destruction are the two ends of the same moment and everything between creation and the next destruction is the journey of life. The universe's *dharma* is to be created and to live out its life until its inevitable destruction, and then be created once again. We're each a downscaled version of the universe.'

'Surely these are just theories, Panditji?'

'Of course, but they explain a lot of things that otherwise are too hard to comprehend. What makes us humans special is that we can choose how to control Good and Evil. Humans have been blessed with intelligence, the Almighty's greatest gift, and this allows us to make choices. We have the power to consciously choose Good and improve our lives. We also have the ability to stop Evil before it destroys us completely. Other living creatures have nature's will forced upon them, but at times we have the privilege of forcing our will upon nature, like when we created agriculture by creating and using Good. What's forgotten, however, is that many times the Good we create leads to the very Evil that will destroy us.'

'Is that where the Mahadev comes in?'

Gopal smiled. 'Yes: Good emerges from creative thinkers and scientists like Lord Brahma, but only a Vishnu can harness that Good and lead humanity on the path of progress. Paradoxically, imbalance in society is embedded in this very progress. At other times, a Vishnu arises and intervenes to move society away from the Evil towards which Good may be leading it by creating an alternative Good. By diluting the potency – and hence the toxic effects – of the *Somras* waste, Brahaspati was attempting just such an intervention. Had he succeeded, we Vasudevs would inevitably have helped him fulfil that mission and a new way of life based on a benign *Somras* would have been established. Alas, Brahaspati didn't succeed and that path is now closed to us. We have only the path of the Mahadev open now: to confront and then lead people away from the Good that has become Evil.'

'So a Vishnu can make people move away from a Good that

has turned evil by offering an alternate Good. But a Mahadev has to ask people to give up a Good without offering anything in return.'

Gopal clapped his hands at Shiva's ready understanding. '*Exactly!* And that's not an easy thing to do. The *Somras* is still good for a lot of people: it increases their lifespan dramatically and enables them to lead youthful, disease-free and productive lives. But it's evil for society as a whole. What we're doing is asking people to sacrifice their selfish interests for the sake of a greater Good, while offering them nothing in return. This requires an outsider, a leader people will follow blindly. This requires a god who excites fervent devotion. This requires the Mahadev.'

'So you always knew the *Somras* was evil?'

'We knew it would eventually *become* evil. What we didn't know was *when* this would happen. Remember, Good needs to run its course. If we remove a Good from society too soon, we're obstructing the march of civilisation. However, if we remove it too late, we risk the complete destruction of society. So in the battle against Evil, the institution of the Vishnu has to wait for the institution of the Mahadev to decide if the time has come. In our case, a Mahadev emerged and his quest led him to the conclusion that the *Somras* is evil. Therefore, we knew that the time had come for Evil to be removed. The *Somras* has to be taken out of the equation.'

Ganesh, Kartik and Brahaspati stared at the entrance to the elephant stables, ten circular enclosures built of massive stone blocks, each capable of housing up to a thousand animals. Five of the enclosures were for the female elephants and their calves. The other five were reserved for the male war elephants.

The female elephants' enclosures had massive pools of water at their centre, with plenty of room for the beasts to fully submerge themselves, spray themselves with water or have a mud bath. The area around the pools was a social meeting point for the animals, set about with piles of nutritious leaves. The female elephants were taken to the jungle in small herds to forage on fresh vegetation. The female enclosures weren't partitioned; though the animals were allowed to mix freely, they usually grouped into herds, each herd led by its matriarch.

The enclosures for the male elephants were completely different. Each elephant had a partitioned-off section, and the animal's *mahout* lived just above, for the *mahouts* spent practically all their time with their individual beasts, which helped develop the personal attachment. The beasts weren't expected to do any work; instead of keeping their skin clean by rubbing against rocks and trees as the females did, the *mahouts* bathed them daily. Nor were they required to walk to a central area for their meals; instead, freshly cut plants were piled outside their individual shelters. The male elephants had only one task: to train for war.

The central area had been prepared for just that purpose. The pools were much deeper than those used by the females, and here the males were trained to put their natural swimming skills to better use ramming and sinking boats. The pools were surrounded by a vast training ground where the beasts were drilled. They learned how to mow down opposing army lines, and they were toughened up so they could survive the heat of battle. The Vasudevs, aware of the widespread use of low-frequency drums to drive the elephants crazy, had developed an innovative type of earplug – and just to ensure the drums would no longer be a problem, the animals were also subjected to a daily interlude of low-frequency drumming, to help them grow accustomed to the sounds.

The Vasudev Kshatrya led Ganesh, Kartik and Brahaspati into one of the male elephant enclosures and took them to one of the animals of which he was personally proud. As he reached the enclosure, he called out to the *mahout* to bring the elephant out of his shelter and the beast emerged with the *mahout* sitting proudly just behind its head. To Ganesh's surprise, the elephant's eyes had been covered by flaps attached to its headgear. Their guide explained that the blinkers could be easily removed by the *mahout*; they were used when the *mahout* wanted the elephant to act solely on his instructions rather than on the basis of what it could see. A metallic cylindrical ball was secured to the elephant's trunk with a bronze chain.

The Vasudev proceeded to set up a circular wooden board as a target. It was roughly three times the size of a human head. 'You may want to step back,' he warned, and as his visitors stepped back, he nodded at the *mahout*, who gently pressed his feet into the back of the elephant's ears, issuing a series of instructions.

The elephant stepped languidly up to the wooden target, shook his head as if acknowledging the orders and then, with lightning speed, he swung his mighty trunk, hitting the wooden board smack in the centre with the metallic ball and smashing the target to smithereens.

Kartik whistled softly in appreciation.

'Can we make the target a little more interesting?' Ganesh asked the Vasudev.

The Vasudev immediately agreed and summoned another wooden target, this one mounted on wheels. A smaller circle was painted on the wooden board, roughly the size of a human head, and the metallic ball attached to the elephant's trunk was coated in bright red paint, so they'd know exactly where the ball hit the target. This time, as the elephant tried to strike the smaller circle, two soldiers pulled on the ropes to move the board around, simulating a man trying to avoid the elephant's blow. If the elephant could be used to kill a specific man rather than for mass butchery, Ganesh explained, then one could target the leader of an opposing army and render it headless.

Everyone stepped back. The *mahout* kept his eyes on the board as the elephant moved slowly towards the target. The soldiers with the ropes were alternately pulling and releasing their lines, keeping the target in constant motion. Suddenly, the *mahout* dug in deep with his right foot and the elephant swung his mighty trunk. The metallic ball hit the wooden board dead-centre, and they could all see from the red mark that it was a killer blow.

'By the great *Pashupatinath* himself,' exclaimed Ganesh, invoking the legendary Lord of the Animals, 'what an elephant!'

CHAPTER 8

Who is Shiva?

'What if I'd arrived at a different answer?' asked Shiva.

'Then we'd have known that it's not yet time for Evil to rise,' replied Gopal, 'and that the *Somras* is still a force for Good.'

'Isn't that rather simplistic? Did you really believe that some random, untested foreigner would arrive at the right answer to the most important question of this age? Is this the way the system works?'

Gopal smiled. 'Not exactly, no. The system's very different. If I'm not mistaken, one of the Vasudev pandits has already told you about the Vayuputras. Just we Vasudevs are the tribe left behind by the previous Vishnu, the Vayuputras are the tribe left behind by the previous Mahadev, Lord Rudra. The institutions of the Vishnu and the Mahadev work in partnership with each other; we Vasudevs defer to them on the question Lord Manu reserved for them: What is Evil? And the Vayuputras defer to us on the question reserved for us: What is the next

great Good? The Vayuputras control the institution of the Neelkanth. They train potential candidates for the role, and if they
believe Evil has risen, they allow a Neelkanth to be identified.'

'Kali did tell me about this – but how do the Vayuputras make
a man's throat turn blue at a time of their choosing?'

'I've heard that they administer some medicine to the candidate as he enters adolescence. The effect of this medicine remains
dormant in his throat for years, only manifesting at a certain age,
when he drinks the *Somras*. I believe the *Somras* reacts with the
traces of the medicine already present to make the man's neck
appear blue. All these activities have to be done at specific times
in the man's life if this is to happen the way it's supposed to. For
example, if a man drinks the *Somras* more than fifteen years after
entering adolescence, his throat won't turn blue, not even if he
took the Vayuputra medicine as a child.'

Shiva's eyes opened wide. 'This is seriously complicated!'

'It's a means by which the system can be controlled. The
Vayuputras alone know the process. People's blind faith in the
legend ensures they'll follow the Neelkanth when he arrives and
remove Evil from the equation. We Vasudevs have believed for
some time now that the *Somras* was turning evil, but we don't
control the institution of the Neelkanth; that's in the hands of
the Vayuputras – but they believed the *Somras* was still good,
and so they refused to release their Neelkanth nominee. So even
though we were convinced it was time for the Neelkanth to
appear, it didn't happen.'

'Did you present your case to the Vayuputras?'

'Of course! But we could not get them to agree. The only alternative available to us was to try to find a solution by the Vishnu method, by creating another Good, and that's what we were trying to do when something happened that stunned everyone – including the Vayuputras.'

Shiva pointed at himself. 'I suddenly emerged out of nowhere.'

'Nobody really understood what had happened. We knew you weren't a Vayuputra-authorised candidate, and in fact, many Vayuputras believed you were a fraud, and you'd be exposed soon enough. Some even wanted you assassinated in the interests of the institution of the Neelkanth. But the Vayuputras' leader, the Mithra, prevailed upon them and decreed that you be allowed to live out your *karma*.'

'Why would the Mithra do that?'

'I don't know – it's a mystery. There was plenty of debate amongst the Vasudevs as well, believe me! Some believed your emergence proved us right, that we should use you to eliminate the *Somras*, while others believed you, an unknown entity, might use the Neelkanth legend to create chaos, so we should have nothing to do with you. There are also those amongst us who believe it's not our job to determine the fate of Evil; that's the sole preserve of the Neelkanth. Still others debated against us that you were – my apologies' – he made a namaste to Shiva – 'a mere barbarian, and chances were you'd arrive at an incorrect conclusion as to what constituted Evil. But the view that finally prevailed was that if the Parmatma has chosen to make you the Neelkanth, he'll also lead you to the right answer, and that we should, with all humility, accept it.'

'And I arrived at the *Somras*.'

'Doesn't that make the decision obvious? You weren't selected for this task and yet somehow you were given the Vayuputra medicine at the right age. Furthermore, you also arrived in Meluha and were given the *Somras* at the appropriate time, which made your throat turn blue. You weren't trained for the role of Neelkanth; nobody gave you the answer to the key question. We consciously refrained from saying *anything* that might create a bias in your mind. We were very careful in our communications with you regarding your task. And yet you arrived at the right answer. Isn't this ample proof that you've been chosen by the Parmatma and that you are, truly, the Mahadev? Doesn't it make our decision easy, then – that in following you, we're following the Parmatma Himself?'

Shiva leaned back in his chair, rubbing his forehead. His brow suddenly felt very uncomfortable.

— ᛉ ꝏU♀☀ —

On returning from their short tour of Ujjain, Brahaspati, Ganesh and Kartik joined Sati, Nandi and Parshuram at the guest house.

'How is the city, Brahaspatiji?' asked Sati.

'Beautiful and well organised,' he replied. 'This city is a better rendition of Lord Ram's principles than even Meluha and Panchavati.'

'My sons,' she said to Ganesh and Kartik, 'did you like the city?'

Ganesh's tactical mind was reflected in his opinion. 'Ujjain's a nice enough city, but what fascinated me were the elephant stables. We watched the *mahouts* tend to these beasts of war. Each one of the five thousand elephants is equivalent to a thousand foot-soldiers. I dare say our strength has vastly increased, given that the Vasudevs follow the Neelkanth. With these elephants on our side, we're not so precariously placed as we were before.'

'Precariously placed?' said Parshuram. 'Lord Ganesh, forgive me for disagreeing with you, but how can you say that? We have the Neelkanth on our side, which means that a vast majority of Indians will be with us. I'd say the odds overwhelmingly favour us.'

'Parshuram, I've always admired your bravery and your utter devotion to the Neelkanth, but hope alone doesn't win battles. Only an honest evaluation of one's weaknesses, followed by their mitigation, can win the day.'

'What weaknesses can we have?' he exclaimed. 'We're led by the Neelkanth. The people will follow him.'

'The people will follow the Neelkanth, but their kings won't. And remember, the people don't control the armies, kings do. Emperor Daksha's already against us, and so is Emperor Dilipa. They've united Meluha's technological wizardry with Swadweep's sheer numbers – that makes for a very strong and formidable army.'

'But *dada*,' argued Kartik, 'even the most capable army is of little use if it's led by incapable leaders. Do you see any good generals on their side? I see none.'

Ganesh glanced at Brahaspati and Nandi before turning back to Kartik. 'They have the best. They have Lord Parvateshwar.'

Sati burst in angrily, 'Ganesh, I've asked you to refrain from insulting *Pitratulya*.'

'I know he's like a father to you, *maa*,' said Ganesh politely, 'but the truth is that Lord Parvateshwar will fight for Meluha.'

'No, he won't. Your father trusts him completely. How can you believe he'll run off and join those who tried to kill the Neelkanth?'

'*Maa*, Parvateshwarji has too much honour to run off. He'll leave openly, once he's revealed his intentions to *baba*. And trust me, *baba* will let him go. He won't even *try* to stop him, for they're both honourable men who'd rather bring harm upon themselves than forsake their honour.'

'He is indeed an honourable man, Ganesh,' said Sati, 'so won't that sense of duty bind him to the Neelkanth's path?'

'No. Parvateshwarji's with *baba* because he's inspired by him, not because he's honour-bound to follow him. He's supremely committed to one value alone, as are all Meluhans, and that's the protection of Meluha. Just ask any of the Meluhans here.'

Nandi's eyes flashed with anger as the normally affable man stared at Shiva's son with unblinking eyes. 'Lord Ganesh, I've already made my choice. I live for the Neelkanth and I'll die for the Neelkanth. If that means I have to oppose my country, so be it. I'll face my *karma* for having betrayed my country but I won't tolerate you questioning my loyalty again.'

Ganesh immediately reached out to Nandi. 'I wasn't questioning your loyalty, brave Nandi. I was wondering how you think General Parvateshwar will react.'

'I don't know what the general thinks. I only know what *I* think,' Nandi bristled.

'Well, *I* know how Parvateshwar thinks,' said Brahaspati. 'I realise this will hurt you, Sati, but Ganesh is right: Parvateshwar won't abandon Meluha. In fact, he'll battle to his final breath all those who seek to hurt Meluha. And if Shiva does decide that the *Somras* is evil, then Meluha will be our primary enemy. The battle lines are already drawn, my child.'

Wordlessly, Sati looked out of the window towards the Vishnu Temple and sighed.

— ⋏ ꞉U⌖⦿ —

Shiva rubbed his throbbing brow as he pondered the mysteries of his childhood.

Gopal leaned towards him. 'What is it, great Neelkanth?'

'It's not the hand of Fate's doing that I emerged as the Neelkanth, Panditji,' he said. 'Nor is it the grand plan of the Parmatma. I suspect it was my uncle's doing – though how he did all this is a mystery to me.'

'What do you mean?'

'My uncle gave me some medicine when I was a child: I suffered this severe burning pain between my brows from when

I was very young, and my uncle's medicine helped to calm the burning sensation. The throbbing persists to this day, but it's not as bad as it used to be. I've never forgotten his words as he prepared the medicine because they were so strange. He chanted, "We will always remain faithful to your command, Lord Rudra. This is the blood-oath of a Vayuputra." Then he pricked his index finger and let his blood drip into the potion. He gave this mixture to me and told me to rub it into my throat.'

Gopal had been listening, fascinated, his eyes pinned on Shiva, but now he glanced at the Vasudev pandit from the Ayodhya Temple, who was sitting in the first row of the assembly.

The Ayodhya Vasudev asked, 'Great Neelkanth, what was your uncle's name?'

'Manobhu,' said Shiva.

'In the great name of Lord Ram!' the Vasudev exclaimed.

'What is it?' asked Shiva, looking around at the stunned faces.

'*Lord Manobhu* was your uncle?' asked Gopal.

'*Lord* Manobhu?'

'He was a Vayuputra lord – one of the Amartya Shpand, a member of the council of six wise men and women who rule the Vayuputras under the leadership of the Mithra.'

'*He was a Vayuputra lord?*' Shiva sounded as stunned as the Vasudevs looked.

'Indeed he was. Many years ago, when we were still trying to convince the Vayuputras that the *Somras* had turned evil, Lord Manobhu was the only one amongst the Amartya Shpand who agreed with us, but the other members of the council didn't support him, and the Mithra also overruled him.'

'So what did he do?'

'I remember that conversation as if it happened yesterday,' said Gopal. 'Lord Manobhu and I had spoken for hours about the *Somras* and when it became obvious that we wouldn't be able to convince the council, he promised that he would ensure a Neelkanth would arise when the time came. When I asked him how he would do it, he said that Lord Rudra would help him. He made me promise that when the Neelkanth did rise, the Vasudevs and I would support him wholeheartedly, and of course I assured him that this was our sworn duty in any case.'

'And then?'

'Lord Manobhu disappeared. Nobody knew what happened to him. Some believed he'd returned to his homeland, since he'd been isolated in the Vayuputra Council. Some thought he'd been killed. I was inclined to believe the latter, for only death could have stopped a man like him from fulfilling his promise. But he didn't fail, did he? He created you. Where is he now? How did he contrive to get you invited to Meluha to receive the *Somras*?'

'He didn't,' said Shiva sadly. 'He died many years ago, at a peace conference, in a cowardly ambush mounted by the Pakratis, our local enemies in Tibet.'

'Then how were you invited into Meluha within the required period? Your throat could turn blue only if you drank the *Somras* within fifteen years of entering adolescence.'

'I don't know,' answered Shiva. 'Nandi just happened to come to Mansarovar at that time, asking for immigrants to accompany him to Meluha.'

Gopal looked up at the central pillar of the temple, towards the idols of Lord Ram and Lady Sita. 'It's obvious, then: it was the will of the Almighty that events unfolded the way they did.'

Shiva looked at Gopal, his eyes revealing his scepticism that his life was somehow all part of a divine plan.

Gopal tactfully changed the topic. 'My friend, you said that your brow has throbbed from a very young age. Did it happen after a specific incident? Did your uncle give you something that precipitated the burning sensation?'

Shiva frowned. 'I don't think so. I've had it for as long as I can remember – from when I was born. Whenever I got upset, my brow started throbbing.'

'Would this happen when your heart rate went up dramatically?'

Shiva thought about it for a second. 'Yes: whenever I'm angry or upset, my heart does beat quite dramatically. Or when I think of Sati – but that's a happy heartbeat.'

Gopal smiled. 'That means that your third eye has been active from the time of your birth – it's very rare. And that only adds to my conviction that you've truly been chosen by the Parmatma.'

'What's this "third eye"?'

'It's the area of your forehead between your brows. It's believed that there are seven chakras or vortices within the human body which allow the reception and transmission of energy. The sixth chakra is called the *ajna chakra*, the vortex of the third eye. These chakras are activated by yogis after years of practise, and they can also be activated by certain medicines; the Vayuputras activate the third eye of those amongst their children who are potential candidates for Neelkanth. But in all my one hundred and forty years, I've never before heard of a child born with his third eye active.'

'What's so special about that? It just causes me trouble – it burns dreadfully.'

Gopal smiled. 'That's just an inconsequential side effect. I believe the fact that your third eye was active from birth might have led your uncle to think you could be the Chosen One. After all, it set your body up to easily accept the Vayuputra medicine.'

At Shiva's raised eyebrows he checked, and explained, 'The Parihan system of medicine believes that the pineal gland, a peculiar gland located deep within our brain between the two cortical hemispheres, is the third eye. It's a little like an eye in that it is impacted by light: darkness activates it and light inhibits it. A hyperactive pineal gland is regenerative, and this is probably what allowed the *Somras* not only to lengthen your life but also to repair your injuries. Furthermore, the pineal gland isn't protected by the blood-barrier system—'

'Which is?' Shiva interrupted.

'Blood flows freely throughout the body, but it encounters a barrier when it approaches the brain, maybe to prevent germs and infections from affecting the brain, the seat of the soul. However, the pineal gland, despite being lodged between the two hemispheres, isn't protected by the blood-barrier system

– that's why your third eye throbs when you're upset. It's the result of blood gushing through your hyperactive pineal gland.'

Shiva nodded slowly. 'Does this happen to others?'

'Only amongst those who practise yoga for decades to train their third eye, or those who are given medicines to stimulate it. As I said, I've never heard of a person being born with an active third eye – it's unprecedented.'

Shiva shifted uneasily in his chair. 'So a congenital accident set me up for this role? My uncle might have got it all wrong – I could still be an erroneous choice. Maybe I won't achieve the purpose set before me—'

'I'm sure your uncle didn't give you the medicine just because of your active third eye,' Gopal said calmly. 'He would also have judged your character and found you worthy. He must have trained you for this.'

'I was trained by him, no doubt about that.' Shiva laughed. 'He taught me ethics, warfare, psychology, the arts – but he never said anything to me about this task.'

'You must concede that he did an excellent job, though, for you've done well as the Neelkanth.'

'Just luck,' said Shiva wryly.

'Great Neelkanth, a non-believer will credit luck for his achievements, but one who believes in the Parmatma, as I do, knows that the Neelkanth has achieved all that he has because the Parmatma willed it. And that means the Neelkanth will complete his journey and eventually succeed in taking Evil out of the equation.'

Shiva smiled. 'Sometimes faith can lean towards over-simplicity.'

Gopal returned his smile. 'Maybe simplicity is exactly what this world needs right now.'

Shiva looked at the audience of Vasudev pundits, who'd been listening to their conversation with rapt attention. 'Well, many of my doubts have been put to rest. The *Somras* is the greatest Good and will therefore one day inevitably emerge as the greatest Evil. But how do we know the moment has arrived? How can we be sure?'

One of the Vasudev pundits answered, 'We can never be completely sure, great Neelkanth. But if you'll allow me to express an opinion, we've experienced a Good which has enjoyed a glorious journey for thousands of years, and humanity has grown tremendously with its munificence. However, we also know that it's close to becoming an Evil now. It's possible that if the *Somras* is taken out of the equation a little early, the world would lose out on a few hundred years of additional good that it might do. But that pales in comparison to the enormous contribution it's already made over thousands of years. On the other hand, the *Somras* is getting closer to Evil, and it is likely to lead to chaos and destruction – in fact, it's already causing it in substantial measure. I'm not referring just to the plague of Branga or the deformities of the Nagas. It's believed that the *Somras* is also responsible for the drastic fall in the Meluhans' own birth rate.'

'Really?'

'Yes, indeed,' answered Gopal. 'Perhaps by refusing to

embrace death, they are paying the price of not seeing their own genes propagate.'

Shiva looked at the massive images of Lord Ram and Lady Sita that formed the carved central pillar. They appeared to be smiling at him and as he accepted their blessings, his eyes were drawn towards a grand painting depicting Lord Ram at the feet of Lord Rudra against the backdrop of holy Rameshwaram. Shiva smiled at the giant circle of life. He joined his hands together in a respectful namaste, closed his eyes and prayed: *Jai Maa Sita. Jai Shri Ram.*

He sounded resolute as he opened his eyes and looked at Gopal. 'I've made my decision. We'll strive to avoid war and needless bloodshed, but should our efforts prove futile, we'll fight to the last man. We will end the reign of the *Somras.*'

CHAPTER 9

The Love-Struck Barbarian

'Your uncle was a Vayuputra lord?' asked Sati, amazed. She had listened silently as Shiva related his entire conversation with the Vasudevs, and the decision he'd arrived at.

'Not just any old lord,' said Shiva with a smile. 'An Amartya Shpand!'

She raised her arms and rested them on Shiva's muscular shoulders, her eyes teasing. 'I always knew there was something special about you – that you couldn't be just another rough tribesman. And now I have proof. You have a pedigree!'

He laughed loudly, holding her close. 'Rubbish! You thought I was an uncouth barbarian when you first laid eyes on me!'

Sati went up on her tiptoes and kissed his lips warmly. 'Oh, you're still an uncouth barbarian—'

Shiva raised his eyebrows.

'—but you're *my* uncouth barbarian!'

His face lit up with the crooked smile he reserved for Sati:

the smile that made her weak at the knees. He held her tight and lifted her up so her lips were close to his. With her feet dangling in the air, they kissed warmly and deeply.

'You are my life,' he whispered.

'You are the sum of all my lives,' said Sati as Shiva continued to hold her up in the air, embracing her tightly.

'So, are you going to put me down at some point?' asked Sati.

Shiva shook his head in reply. He was in no hurry.

She smiled and rested her head on his shoulder, content to let her feet dangle in mid-air as she played with Shiva's hair.

— ⚊ ⚇U⚉⊕ —

'Here you go,' said Sati, handing Shiva a glass of milk.

He liked his milk raw: no boiling, no jaggery, no cardamom, just plain milk. He drained the glass in large gulps, handed it to Sati and sank back on his chair with his feet up on the table. Sati put the glass down and sat next to him. Shiva looked across the balcony towards the Vishnu Temple, then took a deep breath and turned to Sati. 'I agree with you – much as I respect Ganesh's tactical thinking, this time he's wrong. Parvateshwar won't leave me.'

Sati nodded emphatically in agreement. 'Without an inspirational leader like him, the armies of Meluha and Swadweep, though strong, will lack motivation as well as sound battle tactics.'

'True. But let's hope the people themselves will rise up in rebellion and that there'll be no need for war.'

'How can we ensure that, though? If you send the proclamation banning the *Somras* to the kings, they'll make sure the general public never hears it.'

'I discussed that very thing with the Vasudevs. My proclamation should not only reach the royalty but every citizen of India and the best way to ensure that is to display the proclamation in all the temples. All Indians visit temples regularly, and whenever they do, they'll read my decree.'

'And I'm sure the people will be with you. Let's hope the kings listen to the will of their subjects.'

'That's my fervent hope. I can't think of any other way to avoid war. I expect unflinching support only from the royalty of Kashi, Panchavati and Branga. Every other king will make his choice based on selfish interests alone.'

Sati held Shiva's hand and smiled. 'But we have the King of Kings with us – the Parmatma himself. We won't lose.'

'We can't afford to lose,' said Shiva. 'The fate of the nation is at stake.'

— ◊ ◍ �∪ ⊕ ◉ —

'Are you sure you can do this, Kartik?' asked Ganesh.

Kartik looked up at his brother with eyes like still waters. 'Of course I can. I'm your brother.'

Ganesh smiled and stepped away from the elephant-mounting platform. Kartik and another diminutive Vasudev soldier were sitting on a *howdah* atop one of the largest bull elephants in the Ujjain stables. The *howdah*'s standard structure had been altered:

the roof had been removed and the side walls were only half the usual height, which reduced the riders' protection but dramatically improved their ability to fire weapons. Kartik had come up with an innovative idea, envisioning a deliberate and coordinated movement of war elephants as opposed to a wild charge, using the elephants as more than just a battering ram for enemy lines. This way the beasts could also be used as high platforms from which to fire in all directions. The choice of weapons, however, remained unresolved. Arrows discharged from elephant-back could never be numerous enough to cause serious damage, so the Vasudev military engineers had come up with a solution: an innovative flame-thrower using a refined version of the black liquid fuel imported from Mesopotamia. This devastating weapon spewed a continuous stream of fire, burning everything in its path. The fuel tanks occupied a substantial part of the *howdah*, leaving just enough room for two infantrymen to wield a flame-thrower each. The new weapons were not only heavy but also released intense heat while operational, so they required operators with stamina – but the limited space inside the *howdah* also meant the operators had to be short too. Kartik had volunteered to be one of the sodiers manning this potential inferno.

Ganesh stood at a distance along with Parshuram, Nandi and Brahaspati. 'Are you ready, Kartik?' he shouted to his brother.

Kartik cried back, 'I was born ready, *dada*.'

Ganesh smiled as he turned towards the Vasudev commander. 'Let's begin, brave Vasudev.'

The commander nodded and waved a red flag.

Kartik and the Vasudev soldier he was paired with immediately struck a flame and lit the weapons, and two devilishly long streams of fire burst out, covering almost thirty yards on either side of the elephant. A covering secured around the elephant's sides ensured it was protected from the heat. Kartik and the Vasudev had been tasked with reducing some thirty mud statues to ashes to test the weapon's range and accuracy. Though heavy, the fire-weapons were surprisingly manoeuvrable. The *mahout* concentrated on following Kartik's orders and the mud soldiers were destroyed in no time.

'These could be devastating in war, Lord Ganesh,' said Parshuram. 'What do you think?'

Ganesh smiled as he borrowed a phrase from his father. 'Hell, yes!'

— ✶ ⒨Ⓤ✦⊕ —

'We've transcribed your proclamation, Lord Neelkanth,' said Gopal, handing over a papyrus scroll.

> *To all of you who consider yourselves children of Manu and followers of the Sanatan Dharma: this is a message from Shiva, your Neelkanth.*
>
> *I have travelled through all the kingdoms of our great land and met with all the tribes who populate our fair realm. I have been searching for the ultimate Evil, for that is my task. Father Manu told us that Evil isn't a distant demon. It works its destruction close*

to us, amongst us, within us. He was right. He told us that Evil doesn't come from down below to devour us. Instead, we help Evil destroy our lives. He was right. He told us that Good and Evil are two sides of the same coin, and that, one day, the greatest Good will transform into the greatest Evil. He was right. Our greed for Good turns it into Evil. This is the universe's way of restoring balance. It's the Parmatma's way of controlling our excesses.

I have come to the conclusion that the Somras is now the greatest Evil of our age. All the Good that we could wring from it has been wrung. It is time to stop using it, before the power of its Evil destroys us all. It has already caused tremendous damage, from killing the Saraswati River to the emergence of birth deformities and the diseases that plague some of our kingdoms. For the sake of our descendants, for the sake of our world, we cannot use the Somras any more.

Therefore, by my order, use of the Somras is banned forthwith.

To all those who believe in the legend of the Neelkanth: follow me. Stop using the Somras.

To all those who refuse to stop using the Somras: know this: you will become my enemy.

I will not rest until the use of the Somras is ended. This is the word of your Neelkanth.

'This will be distributed to all the pandits in all the Vasudev temples across the Sapt Sindhu,' said Gopal. 'Our Vasudev Kshatriyas will travel to other temples across the land too, carrying your proclamation carved on stone tablets which they'll fix on the walls. They'll all be put up on the same night, one year from now. The kings will have no way to control the message since everyone will receive your command simultaneously. Your word will reach the people.'

This was exactly what Shiva wanted. 'Perfect, Panditji. This will give us one year to get ready. I'd like to be in Kashi when this proclamation's released.'

'Yes, my friend – and until then, we need to prepare for war.'

'I also need to use this year to uncover the identity of my true enemy.'

Gopal frowned. 'What do you mean, great Neelkanth?'

'I don't believe either Emperor Daksha or Emperor Dilipa are capable of mounting a conspiracy on this scale. They're obviously following someone's lead. That person is my real enemy and I need to find him.'

'I thought you already knew who your real enemy is.'

'Do you know his identity?'

'I do. And you're right – he's truly dangerous.'

'Is he so capable, Panditji?'

'A lot of people are *capable*, Neelkanth. What makes a capable person truly dangerous is his conviction. If we believe that we're fighting on the side of Evil, there is moral weakness in our mind. Somewhere deep within, the heart knows that we're wrong. But what happens if we actually believe in the righteousness of our cause? What if your enemy genuinely believes that he's the one fighting for Good and that you, the Neelkanth, are fighting for Evil?'

Shiva raised his eyebrows. 'Such a person will never stop fighting. Just like I won't.'

'Exactly.'

'Who is this man?'

'He's a maharishi — in fact, most people in India revere him as a *Saptrishi Uttradhikari*,' said Gopal, using the Indian term for the successors of the seven great sages of old. 'His scientific knowledge and devotion to the Parmatma are second to none in the modern age. His immense spiritual power makes emperors quake in his presence. He leads a selfless, frugal life in a Himalayan cave and descends to the plains only when he feels that India's interests are threatened. And he's spent the whole of the past year in either Meluha or Ayodhya.'

'Does he genuinely believe the *Somras* is good?'

'Yes. And he believes that you're a fraud, for he knows the Vayuputras didn't select you. In fact, we believe that the Vayuputras are on his side, for who else could have given him the *daivi astras* that were used in the attack at Panchavati?'

'Is there any possibility that he might have made the *daivi astras* himself? That's what I assumed must have happened.'

'Trust me, that's just not possible. Only the Vayuputras have the know-how to make the *daivi astras*, no one else — not even us.'

Shiva stared at Gopal, stunned. 'I didn't expect the Vayuputras to support me — I'm not one of them, after all — but I thought they'd at least remain neutral.'

'No, my friend; we must assume that the Vayuputras are on your enemy's side. They may even be in agreement that the *Somras* is still good.'

Shiva took a deep breath. This man sounded formidable. 'Who is he?'

'He is Maharishi Bhrigu.'

Bhrigu observed intently as the Meluhan soldiers practised their art. Daksha stood next to him with his eyes pinned to the ground. Mayashrenik, the Meluhan army's stand-in general in Parvateshwar's absence, was a few yards ahead of them.

'Your soldiers are exceptional, your Majesty,' said Bhrigu.

Daksha offered no reply, just continued to study the ground.

Bhrigu tried again. 'Your Majesty, your soldiers are very well trained.'

Daksha finally looked at Bhrigu. 'Of course, my Lord, but I already told you there's no need to worry. To begin with, a war is unlikely. But even the possibility of war leaves little to fear, for I have the combined Ayodhyan and Meluhan armies at my command, which—'

'We have much to fear,' interrupted Bhrigu. 'Your soldiers are well trained, but they're not well led.'

'But Mayashrenik—'

'Mayashrenik's no leader. He's a great second-in-command – he'll follow orders unquestioningly and implement them effectively – but he can't lead.'

'But—'

'We need someone who can think, someone who can strategise, someone who is willing to suffer for the sake of the greater good. We need a real leader.'

'But *I'm* their leader.'

Bhrigu looked contemptuously at Daksha. 'You're no leader either, your Majesty. Parvateshwar's a leader, but you sent him off with that fraud Neelkanth. I don't know if the general's still alive, or – even worse – if he's switched loyalties to that barbarian from Tibet.'

Daksha took offence at Bhrigu's criticism. 'Parvateshwar's not the only great warrior in Meluha, my Lord. Vidyunmali's a capable strategist and would make a great general.'

'I don't trust Vidyunmali. And, frankly, your Majesty is hardly the best judge of people.'

Daksha promptly went back to studying the piece of ground that had held his fascination a few moments earlier.

Bhrigu took a deep breath. This discussion was pointless. 'Your Majesty, I'm going to Ayodhya. Please make the arrangements.'

'Yes, Maharishiji,' said Daksha.

— ⚝ ⃝ ᚢ ⚐ ⚙ —

Bhagirath and Anandmayi had reached the last clearing of Dandak Forest before the Madhumati River. They were still a few months' travel from Branga and Kashi, but the remainder of the journey was the last thing on Bhagirath's mind.

'What do you think they've been talking about for so long?' asked Bhagirath.

Anandmayi followed the direction of Bhagirath's gaze towards Ayurvati and Parvateshwar, who appeared to be in the middle of an intense debate. They were gesticulating wildly, but true to Meluhan character, their voices remained soft, polite and inaudible from where the two observers were standing.

Anandmayi shook her head. 'I can't hear a word they're saying.'

'But I can take a good guess,' said Bhagirath. 'I hope Ayurvati wins this one.'

Anandmayi frowned at him.

'Ayurvati's already made her decision,' said Bhagirath. 'She's with us. She's with the Mahadev. And now, I think, she's trying to convince Parvateshwar to make the same choice.'

Anandmayi knew her brother was probably right, but her love for Parvateshwar was forcing her to hope he was wrong. 'Bhagirath, Parvateshwar hasn't made his decision yet. He's devoted to the Mahadev. Don't assume—'

'Trust me, if it comes to a war and he has to choose between Lord Shiva and his precious Meluha, your husband will choose Meluha.'

'Bhagirath, shut up!'

Bhagirath sighed, irritated by his sister's obstinacy in the face of the obvious. 'I'm only speaking the truth.'

'That's a matter of opinion.'

'I'm the crown prince of Ayodhya – many would say my opinion *is* the truth.'

Anandmayi playfully tapped her brother's head, amused despite herself. 'And as the crown prince's elder sister, I have the right to shut him up any time I choose!'

'Parvateshwar, you haven't thought this through,' said Ayurvati.

Parvateshwar smiled sadly. 'I haven't been thinking about much else for the last few months. I know which path I must take.'

'But will you be able to act against the living god you worship?'

'I have no other choice.'

'But Lord Ram said we must protect our faith. The Mahadevs and the Vishnus are our living gods. How can we protect our religion if we don't fight alongside our living gods?'

'You're confusing faith and religion. They're two completely different things.'

'No, they're not.'

'Yes, they are. The Sanatan Dharma is my religion, but it's not my faith. My faith is my country. My faith is Meluha and only Meluha.'

Ayurvati sighed and looked up at the sky before turning back to Parvateshwar. 'I know how devoted you are to the Neelkanth. Can you truly go to war against the Lord? Do you have it in your heart to harm him?'

Parvateshwar sighed deeply, his eyes moist. 'I will fight all who seek to harm Meluha. If Meluha must be conquered, it will be over my dead body.'

'Parvateshwar, do you really think the *Somras* isn't evil? That it shouldn't be banned?'

'I know it should be banned. I've already stopped using it — I stopped using it the day Brahaspati told us about all the evil it's caused.'

'Then why are you willing to fight to defend this *halahal*?' asked Ayurvati. The old Sanskrit term meant the most potent poison in the universe.

'I'm not defending the *Somras*,' said Parvateshwar. 'I'm defending Meluha.'

'But both of those things are on the same side,' said Ayurvati.

'And that's my misfortune. But defending Meluha's my life's purpose — it's what I was born to do.'

'Parvateshwar, Meluha isn't what it used to be — you know full well that Emperor Daksha is no Lord Ram. You're fighting for an ideal that doesn't exist any more. You're fighting for a country whose greatness lives only in memory. You're fighting for a faith that's been corrupted beyond repair.'

'That may be so, Ayurvati, but this is my purpose: to fight and die for Meluha.'

Ayurvati shook her head in irritation, but her voice remained unfailingly polite. 'Parvateshwar, you're making a big mistake. You're pitting yourself against your living god. You're defending the *Somras* even though you believe it's turned evil.

And you're doing all this to serve some "purpose". Does the purpose of defending Meluha justify all the mistakes you know you're making?'

Parvateshwar spoke softly: '*Shreyaan sva dharmo vigunaha para dharmaat svanushthitat.*'

Ayurvati smiled ruefully as he recited the old Sanskrit *shloka* attributed to Lord Hari, after whom the city of Hariyupa was named: *It's better to make mistakes on the path one's soul is meant to walk than to live a perfect life on a path not meant for one's soul.* He meant that a person should discharge his own *swadharma*, his personal *dharma*, even if it was faulty, rather than attempt to live a life meant for another.

'How can you be sure that this is your duty?' she said, unwilling to give up. 'Should you merely remain true to the role the world's foisted upon you? Aren't you just blindly obeying something society's forcing you to do?'

'Lord Hari also said that those who allow others to dictate their own duties aren't living their own lives. They're living someone else's.'

'But that's *exactly* what you are doing. You're allowing others to dictate your duties. You're allowing Meluha to dictate the purpose of your soul.'

'No, I'm not.'

'Yes, you are. Your heart's with Lord Shiva. Can you deny that?'

'No – my heart's with the Neelkanth.'

'Then how do you know that protecting Meluha is your duty?'

'Because I *know*,' said Parvateshwar firmly. 'I just *know* that's my duty. Isn't that what Lord Hari said? Nobody in the world, not even God, can tell us what our duty is. Only our soul can do that. All we have to do is surrender to the language of silence and listen to the whisper of our soul. My soul's whisper is very clear: Meluha's my faith; protecting my motherland is my duty.'

Ayurvati ran her hand over her bald pate and stroked her *choti*, the knot of hair that signified her Brahmin antecedents. She turned to look at Anandmayi and Bhagirath, who were still standing in the distance. 'You'll be on the losing side, Parvateshwar,' she said at last.

'I know.'

'And you'll be killed.'

'I know. But if that's my purpose, then so be it.'

Ayurvati touched Parvateshwar's shoulder compassionately.

Parvateshwar smiled wanly. 'It will be a glorious death. I shall die at the hands of the Neelkanth.'

CHAPTER 10

His Name Alone Strikes Fear

Reclining in an easy chair beside Sati, his legs outstretched and resting on a low table, Shiva contemplated the Ujjain Temple from their chamber balcony. Ganesh was leaning against the doorway, while Kartik had perched on the railing. Shiva had just revealed the identity of their real enemy.

Now he looked up at the evening sky before turning to Sati. 'Say something.'

'What can I say?' asked Sati. '*Lord Bhrigu* . . . Lord Ram, be merciful—'

'He can't be all that powerful.'

Sati looked sternly at Shiva. 'He's one of the *Saptrishi Uttradhikaris*. His spiritual powers and scientific knowledge are legendary. But it's not fear of his powers that's shaken me. It's the fact that a man of his strength of character has chosen to oppose us.'

'What do you mean?'

'He's singularly unselfish and a man of unimpeachable moral integrity.'

'And yet he sent five ships to assassinate us.'

'Indeed. He must truly believe that the *Somras* is good, and that we are evil for trying to stop its usage. If he's so convinced of that, is it possible we're wrong?'

Kartik opened his mouth to interject, but Shiva raised his hand. 'No,' he said. 'I'm sure the *Somras* is evil and has to be stopped. There's no turning back.'

'But Lord Bhrigu—' she said again.

'Sati, why would a man of such immense moral character use the *daivi astras*, which we all know have been banned by Lord Rudra himself?'

Sati stared at him silently.

'Lord Bhrigu's attachment to the *Somras* has made him do this,' said Shiva. 'He thinks he's acting for the greater good, but in truth, he's become attached to the *Somras*. Attachment makes people forget not only their moral duties but even who they really are.'

Kartik finally spoke up. '*Baba*'s right. And if the *Somras* can do this to a man of Lord Bhrigu's stature, then surely it must be evil.'

Shiva nodded agreement with his son. 'What we're doing is right. The *Somras* must be stopped.'

Sati remained silent.

'We need to focus our minds on the impending war,' said Shiva. 'With a leader of Lord Bhrigu's character in charge of the armies of Meluha and Ayodhya, the odds are truly stacked against us. How do we fight this?'

'Divide their capabilities,' said Kartik.

'Go on.'

Kartik went into his bedchamber and returned with a map. '*Baba*, would you please . . . ?'

As Shiva lifted his feet off the table, Kartik spread out the map. '*Dada* and I agreed that their strength lies in the combination of Meluha's technological wizardry with Ayodhya's sheer numbers. If we can divide them, it would even out the odds.'

'Lord Bhrigu's played his cards well by persuading Meluha and Ayodhya to conspire to assassinate us at Panchavati,' said Shiva ruefully. 'When they learn that I'm still alive, they'll be compelled to treat me as their common foe and maintain the alliance. After all, an enemy's enemy is a friend.'

Kartik smiled. 'I wasn't talking about breaking their alliance, *baba*, but dividing their capabilities.'

Sati, who had been studying the map, was suddenly struck by the obvious. 'Magadh!'

'Exactly,' said Kartik as he tapped on the location of Magadh. 'Swadweep's roads are either pathetic or nonexistent, which is why armies, especially big ones, use rivers to mobilise. The Ayodhyan army won't come to Meluha's aid by cutting through dense forests. They'll sail down the Sarayu, then up the Ganga to the newly built road Meluha's constructed to Devagiri.'

Shiva nodded. 'The Ayodhyan ships would have to pass

Magadh, at the confluence of the Sarayu and Ganga Rivers. If Magadh creates a blockade there, the ships won't be able to pass. We can hold back their massive army with only a small naval force from Magadh.'

'Exactly.'

Smiling, Shiva patted Kartik's shoulder. 'I'm impressed, my boy.'

Kartik grinned at his father's praise.

'First we have to rally Prince Surapadman to our side,' said Sati. 'Bhagirath told me that the Magadhan prince makes all the decisions, not his father, King Mahendra.'

Shiva glanced at Ganesh for his reaction.

Ganesh remained silent. He appeared a little unsettled by this new development.

'That's a good idea,' said Gopal as Shiva explained Kartik's plan. 'It should be relatively easy to bring Magadh to our side,' he continued, looking at Shiva, Sati, Ganesh and Kartik in turn. 'King Mahendra is old and indecisive, but his son, Surapadman, is a fearsome warrior and a brilliant tactician – and most importantly, he's a calculating and ambitious man.'

'His ambition should make him smell the opportunities in the coming war,' Shiva took over. 'He can use it to bolster his position and declare independence from Ayodhya.'

'Exactly,' said Sati. 'Whatever his reasons for choosing to support us, an alliance with him will help us win the war.'

Gopal noticed that Ganesh was a little pensive. 'Lord Ganesh?'

As Ganesh reacted with a start, the Chief Vasudev looked at him closely and asked, 'Is there something about this plan that troubles you?'

Ganesh shook his head. 'Nothing that needs to be discussed right now, Panditji.' He was worried that he'd inadvertently ruined any likelihood of an alliance with Magadh by killing the elder Magadhan prince, Ugrasen. He'd done so to save an innocent mother and her son from Ugrasen's depredations, but he had to hope that Surapadman was unaware of the identity of his brother's murderer.

Seeing Ganesh's continued unease, Kartik spoke up. '*Dada* and I have discussed this and we don't think we should assume Magadh will join us. We must be prepared to conquer Magadh as well, if need be.'

'Hopefully that situation won't arise, my son,' said Shiva. Turning to Ganesh, he added, 'But yes, we should make contingency plans to fight Magadh. It could be one of our opening gambits in the war.'

'Then I shall start making plans for our journey to Magadh,' said Gopal.

'Are you coming with us, Panditji?' Shiva was surprised. 'That will reveal your allegiance openly.'

'The time for remaining hidden is past, my friend,' said Gopal. 'The battle with Evil is upon us and we must all declare which side we're on. There are no bystanders in a holy war.'

Parvateshwar and Anandmayi held hands and whispered to each other as they rode their favourite steeds. He'd just told her that if it came to war, he'd have no choice but to fight on Meluha's side, and Anandmayi, in turn, had told him that she would have to oppose Meluha.

'Aren't you even going to ask me why?' she asked.

Parvateshwar shook his head. 'I don't need to. I know how you think.'

Anandmayi looked at her husband, her eyes moist.

'And I guess you know how I think, too,' said Parvateshwar. 'You didn't ask me for an explanation, either.'

Anandmayi smiled sadly at her husband and squeezed his hand.

'What do we do now?' he asked.

Anandmayi took a deep breath. 'Keep riding forward together.'

Parvateshwar stared at his wife.

'For as long as our paths allow us . . .'

Shiva leaned against the side as the ship sailed gently down the Chambal. Dense forest lined the banks on either side and there was no sign of human habitation for miles in any direction. He looked back at the five ships directly behind his own vessel, a small contingent of the fifty-ship Vasudev fleet. It had taken the Vasudevs a mere two months to mobilise for departure.

'What are you thinking, my friend?' asked Gopal.

'I'm thinking that the primary source of Evil is human greed. It's our greed to extract more and more from Good that turns it into Evil. Wouldn't it be better if this was controlled at the source, somehow? Can we really expect humans to not be greedy? How many of us would be willing to give up our desire to live for two hundred years? The *Somras* has dominated for many thousands of years and it has achieved both good and evil, but soon it'll be of no practical use to anyone. Isn't it fair to say that it's served no purpose in the larger scheme of things? Perhaps things would have been better had the *Somras* never been invented. Why embark on a journey when you know that the destination takes you back to exactly where you began?'

'Are there any journeys which don't take you back to where you began?'

Shiva frowned. 'Of course there are.'

Gopal shook his head. 'If you aren't back to where you began, all it means is that the journey isn't over. Maybe it'll take one lifetime, maybe many, but you will end your journey exactly where you began: that's the nature of life. Even the universe will end its journey exactly where it began: in an infinitesimal black hole of absolute death. And on the other side of that death, life will begin once again with a massive big bang. And so it will continue, in a never-ending cycle.'

'So what's the point?'

'That is the biggest folly of all, great Neelkanth – to think that we're on this path in order to get somewhere.'

'Aren't we?'

'No. The purpose is not the destination but the journey itself. Only those who understand this simple truth can experience true happiness.'

'Are you saying that neither the purpose nor the destination matter? That the *Somras* had to create Good and Evil in equal measure before being eliminated by a Neelkanth? If one believes this, then in the larger scheme of things, the *Somras* has achieved nothing.'

'Let me try to explain it another way. Do you understand the process that makes the rains fall in India?'

'Of course – one of your scientists explained it to me. The sun heats the sea, making the water rise in the form of water vapour which coalesces into clouds, which are then blown overland by monsoon winds. The clouds rise when they hit the mountains, which cools them and turns the vapour back into water, which falls as rain.'

'Perfect – but you've only covered half the journey. What happens after the water has rained upon us?'

Shiva's knowing smile suggested that he was beginning to follow the Chief Vasudev's train of thought.

Gopal continued, 'The water finds its way into streams, then rivers, and finally, the rivers flow back into the sea. Some of the water that falls as rain is used by humans, animals, plants – anything that needs water to stay alive – but ultimately, even the water we use escapes into the rivers and then back into the sea. The journey always ends exactly where it began. Now, can we say that the water's journey serves no purpose? What would happen to us if the sea decided there's no point to this journey because it ends exactly where it begins?'

'We'd all die.'

'Exactly. Now, one might be tempted to think that water's journey results in only Good, right? Whereas the *Somras* has caused both Good and Evil.'

Shiva smiled wryly. 'I am indeed tempted to think that, but I'm sure you're about to disabuse me of any such notion.'

Gopal's smile was equally dry. 'What about the floods caused by rains? What about the spread of disease that comes with the rains? If we were to ask those who have suffered floods and disease, they might well hold that rain is evil.'

'Excessive rains *are* evil,' corrected Shiva.

Gopal smiled and conceded his point. 'True enough. So water's journey from the sea back into the sea serves a purpose, for it makes the journey of life possible on land. Similarly, the journey of the *Somras* served a purpose for many, including you, for your purpose is to end the journey of the *Somras*. What would you be doing if the *Somras* hadn't existed?'

'I can think of so many things! Lazing around with Sati, for example. Or whiling away my time immersed in dance and music. Now *that* would be a good life . . .'

Gopal laughed softly. 'But, seriously, hasn't the *Somras* given your life purpose?'

Shiva smiled. 'Yes, it has.'

'And your journey has given my life purpose – for what's the point of being Chief Vasudev if I can't help the next Mahadev?'

Shiva smiled and patted Gopal's back.

'It's the journey rather than the destination that lends meaning to our lives, great Neelkanth. Being faithful to our path will lead to consequences both good and evil, for that's the way of the universe.'

Shiva thought about Gopal's words for a few moments. 'So from that perspective, my journey might have a positive effect on the future of India, but it'll have a negative effect on those who're addicted to the *Somras*. Perhaps that's my purpose.'

'Exactly. Lord Vasudev cautioned that we should be under no illusion that we are in control of our own breathing. We should realise the simple truth that we're "being breathed" – we're being kept alive because our journey serves a purpose. When our purpose is served, our breathing will stop and the universe will change our form to something else, so that we may serve another purpose.'

Shiva smiled. 'Then the only thing worth waiting for is release from this cycle of rebirths.'

'Exactly.'

CHAPTER 11

The Branga Alliance

Parvateshwar's entourage had sailed up the Madhumati to the point where it separated from the mighty Branga River and there they dropped anchor to await Bhagirath's return.

Bhagirath's ship had turned east and sailed down the Branga's main tributary, the massive Padma. A week later, his ship docked at the port of Brangaridai, the capital city of the Branga kingdom.

King Chandraketu had been informed of Bhagirath's arrival and had ensured that the Prince of Ayodhya was escorted to his palace with all due honour. When Bhagirath was led into the private palace rather than the formal court, he realised that Chandraketu wasn't treating him as the crown prince of Swadweep but as a friend.

Bhagirath found him waiting at the palace door, along with his wife and daughter. The King of Branga folded his hands in a formal namaste. 'How are you, brave Prince of Ayodhya?'

Bhagirath smiled and bowed his head as he returned the namaste. 'I'm well, your Majesty.'

Chandraketu smiled fondly at his consort. 'Prince Bhagirath, this is my wife, Queen Sneha.'

Bhagirath bowed to Sneha. 'Greetings, your Majesty.' The chivalrous Bhagirath then went down on one knee to face the six-year-old girl who was watching him with wide eyes. 'And who might this lovely lady be?'

'This is my daughter, Princess Navya,' said Chandraketu with an indulgent smile.

'Namaste, young lady,' said Bhagirath.

Navya slid shyly behind her mother, hiding her face.

'I'm a friend of your father's, my child,' Bhagirath said gently. 'You don't need to be afraid of me.'

'You smell funny . . .' whispered Navya, sticking her face out from behind her mother's skirts.

Bhagirath, startled, burst into laughter.

Chandraketu folded his hands together. 'My apologies, Prince Bhagirath. She can be a little direct sometimes.'

Bhagirath controlled his mirth. 'No, no; she's only speaking the truth.' To Navya, he said, 'But young lady, I was always taught to be polite to strangers. Don't you agree that's important, too?'

'Politeness doesn't mean lying,' said Navya primly. 'Lord Ram said we should always speak the truth. *Always*.'

Bhagirath raised his eyebrows in surprise before glancing at Chandraketu. 'Wow. Quoting Lord Ram at this age? She's smart.'

'She is that,' said Chandraketu proudly.

Bhagirath smiled fondly at Navya. 'Of course you're right, my child. I carry the odour of a long and rigorous voyage. I'll be sure to bathe before I meet with you again. You won't find my smell offensive then, I'll wager.'

Chandraketu laughed. 'Be warned, great prince. Navya's never lost a bet.'

The princess looked up at her mother. 'He doesn't seem all that bad, *maa*. I guess not all Ayodhyan royals are bad—'

Bhagirath laughed again and waved away Queen Sneha's apologies. 'King Chandraketu, I think we should retire to your chambers before any more assaults are made upon my dignity.'

— ⚕ ⑩Ʋ♀ ✪ —

'*Baba*,' whispered Ganesh nervously as he entered Shiva's cabin aboard the central ship of the joint Vasudev–Naga convoy.

Shiva looked up as he put the palm-leaf book aside. 'What is it, my son?'

'I need to speak with you,' he said, still whispering.

As Shiva pointed to the chair next to him and lifted his feet off the table, Ganesh took a deep breath. '*Baba*, there may be some complications with Magadh.'

Shiva smiled. 'I was wondering when you were going to bring that up.'

Ganesh frowned. 'You already know?'

'I know Ugrasen was killed by a Naga, and I understand that may complicate things.'

Ganesh kept silent as Shiva went on, 'Do you know who killed him? If it was a criminal act, we should support Surapadman. Not only would justice be served, but it would also help to convince Magadh to join us.' Shiva frowned when his son remained silent. 'Ganesh?'

'It was me,' confessed Ganesh.

Shiva's eyes widened. 'Well – that certainly does complicate matters . . . Did you have a good reason to kill him?'

'I did, *baba*.'

'What was it?'

'The Chandravanshi nobility have always patronised the tradition of bull-racing. In the quest for the lightest riders, innocent young boys are being kidnapped and forced to ride the bulls, and it's left innumerable children maimed – and many have died very painful deaths.'

Shiva stared at Ganesh in horror. 'What kind of barbaric people would do that to children?'

'Men like Ugrasen. I found him trying to kidnap a young boy, one of the forest tribes. The boy's mother was refusing to let him go, so Ugrasen and his men were on the verge of killing her. I had no choice . . .'

Shiva recalled something Kali had mentioned. 'Is this when you were seriously injured?'

'Yes, *baba*.'

Shiva breathed deeply. Ganesh had once again shown tremendous character, fighting injustice even at the risk of his own life. Shiva was proud of his son. 'You did the right thing,' he said warmly.

'I'm really sorry if I've complicated the issue—'

Shiva shook his head.

'What are you thinking, *baba*?'

'The ways of the world are really strange,' said Shiva. 'You protected an innocent child and his mother from an immoral prince. The Magadhans, however, didn't hesitate to spread the lie that Ugrasen died defending Magadh from a Naga terrorist attack, and people chose to believe that lie.'

Ganesh shrugged dismissively. 'The Nagas have always been treated this way. The lies never stop.' He paused, then asked, 'What do we do now?'

'We'll stick to the plan. Let's hope that Surapadman's ambitious enough to realise where Magadh's interests lie. But you should remain in Kashi – don't come with us to Magadh.'

'Yes, *baba*.'

Chandraketu clenched his fists and tried hard to suppress the anger welling up within him. Bhagirath's news, that the *Somras* waste was responsible for the plagues that had been devastating Branga for generations, had enraged him.

'By all the fury of Lord Rudra,' he growled, 'my people have been dying for decades, our children have suffered from horrific diseases and our aged have endured agonising pain – and all so that privileged Meluhans can live for two hundred years?'

Bhagirath remained silent and allowed Chandraketu to vent his righteous anger.

'What does the Lord Neelkanth have to say about this? When do we attack?'

'I'll send word to you when the time comes, your Majesty,' said Bhagirath, 'but it'll be soon, perhaps only a few months from now. You must mobilise your army and be ready.'

'We'll not only mobilise our army, but every single Branga who can fight. This isn't just a war for us – this is vengeance for our ancestors too.'

'My sailors are unloading some gifts from the Nagas and from Parshuram at the Brangaridai docks. As the Neelkanth promised, all the materials required to make the Naga medicine are being delivered to you. A Naga scientist is also going to stay here and teach you how to make the medicine yourselves. These materials, combined with the herbs you already have in your kingdom, should keep you supplied with the Naga medicine for three years.'

Chandraketu smiled slightly. 'The Lord Neelkanth has honoured his word. He is a worthy successor to Lord Rudra.'

'That he is.'

'But I don't think we'll need that much medicine. The combined might of Ayodhya and Branga will ensure Meluha's defeat well within three years. We'll stop them from manufacturing the *Somras* and destroy their waste facility in the Himalayas. Once the waste stops poisoning the Brahmaputra, there'll be no more plague and no further need for any medicine.'

Bhagirath narrowed his eyes, hesitating.

'What is it, Prince Bhagirath?'

'Your Majesty, Ayodhya's probably not going to be fighting alongside us in this war.'

'What? Are you saying Ayodhya may side with Meluha?'

'They've already thrown in their lot with Meluha.'

'Then why—?'

Bhagirath completed the question. 'Why am I acting against my own father and kingdom?'

'Exactly.'

'I follow my Lord, the great Neelkanth. His path is true, and I will walk on it – even if it means fighting my own kinsmen.'

Chandraketu rose and bowed to Bhagirath. 'It takes a special form of greatness to fight your own people for the ideal of justice. As far as I'm concerned, you're fighting for justice for the Brangas. I'll remember this gesture, Prince Bhagirath.'

Bhagirath was happy with the way the conversation had progressed. He'd accomplished the task Shiva had given him, and in a manner that had also won him the personal allegiance of the fabulously wealthy King of Branga. This alliance would prove useful when he came to make his move for the Ayodhyan throne. Remembering Chandraketu's sentimental nature, he thought it wise to seal the alliance with blood.

He pulled out his knife, slit his palm and held it out to the king. 'May my blood flow in your veins, my brother.'

A moist-eyed Chandraketu immediately pulled out his own

knife, slit his palm and grasped Bhagirath's bloodied hand. 'And may my blood flow in yours.'

— ⚹ ◍∪✚✸ —

Brahaspati, Nandi and Parshuram, sitting aft on the deck of the Vasudev–Naga fleet's lead ship, watched Ganesh and Kartik practising their swordsmanship aboard the vessel behind them.

Brahaspati's emotions were tinged with bitter regret. 'My mission's gained a leader but I've lost a friend.'

'Of course you haven't, Brahaspatiji,' said Nandi. 'The Lord Neelkanth still loves you.'

Brahaspati raised his eyebrows and smiled. 'Nandi, lying doesn't become you.'

Nandi laughed softly. 'If it makes you feel any better, I can tell you that Lord Shiva missed you dearly when he believed you were dead. You were always on his mind.'

'I wouldn't have expected any less,' said Brahaspati. 'But I don't think he understands why I did what I did.'

'To be honest,' said Nandi, 'neither do I. I concede that it was important to fake your death, but you probably should have told Lord Shiva the truth sooner.'

'I couldn't,' said Brahaspati. 'Shiva is Emperor Daksha's son-in-law, and Daksha's my primary enemy. Had Daksha learned I was alive, he'd have sent assassins after me to finish the job and I wouldn't have lived long enough to conduct the experiments I needed to. And I had no way of knowing whether Shiva would have enough faith in me to not reveal anything to Daksha.'

Parshuram tried to console Brahaspati. 'He's forgiven you – trust me, he has.'

'He may have forgiven me, but I don't think he understands me yet,' said Brahaspati. 'I hope a time will come when I get my friend back.'

'It will,' said Parshuram. 'Once the *Somras* is destroyed, we'll all go with the Lord to Mount Kailash and live happily ever after.'

Nandi smiled. 'Mount Kailash is far less hospitable than you imagine, Parshuram. I should know – I've been there. It's no paradise.'

'Any place would be paradise so long as we sit at the feet of Lord Shiva.'

— ⋏ ⚭∪⇞⊕ —

'Are you wearing *kajal* around your eyes?' asked Shiva, surprised. He had been gazing fondly at his children from his vantage point of the high private deck, watching as they sparred with each other on the main deck, their swords flashing in the sunlight. Sati was leaning against him, briefly lost in the moment. Shiva had rarely seen Sati use make-up; her beauty was so perfect he believed it needed no embellishment.

Sati looked up at Shiva with a shy smile. Her pronounced Suryavanshi personality had been subtly influenced by the Chandravanshi women, particularly Anandmayi, and she was discovering the pleasures of beauty, especially when experienced through the appreciative eyes of the man she loved. 'Yes. I thought you hadn't noticed.'

The kohl accentuated Sati's large almond-shaped eyes and her bashful smile made her dimples spring to life.

Shiva was mesmerised. 'It looks lovely . . .'

Sati kissed him lightly. That was the right reaction.

Ganesh and Kartik were engaged in a furious duel on the foredeck, fighting with real weapons instead of wooden swords – they believed the risk of serious injury helped focus their minds and improved their practice. They always pulled back from a killing strike, demonstrating to the other that an opening had been found.

Using his smaller size to his advantage, Kartik pressed close to Ganesh, cramping him and making it difficult for his taller opponent to strike freely. Ganesh stepped back and swung his shield down in an apparently defensive motion, but halted the movement just short of Kartik's shoulder.

'Kartik, my shield contains a knife,' said Ganesh as he pressed a lever to release the blade. 'This strike is mine. I've said this to you before: fighting with two swords is too aggressive. You should use a shield. You ended up leaving an opening for me.'

Kartik smiled. 'No, *dada*. The strike is mine. Look down.'

Ganesh's eyes flicked to his chest as he felt a light touch of metal against his skin. Kartik was holding his left sword reversed and a small blade was sticking out of the hilt-end. He'd managed to turn the sword around, release the concealed knife and bring it in close, all the while giving Ganesh the illusion that he was feinting and leaving his left flank open. Shiva's elder son had assumed Kartik had pulled his left sword out of combat.

Ganesh's eyes widened – he was seriously impressed with his brother. 'How in Lady Bhoomidevi's name did you manage that?'

Shiva, who had seen the entire manoeuvre from his vantage point on the upper deck, was equally impressed with Kartik. He pulled away from Sati and shouted, 'Bravo, Kartik!'

Sensing angry eyes boring into him, Shiva immediately returned his attention to Sati, who was glaring at her husband irritably and holding her breath, her lips still puckered.

'I'm so sorry – I'm so sorry,' said Shiva, trying to draw close and kiss Sati again.

Sati pushed Shiva's face away with mock irritation. 'The moment's passed—'

'I'm so sorry. It's just that what Kartik did was—'

'Huh,' said Sati.

'It won't happen again—'

'It had better not—'

'I'm sorry—'

Sati rested her head against Shiva's chest.

Shiva pulled her close. 'I love the *kajal*. I didn't think it was possible for you to look even more beautiful.'

Sati looked up at Shiva and rolled her eyes, then slapped him lightly on his chest. 'Too little, too late.'

CHAPTER 12

Troubled Waters

'How did it go?' asked Anandmayi as Bhagirath rejoined Parvateshwar's vessel. Parvateshwar, Anandmayi and Ayurvati had been waiting for Bhagirath on the aft deck, eager for the news from Branga.

Bhagirath glanced at Parvateshwar and Ayurvati, then said to Anandmayi, 'How do you think it went?'

'Did you tell him everything?' asked Ayurvati.

'Of course! I did exactly what the Lord Neelkanth asked me to do,' he replied.

Parvateshwar sighed deeply and walked away.

Anandmayi watched her husband leave, then turned back to her brother. 'So what did he say, Bhagirath?'

'King Chandraketu's livid that his people have been suffering from a murderous plague so that the Meluhans can live extra-long lives.'

'I hope you also told him that most Meluhans didn't know

this,' said Ayurvati. 'Had we known the *Somras* was causing this evil in Branga, we'd never have used it.'

Bhagirath looked disbelievingly at Ayurvati and sarcastically remarked, 'I informed him that most Meluhans were ignorant of the devastation their addiction had caused. Strangely, it didn't appear to lessen King Chandraketu's anger.'

Ayurvati remained silent.

Anandmayi said irritably, 'Can you stop being judgemental for a moment and tell me what's going to happen in Branga now?'

'King Chandraketu's going to concentrate on manufacturing the medicines his people need,' said Bhagirath, 'but he's also begun to mobilise his troops for war. He'll be ready and waiting in three months for the Lord Neelkanth's orders.'

Tears welled up in Ayurvati's eyes as she looked wistfully at Parvateshwar in the distance. She felt the anguish in his heart, for hers was just as heavy.

'Your Majesty,' said Siamantak, the Ayodhyan prime minister, as he entered Emperor Dilipa's chambers, 'I've just received word that Maharishi Bhrigu is on his way here.'

'Lord Bhrigu?' Dilipa was surprised. 'Coming here?'

'The advance boat has just arrived, your Majesty,' said Siamantak. 'Lord Bhrigu should be here by tomorrow.'

'Why wasn't I informed sooner?'

'I didn't know until now that he was on his way, your Majesty.'

'Meluha should have informed us in advance before sending Lord Bhrigu here.'

'That's Meluha for you, my Lord. Discourteous, as always.'

Dilipa ran his hands nervously across his face. 'Is there any news from the shipyard? Are our vessels close to completion?'

Siamantak swallowed anxiously. 'No, your Majesty. You asked me to pay attention to the pavement-dweller issue and—'

'I know what I asked you to do!' the emperor shouted. 'Just answer my question with a simple yes or no!'

'My humble apologies, your Majesty. No, the ships are nowhere near completion.'

'When will the job be done?'

'If we put everything else on hold, then I guess we should be ready in another six to nine months.'

Dilipa appeared to breathe easier. 'That's not so bad. Nothing's going to happen in the next nine months.'

'Yes, your Majesty.'

Emperor Dilipa and Maharishi Bhrigu were at the Ayodhya shipyard. The Meluhan brigadier, Prasanjit, who had accompanied Bhrigu, stood at a distance.

Declining the hospitality awaiting him on landing, Bhrigu had headed directly for the shipyard. A flustered Dilipa had followed him, courtiers and all. When they arrived, he gestured for Siamantak and everyone else to remain at a distance. He knew Bhrigu was angry, and expected an earful.

'Your Majesty,' said Bhrigu slowly, keeping his temper on a tight leash, 'you promised me that your ships would be ready by now.'

'I know, my Lord,' said Dilipa softly, 'but surely a short delay won't hurt us. It's been many months since our attack on Pancha-vati and there's been absolutely no news of the Neelkanth. I'm sure we've succeeded, so we don't really need to be nervous. I honestly believe the likelihood of a war is substantially reduced.'

Bhrigu said angrily, 'Your Majesty, may I request that you leave the thinking to me?'

Dilipa immediately fell silent.

'Wasn't it your suggestion to commandeer Ayodhya's trade ships and refit them for war?'

'Yes, my Lord,' said Dilipa.

'And didn't I predict that we're not likely to be fighting naval battles on the Ganga? Didn't I tell you that we'll only need transport ships, for which your trade ships were good enough already?'

'You did, my Lord.'

'Yet you still insisted that we must have battleships, just in case.'

'Yes, my Lord.'

'And I agreed on one condition: that the battleships would be ready in six months. Correct?'

'Yes, my Lord.'

'Seven months have passed. You've stripped down the trade ships but haven't refitted them yet. So now, seven months later, not only do we have no battleships, but we're also without any transport ships.'

'I know it looks very bad, my Lord,' said Dilipa, wiping his perspiring brow with his fingers, 'but the pavement-dwellers here went on a hunger strike.'

Bhrigu raised his hands in exasperation. 'What does that have to do with the ships?'

'My Lord,' Dilipa explained patiently, 'in my benevolence, I decreed that no Ayodhyan shall be roofless. This onerous but noble task was assigned to the Royal Committee of Internal Affairs, which looks after both housing and the royal shipyard. The committee has been seriously debating this grand housing scheme for the past three years. Following our last conversation, however, I directed the committee to focus on building ships. The pavement-dwellers protested the neglect of the free housing scheme. Public order being paramount, I redirected the committee to concentrate on the housing scheme again. I'm glad to say that the seventh version of the housing report, which judiciously takes into account the views of every citizen, should be ready soon. Once accepted, the committee can then give its undiluted attention to the matter of building ships.'

Bhrigu was staring wide-eyed at the emperor, stunned.

'So you see, my Lord,' said Dilipa, 'I know this doesn't look good, but everything will be set right very soon. In fact, I expect the committee to start debating the shipyard issue within the next seven days.'

Bhrigu spoke softly, but his rage was at boiling point. 'Your

Majesty, the future of India is at stake and your committee is *debating*?'

'But my Lord, debates are important. They help us to incorporate all points of view, or else we might make decisions that aren't—'

'In the name of Lord Ram, you are the *king* – not just the *king*, the *emperor*! Fate has placed you in that exalted position so that you can make decisions *for* your people!'

Dilipa fell silent.

Bhrigu was silent for a few seconds while he tried to control his anger, then he spoke in a low voice. 'Your Majesty, what you do within your own kingdom is your problem, but I want the refitting of these ships to begin today. Do you understand?'

'Yes, Maharishiji.'

'How soon can the ships be ready?'

'In six months, if my people work every day.'

'Make those imbeciles work day and night and have them ready in three. Am I clear?'

'Yes, my Lord.'

'Also, please have your cartographers map the jungle route from Ayodhya to the upper Ganga.'

'But why—?'

Bhrigu sighed in exasperation. 'Your Majesty, I expect Meluha to be the real battleground, not Ayodhya. I wanted these ships ready in case we needed to transport your army to Meluha at a moment's notice. Since they're not ready yet, we need an alternative plan in case war is declared within the next few months. That means your army will have to cut through the jungle in a north-westerly direction until they reach the upper Ganga, close to Dharmakhet. Beyond that, you can use the Meluhans' new road to reach Devagiri. Cutting through the jungle will be slow work and will likely take many months, but it's better than no reinforcements reaching Meluha at all. To ensure that your army doesn't get lost in the jungle, they'll need good maps. I'm sure your commanders will want to reach Meluha in time to help your allies.'

Dilipa nodded sliently.

'As I said, I'll be surprised if Ayodhya's attacked directly.'

'Of course – why would anyone attack Ayodhya?' asked Dilipa. 'We haven't harmed anyone.'

In truth, Bhrigu wasn't certain that Ayodhya wouldn't be attacked, but he didn't care. His only concern was the *Somras*. Meluha had to be protected in order to protect the *Somras*. He'd gladly have convinced Dilipa to order the Ayodhyan army to leave for Devagiri right away, had such a thing been logistically possible.

'I'll order the cartographers to map the route through the jungles, my Lord,' said Dilipa.

'Thank you, your Majesty,' said Bhrigu, smiling for the first time since his arrival. 'By the way, I notice that your wrinkles are disappearing. Has the blood in your cough reduced?'

'Disappeared, my Lord. Your medicines are truly miraculous.'

'A medicine is only as good as the patient's responsiveness. All the credit is due to you, your Majesty.'

'You're too kind, my Lord. You've worked magic with my ailing body. But my knee continues to trouble me. It still hurts when I—'

'We'll take care of that as well. Don't worry.'

'Thank you, my Lord.'

Bhrigu gestured to Prasanjit, who was still waiting patiently behind them. 'I've brought this Meluhan brigadier to train your army in modern warfare techniques.'

'But—'

'Please ensure that your soldiers listen to him, your Majesty.'

'Yes, my Lord.'

— ⚚ ⦶⦶∪⦵⦾ —

The two ships carrying Parvateshwar and his companions had just docked at the river port of Vaishali, Branga's immediate neighbour. Shiva had asked Parvateshwar to speak to King Maatali and secure his support for the Neelkanth, but as Parvateshwar had decided he must oppose the Mahadev and protect Meluha, he thought it would be unethical of him to approach the king. He asked Anandmayi to carry out the mission instead and decided to use the time to practise his sword skills with Uttanka on the lead ship.

Bhagirath, Anandmayi and Ayurvati were standing aft while they waited for the gangplank to be lowered onto the Vaishali dockside. They gazed at the exquisite Vishnu Temple dedicated to Lord Matsya, which had been built very close to the river harbour, and bowed low towards the first Lord Vishnu.

'You'll have to excuse me, sister,' said Bhagirath.

'Are you planning to leave for Ayodhya right away?' asked Anandmayi.

'Why delay the inevitable? I'm taking the second ship up the Sarayu to Ayodhya. The Vaishali king's allegiance is a given – he's blindly loyal to the Neelkanth, so your meeting with him will be a mere formality. I might as well get on with the other task the Lord Neelkanth's given me.'

'Fair enough,' said Anandmayi.

'Go with Lord Ram's blessings, Bhagirath,' said Ayurvati as he waved them goodbye.

— ☧ ◍U⚲⊛ —

The lead ships of Shiva's convoy berthed at Kashi's Assi Ghat, while the rest docked nearby at the Brahma Ghat. King Athithigva was waiting with a large retinue for the ceremonial reception to begin. On cue, drummers began to beat a steady rhythm and conches blared as Shiva stepped onto the gangplank. Ceremonial *aartis* and a cheering populace added to the festive air. Their living god had returned.

King Athithigva bowed low and touched Shiva's feet as soon as he stepped onto the Assi Ghat.

'*Ayushman bhav*, your Majesty,' said Shiva, blessing King Athithigva with a long life.

Athithigva smiled, his hands folded in a respectful namaste. 'A long life's not much use if we're not graced with your presence here in Kashi, my Lord.'

Shiva, always uncomfortable with such deference, quickly changed the subject. 'How have things been going, your Majesty?'

'Very well. Trade's been good. But rumours have been going around that the Neelkanth's about to make a big announcement. Is that so, my Lord?'

'Let's wait till we get to your palace, your Majesty.'

'Of course,' said Athithigva. 'By the way, I've received word via a fast sailboat that Queen Kali's on her way to Kashi – she's only a few days' journey behind you.'

With raised eyebrows, Shiva instinctively looked upriver, in the direction from which Kali's ship would arrive. 'It'll be good to have her here – we have a lot of planning to do.'

CHAPTER 13

Escape of the Gunas

Shiva embraced Veerbhadra delightedly as Sati hugged Krittika. The couple had just joined Shiva in their private chamber in the Kashi palace.

Veerbhadra and Krittika's journey through Meluha had been uneventful. Their reception at the village where the Gunas had been housed had taken them by surprise: there were no soldiers, no alarms, nothing out of the ordinary. Clearly, the Gunas weren't being targeted as leverage to use against the Neelkanth. The Meluhans' system had achieved exactly what they'd conceived – everybody was being treated in accordance with the law, with no special provisions for any particular individuals or groups.

'Did you run into any trouble?' asked Shiva.

'None,' said Veerbhadra. 'The tribespeople were living just like everyone else, in comfortable egalitarianism. We quickly bundled them into a caravan and left quietly. We arrived in Kashi a few months later.'

'That means they don't know yet that I escaped the attack at the Godavari,' said Shiva. 'If they did, they'd have arrested the Gunas long before you got there.'

'That would make sense from a strategic point of view.'

'Of course, if any Meluhan happens to check the Guna village and finds them missing, they'll assume I'm still alive and planning a confrontation.'

'Another logical conclusion. But there's nothing we can do about that, is there?'

'I'm afraid not,' Shiva agreed.

'*Didi!*' Kali smiled warmly as she embraced her sister.

'How are you, Kali?' asked Sati.

'I'm tired. My ship had to race down the Chambal and Ganga to catch up with you!'

'It's good to see you, Kali,' said Shiva.

'Likewise,' said Kali. 'How was Ujjain?'

'A city worthy of Lord Ram,' said Shiva.

'Is it true that some of the Vasudevs have accompanied you here?'

'Yes, including the Chief Vasudev himself, Lord Gopal.'

Kali whistled softly. 'I didn't even know the Chief Vasudev's name until the other day, and now it looks like I'll be meeting him soon. The situation must be really grim for him to emerge from his seclusion like this.'

'Change doesn't happen easily,' said Shiva. 'I'm not expecting the supporters of the *Somras* to just fade into the sunset. The Vasudevs believe the war's already begun, regardless of whether it's been formally declared or not, and that it's just a matter of time before actual hostilities break out. I'm inclined to agree with them.'

'Is that why my ship was dragged into the Assi River?' asked Kali. 'It's more of a stream than a river – I was worried we might not make it into the harbour!'

'That was Lord Athithigva's idea,' said Shiva. 'He thinks our enemies may hesitate to attack the city itself because they believe Lord Rudra's spirit protects Kashi.'

'Hence the decision to move all our ships into the Assi,' said Sati. 'The channel at the river's mouth where it flows into the Ganga is very narrow, so only one enemy ship can come through at a time. That means we can defend our own ships more easily. Also, the Assi flows through the city of Kashi, and as Shiva said, most Chandravanshis won't want to venture within the city because they believe that Lord Rudra's spirit will curse them for harming Kashi, even by mistake.'

Kali raised her eyebrows. 'Using an enemy's own superstition against him? I like it!'

'Sometimes good tactics can work better than a sword's edge,' said Shiva with a grin.

'Ah,' said Kali. 'You're only saying that because you've never encountered my sword!'

Shiva and his companions waited in the main hall of the grand
Kashi Vishwanath Temple. Athithigva had accompanied the
head pandit into the inner sanctum to offer *prasad* to the idols
of Lord Rudra and Lady Mohini. They soon returned with the
ritual offerings, which had now received the gods' blessings.

'May Lord Rudra and Lady Mohini bless our enterprise,' said
Athithigva, offering the *prasad* to Shiva.

Shiva took the *prasad* with both hands, swallowed it whole
and ran his right hand over his head, offering his thanks to the
lord and lady for their blessings, while the temple pandit distributed the *prasad* to everybody else. Then, the ceremonies over,
the pandit was led out of the temple by Kashi policemen and
the entrance sealed before Athithigva sat down with the group
to discuss the strategy for the approaching war. No one would
be allowed inside for the duration of the meeting.

'My Lord, my people are forbidden to commit any acts of
violence except in self-defence,' said Athithigva. 'Consequently,
we can't actively participate in your campaign – but all of my
kingdom's resources are at your disposal.'

Shiva had no intention of leading the peace-loving Kashi
people into battle – he knew they wouldn't make good soldiers.
'I know of your vows, King Athithigva. I wouldn't ask anything
of your people that they'd be honour-bound to refuse to do. But
you must be ready and able to defend Kashi if it's attacked, for
we intend to store many of our war resources here.'

'We'll defend it to our last breath, my Lord,' said Athithigva.

Shiva nodded, although he didn't really expect the Chandravanshis to attack Kashi. Turning to Gopal, he said, 'Panditji, there are many things we need to discuss. To begin with, how do we keep the Chandravanshis out of the theatre of war in Meluha? Secondly, what strategy should we adopt with Meluha?'

'I think Lord Ganesh and Kartik's suggestion is an excellent idea,' said Gopal. 'Let's hope we can secure Magadh's allegiance.'

'Easier said than done,' said Kali. 'Surapadman's father will compel him to seek vengeance for the death of his stupid brother, Ugrasen, and I have no intention of handing Ganesh over for what was a just execution.'

'So what do you suggest, Kali?' asked Sati.

'I say we either fight Magadh right away or tell them that we'll investigate Ugrasen's death and hand over the Naga culprit as soon as we lay our hands on him.'

Sati held Ganesh's hand protectively.

Kali laughed softly. '*Didi*, all I'm suggesting is that we make Surapadman *think* we're going to hand him over – that way we can buy some time and attack Ayodhya.'

'Are you suggesting that we lie to the Magadhans, your Highness?' asked Gopal.

Kali frowned at him. 'Only that we should be economical with the truth, great Vasudev. The future of India is at stake and many people are counting on us. If we have to taint our souls with a sin for the sake of greater good, then so be it.'

'I won't lie,' said Shiva. 'This is a war against Evil. We're on the side of Good. Our fight must reflect that.'

'*Baba*,' said Ganesh, 'you know I'd agree with you under

normal circumstances, but do you think the other side's holding itself to such high standards? Wasn't the attack on us at Panchavati an act of pure deception and subterfuge?'

'I don't believe it's wrong to attack an unprepared enemy,' said Shiva. 'Their use of *daivi astras* was questionable, I'll admit. Even so, two wrongs don't make a right. I won't lie to win this war. We'll win it the right way.'

Kartik remained silent. While he agreed with the pragmatism of Ganesh's words, he was also inspired by Shiva's moral clarity.

Gopal smiled at Shiva. '*Satyam vada. Asatyam mavada.*'

'What does that mean?' asked Shiva.

Kali spoke up. 'It's an old Sanskrit saying: Speak the truth; never speak the untruth.'

Sati smiled. 'I agree.'

'Well, I know some old Sanskrit sayings, too,' said Kali. '*Satyam bruyat priyam bruyat, na bruyat satyam apriyam.*'

Shiva raised his hands in dismay. 'Can we dispense with this old Sanskrit one-upmanship? I can't understand a word you're saying.'

Gopal translated for Shiva. 'Queen Kali said, "Speak the truth in a pleasing manner, but never speak that truth which is unpleasant to others."'

'It's not my line,' said Kali, turning to Shiva. 'I'm sure it can be traced back to some ancient sage. But I think it makes sense. We don't have to reveal to Surapadman that we know who killed his brother. All we're trying to do is motivate him to hold off choosing his friends and his enemies until after we've attacked Ayodhya. That way his ambition will guide him in the direction we desire.'

'Ayodhya's walls are impregnable,' warned Gopal, drawing their attention to another factor that required consideration. 'We might be able to lay siege to the city, but we won't be able to destroy it.'

'True,' said Ganesh. 'But our aim isn't to destroy Ayodhya – it's to prevent their navy from ferrying their soldiers to Meluha. Our main battle will be in Meluha.'

'But what if Surapadman attacks us from the rear after we've laid siege on Ayodhya?' asked Gopal. 'We'd be trapped between them – we might be destroyed.'

'Actually, no,' said Ganesh. 'Surapadman attacking us from behind would make things easier for us. When he leaves Magadh, we'll make our move.'

Shiva, Kartik and Sati nodded approvingly. They understood Ganesh's plan.

'That's brilliant,' exclaimed Parshuram, and he took aside those who needed further explanation.

Kali returned to the conversation about lying she'd been having with Shiva. 'Don't tell Surapadman the whole truth, just the parts that'll make him pause. His ambition will do the rest. We need him to allow our ships to pass through the confluence of the Sarayu and Ganga on their way to Ayodhya. Once that's done, we'll achieve our objective one way or the other – either by holding Ayodhya back or by destroying the Magadhan army.'

'But what about Meluha?' Shiva asked. 'Should we launch a frontal attack with all our military strength? Or should we adopt diversionary tactics to distract their armies while a small group searches for the secret *Somras* facility and destroys it?'

'Our Branga and Vaishali forces will fight in Magadh and Ayodhya, leaving the Vasudevs and the Naga armies for the Meluhan campaign,' said Sati. 'So we'll have much smaller forces in Meluha. Of course, they'll be exceptionally well trained, with superb technological skills, like the fire-spewing elephant corps the Vasudevs have developed. But we have to respect the Meluhan forces: they're equally well trained and technologically adept.'

'Are you suggesting that we avoid any direct attack?' asked Shiva.

'Yes,' said Sati. 'Our main aim has to be to destroy the *Somras* manufacturing facility. It'll take them years to rebuild it, which will be more than enough time for your word to prevail amongst the people. The average Meluhan is devoted to the legend of the Neelkanth. The *Somras* will die a natural death. But if we attack directly, the war with Meluha will drag on, and the longer it drags on, the more innocent people will die. Also, the Meluhans will begin to look upon the war as an attack on their beloved country rather than the *Somras*. I'm sure there'll be large numbers of Meluhans willing to turn against the *Somras*, but if we challenge their patriotism, we have no chance of winning.'

Kali was smiling.

'What?' asked Sati.

'I notice you said "they" instead of "we" when you referred to the Meluhans,' said Kali.

Sati looked perplexed. She still believed Meluha was her homeland. 'Um, that's unimportant . . . It's still my country—'

'Sure it is,' said Kali with a smile.

Gopal cut in, 'Just for the sake of argument, let's imagine what might happen if there's an all-out war.'

'That's something we must strive to avoid,' said Shiva. 'Sati's making a very valid point.'

'Nevertheless, let's consider what Lord Bhrigu and Daksha might be thinking,' said Gopal. 'I agree that it's in our best interests to avoid a direct war, but it's in their interest to have one, and a destructive one at that. They'll want tensions to escalate so they can confuse the people. They'll say that the Neelkanth has betrayed Meluha – and, as Lady Sati just pointed out, the Meluhans' patriotism could easily drown out their faith in the Neelkanth.'

'I agree that Lord Bhrigu may want to escalate the situation,' said Shiva. 'What I don't understand is how he hopes to control it once he has. I've seen the Meluhan army up close. Yes, it's a well-drilled force with an efficient chain of command. But the problem with such armies is their utter dependence on a good commander. Their general, Parvateshwar, is with us. Trust me – they don't have another man like him. If Lord Bhrigu's as intelligent as you say he is, he'll know that, too.'

Ganesh and Kartik sighed at the same time.

Shiva glared at his sons.

'*Baba* . . .' said Kartik.

'Dammit!' exclaimed Shiva. 'You will *not* doubt his loyalty! Am I clear?'

Ganesh and Kartik bowed their heads, their mouths pursed mutinously.

'Am I clear?' Shiva repeated.

Kali frowned at him, but remained silent.

Shiva turned back to Gopal. 'We have to avoid provocation. Our military formations must be solidly defensive in order to deter them from staging an open confrontation. The main task for our army is to distract them while a smaller unit searches the towns along the Saraswati for signs of the *Somras* manufacturing facility. Once we've destroyed that facility, we'll win the war.'

'Nandi,' said Sati, summoning the Meluhan major to join the discussion.

Nandi laid out a map of Meluha, and everyone peered at it.

'Look here,' said Sati. 'The Saraswati ends in an inland delta. The Meluhans won't be able to move their massive fleet from Karachapa into the Saraswati. Their defence deployment covers just two possible threats: a naval attack via the Indus or a land-based army attack from the east. That's why they only maintain a small fleet on the Saraswati.'

Shiva grasped what Sati was thinking. 'They're unprepared for any naval attack on the Saraswati—'

'You must understand that they have good reason not to expect an attack from that direction. They're assuming that the Saraswati's safe from enemy ships – no enemy-controlled rivers flow into it and the Saraswati doesn't open to the sea any more.'

'But isn't that the problem?' Athithigva was confused. 'How will we get ships into the Saraswati?'

'We won't,' said Shiva. 'We'll capture the Meluhan ships stationed in the Saraswati instead.'

'That's the last thing they'll be expecting,' Kali pointed out, 'which is why it'll work.'

'Exactly,' said Sati. 'All we have to do is capture Mrittikavati, which is where most of the Saraswati command of the Meluhan navy is stationed. Once we have those ships, we'll control the Saraswati. We can sail along it unchallenged while we search for the *Somras* manufacturing facility.'

'The facility must be located somewhere along the Saraswati,' said Brahaspati.

'This sounds like a good plan,' said Gopal, 'but how do we capture their ships? Where will we enter their territory? Mrittikavati's not a border town. We'll have to march in with an army, and we'll obviously face resistance from the border town of Lothal.'

'I've never heard of Lothal,' said Kartik.

'Lothal is the port that serves Maika,' said Gopal. 'They're practically twin cities. Maika is where all the Meluhan children are born and raised, and Lothal is the local army base.'

'Don't worry about Maika or Lothal,' said Kali. 'They'll be on our side.'

Her statement took Gopal, Shiva and Sati by surprise, and they asked Kali to explain her thinking.

'If there are any Meluhans who'll sympathise with us, it'll be the people of Maika,' said Kali. 'They've seen the Naga children suffer. They've tried to help us on many occasions, even breaking their own laws in the process. The present governor of Maika, Chenardhwaj, is also the administrator of Lothal. He was transferred from Kashmir a few years back and I know he's loyal to the institution of the Neelkanth. Furthermore, I saved his life once. Trust me, both Maika and Lothal will be with us when hostilities break out.'

'I remember Chenardhwaj,' said Shiva. 'All right, then, we'll utilise Lothal's resources to conquer Mrittikavati. Then we'll use their ships to search the towns along the Saraswati. But remember – we must avoid a direct clash at all costs.'

CHAPTER 14

The Reader of Minds

'Do you believe we can convince him?' Shiva asked Gopal as they were preparing to leave for Magadh.

'I'd have been worried if we were meeting Lord Bhrigu,' said Gopal, 'but it's only Surapadman.'

'What's so special about Lord Bhrigu?' asked Shiva. 'He's only human. Why are you all so wary of him?'

'He's a maharishi, Shiva,' said Sati. 'In fact, as Gopalji mentioned earlier, Lord Bhrigu's believed by many to be greater than a maharishi – they say he's a *Saptrishi Uttradhikari*.'

'You should respect the man, not his position,' said Shiva, before turning to Gopal. 'I'll ask you again, my friend – why are you so wary of him?'

'Well, for a start, he can read minds,' said Gopal.

'So?' asked Shiva. 'You and I can do that, too. Every Vasudev pandit can, in fact.'

'True, but we can only do so while we're inside one of our

temples. Lord Bhrigu can read the minds of anyone around him, regardless of where he is.'

'How can he do that?' asked Ganesh, surprised.

'Our brains transmit radio waves when we think,' explained Gopal. 'These thoughts can be detected by a trained person, provided he's within the range of a powerful transmitter. But it's believed that a maharishi's abilities are more advanced. They don't need to wait till our thoughts are converted into radio waves to be able to detect them. They can read our thoughts even as we formulate them.'

'But how, exactly?' persisted Ganesh.

'Thoughts are just electrical impulses in our brains,' said Gopal. 'These impulses make the pupils of our eyes move minutely. A highly trained person – such as a maharishi, for example – can discern these movements in our pupils and de-cipher them to read our thoughts.'

'Lord Ram, be merciful,' whispered Kartik.

'I still don't understand how this is possible,' said Shiva. 'Are you saying all our thoughts are exposed by the movements of our pupils? What language would that communication be in? This makes no sense.'

'My friend,' said Gopal, 'you're confusing the language of communication with the internal language of the brain. San-skrit, for example, is a language of communication. You use it to communicate with others. You also use it to communicate with your own brain, so that your conscious mind can understand your inner thoughts. But the brain itself uses only one language for its own workings. This is a universal language shared by all brains of all known species. And the alphabet of this language has two letters, or signals.'

'Only two?' asked Sati

'Yes,' said Gopal, 'only two – "electricity on" and "electricity off". Our brains have millions of thoughts and instructions running through them simultaneously, but only one of these thoughts can capture our conscious attention in any given moment. This particular thought is reflected in our eyes through the language of the brain. A maharishi can read this conscious thought, so one must be very careful what one consciously thinks in the presence of a maharishi.'

'So the eye is indeed the window to one's soul,' said Ganesh.

Gopal smiled. 'It would appear so.'

Shiva grinned. 'Well, I'll have to make sure I keep mine shut when I meet Lord Bhrigu.'

Gopal and Sati laughed with him.

'Nevertheless, we will win,' said Gopal.

'Yes,' said Ganesh. 'We're on the side of Good.'

'That's true, without doubt,' said Gopal 'but that's not the reason, Lord Ganesh. We'll win because of your father.'

'No,' said Shiva. 'It can't just be down to me. We'll win because we're all in this together.'

'It's you who brings us together, great Neelkanth,' said Gopal. 'Lord Bhrigu may be as intelligent as you are – more intelligent, perhaps – but he's not a leader like you. He misuses his brilliance to intimidate his followers. They don't idolise him – they're scared of him. You, on the other hand, are able to draw out the best in your followers, my friend. Don't think I didn't know exactly what you were doing a few days back. You'd already decided on your course of action, but you still had that discussion with us, which allowed us to feel we had a part in the decision. Somehow, you guided us all to say what you wanted to hear, yet you made each one of us feel as if it was our own decision. That's true leadership. Lord Bhrigu may have a bigger army than ours, but he fights alone. Our entire army will fight as one. That, great Neelkanth, is a supreme tribute to your leadership.'

Shiva quickly changed the topic, embarrassed as always when complimented. 'You're being too kind, Gopalji. In any case, I think it's time to leave — Magadh awaits us.'

'Bhagirath's *here*?' said Emperor Dilipa.

'Yes, my Lord,' said Siamantak.

'But how did he—?'

'Prime Minister Siamantak,' said Bhrigu, interrupting Dilipa. 'I'd be delighted to meet him. Are Princess Anandmayi and her husband travelling with him?'

'No, my Lord,' said Siamantak. 'He's come alone.'

'That's most unfortunate,' said Bhrigu. 'Please, bring him into our presence with every honour due to one of his rank.'

'As you wish, my Lord,' said Siamantak as he bowed to Bhrigu and Dilipa before leaving the room.

As soon as he'd closed the door, Bhrigu said, 'Your Majesty, you must learn to control your reactions. Siamantak is unaware of the attack at the Godavari.'

'I'm sorry, my Lord,' said Dilipa. 'It's just such a shock.'

'Not to me, it isn't.'

Dilipa frowned. 'Did you anticipate this, my Lord?'

'I can't say I expected this specifically, but I had a strong suspicion that our attack had failed. The only question was how my suspicion would be confirmed.'

'I don't understand, my Lord. There are so many disasters that could have befallen our ships—'

'The destruction of our ships isn't the only factor in the equation. There's something else. I asked Kanakhala to try and locate the Gunas.'

'Who are the Gunas?'

'The tribe of that fraud Neelkanth. The Gunas were immigrants in Meluha. Meluha has standard policies for all immigrants, one of which is that their records are kept secret. This system ensures that they're not targeted or oppressed, but it also meant that the royal record-keeper was refusing to tell his own prime minister where the Gunas had been settled.'

'How can the record-keeper do that? The prime minister's word is the order of the emperor – and his word is law!'

'Meluha's not like your empire, Lord Dilipa,' said Bhrigu with a smile. 'They have this irritating habit of sticking to the rules.'

Bhrigu's sarcasm was lost on Dilipa. 'So what happened, my Lord? Did you find the Gunas?'

'At first, Kanakhala was quite certain that the Gunas were in Devagiri. But when her initial search of the city yielded nothing, she had no choice but to approach Emperor Daksha, who passed an order through the *Rajya Sabha*, the Royal Council, that forced the Meluhan record-keeper to reveal the Gunas' location – but by the time we reached their village, they were gone.'

'Gone where?'

'I don't know. I was told this happens quite often. Many immigrants are unable to adapt to Meluha's civilised but regimented lifestyle and choose to return to their homelands. Consequently I was asked to believe that the Gunas must have gone back to the Himalayas.'

'And do you believe that?'

'Of course not. I think the fraud Neelkanth must have spirited his tribe away before declaring war. But what could I do? I didn't know where the Gunas were.'

'But why is Bhagirath here? Why would the Neelkanth reveal his hand?'

'*Fraud* Neelkanth, your Majesty,' said Bhrigu.

'I'm sorry, my Lord,' said Dilipa.

Bhrigu looked up at the ceiling. 'Yes, why has Shiva sent him here?'

'My god!' whispered Dilipa. 'Could he have been sent here to assassinate me?'

Bhrigu shook his head. 'That's unlikely, your Majesty. I don't think killing you would serve any larger purpose.'

Dilipa opened his mouth to say something but decided instead to remain silent.

'Yes,' continued Bhrigu, narrowing his eyes, 'we do need to know why Prince Bhagirath's here. I look forward to meeting him.'

'Father,' said Bhagirath as he walked confidently into Dilipa's chamber.

Dilipa did his best to smile, but he had little love for his son. 'How are you, Bhagirath?'

'I'm well, Father.'

'How was your trip to Panchavati?'

Bhagirath glanced at the old Brahmin sitting beside his father and wondered who he was, then returned his attention to his father. 'It was an uneventful trip, Father. Perhaps the Nagas are not as bad as we think. Some of us have returned early. The Lord Neelkanth will join us later.'

Dilipa frowned as if surprised and glanced at Bhrigu.

Bhagirath arched an eyebrow before offering Bhrigu a namaste and a quick bow of his head. 'Please accept my apologies for my bad manners, Brahmin. I was overwhelmed with emotion on seeing my father.'

Bhrigu looked deep into Bhagirath's eyes.

Bhagirath's consumed with curiosity about who I am. I'd better put this to rest so that his conscious mind can move on to more useful thoughts.

'Perhaps it is I who should apologise,' said Bhrigu. 'I haven't introduced myself. I'm a simple sage from the Himalayas. I go by the name of Bhrigu.'

Bhagirath straightened up in surprise. Of course he knew who Bhrigu was, although he'd never met him. Bhagirath stepped forward and bowed low to touch the sage's feet. 'Maharishi Bhrigu, it is my life's honour to meet you. I'm fortunate to have the opportunity to seek your blessings.'

'*Ayushman bhav*,' said Bhrigu, blessing Bhagirath with a long life.

Bhrigu then placed his hands on Bhagirath's shoulders and pulled him up, once again looking directly into his eyes.

Bhagirath's realised that his imbecile of a father isn't the true leader – I am. And he's scared. Good. Now all I have to do is give him some more things to think about.

'I trust the Neelkanth's well?' asked Bhrigu. 'I've still not had the pleasure of meeting the man the commoners believe to be the saviour of our times.'

'He's well, my Lord,' said Bhagirath, 'and worthy of the title he carries. In fact, some amongst us believe he even deserves the title of Mahadev.'

So, Bhagirath volunteered to come here to discover the identity of the true leader of the opposition. Interesting. The Tibetan barbarian knows all too well that this fool Dilipa couldn't have been the one in charge. He's more intelligent than I thought.

'Allow posterity to prevail upon the present in deciding the honour and title bestowed upon a man, my dear Prince of Ayodhya,' said Bhrigu. 'Duty must be performed for its own sake, not for the power and pelf it might bring. I'm sure even your Neelkanth is familiar with Lord Vasudev's nugget of wisdom which encapsulates this thought: *Karmanye vaadhikaa raste maa phaleshu kadachana.*'

'Oh, the Neelkanth's the embodiment of that notion, Maharishiji,' said Bhagirath. 'He never calls himself the Mahadev. It is we who address him as such.'

Bhrigu smiled. 'Your Neelkanth must be truly great indeed to inspire such loyalty, brave Prince. By the way, how did you like Panchavati? I've never had the pleasure of visiting that land.'

'It's a beautiful city, Maharishiji.'

They were attacked on the outskirts of Panchavati . . . So our ships did make it through to them — but their devil boats got us. Well, at least our information about the location of Panchavati is correct.

'With Lord Ram's blessings,' said Bhrigu, 'I will visit Panchavati myself someday.'

'I'm sure the Queen of the Nagas would be honoured to receive you, my Lord,' said Bhagirath.

Bhrigu smiled. *Kali would kill me, given half a chance. Her temper's even more volatile than Lord Rudra's legendary anger.*

'Unfortunately, Prince Bhagirath,' said Bhrigu, 'I must raise an iniquity you've committed.'

Bhagirath folded his hands together in an apologetic namaste. 'I apologise profusely if I've offended you in any way, my Lord. Please, tell me how I can set it right.'

'It's very simple,' said Bhrigu. 'I was very much looking forward to meeting the emperor's daughter and her new husband – but you haven't brought Princess Anandmayi here with you.'

'I must apologise for my oversight, my Lord,' said Bhagirath. 'I rushed here to pay obeisance to my respected father, whom I have not seen for a long time. Princess Anandmayi has dutifully accompanied her husband General Parvateshwar to Kashi.'

Bhrigu suddenly held his breath as he read Bhagirath's thoughts. *Parvateshwar wants to defect? He wants to return to Meluha?*

'I guess I'll have the pleasure of meeting Princess Anandmayi and General Parvateshwar only when the Almighty wills it,' said Bhrigu.

The smile on Bhrigu's face left Bhagirath feeling distinctly uneasy.

'Hopefully that will be soon enough, my Lord,' said Bhagirath. 'If I may be excused, I have other meetings to attend, after which I must head to Kashi to take care of some unfinished tasks.'

Dilipa was about to say something when Bhrigu raised his hand and placed it on Bhagirath's head. 'Of course, brave Prince. Go with Lord Ram.'

As soon as Bhagirath had left, Dilipa said, 'Why did you let him go, my Lord? We could have arrested him. Interrogation would surely have revealed what happened in Panchavati.'

'I already know what happened,' said Bhrigu. 'Our ships did reach Panchavati and our men even managed to kill a large number of their convoy. But Shiva's still alive, and our ships were destroyed in the battle.'

'Even so, we shouldn't allow Bhagirath to leave. Why are we letting one of their main leaders return to them unharmed?'

'I have blessed him with a long life, your Majesty. I'm sure you don't want me to be proven a liar.'

'Of course not, my Lord.'

Bhrigu looked at Dilipa and smiled. 'I know what you're thinking, your Majesty. Trust me, in war, as in chess, one sometimes sacrifices a minor piece for the strategic advantage of capturing a more important piece several moves later.'

Dilipa frowned.

'Let me make myself very clear, your Majesty,' said Bhrigu. 'Prince Bhagirath must not be harmed in Ayodhya. I imagine he'll leave your city within a day. He should leave safe and sound. I want them to think that we're none the wiser after his brief visit.'

'Yes, my Lord.'

'Provision a fast sailboat for me – I must leave for Kashi immediately.'

'Yes, my Lord.'

'Please have the manifest of my ship state that I'm going to Prayag. Bhagirath still has friends in Ayodhya, and I don't want him to know that I'm leaving for Kashi. Is that clear?'

'Of course, my Lord. I'll have Siamantak take care of this immediately.'

CHAPTER 15

The Magadhan Issue

Andhak, the Magadhan minister for ports, led Shiva, Sati and Gopal into the guest chambers of Surapadman's royal palace, and the Chief Vasudev waited for him to leave before remarking, 'It's interesting that we're being housed in Prince Surapadman's private residence rather than King Mahendra's palace.'

'Surapadman wants to make sure he's the exclusive channel of information between us and his father,' said Sati. 'That'll allow him to be selective about what the king hears, which actually makes me more hopeful of success.'

'I'm far less hopeful,' countered Shiva. 'Surapadman's the real power in Magadh. In addition to being the crown prince, he's also the keeper of the king's seal. But even he might be wary of his father's reaction when he learns of the secret behind Prince Ugrasen's death. Perhaps that's why he wants to talk to us here, in private.'

'Perhaps,' said Gopal. 'Maybe that's also why we were

received in Magadh by Andhak rather than King Mahendra's prime minister.'

'I agree,' said Shiva. 'I believe Andhak's loyal to Surapadman.'

'All we can do is hope for the best,' said Sati.

As Shiva, Sati and Gopal entered the prince's court, Surapadman rose from his ceremonial chair to greet them. He walked up to the Neelkanth and knelt down to place his head on Shiva's feet. 'Bless me, great Neelkanth.'

'*Sukhinah bhav,*' said Shiva, placing his hand on Surapadman's head and blessing him with happiness.

Surapadman looked up at Shiva. 'I hope by the time this conversation ends, my Lord, that you'll find it in your heart to bless me with victory along with happiness.'

Shiva smiled and placed his hands on Surapadman's shoulders as he rose. 'Please allow me to introduce my companions, Prince Surapadman. This is my wife, Sati.'

Surapadman bowed low towards her, and she politely returned Surapadman's greeting.

'And this is my close friend, Chief Vasudev Gopal,' said Shiva.

Surapadman's hands came together in a respectful namaste as his eyes widened with surprise. 'Lord Ram, be merciful!'

'Pray to him,' said Gopal, 'and he will be.'

Surapadman smiled. 'My apologies, Gopalji. My informants have always assured me that the legendary Vasudevs are real, but I didn't believe they'd interfere with worldly affairs unless an existential crisis was upon us.'

'Such a time is indeed upon us, Surapadman,' said Gopal, 'and all true followers of Lord Ram must ally themselves with the Neelkanth.'

Surapadman remained silent.

'Let's make ourselves comfortable, brave Prince of Magadh,' said Shiva.

Surapadman led them to the centre of the court where ceremonial chairs had been placed in a circle. Gopal noted that Andhak was the only official from the royal Magadhan court in attendance. Perhaps the rumours that he would soon be taking command of the Magadhan army were true, after all. Gopal also speculated that the rest of the Magadhan court didn't really support the Neelkanth. Given Magadh's traditional rivalry with Ayodhya, they might have been expected to choose the opposite side and ally themselves with the Neelkanth. But Ugrasen's murder appeared to have changed everything.

'What can I do for you, my Lord?' asked Surapadman.

'I'll come straight to the point, Prince Surapadman,' said Shiva. 'Your elite intelligence officials must already have briefed you that war is likely.'

Surapadman nodded but remained silent.

'Perhaps you've also been made aware that Ayodhya hasn't chosen sides wisely,' said Gopal.

'Indeed I am,' said Surapadman, allowing himself a hint of a smile. 'But given Ayodhya's penchant for indecision and confusion, few can be sure which side they'll eventually find themselves on!'

Sati smiled. 'And what do you intend to do, brave Prince?'

'My Lady,' said Surapadman, 'I believe in the legend of the Neelkanth. And the Lord has shown that he's a worthy inheritor of the title of the Mahadev.'

Shiva shifted in his seat awkwardly, still not comfortable with being compared to the great Lord Rudra.

'Furthermore, Ayodhya is a terrible overlord,' continued Surapadman. 'Their supremacy needs to be challenged in the interests of Swadweep, and only Magadh has the ability to do that.'

'I can see that only mighty Magadh has the strength to confront Ayodhya,' said Sati.

'And there you have it,' said Surapadman. 'I've given you two good reasons why I should choose to stand with the Neelkanth.'

Shiva, Gopal and Sati remained silent, waiting for the inevitable 'but'.

'And yet,' said Surapadman, 'circumstances have made my situation a little more complex.'

Turning to Shiva, Surapadman continued, 'My Lord, you must already be aware of my dilemma. My brother, Ugrasen, was killed in a Naga terrorist attack and my father's hell-bent on seeking vengeance.'

Shiva spoke softly in deference to the sensitivity of the issue at hand. 'Surapadman, I think the incident—'

'My Lord,' said Surapadman, 'please forgive me for interrupting you, but I know the truth.'

'I'm not sure you do, Prince Surapadman. If you did, your reaction would have been different.'

Surapadman glanced briefly at Andhak and continued, 'My Lord, Andhak and I have investigated the case personally. We've visited the spot where my brother and his men were killed. We know what happened.'

Sati couldn't help enquiring, 'Then why—?'

'What can I do, my Lady?' asked Surapadman. 'My father's a grieving old man who has convinced himself that his favourite son was a noble and valiant Kshatriya who died while defending his kingdom from a cowardly Naga attack. How can I tell him the truth? How do I tell him that Ugrasen was actually a compulsive gambler who was trying to kidnap a hapless boy-rider so he could win some money? Should I tell my father that my brother tried to murder a mother who was protecting her own child? That the apparently wicked Nagas were really heroes who saved a subject of his kingdom from his own son's villainy? Do you think he'll even listen to me?'

'There is nobility in truth,' said Sati, 'even if it hurts.'

Surapadman laughed softly. 'This isn't Meluha, my Lady. Meluhans' devotion to "the truth" is seen by many here as nothing but rigidity of thought. Chandravanshis prefer to choose from several alternative truths which may simultaneously coexist.'

Sati remained silent.

Surapadman turned to Shiva. 'My Lord, my father thinks I'm an ambitious warmonger who's impatient to ascend the throne.

He preferred my elder brother, who was more attuned to my father's views. I think he suspects me of engineering Ugrasen's death in pursuit of my own goals.'

'I'm sure that's not true,' said Shiva. 'You're his more capable son.'

'It takes a very self-assured man to appreciate the talents of another, my Lord,' said Surapadman, 'even when it comes to one's own progeny. Ironically, the Nagas have actually helped me, for my path to the throne is now clear. All I have to do is wait for my father to pass on – that and desist from doing anything that will cause him to disinherit me and offer the throne to some other relative. With that in mind, if I were to tell my father that his favourite son's murder by the "evil" Nagas was absolutely justified, I'd probably go down in history as the stupidest royal ever.'

Gopal smiled slightly. 'It appears we're at an impasse, Prince Surapadman. What do we do?'

Surapadman narrowed his eyes. 'Just give me a Naga.'

'I can't,' said Shiva.

'I'm not asking for the one who actually killed Ugrasen, my Lord,' said Surapadman. 'I guess he must be someone important. All I'm asking for is a random Naga. I'll present him to my father as Ugrasen's killer and we'll have him executed forthwith. My father will then happily retire and go into *sanyas* to pray for my brother's soul. And I, along with all the resources of Magadh, will stand beside you. I know the Brangas are with you. Victory is assured if Magadh and Branga are on the same side. You will win the war, my Lord, and Evil will be destroyed. All you need to do is sacrifice an insignificant Naga who's already suffering for the sins of his past lives. We'll actually be giving him an opportunity to earn good *karma*. What do you say?'

Shiva didn't hesitate for a second. 'I can't do that.'

'My Lord—'

'I *won't* do that.'

'But—'

'No.'

Surapadman leaned back in his chair. 'We do indeed appear to be at an impasse, great Vasudev. My father won't allow me to fight in an army that includes the Nagas unless we can assuage his thirst for vengeance.'

Shiva spoke up before Gopal could respond. 'What if you don't pick either side?'

Surapadman frowned, intrigued.

'Convince your father to remain neutral,' continued Shiva. 'Allow my ships to proceed to battle with Ayodhya. If we're able to beat them, then your primary enemies are weakened. If they beat us, our army, including the Nagas, would be in retreat. Your imagination can fill in the rest. You win both ways.'

Surapadman smiled. 'That does have an attractive ring to it.'

Parvateshwar was sitting on the balcony of his chamber, which was in a different wing of the massive Kashi palace from Shiva's accommodations. Anandmayi and Ayurvati had gone to meet

Veerbhadra and the Gunas, and the Meluhan general was staring out towards the Ganga flowing in the distance.

'My Lord,' called the doorman.

Parvateshwar turned. 'Yes?'

'A messenger has just delivered a note for you.'

'Bring it to me.'

'Yes, my Lord.'

As the doorman entered, Parvateshwar asked, 'Who brought the message?'

'The main palace door-keeper, my Lord.'

Parvateshwar raised his brows. 'And who gave the message to the palace door-keeper?'

The doorman looked lost. 'How would I know, my Lord?'

Parvateshwar sighed. These Swadweepans had no sense of systems and procedures. It was a wonder that their enemies didn't just stroll into their key installations and take them over before anyone noticed. He took the neatly sealed papyrus scroll from the doorman and dismissed him. Parvateshwar didn't recognise the symbol on the seal. It appeared to be a star, the kind used in ancient astrological charts. He shrugged and broke it open. The script surprised him — it was one of the standard Meluhan military codes, more specifically one used exclusively by senior Suryavanshi military officers to convey top-secret messages during times of war. The text was short and simple:

Lord Parvateshwar, it's time to prove your loyalty to Meluha. Meet me in the garden behind the Sankat Mochan Temple at the end of the third prahar. *Come alone.*

Parvateshwar's breath caught in his throat and he glanced instinctively towards the door, but he was alone. He tucked the scroll into the pouch tied to his waistband.

He knew what he had to do.

— ⚜ ◍ ∪ ⚐ ⊛ —

The sounds of bells, drums and prayer chants fill the morning air, day after day, at the Sankat Mochan Temple. Having thus awoken Lord Hanuman, the devotees then sing *bhajans*, as Lord Hanuman did to gently wake his master, Lord Ram. At the end of this elaborate *puja*, the great seventh Vishnu proceeds to grant *darshan*, the divine pleasure of beholding him.

The silence at dusk, however, was a stark contrast to the exuberance of the dawn, and it was dusk when Parvateshwar strode into the great temple.

He looked back to ensure nobody was following him, then walked swiftly towards the garden behind the temple. All was quiet. Parvateshwar approached a tree at the far end of the garden and sat, leaning against it.

'How are you, General?' asked a soft, polite voice.

Parvateshwar looked up. 'I'll feel a lot better when I see you.'

'Are you alone?'

'I wouldn't have come had I not been alone.'

After silence stretched for several minutes, Parvateshwar got up to leave. 'If you're a true Meluhan, you'd know that Meluhans don't lie.'

'Wait, General,' said Bhrigu as he emerged from the shadows.

Parvateshwar was stunned. He recognised the *Saptrishi Uttra-dhikari* immediately. He knew that, despite wielding tremendous influence, Bhrigu had never interfered in Meluha's affairs before, and he found it difficult to believe that he would now involve himself in the mundane matters of the material world.

'I'm taking a huge risk by meeting you face to face,' said Bhrigu. 'I had to be sure that you're alone.'

'What are you doing here, Maharishiji?' asked Parvateshwar, bowing to the great sage.

'I'm doing my duty. As you are doing yours.'

'But you've never interfered in earthly matters before.'

'I have,' said Bhrigu, 'but only rarely. And this is one of those rare occasions.'

Parvateshwar remained silent. *So Bhrigu's the true leader. He sent the joint Meluha–Ayodhya fleet to attack Lord Shiva's convoy by stealth outside Panchavati.* Parvateshwar's respect for Bhrigu went down a notch. The great sage was human after all.

'You already know what you have to do,' said Bhrigu. 'I know you won't support the fraud Neelkanth in attacking your beloved motherland.'

Parvateshwar bristled with anger. 'Lord Shiva is no fraud! He's the finest man to have walked the earth since Lord Ram!'

Bhrigu stepped back, astonished. 'Perhaps I was wrong. Perhaps you don't love Meluha as much as I thought.'

'Lord Bhrigu, I will die for Meluha,' said Parvateshwar, 'for it is my duty to do so. But please don't make the mistake of thinking that I despise the Lord Neelkanth. He's my living god.'

Bhrigu frowned, even more surprised, and looked into Parvateshwar's eyes. The normally restrained sage's mouth fell open ever so slightly. He realised he was looking at a rare man who said exactly what he was thinking. Bhrigu's manner changed and he became more respectful. 'My apologies, great General. I can see that your reputation does you justice. I misunderstood you. Sometimes the hypocritical nature of the world makes us immune to a rare sincere man.'

Parvateshwar remained silent.

'Will you fight for Meluha?' asked Bhrigu.

'To my last breath,' whispered Parvateshwar. 'But I will fight according to Lord Ram's laws.'

'Of course.'

'We won't break the rules of war.'

Bhrigu nodded silently.

'I suggest, Maharishiji,' said Parvateshwar, 'that you return to Meluha. I'll follow in a few weeks.'

'It wouldn't be wise to remain here, General,' said Bhrigu. 'If anything were to happen to you, the consequences for Meluha would be disastrous. Your army needs a good leader.'

'I can't leave without asking my Lord's permission to do so.'

Bhrigu thought he must have misheard. 'Excuse me? Did

you say you want to ask for the Neelkanth's permission before leaving?' He was careful not to say, 'fraud Neelkanth'.

'Yes,' answered Parvateshwar.

'But why would he allow you to leave?'

'I don't know if he will, but I know I can't leave without his permission.'

Bhrigu spoke carefully. 'Lord Parvateshwar, I don't think you realise the gravity of the situation. If you tell the Neelkanth that you're going to lead his enemies, he'll kill you.'

'No, I don't believe he will. But if he chooses to do so, then that will be my fate.'

'My apologies for sounding rude, but this is foolhardy.'

'No, it's not. This is what a devotee does if he chooses to leave his Lord.'

'But—'

'Lord Bhrigu, this sounds peculiar to you because you haven't met Lord Shiva. His companions don't follow him out of fear. They do so because he's the most inspiring presence they've ever encountered in their lives. My fate has put me in a position where I'm being forced to oppose him, and it's breaking my heart. I need his blessing and his permission to give me the strength to do what I have to do.'

Bhrigu's slow nod revealed a glimpse of grudging respect. 'The Neelkanth must be a special man indeed to inspire such loyalty.'

'He's not just a special man, Maharishiji. He's a living god.'

CHAPTER 16

Secrets Revealed

'I think we've achieved what we came here for,' said Sati after she, Gopal and Shiva had retired to their chambers in Surapadman's palace. As a gesture of goodwill, Surapadman had persuaded them to stay for a few days to give him time to ready some weapons for Shiva's army.

'I agree,' said Gopal. 'Surapadman's offer of weapons, though token in nature, is symbolic of his alliance with us.'

'No one else from the Magadhan court has visited us, though,' said Shiva. 'I hope King Mahendra doesn't persuade Surapadman to do something unwise.'

'Do you think he might try to prevent our ships from passing through to Ayodhya?' asked Gopal.

'I can't be sure,' said Shiva. 'He'll probably cooperate with us, but it depends on how his father reacts.'

'Let's hope for the best,' said Sati.

'What about my proclamation, Panditji?'

'It'll be ready and distributed in a few weeks from now,' said Gopal. 'Vasudev pandits across the country will give us constant updates regarding the reactions of the people and the nobility.'

'But what if the Vasudev pandits are discovered?'

'They won't be. The nobility may be aware that the Vasudev tribe has allied with the Neelkanth, but they won't know the identity of the Vasudevs within their kingdoms.'

Shiva let out a long, slow breath. 'And so it shall begin.'

— ⚡ ⊙ ∪ ⚹ ⊕ —

Bhagirath arrived in Kashi late in the evening and proceeded directly to the palace, where he was informed that Shiva had gone to Magadh to explore an alliance with Surapadman. He shared his news with Ganesh and Kartik in the Neelkanth's absence.

'The Ayodhyans appear to have a back-up plan,' said Bhagirath. 'They're expecting Magadh to prevent their ships from carrying their soldiers up the Ganga to Meluha. Consequently, they intend to cut north-west through the forests straight to Dharmakhet and cross the Ganga there, then use the newly built road to march to Meluha.'

'That's logical,' said Ganesh, 'but it'll be slow going. The war may well be over by the time they get there.'

'True,' said Bhagirath.

Ganesh leaned forward. 'But I can see you have more news for me.'

Bhagirath could hardly contain himself. 'I know the identity of the one who leads our enemies.'

'Maharishi Bhrigu?' suggested Kartik.

Bhagirath was amazed. 'How did you know?'

'*Baba*'s friends, the Vasudevs, told us,' answered Ganesh.

Bhagirath had heard stories about the legendary Vasudevs but never really believed them. 'So they actually exist?'

'Indeed they do, brave Prince,' said Kartik.

Bhagirath smiled. 'With friends like them, Lord Shiva doesn't need followers like me!'

Ganesh laughed. 'He couldn't have known when he agreed to your suggestion that the Vasudevs would reveal the identity of the main conspirator.'

'Of course,' said Bhagirath. 'But at least we now know about the Ayodhyans' back-up plan for getting to Meluha.'

'Yes, that's useful information, Bhagirath,' said Ganesh.

Kartik suddenly sat up straight. 'Prince Bhagirath, did you meet Maharishi Bhrigu in person?'

'Yes.'

Kartik looked at Ganesh with concern.

'What's the matter?' asked Bhagirath.

'Did he look into your eyes while speaking with you, Bhagirath?' asked Ganesh.

'Where else would he be looking while he was talking to me?'

Kartik rolled his eyes towards the ceiling. 'Lord Ram, be merciful.'

'What have I missed?' asked a confused Bhagirath.

'We've been told that Lord Bhrigu can read a person's mind by looking into their eyes,' said Kartik.

'What? That's impossible!'

'He's a *Saptrishi Uttradhikari*, Bhagirath,' said Ganesh. 'Very few things are impossible for him. If he was looking into your eyes, chances are he's read your conscious thoughts, and he may have gleaned some very sensitive information about our plans.'

'Good Lord!' whispered Bhagirath.

'I want you to carefully recall what you were thinking about while speaking with Lord Bhrigu,' said Ganesh.

'I spoke about—'

Kartik interrupted Bhagirath. 'It doesn't matter what you said. What matters is what you *thought*.'

Bhagirath closed his eyes and tried to remember. 'I recall thinking that my imbecile father couldn't have been the true leader of the conspiracy.'

'That's no secret,' said Ganesh. 'What else crossed your mind?'

'I remember a feeling of dread when I realised that Lord Bhrigu's the true leader.'

'Ideally you wouldn't have let him know your fears,' said Kartik, 'but this information can't really harm us, either.'

'I recall thinking that Lord Shiva had sent me to Ayodhya to discover the identity of the true leader.'

'Bhrigu would have worked that out for himself already,' said Ganesh.

Then Bhagirath said, 'I thought about being attacked by the

joint Meluha–Ayodhya ships at Panchavati and how we repelled the attack.'

Ganesh cursed under his breath.

Bhagirath looked at Ganesh apologetically. 'So Maharishi Bhrigu knows about Panchavati's defences now . . . I'm so sorry, Ganesh.'

Kartik patted Bhagirath's arm reassuringly. 'You didn't intend for this to happen, Prince Bhagirath. Was there anything else?'

'Oh, Lord Rudra!' whispered Bhagirath.

Ganesh's eyes narrowed. 'What?'

'I thought about Parvateshwar wanting to defect to Meluha,' said Bhagirath.

Ganesh stopped breathing while Kartik held his head. 'What now, *dada*?'

'Bring *mausi* here immediately, Kartik,' said Ganesh. 'We know what we have to do, but *baba*'s wrath will be terrible. Kali can stand up to him. We need to know if the Naga queen agrees with us.'

Kartik left the room at once.

Bhagirath stared at Ganesh in shock. 'I hope you're not thinking what I fear you're thinking.'

'Do we have a choice, Bhagirath? Maharishi Bhrigu will try to contact Parvateshwar at the first opportunity and whisk him away.'

'Ganesh, Parvateshwar's my sister's husband. We can't kill him!'

Ganesh threw up his hands in exasperation. '*Kill* him? What are you talking about, Bhagirath? I only want to arrest General Parvateshwar so that he can't escape.'

Bhagirath opened his mouth to reply, but Ganesh interrupted him. 'We have no choice. If Parvateshwar defects to their side, it'll be disastrous for us. He's a brilliant strategist.'

Bhagirath sighed. 'I won't argue with you – we must do what needs to be done. But we can't kill him. I won't be responsible for making my sister a widow.'

'I wouldn't dream of killing a man like Parvateshwar, Bhagirath, but we've got to arrest him immediately. For all we know, Maharishi Bhrigu may already be attempting to make contact with him.'

— ✶ ◍U⛢ ⊛ —

A moonless night shrouded the eerily quiet Assi Ghat. The Port of Eighty did receive a small number of ships after dusk, but the darkness had kept away even the few captains brave enough to attempt night dockings.

Parvateshwar was walking back from the Ghat, silent and pensive. He had just escorted Bhrigu to a waiting rowing boat which would take him to a ship anchored in the middle of the river. Bhrigu intended to stop at Prayag for a short time and then proceed to Meluha.

'General Parvateshwar!'

Parvateshwar looked up to see Kali approaching. Flickering torchlight revealed that she was accompanied by Ganesh, Kartik and about fifty soldiers. He smiled. 'You've brought fifty soldiers to take down one man?' he asked, his hand resting on his sword-hilt. 'You think too highly of me, Queen Kali.'

'Are you going somewhere, General?' asked Kali as the soldiers rapidly surrounded him, making escape impossible.

Parvateshwar was about to answer when he saw a familiar figure next to Kartik. 'Is that you, Bhagirath?'

'It is,' Bhagirath replied. 'This is a sad day for me.'

'I'm sure it is,' said Parvateshwar sarcastically, before addressing Kali again. 'So what's your plan, Queen Kali? Kill me now or wait until the Lord Neelkanth returns?'

'So you admit you're a traitor,' said Kali.

'I admit to nothing since you haven't asked me anything.'

'I did ask if you're going somewhere.'

'If I were, I wouldn't be walking *away* from the Assi Ghat, your Majesty.'

'Have you met with Maharishi Bhrigu?' asked Ganesh.

Parvateshwar never lied. 'Yes.'

Kali sucked in a sharp breath and reached for her sword.

'*Mausi*,' said Ganesh, pleading with the Naga queen to keep her temper under control. 'Where's the maharishi, General?'

'He's on a boat,' said Parvateshwar, 'probably on his way to Meluha.'

'You know what comes next, don't you?' asked Kali.

'Do I get a soldier's death?' asked Parvateshwar. 'Will you attack me one by one so I may have the pleasure of killing a few of you before I die? Or will you just pounce on me like a pack of cowardly hyenas?'

'Nobody's getting killed, General,' said Ganesh. 'We Nagas are no strangers to justice. Your treachery will be proven in court and then you'll be punished accordingly.'

'No Naga's going to judge me,' said Parvateshwar. 'I recognise only two courts: the one sanctioned by the laws of Meluha and that of the Lord Neelkanth.'

'Then you shall receive justice from the Neelkanth when he returns,' said Kali, before turning towards the soldiers. 'Arrest the general.'

Parvateshwar didn't argue. He stretched out his hands as he looked at the crestfallen face of the man handcuffing him. It was Nandi.

— ⚔ ⬤U⚶⊛ —

'I met with the ship's captain earlier this evening,' said Sati as she, Shiva and Gopal were dining in their chamber at Magadh. 'All the weapons have been loaded. We can sail for Kashi tomorrow morning.'

'So we can begin our campaign in the next few weeks,' Shiva said, pleased.

Gopal had anticipated this. 'I've already sent a message to the pandit of the Narsimha Temple in Magadh. He'll relay it to King Chandraketu, who will set sail with his armada and await further instructions at the port of Vaishali.'

'Bhagirath, Ganesh and Kartik will travel with them to Ayodhya,' said Shiva. 'Ganesh will lead the Eastern Command.'

'A wise choice,' said Gopal.

'The Western Army – the Vasudevs, the Nagas and those Brangas who've been assigned to the Nagas – will attack Meluha under my command. We'll set sail along with Kali and Parvateshwar within a week of reaching Kashi.'

'I've already sent a message to Ujjain,' said Gopal. 'The army's marched out carrying dismantled sections of our ships, which will be reassembled on the Narmada. We'll sail together to the Western Sea and then further up the coast, to Lothal.'

'What about your war elephants, Panditji?' asked Sati. 'How will they reach Meluha?'

'Our elephant corps will set out from Ujjain through the jungles and meet us at Lothal,' answered Gopal.

'Gopalji,' said Shiva, 'can the Narsimha Temple pandit also send a message to Suparna in Panchavati? Kali's appointed her commander of the Naga army in her absence. They should meet us at the Narmada.'

'It shall be done, Neelkanth,' said Gopal.

CHAPTER 17

Honour Imprisoned

An underground chamber beneath the royal palace had been converted into a temporary prison for General Parvateshwar. While the public prisons of peaceful Kashi were humane, it would have been a slight to a man of Parvateshwar's stature to be imprisoned along with common criminals. The spacious chamber, though luxuriously appointed, was windowless. In a surfeit of caution, Parvateshwar's hands and legs had been securely shackled. A platoon of crack Naga troops stood guard at the single exit and two senior officers watched over Parvateshwar at all times.

Nandi and Parshuram kept first watch. 'My apologies, General,' said Parshuram.

'You don't need to apologise, Parshuram. You're following orders – that's your duty.'

Nandi was sitting opposite Parvateshwar, but he kept his face averted.

'Are you angry with me, Major Nandi?' asked Parvateshwar.

'What right do I have to be angry with you, General?'

'If I've done something that's troubled you, then you have every right to be angry. Lord Ram asked us to always be true to ourselves.'

Nandi remained silent, and Parvateshwar smiled ruefully, then looked away.

At last Nandi gathered the courage to speak. 'Are you being true to yourself, General?'

'Yes, I am.'

'Forgive me, but I disagree. You're betraying your living god.'

With visible effort, Parvateshwar kept his temper in check. 'Only the very unfortunate must choose between their god and their *swadharma*.'

'Are you saying that your personal *dharma*'s leading you away from Good?'

'I'm saying no such thing, Major Nandi. But my duty to Meluha is most important to me.'

'Rebelling against your god is treason.'

'Some may hold that rebelling against your country is a greater treason.'

'Again, I respectfully disagree. Of course Meluha's important to me – I would readily die for my country. But I won't fight my living god for the sake of Meluha. That would be completely wrong.'

'I'm not saying you're wrong, Major Nandi.'

'Then you admit to being wrong yourself?'

'I didn't say that, either.'

'How can that be, General?' asked Nandi. 'We're talking about polar opposites. One of us has to be wrong.'

Parvateshwar smiled. 'That's such a staunch Suryavanshi belief: that the opposite of truth has to be untruth.'

Nandi remained silent.

'But Anandmayi's taught me something profound,' said Parvateshwar. 'There's *your* truth and there's *my* truth. As for universal truth: it doesn't exist.'

'Universal truth *does* exist,' insisted Parshuram, 'though it's always been an enigma to human beings. And it'll remain an enigma for as long as we're bound to our mortal bodies.'

— ※ ◍U⚡⦾ —

Anandmayi stormed into Bhagirath's chambers in the Kashi palace, brushing the guard aside. 'What the hell have you done?' she shouted.

Bhagirath immediately rose and approached his sister. 'Anandmayi, we had no choice—'

'He's my *husband*! How dare you?'

'Anandmayi, it's very likely that he'll share our plans with—'

'Don't you know Parvateshwar better than that by now? Do you think he'd *ever* do anything unethical? He's always walked away whenever you began to speak about the Lord Neelkanth's orders – he has no knowledge of any of your "confidential" military plans!'

'You're right, sister. I'm sorry.'

'Then why is he under arrest?'

'Anandmayi, it wasn't my decision—'

'Rubbish! Why is he under arrest?'

'He might escape if—'

'Do you think he couldn't have escaped already if he wanted to? He's waiting to meet with the Lord Neelkanth. Only then will he leave for Meluha.'

'That's what he said, but—'

'But? What the hell do you mean, "but"? Do you think Parvateshwar would choose to lie? Do you think he's even *capable* of lying?'

'No.'

'If he's said he won't leave until Lord Shiva returns, then, believe me, he's not going anywhere!'

Bhagirath remained silent.

Anandmayi moved very close to her brother. 'Are you planning to assassinate him?'

'No, Anandmayi!' Bhagirath was shocked. 'How can you even think I'd do such a thing?'

'Don't pull your injured act on me, Bhagirath. If anything happens to my husband, even by accident, you know that the Lord Neelkanth's anger will be terrible. You and your allies may discount me, but you're scared of *him*. Remember his rage before you do something stupid.'

'Anandmayi, we're not—'

'The Lord Neelkanth will be back in a week. Until then,

I'm going to keep a constant vigil outside the chamber where you've imprisoned my husband. If anyone wants to harm him, he'll have to fight me first.'

'Anandmayi, nobody's going to . . .'

She turned and strode away stiffly as Bhagirath's attempt to reassure her trailed off mid-sentence. She pushed aside the diminutive Kashi soldier standing in her path and slammed the door behind her as the soldier fell to the ground.

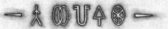

Ayurvati placed a comforting hand on Anandmayi's shoulder. The Ayodhyan princess was sitting outside the chamber where Parvateshwar had been imprisoned, where she'd been for the last few days.

'Why don't you go to your room and sleep,' said Ayurvati. 'I'll sit here for you.'

A determined Anandmayi shook her head. Wild horses couldn't drag her away.

'Anandmayi—'

'They won't even let me see him, Ayurvati,' said Anandmayi with a sob.

Ayurvati sat down next to her. 'I know—'

Anandmayi turned towards the Naga soldiers standing guard at the door and shouted, 'My husband's no criminal!'

Ayurvati took Anandmayi's hand in hers. 'Calm down – these soldiers are only following orders—'

'But he's not a criminal . . . He's a good man . . .'

'I know.'

Anandmayi rested her head on Ayurvati's shoulders and began to cry.

'Hush now, calm down,' said Ayurvati soothingly.

Anandmayi raised her head and looked at Ayurvati with tear-reddened eyes. 'I don't care if the entire world turns against him. I don't even care if the Neelkanth turns against him. I'll stand by my husband. He's a good man . . . a good man!'

'Have faith in the Neelkanth, Anandmayi. Have faith in his justice. Speak to him the moment he arrives in Kashi.'

The sun was directly overhead as Shiva's ship prepared to dock at Assi Ghat. Shiva, Sati and Gopal were standing at the balustrade.

'I don't understand why King Athithigva has to organise such a grand reception every time I come here,' said Shiva as he looked at the giant canopy and vast throngs of people waiting for him to disembark.

Gopal smiled. 'I don't think Lord Athithigva orders his people to assemble, my friend. The people gather of their own accord to welcome their Neelkanth.'

'Yes, but it's so unnecessary,' said Shiva. 'They shouldn't be taking a break from their work to welcome me. If they really want to honour me, they should work even harder at their jobs.'

Gopal laughed. 'People tend to do what they want to do rather than what they should be doing.'

The ship was now close enough for them to see the expressions of the people on the dock, and even of the nobility standing further away on higher ground.

'Something's not right,' said Sati.

'Why is everyone looking so troubled?' asked Gopal.

Shiva studied the crowds carefully. 'Something's definitely amiss.'

'King Athithigva's agitated,' said Sati.

'And Kali, Ganesh, Kartik and Bhagirath are engaged in a heated discussion,' said Shiva. 'I wonder what that's all about.'

Sati tapped Shiva's arm lightly. 'Look at Anandmayi.'

'Where is she?' asked Shiva, not finding her in the area cordoned off for the nobility.

'She's in the crowd,' said Sati, gesturing with her eyes. 'Right where the ship's gangplank will be secured.'

'I suspect she wants to talk to you the moment you step off the ship, my friend,' said Gopal.

'She looks really upset, Shiva,' said Sati.

Shiva scanned the entire port area, then asked softly, 'Where's Parvateshwar?'

The guards stepped aside as the Neelkanth stormed into the temporary prison. Sati, Gopal, Anandmayi and Kali could barely keep up with him.

He found Veerbhadra, Parshuram and Nandi deep in conversation with the fettered Parvateshwar.

'What in the name of the Holy Lake is the meaning of this?' shouted Shiva, livid.

'My Lord,' said Parvateshwar, the chains clinking as he rose. Nandi, Veerbhadra and Parshuram stood, too.

'Remove his chains!'

'Shiva,' said Kali softly, 'I don't think that's wise—'

'Remove his chains *now*!'

Nandi and Parshuram immediately set to work and the chains were removed with great haste. Parvateshwar rubbed his wrists to restore circulation.

'Leave me alone with Parvateshwar.'

'Shiva—' said Veerbhadra.

'Am I not making myself clear, Bhadra? Everybody leave *right now*!'

Kali shook her head disapprovingly but obeyed. The others followed her without any sign of protest.

Shiva turned to Parvateshwar, his eyes blazing with fury.

Parvateshwar was the first to speak. 'My Lord—'

Shiva raised his hand and Parvateshwar fell silent immediately. Shiva looked away as he paced back and forth, breathing deeply to calm his mind. He remembered his Uncle Manobhu's words.

Anger is your enemy. Control it. Control it.

Much as he tried, however, Shiva could feel the fury welling up within him like a coiled snake preparing to strike. But his mind also told him that the issue at hand was far too important to allow anger to cloud his judgement.

Once he'd breathed some calm into his mind and heart, Shiva turned to Parvateshwar. 'Tell me this isn't true. Just say it and I'll believe you, regardless of what anyone else claims.'

'My Lord, this is the most difficult decision I've ever had to make in my life.'

'Do you intend to fight me, Parvateshwar?'

'No, my Lord. But I'm duty-bound to protect Meluha. I hope some miracle will ensure that you and Meluha don't end up on opposite sides.'

'Miracle? *Miracle?* Are you a child, Parvateshwar? Do you think it's possible for me to compromise with Meluha where the *Somras* is concerned?'

'No, my Lord.'

'Do you think the *Somras* isn't evil?'

'No, my Lord. The *Somras* is evil. I stopped using it the moment you said that it was evil.'

'Then why would you fight to protect the *Somras*?'

'I will only fight to protect Meluha.'

'But they're on the same side!'

'That is my misfortune, my Lord.'

'You stubborn—' Shiva checked himself at the last moment. Parvateshwar remained silent. He knew the Neelkanth's anger was justified.

'Is Bhrigu forcing you to do this? Has he captured somebody important to you? We can take care of that. No one important to you will be hurt as long as I'm alive.'

'Maharishi Bhrigu isn't forcing me in any way, my Lord.'

'Then who in Lord Rudra's name is making you do this?'

'My soul. I have no choice. This is what I must do.'

'That doesn't make any sense, Parvateshwar. Do you actually believe that your soul is forcing you to fight for Evil?'

'My soul is only making me fight for my motherland, my Lord. This is a call I can't refuse. It's my soul's purpose.'

'Your soul is taking you down a dangerous path, Parvateshwar.'

'Then so be it. No danger should distract a person from walking their path.'

'What nonsense is this? Do you think Bhrigu cares about you? All he cares about is the *Somras*. Trust me, once your purpose is served, you'll be killed.'

'All of us will die when we have served our purpose – that's the way of the universe.'

Shiva covered his face with his hands in sheer frustration.

'I know you're angry, my Lord,' said Parvateshwar, 'but your purpose is to fight Evil, and you must do everything you can to accomplish that task.'

Shiva's hands dropped to his sides and he stared at Parvateshwar in silence.

'All I'm asking is for you to understand that I must serve my purpose, just as you must serve yours. Your soul won't allow you to rest until you've destroyed Evil. My soul won't allow me to rest until I've done everything I can to protect Meluha.'

Shiva ran his hands over his face, trying desperately to remain calm. 'Do you think I'm wrong, Parvateshwar?'

'Please, my Lord – how could I ever think that? You'd never do anything wrong.'

'Then can you please explain the strange workings of your mind? You won't walk with me even though you admit that my path is right. Instead, you insist on walking a path that will lead you to your death. In the name of Lord Rudra, why?'

'*Svadharma nidhanam shreyaha para dharmo bhayaavahah*,' said Parvateshwar. 'Death in the course of performing one's own duty is better than following another's path, for that is truly dangerous.'

Shiva stared hard at Parvateshwar for what felt like an eternity, then turned around and bellowed, 'Nandi! Bhadra! Parshuram!'

The three men rushed in.

'General Parvateshwar will remain our prisoner,' said Shiva.

'As you command, my Lord,' said Nandi, saluting Shiva.

'And Nandi, the general will not be chained.'

CHAPTER 18

Honour or Victory?

'I say we have no choice,' said Kali. 'I agree we can't kill him, but he must remain here as our prisoner until the war's over.'

Shiva and his family, along with Gopal, were assembled in the Neelkanth's private chambers at the Kashi palace.

Ganesh glanced at a seething Sati and decided to hold his tongue.

Kartik, however, had no such compunctions. 'I agree with *mausi*.'

Shiva looked sternly at Kartik, who said, 'I know this is a difficult decision. Parvateshwarji has behaved with absolute honour. He removed himself from our strategy discussions. He could have escaped on multiple occasions, but didn't. He waited until you returned so he could ask for your permission to leave. But you're the Neelkanth, *baba*. You carry the responsibility for the whole of India on your shoulders. Sometimes, for the sake of the larger good, one has to do things that may not appear to be right at the time. Perhaps a laudable end can justify some questionable means.'

Sati glared at her younger son. 'Kartik, how can you think that a great end justifies questionable means?'

'*Maa*, can we accept a world where the *Somras* continues to thrive?'

'Of course we can't,' said Sati. 'But do you think this struggle is only about the *Somras*?'

Ganesh finally spoke up. 'Of course it is, *maa*.'

'No, it's not,' said Sati. 'It's also about the legacy we'll leave behind, how Shiva will be remembered. People from across the world will analyse every aspect of his life and draw lessons from his actions. They'll aspire to be like him. Didn't we all criticise Lord Bhrigu for using the *daivi astras* in the attack on Panchavati? The maharishi must have justified his actions with arguments similar to the ones you're advocating. If we behave in the same way, then how are we any different from him?'

'People only remember victors, *didi*,' said Kali. 'History's written by victors, and they can write it however they want. The losers are always remembered the way the victors portray them. What's important right now is for us to ensure our victory.'

'Permit me to respectfully disagree, your Highness,' said Gopal. 'It's not true that only victors determine history.'

'Of course it is,' said Kali. 'There's a Deva version of events and an Asura version. Which version do we remember?'

'If you're talking about present-day India, then yes, the Deva version is the one that's remembered,' said Gopal. 'But even today, the Asura version's still well known outside India.'

'But we live *here*,' said Kali. 'Why should we bother about the beliefs that prevail elsewhere?'

'Perhaps I've not made myself clear, your Highness,' said Gopal. 'It's not just about the place, but also about the time. Will the Deva version of history always be remembered the way it is now? Or is it possible that different versions will emerge? Remember, if there's a victor's version of events, then there's also a victim's narrative. For as long as the victors remain in power, their version holds ground. But if history's taught us one thing, it's that communities rise and fall just as surely as the tides ebb and flow. There comes a time when victors are not as powerful as they once were, a time when the victims of the old regime become the elite of the day. Then one finds that the narratives change just as dramatically. The victims' version becomes the popular version over time.'

'I disagree,' said Kali dismissively. 'Unless the victims escape to another land, like the Asuras did, they'll always remain powerless, their experiences dismissed as myths.'

'Not quite,' said Gopal. 'Let me talk about something that's close to your heart. In these times in which we live, the Nagas are feared and cursed as demons. Many millennia ago, they were respected. After winning this war, they'll become respectable and powerful once again as loyal allies of the Neelkanth. Your version of history will then begin to gain currency again, won't it?'

Unconvinced, Kali chose to remain silent.

'An interesting factor is the conduct of the erstwhile victims in the new era,' said Gopal. 'Armed with fresh empowerment, will they seek vengeance on the surviving members of the old elite?'

'Of course the victims will nurse hatred in their hearts. Would you expect them to be filled with the milk of human kindness?' asked Kali, sarcastically.

'You hate the Meluhans, don't you?'

'Yes, I do.'

'But how do you feel about Meluha's founding father, Lord Ram?'

Kali was quiet. She held Lord Ram in deep reverence.

'Why do you revere Lord Ram but reject the people he left behind?' asked Gopal.

Sati spoke up on her sister's behalf. 'Because, unlike present-day Meluhans, Lord Ram treated even his enemies honourably.'

Sati's calm tone and wise words filled Shiva with quiet pride.

'A man becomes a god when his vision moves beyond the bounds of victors and vanquished,' said Sati. 'Shiva's message has to live on forever, and that can only happen if both the winners and the losers find validation in his words and actions. That he must win is a given. But equally critical is that he wins the right way.'

Gopal was quick to support Sati. 'Honour must beget honour. That's the only way.'

Shiva walked to the balcony and gazed at the massive Kashi

Vishwanath Temple on the Sacred Avenue and beyond it towards the holy Ganga.

Everyone was poised for his decision.

He turned and said quietly, 'I need some time to think. We'll meet again tomorrow.'

Sati looked down into the clear waters of the lake below her. The fish swam rapidly, keeping pace with her as she flew towards the distant bank.

She looked up and saw a massive black mountain, different in hue from all the surrounding mountains and topped by a white cap of snow. As she drew close, her vision fell upon a yogi on the lake shore. He was wearing a tiger-skin skirt and his long, matted hair had been tied up in a bun. His muscular body was covered with battle scars. A small halo, almost like the sun, shone behind his head. A crescent moon was lodged in his hair and a snake slithered around his neck. A massive trident stood sentinel beside him, its shaft half-buried in the ground. The yogi's face was blurred, though. And then the mists cleared.

'Shiva!' said Sati.

Shiva smiled at her.

'Is this your home? Kailash?'

Shiva nodded, never once taking his eyes off her.

'We shall come here one day, my love. When it's all over, we shall live together in your beautiful land.'

Shiva's smile broadened.

'Where are Ganesh and Kartik?'

Shiva didn't answer.

'*Shiva, where are our sons?*'

Suddenly, Shiva started to age. His handsome face was rapidly overrun by wrinkles and his matted hair turned white. Then his massive shoulders began to droop, his taut muscles wasting before Sati's very eyes.

Sati smiled. 'Will we grow old together?'

Shiva's eyes flew wide open as if he was looking at something that didn't make sense.

Sati glanced down at her reflection in the waters and frowned in surprise. She hadn't aged a day. She looked at her husband again. 'But I've stopped using the Somras. What does this mean?'

Shiva was horror-struck. Tears were flowing fiercely down his wrinkled cheeks and his face was twisted in agony. He reached out his hand and screamed: 'Sati!'

Sati looked down. Her body was on fire.

'Sati!' he screamed again as he rose and began running towards the lake. 'Don't leave me!'

Still facing Shiva, Sati began to fly backwards, faster and faster, the wind fanning the flames on her body. But even through the blaze she could see her husband running desperately towards her.

'Sati!'

Sati woke up with a start. The beautifully carved Kashi palace ceiling looked ethereal in the flickering torchlight. The only sound was the water trickling down the porous walls, cooling the hot, dry breeze as it flowed in through an open window. Sati instinctively reached out to her left. Shiva wasn't there.

Alarmed, she was up in a flash. 'Shiva?'

She heard him call from the balcony. 'I'm out here, Sati.'

Walking across the room, she could just make out Shiva's silhouette in the darkness as he leaned back in his chair, focused on the Vishwanath Temple in the distance. Nestling comfortably against him on the armrest, she reached out her hand and ran it lovingly through her husband's locks.

It wasn't a full-moon night, but there was enough light for Shiva to clearly see his wife's expression.

'What's the matter?' he asked.

Sati shook her head. 'Nothing.'

'Something's wrong – you look upset.'

'I had a strange dream.'

'What happened?'

'I dreamt that we were separated.'

Shiva smiled and pulled Sati closer to him, embracing her. 'You can dream all you want, but you're never getting away from me.'

Sati laughed. 'I don't intend to.'

Shiva held his wife in his arms and returned his gaze to the Vishwanath Temple.

'What are you thinking?' asked Sati.

'That marrying you is the best thing I've ever done.'

Sati smiled. 'I'm not going to disagree with you, but what prompted that thought?'

Shiva caressed Sati's face. 'Because I know that, for as long as you're with me, you'll always keep me centred on the right path.'

'So, you've decided to do the right thing with—'

'I have.'

Sati nodded in satisfaction. 'We *will* win, Shiva.'

'Yes, we will. But it has to be done the right way.'

'Absolutely,' said Sati, and quoted Lord Ram: '"There is no wrong way to do the right thing."'

— ⚹ ⓂⓊ⊕ ◉ —

A select assembly awaited Parvateshwar's arrival in the court of Kashi during the second *prahar*. The Kashi nobility were represented by Athithigva alone. Shiva sat impassively, his closest advisors around him in a semicircle: Gopal, Sati, Kali, Ganesh and Kartik. Bhagirath and Ayurvati stood at a distance. Anandmayi was missing.

Shiva nodded to Athithigva.

Athithigva called out loudly, 'Bring the general in.'

Parshuram, Veerbhadra and Nandi escorted Parvateshwar into the hall. The Meluhan general was unchained, as Shiva had ordered. He glanced briefly at Sati before turning to Shiva. The Neelkanth's rigid face was inscrutable. Parvateshwar expected to be put to death. He knew Shiva wouldn't want to do it, but the others would have convinced him of the necessity of getting rid of him.

Parvateshwar also knew that, regardless of what happened to him, he would treat the Neelkanth with the honour the Lord deserved. The general clicked his heels together and brought his balled right fist up to his chest. And then he completed the Meluhan military salute by bowing low towards the Neelkanth. He didn't bother to so honour anyone else in the room.

'Parvateshwar,' said Shiva.

Parvateshwar immediately looked up.

'I don't want to drag this out,' said Shiva. 'Your rebellion has shocked me, but it's also reinforced my conviction that we are definitely fighting Evil, and it won't make things easy for us. It can lead even the best amongst us astray, if not through inducements then through dubious calls of honour.'

Parvateshwar continued to stare at Shiva, waiting for the sentence.

'But when one fights against Evil, one has to fight with Good,' said Shiva. 'Not just on the side of Good, but with Good in one's heart. Therefore I've decided to allow you to leave.'

Parvateshwar couldn't believe his ears.

'Go now,' said Shiva.

Parvateshwar was only half listening. This magnificent gesture from the Neelkanth had brought tears to his eyes.

'But let me assure you,' continued Shiva coldly, 'the next time we meet, it'll be on a battlefield. And that will be the day I kill you.'

Parvateshwar bowed his head once again, his eyes clouded with tears. 'That will also be the day of my liberation, my Lord.'

Shiva remained stoic.

Parvateshwar looked up at Shiva. 'But for as long as I live, my Lord, I shall fight to protect Meluha.'

'Go!' said Shiva.

Parvateshwar smiled at Sati. She brought her hands together in a polite but expressionless namaste. Parvateshwar mouthed the word '*Vijayibhav*' silently, blessing his goddaughter with victory.

As he turned around to leave, he saw Ayurvati and Bhagirath standing by the door. He walked up to them.

'My apologies, Parvateshwar,' said Bhagirath.

'I understand,' replied Parvateshwar, his face impassive.

Ayurvati just shook her head. 'Do you realise you're leaving one of the most magnificent men ever born?'

'I do,' said Parvateshwar. 'But I'll have the good fortune of dying at his hands.'

Ayurvati sighed deeply and patted Parvateshwar's shoulder. 'I'll miss you, my friend.'

'I'll miss you, too.'

Parvateshwar quickly scanned the room. 'Where's Anand-mayi?'

'She's waiting for you at the port,' said Bhagirath, 'beside the ship that will take you away.'

Parvateshwar nodded. He looked back one last time at Shiva and then walked away.

— A ᛗU⊕⊛ —

The harbour master approached Parvateshwar as soon as he reached the Assi Ghat. 'General, your ship's berthed over there.'

He began walking in the direction indicated and saw Anand-mayi standing by the gangplank of a small vessel, obviously a merchant ship.

'Did you know I'd be allowed to leave honourably?' he asked, smiling as he reached her.

'When they told me this morning to arrange a ship to sail up the Ganga,' said Anandmayi, 'I surmised it wasn't to carry your corpse all the way to Meluha and display it to the Suryavanshis.'

Parvateshwar laughed.

'Also, I never lost faith in the Neelkanth,' said Anandmayi.

'Of course not,' said Parvateshwar. 'He's the finest man born since Lord Ram.'

Anandmayi looked at the ship. 'It's not much, I admit. It won't be comfortable, but it's fast.'

Parvateshwar suddenly stepped forward and embraced his wife. The gesture surprised her – Parvateshwar wasn't a man given to public displays of affection – and it took her a moment to respond. She smiled warmly and caressed his back. 'It's all over now.'

Parvateshwar pulled away from her a little, but kept his arms around his wife. 'I'll miss you.'

'Why?' asked Anandmayi.

'You've been the best thing that ever happened to me,' he said, tears in his eyes.

Anandmayi raised her eyebrows and laughed. 'And I'll con-tinue to happen to you. Let's go.'

'Let's go?'

'Yes.'

'Where?'

'Meluha.'

'You're coming to Meluha?'

'Yes.'

Parvateshwar stepped back. 'Anandmayi, the path ahead is dangerous. I honestly don't think Meluha can win.'

'So?'

'I can't permit you to put your life in danger.'

'Did I seek your permission?'

'Anandmayi, you can't—'

Parvateshwar stopped speaking as Anandmayi took his hand, turned around and started walking up the gangplank. Parvateshwar followed quietly with a smile on his face and tears in his eyes.

CHAPTER 19

Proclamation of the Blue Lord

'I have a brilliant plan,' said Daksha to Veerini.

Warily Veerini put the morsel of *roti* and vegetables she'd been about to eat back on her plate and stole a quick glance towards the attendants standing guard at the door.

'What plan?' asked Veerini.

'Believe me,' said an excited Daksha, 'if we can implement it, the war will be over before it's begun.'

'But Lord Bhrigu—'

'Even Lord Bhrigu will be impressed. We'll be rid of the Neelkanth problem once and for all.'

'Wasn't it the Neelkanth *opportunity* not so very long ago?' she asked sarcastically.

'Don't you understand what's happening?' snapped Daksha, irritated now. 'Do I have to explain everything to you? War's about to break out. Our soldiers are training day and night.'

'Yes, I'm aware of that. But I think we should keep out of it and leave the matter entirely to Lord Bhrigu.'

'Why? Lord Bhrigu's not the Emperor of India – *I* am.'

'Have you told Lord Bhrigu that?'

'Don't provoke me, Veerini. If you're not interested in hearing my idea, just say so.'

'I'm sorry, but I think it's better to leave all the decision-making to Lord Bhrigu. Our only concern should be our family.'

'There you go again!' said Daksha, raising his voice. 'Family! Family! Family! Don't you care about how the world will see me? How history will judge me?'

'Even the greatest of men can't dictate how posterity will judge them.'

Daksha pushed his plate away and shouted, '*You're* the source of all my problems! It's your fault that I haven't been able to achieve my full potential!'

Veerini glanced at the attendants again, then turned back towards her husband. 'Keep your voice down, Daksha. Don't make a mockery of our marriage.'

'Ha! This marriage has been a mockery from the very the beginning! If I'd had a more supportive wife, I'd have conquered the world by now!' With that, Daksha got up angrily and stormed out.

— ⚵ ⓌⓊ⚴⊛ —

'This is a huge mistake,' said Kali to Ganesh and Kartik. 'In his obsession to follow the "right" way, your father may end up losing the war.'

'I disagree, *mausi*,' said Kartik. 'I think *baba* did the right thing. We have to win, but we *must* do it the right way.'

Kali frowned. 'I thought you were in agreement with us,' she said.

'I was, but *maa*'s words convinced me otherwise.'

'In any case, *mausi*,' said Ganesh, 'it's happened, so let's not fret over it. We should focus on the war instead.'

'What other choice do we have?' asked Kali.

'*Baba* told me I'll be leading the campaign in Ayodhya,' said Ganesh. 'Kartik, you'll be with me.'

'We'll destroy them, *dada*,' said Kartik, raising his clenched right fist.

'That we will,' said Ganesh. '*Mausi*, are you sure about Lothal and Maika?'

'I've already asked Suparna to send ambassadors to Governor Chenardhwaj,' said Kali. 'Trust me, he's a friend.'

— ☥ ⦿Ṵ♉⊛ —

Kartik bowed down and touched his mother's feet.

'*Vijayibhav*, my child,' said Sati as she applied the red *tilak* to Kartik's forehead for good luck and victory.

Ganesh, whose forehead already bore the *tilak*, looked at his brother with pride. Kartik might still be a child, but he was already respected as a fearsome warrior by all who had seen him fight. Shiva's two sons were about to set sail down the Ganga to meet their allies in Vaishali. Once their forces were united, they would sail up the Sarayu River and attack Ayodhya.

Ganesh turned towards his father and touched his feet and Shiva smiled as he pulled Ganesh up into an embrace. 'My blessings aren't as potent as those that emerge from your mother's heart, but I know you'll make me proud.'

'I'll try my best, *baba*,' said Ganesh.

Kartik took his turn, and after he'd touched Shiva's feet his father hugged his younger son. 'Give them hell, Kartik!'

Kartik grinned. 'I will, *baba*!'

'You should smile more often, Kartik,' said Sati. 'You look very handsome when you do.'

Kartik's smile widened. 'The next time we meet, I'll be grinning from ear to ear, for our army will have defeated Ayodhya by then!'

Shiva patted Kartik's back, then said to Ganesh, 'If Ayodhya's willing to withdraw its support for Meluha after my proclamation's made public, then I'd rather we didn't attack them.'

'I understand, *baba*,' said Ganesh. 'That's why I'm taking Bhagirath with me. His father may hate him, but many members of the nobility still support their prince. I'm hoping he'll be able to convince them to remain neutral, or even join us.'

'When will the proclamation be made, *baba*?' asked Kartik.

'Next week,' answered Shiva. 'Stay in touch with the Vaishali Vasudev pandit; they'll report the reactions from across Swadweep and that'll give you some idea of what to expect in Ayodhya.'

'Yes, *baba*,' said Kartik.

Shiva turned to Ganesh. 'I hear you've recruited Divodas and the Branga soldiers into the army.'

'I have,' said Ganesh. 'We'll leave aboard five ships and rendezvous with the combined Branga–Vaishali army at Vaishali. I'm told they have two hundred ships. Fifty of them have been seconded to the Western Army under your command; they're on their way to Kashi. The remaining hundred and fifty ships will be with me: we'll be attacking Ayodhya with a hundred and fifty thousand men.'

'That won't be enough to conquer them,' said Sati, 'but we should be able to keep them busy for a while.'

'That's what we're hoping,' said Ganesh.

'We'll hold them back, *baba*,' said Kartik. 'I promise.'

The kings of Kashi had bought the land on the eastern banks of the Ganga River long ago, for it was considered inauspicious territory for any permanent construction and they wished to ensure that no Kashi citizen settled there, by accident or design. Taking the bad fate on himself, King Athithigva had built his eastern palace here to hide his Naga sister, Maya, but the open presence of Ganesh and Kali had given the King of Kashi the courage to let his sister come out of hiding.

'How is she now?' asked Kali, standing at the palace's river gate. She'd come to say goodbye, before she left with the Western Army the next day.

'Your medicines have helped, your Highness,' said Athithigva gratefully. 'At least she's not in terrible pain any more. The Parmatma has sent you as an angel to help my sister.'

Kali smiled sadly, for she knew it was only a matter of time before Maya died – it was a miracle she had lived as long as she had, for Maya was a singular name for conjoined twins fused into one body from the chest down. When Kali had discovered her, she had immediately supplied Naga medicines, hoping they would lessen her suffering.

She laughed a little as she handed Athithigva the rest of her medicines. 'I promise you I'm no angel,' she said. 'If the Parmatma had any sense of justice, he wouldn't make an innocent person like Maya suffer so much. I'm simply doing what I can to set right his injustices.'

Athithigva looked resigned. He was far too pious to curse God, despite knowing what his sister had endured.

Kali's gaze turned towards the Ganga, where the fifty Branga ships had dropped anchor just the previous day. The mighty fleet stretched all the way to the opposite bank. The nervous excitement was almost palpable throughout Kashi: the smell of war was in the air.

She knew their initial progress would be slow, for the armada would first sail west, against the current, before turning southwards along the Chambal River. After disembarking close to the headwaters of the Chambal, the soldiers would march towards the Narmada, where the Vasudev navy awaited them. The third part of the journey would see them sailing down the Narmada to the Western Sea, and then northwards to Meluha.

After a moment she turned her attention back to the king and smiled an apology for her wandering thoughts. 'I'd like to see Maya before I leave,' she said.

— ⚇ ⚇ —

'Your Majesty!' cried Kanakhala, running into Daksha's private office.

Daksha looked up at his prime minister as he slipped the papyrus he was reading back into the drawer of his desk. 'Where's the fire, Kanakhala?'

'Your Majesty,' Kanakhala was obviously carrying something barely concealed within the folds of her *angvastram*, 'you need to see this.' She placed a thin stone tablet on her emperor's desk.

'What's this?' asked Daksha.

'You need to read it, your Majesty.'

To all of you who consider yourselves children of Manu and followers of the Sanatan Dharma: this is a message from Shiva, your Neelkanth.

I have travelled through all the kingdoms of our great land and met with all the tribes who populate our fair realm. I have been searching for the ultimate Evil, for that is my task. Father Manu told us that Evil isn't a distant demon. It works its destruction close to us, amongst us, within us. He was right. He told us that Evil doesn't come from down below to devour us. Instead, we help Evil destroy our lives. He was right. He told us that Good and Evil are two sides of the same coin, and that, one day, the greatest Good will transform into the greatest Evil. He was right. Our greed for Good turns it into Evil. This is the universe's way of restoring balance. It's the Parmatma's way of controlling our excesses.

I have come to the conclusion that the Somras is now the greatest Evil of our age. All the Good that we could wring from it has been wrung. It is time to stop using it, before the power of its Evil destroys us all. It has already caused tremendous damage, from killing the Saraswati River to the emergence of birth deformities and the diseases that plague some of our kingdoms. For the sake of our descendants, for the sake of our world, we cannot use the Somras any more.

Therefore, by my order, use of the Somras is banned forthwith.

To all those who believe in the legend of the Neelkanth: follow me. Stop using the Somras.

To all those who refuse to stop using the Somras: know this: you will become my enemy.

I will not rest until the use of the Somras is ended. This is the word of your Neelkanth.

Daksha looked completely stunned. 'What the hell?'

'I don't understand what this means, your Majesty,' said Kanakhala. 'Do we stop using the *Somras*?'

'Where did you find this?'

'It was hanging on the outer wall of the temple of Lord Indra near the public baths, your Majesty,' said Kanakhala. 'Half the citizens have seen it already, and they'll doubtless have told the other half by now.'

'Where's Maharishi Bhrigu?'

'My Lord, what about the *Somras*? Should I—?'

'*Where's Maharishi Bhrigu?*'

'But if the Neelkanth's issued this order, we have no choice—'

'Dammit, Kanakhala!' shouted Daksha. 'Where is Maharishi Bhrigu?'

Kanakhala was silent for a moment. She didn't like the way her emperor had just spoken to her. She took a breath to calm herself, then said quietly, 'Maharishi Bhrigu left Prayag a little more than a month ago. That was the last I heard of him, your Majesty. It will take him at least two more months to reach Devagiri.'

'Then we'll wait for him to get here before deciding on a course of action,' said Daksha.

'But how can we oppose a proclamation from the Neelkanth, your Majesty?'

'Who is the emperor, Kanakhala?'

'You are, your Majesty.'

'And have I just made a decision?'

'Yes, your Majesty.'

'Then that is the decision of Meluha.'

'But the people have already read this—'

'I want you to put up a notice stating that this proclamation is fraudulent. It can't have been issued by the true Neelkanth, for he would never go against the *Somras*, which was Lord Brahma's greatest invention.'

'But is that true, your Majesty?'

Daksha's eyes narrowed. he was barely keeping his temper in check. 'Kanakhala, just do what I tell you to do or I'll appoint someone else as prime minister.'

Kanakhala looked down so he wouldn't see her anger and brought her hands together in a formal namaste, then turned to leave. She couldn't resist a final parting shot, though. 'What if there are other notices like this?'

Daksha looked up. 'Send bird-couriers across the empire. If anyone sees such a notice anywhere, it must be removed immediately and replaced with the proclamation discrediting it. This notice is bogus, do you understand?'

'Yes, your Majesty,' said Kanakhala.

As she closed the door behind her, Daksha angrily flung the tablet on the floor. 'My idea is the only practical way to stop this. Maharishi Bhrigu *has* to listen to me.'

CHAPTER 20

The Fire Song

Gopal was shown into Shiva's private chamber the moment he arrived, and he joined Shiva and Sati on the balcony.

'What news do you have for me, Panditji?' asked Shiva. 'It's been a week since we put out the proclamation.' He was fervently hoping that the people would follow his command.

'My pandits have sent in their reports from across the country,' the Chief Vasudev started, 'and as we expected, the reactions in Meluha have been very different from those in Swadweep. The Swadweepan public have embraced the proclamation, not least because it feeds into their bias against Meluha. They regard the *Somras* as yet another example of the Meluhans unfairly conspiring to stay ahead of everyone else. And remember, the Swadweepans don't use the *Somras* anyway, so it's no real sacrifice for them.'

'But how have the kings reacted?' asked Sati. 'They're the ones in control of the armies.'

'It's too early to say, Satiji,' said Gopal, 'but I do know that all the kings across Swadweep are engaged in intense consultations with their advisors even as we speak.'

'But the Meluhans have rejected my proclamation, haven't they?' asked Shiva.

Gopal took a deep breath. 'It's not as simple as that. My pandits tell me that the Meluhan public appeared to be genuinely disturbed by your proclamation: there were serious public discussions and many citizens believed they should follow their Neelkanth's instruction. But the Meluhan state is supremely efficient, my friend, and within three days the notices had been taken down – in all the major cities, at least – and replaced by a Meluhan royal order denouncing the proclamation as the work of a fraud Neelkanth.'

'And the people believed it?'

'The Meluhans have trusted their government completely, for many generations,' Sati said. 'They'll always believe what their government tells them.'

'There's another thing,' Gopal pointed out. 'You've been away from Meluha for many years, my friend, and many people are genuinely beginning to wonder if the Neelkanth's forgotten Meluha.'

Shiva sighed. 'So it looks like war is inevitable.'

'Daksha – and, more importantly, Lord Bhrigu – will make sure of that,' said Gopal. 'But at least our message is out there, and hopefully some Meluhans will start asking questions.'

Shiva gazed out at the vessels anchored on the Ganga: Branga, Vasudev and Naga ships. 'We set sail in two days.'

— ⚔ ⦿ ∪ ⚕ ✺ —

'No, no!' Shiva shook his head in dismay. 'You've got it all wrong!'

Light and shadows from the bonfire danced over the faces of Brahaspati, Veerbhadra, Nandi and Parshuram as they stood before Shiva, suitably chastened. It was a moonless night and a cold wind had swept in from the river. The Ganga's waters shimmered in the reflected light of the torches from the Branga fleet.

It was traditional for the Gunas to sing paeans to the five holy elements before embarking on any major campaigns, to invoke their protection and as a mark of their manhood in the face of danger. Shiva's friends had gathered to honour this custom before setting sail at the crack of dawn the following day.

Shiva passed his chillum to Parshuram. It was down to him to teach his friends the fine art of singing. 'The real trick is in here,' he said, pointing at his diaphragm.

'I thought it was in here,' said Veerbhadra teasingly, pointing to his throat.

'*Bhadra!* The vocal cords are basically a wind instrument! Your skill depends on how much control you have over your breath, my friend, and that means your *lungs*. And the *lungs* can be regulated using the diaphragm—'

Nandi sang a note and then asked, 'Am I doing it right, my Lord?'

Shiva looked at Nandi's immense stomach. 'If you can feel your diaphragm pressing on your stomach, then you're doing it right.'

Brahaspati, Parshuram and Nandi were listening with rapt attention, but Veerbhadra's eyes were sparkling with mischief. He didn't much care for singing. 'Shiva, you're taking this far too seriously! It's the thought that counts – as long as I sing it with my heart, I don't think anybody ought to object even if I murder the song!'

Parshuram waved his hand at Veerbhadra before turning to Shiva. 'My Lord, why don't you sing? Show us how it's done?'

As everyone fixed their eyes upon him, Shiva looked up at the sky, rubbed his cold neck and cleared his throat.

'Enough of the theatrics,' said Veerbhadra. 'Get on with it before we all freeze to death.'

Shiva slapped Veerbhadra's arm playfully and with a genial grin, said, 'All right then. Silence!'

Veerbhadra made a show of putting his finger on his lips as Brahaspati glared at him; he ignoried the Meluhan as he took the chillum from Parshuram and inhaled deeply.

Shiva closed his eyes and went within himself. A sonorous hum emerged from the very core of his being and he hit the perfect note and started a lilting melody that enraptured his audience. Each of the elements had a Guna war song, but this one was to *Agni*, the God of Fire, and as they listened, they absorbed the significance of the words of this warrior's prayer, imploring *Agni* for a blessing, which the warrior would repay by feeding his enemies to the hungry flames of a cremation pyre. And as the listeners drank in Shiva's words, they sensed that their Neelkanth's *prakriti* – his true nature – was closer to fire rather than the other elements.

It was a short song, but the audience was spellbound and Shiva ended his performance to a robust round of applause.

'Ah, you still have it in you,' said Veerbhadra affectionately to his oldest friend. 'That cold throat hasn't thrown your voice off.'

Shiva grinned back and took the chillum from Veerbhadra. He was about to inhale the fragrant smoke when he heard someone cough softly near the entrance of the terrace. Everyone turned to find Sati standing there.

Shiva put down the chillum and smiled at her. 'Did we wake you?'

Sati laughed as she took a seat next to her husband. 'You were loud enough to wake the whole city! But the song was so beautiful that I didn't mind being woken up.'

'It's a song from back home,' said Shiva. 'It steels a warrior's heart for battle.'

'I think the singing was more beautiful than the song,' said Sati.

'Why don't you try to sing it, my Lady?' asked Nandi.

'No, no,' said Sati, 'I couldn't—'

'Why not?' asked Veerbhadra.

'I'd love to hear you sing, my child,' said Brahaspati.

'Come on,' pleaded Shiva.

'All right,' said Sati. 'I'll try.'

Shiva picked up the chillum and offered it to her, but she shook her head.

Sati had been listening closely to Shiva. She wasn't sure about the words, but she thought she knew the melody now. She closed her eyes, inhaled deeply and gave herself to the music, beginning, as Shiva had, on that very low, sonorous note. She allowed the words to flow through her, at times flooding from her, at others, allowing them to just hang softly in the air. As she approached the end, she crescendoed, taking the notes higher and higher, finishing the song like a clarion call to war. Even the bonfire appeared to respond to the song's elemental call when Sati sang it.

'Wow!' exclaimed Shiva, embracing her as she finished. 'I didn't know you could sing so beautifully.'

Sati blushed. 'Was it really that good?'

'My Lady!' Veerbhadra looked visibly stunned. 'It was *fantastic*. I always thought Shiva was the best singer in the universe, but you're even better than him.'

'Of course I'm not,' said Sati.

'Of course you are,' said Shiva. 'It was almost as if you'd pulled all the surrounding fire into yourself.'

'And I shall keep it within me,' said Sati. 'We're going to be fighting the war of our lives. We need all the fire we can get!'

— ⚔ ☀ ᛜ ⚙ —

King Maatali of Vaishali had housed Ganesh and Kartik in his private chambers, along with King Chandraketu of Branga and

Prince Bhagirath. They'd received information that Magadh had not yet established a blockade to prevent their ships from sailing to Ayodhya, but the Magadhan army had been put on alert and their training sessions had been doubled. Perhaps Surapadman was simply being cautious and preparing for any eventuality, but the Magadhans might also be planning to attack them once they'd exhausted themselves against the Ayodhyans.

'We can't afford to lose either men or ships at Magadh,' said Ganesh. 'We've got to be prepared for the worst.'

'The way I see it,' said Bhagirath, pointing to the map of the river laid out on the table, 'their primary catapults will be set up in the main fort on the west bank of the Sarayu, here. They have a secondary battlement on the east bank, here, but it's small so I don't think any weapons stationed there will have a particularly long range. So my suggestion would be to sail our ships closer to the eastern bank of the Sarayu.'

'Not too close, though, in case you're mistaken!' said Chandraketu.

'Of course,' said Bhagirath. 'Smaller catapults can still do a fair amount of damage, given the right circumstances.'

'I think we should also have our oarsmen in position when we pass,' said King Maatali. 'That way we're not wholly dependent on our sails if we need to move the ships rapidly.'

'Agreed,' said Ganesh. 'But no matter which side of the river we choose, or how quickly we row, we'll still lose people if they decide to attack. We won't be able to land our men fast enough to retaliate.'

'Why don't we increase their risks?' asked Kartik.

'How?' asked Ganesh.

'Disembark half the soldiers from every ship before we reach Magadh and have them march down the eastern bank alongside our ships. The reduced load will allow our ships to move faster, and the Magadhan battlement on the eastern bank will think twice before doing anything stupid when they see a massive battalion of enemy soldiers marching towards their walls.'

'I like it,' said Bhagirath.

'I've thought of something even simpler,' said Chandraketu. 'The Magadh royals are amongst the poorest in Swadweep. It's a powerful kingdom, but King Mahendra lost a considerable amount of his fortune to his gambling addiction, and his son Ugrasen turned out to be a chip off the old block too.'

'Are you suggesting we bribe them?' asked Bhagirath.

'Why not?'

'For one thing, we'd need a lot of money – a few thousand gold coins won't suffice, not if we're negotiating with the king himself.'

'Will one million gold coins be enough?' Chandraketu asked.

Bhagirath's mouth fell open. 'One *million*?'

'Yes.'

'Just to secure our passage through their territory unharmed?'

'Yes.'

'Lord Rudra be praised: that's the equivalent of almost six months' worth of tax collections for the Magadhan royalty.'

'Exactly. I'll send Divodas to Magadh with half the amount.

The remainder will be handed over once our last ship has passed by safely.'

'But they could use this wealth to buy weapons,' said Kartik.

'They could, but they won't be able to do that quickly enough to use them in the coming conflict,' said Chandraketu. 'And what they do with the money after the war's over is no concern of mine.'

'Can you really afford to give away so much gold, your Majesty?' asked Ganesh.

Chandraketu smiled. 'We have more than enough, Lord Ganesh, but I'd gladly give away every last gold piece to stop the *Somras*.'

'All right,' said Ganesh. 'I see no reason why your plan won't work.'

CHAPTER 21

Siege of Ayodhya

The cool northerly wind was a welcome relief for Shiva as he sat on the deck of the lead ship with Gopal, Sati and Kali. The fifty-six vessels were making steady progress upriver; in a few weeks they'd be approaching the headwaters of the Chambal, where the soldiers would disembark and begin the overland march to the Narmada River, where they would transfer onto waiting Vasudev ships, vessels that had been specially designed to handle the weight of the additional fifty-five thousand soldiers.

'Judging by the maps we've seen,' said Sati, 'we should reach Lothal in three months – right, Panditji?'

Gopal smiled. 'If the winds favour us, we may even make it sooner,' he said.

'Have you heard from the Lothal governor yet?' Shiva asked Kali.

'My ambassador will be waiting for us at the Narmada,' answered Kali. 'Trust me, we'll have no trouble getting into

Lothal. But don't expect many to join our army. Lothal has only about two or three thousand soldiers in total.'

'We don't really need their soldiers,' said Shiva. 'We have enough troops already – more than one hundred thousand men, counting the Vasudev contingent waiting for us at the Narmada, your own Naga army and this Branga force. That's equal to the strength of the Meluhan army.'

'We can easily defeat them,' said Kali.

'I don't intend to attack,' said Shiva.

'I think you should.'

'All we need to do is destroy the *Somras* manufacturing facility, Kali.'

'You'll have the Nagas with you, so there's no need to fear a direct confrontation.'

'I'm not afraid. I just don't see the sense in it. It'll distract us from our main purpose, which is the destruction of the *Somras*. We don't want to destroy Meluha, so please remember that.'

'I'm sure I can count on you to remind me of that every time I forget,' said Kali, making Shiva shake his head at her obstinacy.

The voyage up the Sarayu River turned out to be surprisingly uneventful. Chandraketu's bribe had sealed the deal and the Magadhans left Ganesh's ships alone. The convoy was so massive that the guards on the Magadhan towers spent an entire day watching ships go by.

A week later, Ganesh ordered his ships to drop anchor and

rowed ashore with Kartik, Bhagirath and Chandraketu to meet Divodas, the leader of the Branga immigrants in Kashi, who was waiting there along with twenty men.

As soon as the rowboat grounded Ganesh jumped out and waded through the shallow water to the riverbank, the others close on his heels. The moment he reached the shore he touched his head to the ground, then he looked deep into the forest, remembering a time long ago when he'd hidden behind the trees here and watched his mother.

He turned to his brother. 'Kartik, this is the Bal-Atibal Kund, where *Saptrishi* Vishwamitra taught Lord Ram his legendary skills.'

Kartik's eyes opened wide in awe. He bent down, touched the ground and whispered, '*Jai Shri Ram.*'

Everyone around him echoed his words: '*Jai Shri Ram.*'

'This ground was blessed by *Saptrishi* Vishwamitra and Lord Ram,' said Ganesh, 'but its greatness has been forgotten by many. We may have to redeem the honour of this land with blood.'

Kartik thought for a moment, then said, 'Do you think Surapadman might chase us?'

Ganesh smiled. 'There's a good chance he will. I see the siege of Ayodhya as a bait to draw the prince out of Magadh. Once Surapadman's in the open, we'll destroy his army and capture his city – with the Ganga blockaded at Magadh we'll easily be able to stop Ayodhyan ships. And the battle to decide Magadh's fate should be fought here. This is where I want *you* to attack him.'

'I thought Surapadman would be able to persuade his father to stay out of this?'

'He's a clever man, Kartik. As I understand it, his first instinct was to support us, but in the face of so much opposition from the rest of the nobility, he'll do what's in his best interests now. And he certainly has much to gain. He'll win the favour of his father and his countrymen by taking revenge for his brother's death and he'll arrive on the scene as Ayodhya's saviour – albeit a little late, so that Ayodhya will have been weakened by our attack. And, who knows? He may even capture the Neelkanth's sons . . . Wouldn't that make him Bhrigu's number-one ally?' asked Ganesh with an ironic smile. 'Yes, brother, he will attack and he will learn that clever men should always listen to their instincts.'

Kartik took a deep breath and looked up at the sky before turning back to Ganesh with resolve writ large in his eyes. 'We will turn the river red with blood, *dada*.'

Bhagirath looked at Kartik and felt the now familiar sensation of fascination tinged with fear that ran through him when the young man spoke with such resolve.

'Why have you chosen this particular stretch of riverbank, Lord Ganesh?' asked Chandraketu.

'As you can see, your Majesty,' said Ganesh, 'this stretch is long and narrow, which will lure Surapadman into anchoring his ships along the bank, thus stretching his army thin. The forest's not too far from the shore, which will allow our main army to remain hidden in the trees. We'll leave just a small contingent on the beach.'

Bhagirath smiled. 'That will be very juicy bait. Surapadman will probably think it's a small brigade that's deserted the siege – he'll want to kill them to give his soldiers an easy taste of victory.'

'My thinking exactly,' said Ganesh. 'But the main battle won't be on land. We just have to pin him down here – which will actually take a great deal of courage since he'll have a lot of men with him. That's why I want Kartik here. But Surapadman himself will be defeated on the river itself.'

'How?' asked Chandraketu.

'I'll pull my ships back from Ayodhya and ram his from the front,' said Ganesh. 'I've also asked King Maatali to keep thirty ships in the Sharda River. The Sharda meets the Sarayu downriver from here: once Surapadman's ships have passed the entrance of the Sharda, the Vaishali fleet will fall in behind the Magadhans and attack them from the rear while my own ships ram them from the front. Kartik just has to delay Surapadman here long enough for our ships to arrive and immobilise his fleet.'

'Surapadman will be caught between the hammer and the anvil,' said Chandraketu. 'He won't stand a chance.'

'Sounds like a good plan,' said Bhagirath.

'Success hinges on two things,' said Ganesh. 'Firstly, Kartik has to entice Surapadman to anchor his ships here and attack our soldiers on shore. If Surapadman doesn't fall for that and keeps sailing, we're in trouble. Our ships are light, manouvrable, built for speed; the Magadhans' are built for strength. His bigger boats will easily ram through ours, and we're likely to sustain heavy casualties. I'll be in command of our ships in case that happens.'

'And the second factor?' asked Bhagirath.

'King Maatali must be in position to block Surapadman's retreat to Magadh. That's crucial to the success of this pincer trap.'

Chandraketu doubted neither Kartik's courage nor his strategic mind and he addressed the young warrior with the utmost respect. 'You're on your own, Kartik. It's all up to you now.'

Ganesh smiled proudly at his little brother's bravery as Kartik placed his hand on his sword hilt and swore, 'I'll draw him in, King Chandraketu, and once I do, I assure you I'll obliterate his entire army myself. Our ships won't even need to join the battle.'

— ⚹ ⬯⬰⬱⬲ —

Ganesh reached for another document from the stack on the desk and began to read, then paused to rub his tired eyes. His private cabin was piled high with messages from his informants about the progress of the assault, dozens of missives describing everything from the mood of the Ayodhyan populace to the progress of the armourers in meeting the archers' never-ending demands for arrows. He'd hardly slept since the battle had begun and his body screamed for rest, but these reports couldn't wait. Ayodhya was poised on the brink of surrender and any misstep now could spell disaster.

Kartik and Chandraketu sat patiently by his side, helping to deal with the endless stream of messages while they all anxiously awaited Bhagirath's return, desperate to hear how his mission had fared.

The siege of Ayodhya had begun a month ago, when Ganesh's navy had assaulted the city with textbook precision. A large part of the fleet was now anchored in a double line along the western bank of the Sarayu, safely out of catapult range. The lines of ships went north of Ayodhya, almost as far as the sheer cliff upriver where the Sarayu descended in a waterfall. Small lifeboats had been tied all the way along the river side of Ganesh's convoy, and troops had been stationed ashore on the ships' landside to thwart guerrilla attacks. Guards on board every vessel kept a round-the-clock watch for Ayodhyan devil boats.

Further south, Ganesh had anchored ships across the river in two rows of ten vessels, and five fast-moving cutters patrolled the river further downstream. Any Ayodhyan ship attempting to run the blockade would have to get through a solid double row of twenty enemy ships and then outrun the five speedy cutters waiting downstream.

The defending army had cleared a bit of the forest around Ayodhya to make it impossible for any attacking force to approach the city unseen, but Brigadier Prasanjit, the Meluhan left behind by Maharishi Bhrigu, had failed to convince the Ayodhyans to extend the clearing even further.

Ganesh was able to use that: he had his own men cut a firebreak through the trees, then set fire to the trees between the firebreak and the clearing so the intense heat generated would collapse any tunnels leading from Ayodhya; no food would be smuggled into the city that way.

The fire burned for four days, and it had a significant demoralising effect on the citizens of 'the impenetrable city', for it confirmed the steely resolve of those laying siege.

North of Ayodhya, a waterfall crashing down a sheer cliff served as a natural barrier, making navigation further north on the Sarayu River impossible. The Ayodhyans had built a single narrow channel into their walled shipyard just before the waterfall. The gated channel was easily defendable – but it worked both ways, for it also allowed Ganesh to block their ships' exit route with ease, using logs left over from the forest-clearing. Once he'd ordered a few ships to patrol the river near the channel, to deter the Ayodhyans from trying to remove the logs, the city was effectively sealed off in every direction.

Next, Ganesh turned his attention to the bird-courier system the Meluhans had set up for the Ayodhyans. He placed archers in the treetops outside Ayodhya and along the Sarayu River with orders to shoot every bird in the sky. Working in shifts, the six hundred men patrolled the skies continually, round-the-clock. Groups of trackers retrieved the dead birds, intercepting all messages exchanged between Meluha and Ayodhya and providing fresh meat for the soldiers.

Man-made channels from the Sarayu provided the city's drinking water, with great waterwheels along the banks using the river's own flow to lift water into the channels. The water-wheels were encased in tall walls, and the opening just below the water's surface where the waterwheels' buckets filled up with water was fortified with bronze bars, set too closely together to allow a man to swim in between them.

But that hadn't deterred Ganesh, who came up with an ingenious solution: his engineers provided a number of small wooden barrels, each filled with water, into which was dropped a smaller iron can full of oil. A slow-burning fuse made of waxed hemp was lit just before the oil-can and barrel were sealed, then swimmers towed them across the river under cover of darkness and hid them in the water buckets before returning to camp. The fuse ignited the oil, which in turn brought the water to a boil; the pressure from the trapped steam exploded the barrels, turning iron and wood into devastatingly effective shrapnel, which completely destroyed the wooden buckets – and Ayodha's drinking water system. The remaining wells within the city would never be able to quench the thirst of its innumerable residents.

Ganesh allowed some of the city's medical staff through the barricades to replenish their water supplies, but every day fewer were allowed out, part of his slow squeeze designed to make the Ayodhyans rise up against their king and surrender. Ganesh's men added psychological pressure by berating the water-carriers for going against the wishes of their Neelkanth and siding with Meluha. The soldiers repeatedly told the besieged Ayodhyans that Ganesh wasn't firing missiles into the city because he didn't wish to harm innocent citizens who'd had nothing to do with Emperor Dilipa's decision to defy the Neelkanth.

The daily traffic also enabled the Vasudev pandit of the Ramjanmabhoomi Temple, who'd been in hiding since the start of the siege, to send emissaries to Ganesh with information collected from all the other Vasudev pandits scattered across India.

After two weeks, Ganesh had offered to send Bhagirath to meet the nobles of his father's kingdom, to negotiate a mutually acceptable compromise. The Ayodhyans had accepted the opportunity immediately.

Ganesh stretched his tired arms before glancing at Kartik and Chandraketu, who were seated beside him in his cabin. They'd hardly slept either, but were stalwartly masking their exhaustion and continuing to peruse the documents. Ganesh smiled to himself. *When this is done*, he thought, *we're going to lock ourselves in our cabins and sleep for a week!*

Footsteps sounded outside, followed by a brief knock at the cabin door before it was pushed open to reveal Bhagirath, his hair ruffled from the wind. He bowed slightly to Ganesh before entering and taking a seat next to Chandraketu.

'What news, Bhagirath?' asked Ganesh, pushing the pile of messages to one side.

'I'm afraid it's not good.'

'Really?' asked Chandraketu. 'I'd have thought the Ayodhyan army must be deeply divided by now – I can't think why else we were able to lay siege to the city so easily. There's been no skirmishes, no guerrilla attacks – surely that can only mean that the army doesn't intend to fight?'

Bhagirath shook his head and with a wry smile admitted, 'You don't know Ayodhya, King Chandraketu: it's not the cowardice of their army but the indecisiveness of their nobility that is working in our favour. They can't agree on the best way to attack us! It didn't help that Maharishi Bhrigu brought in a Meluhan brigadier to oversee the Ayodhyans' war preparations – all that's done is to divide the city further. By the time they agreed on a strategy, we were already in control of the river, so there wasn't much they could do after that.'

'So what now?' asked Ganesh. 'Haven't their troubles opened the eyes of some, at least?'

'No, there's tremendous confusion within the city,' said Bhagirath. 'Many Ayodhyans are fanatical devotees of Lord Shiva and they're certain that the Neelkanth won't harm them. They refuse to believe he's ordered this attack – so this blind devotion is actually working against us.'

'So who do they think ordered this attack?' asked Chandraketu.

'They think you did,' said Bhagirath bluntly. 'They're looking at the numbers of Branga soldiers—'

Chandraketu raised his hands in consternation. 'Why would I attack Ayodhya?'

'They believe Branga wants to be overlord of Swadweep,' said Bhagirath. 'In the absence of Lord Shiva, I can't think of anything we can do to convince them otherwise. There are a few who believe the proclamation is authentic, but they're in the minority, and their opinion's out-shouted by a very simple logic: "We've never used the *Somras*, so why would the Neel-kanth attack us? He should attack Meluha." Of course, some of the nobility do use *Somras*, but the general population don't know that.'

'It's the opinion of the nobility that's more important right now,' said Kartik. 'The people don't control the army. So what do the nobles think?'

'The nobility's sharply divided, too,' said Bhagirath. 'Some of them actually want us to succeed, and that would give them a plausible reason to refuse to help Meluha. Others believe surrendering will mean terrible loss of face and they want the army to gallantly strike out and sail to Meluha if only to prove to the rest of Swadweep that Ayodhya has the strength to do what it chooses to do.'

'How do we help those who don't want to come to Meluha's aid?' asked Ganesh.

'It's difficult,' said Bhagirath. 'My father made a brilliant move last week. He promised all of them a lifetime supply of the *Somras*.'

'*What?*' Ganesh exclaimed.

'Yes. He told them that Lord Bhrigu's promised to supply the *Somras* powder to Ayodhya in massive quantities.'

'But how can Maharishi Bhrigu promise that?' asked Kartik. 'Where will the powder come from? Is Meluha's manufacturing facility capable of producing so much?'

'It must be,' said Bhagirath, 'but in any case, this offer was made only to the nobility, so the numbers will be small.'

'Damn the man!' said Ganesh.

'My thoughts precisely,' said Bhagirath. 'This will allow them to live for a hundred more years – no amount of gold can compete with that.'

'So what do we do now?' asked Chandraketu.

Ganesh sighed. 'We prepare for war,' he said. 'They'll soon start making earnest attempts to break the siege.'

CHAPTER 22

Magadh Mobilises

The Vasudevs had built a viewing platform in the branches of a banyan tree overlooking the Narmada River. The leaves had been shorn off, giving Shiva, Sati, Gopal and Kali a panoramic view of the boarding operations as the massive army used great log rafts to get to the Vasudev and Naga fleet anchored in the middle of the river. More than a hundred thousand soldiers – Brangas, Vasudevs and Nagas – were boarding a line of ships that stretched as far as the eye could see. The voyage would be uncomfortable with two thousand men on every ship, but fortunately it wasn't far to Lothal.

'We should be ready to sail by tomorrow, Shiva,' said Kali.

'Has Suparna boarded?' asked Shiva. He wanted to meet the fearsome warrior, leader of the Garuda Nagas. 'I'd like to exchange some thoughts about the Nagas under her command.'

Kali raised her eyebrows. She'd expected to lead the Nagas into battle herself.

'I'd like you to be at my side, Kali,' said Shiva, reading her face and mollifying her. 'I trust you. I'm going to be leading the search party into the Meluhan cities to try and locate the *Somras* manufacturing facility – we'll be working quietly and anonymously while our army keeps the Meluhans busy outside the city.'

'You're very tactful, Shiva,' she said after a moment. 'You know how to get your way without making me feel I've been cut down to size.'

Shiva smiled, but remained silent.

'I know the search for the *Somras* facility is crucial,' she went on, 'so it'll be my honour to accompany you.'

'Excellent,' said Shiva, turning to Gopal. 'Any news from the Vasudevs, Panditji?'

'The siege of Ayodhya's been surprisingly easy so far,' said Gopal. 'Ganesh has a stranglehold over the city, and so far at least, the Ayodhyans haven't fought back.'

'But has King Dilipa changed his stance?'

'Not yet. Ganesh is, very wisely, not resorting to violence, as that might rally the citizens around their king. We'll have to be patient.'

'As long as the Ayodhyan army doesn't come to Meluha's aid, I'm happy. What about Magadh?'

'His ships are ready,' said Gopal, 'but Surapadman's army hasn't been mobilised yet.'

Shiva's eyebrows arched in surprise. 'I didn't think Surapadman would let an opportunity like this pass him by. I imagine King Mahendra will be pressuring him to attack us too.'

'Let's just wait and see what happens,' said Sati. 'Maybe Sura-padman wants Ayodhya and our army to fight first so that he'll be attacking a weakened enemy.'

'Perhaps you're right,' Shiva said contemplatively.

— ⚹ ◗◖U⇧✸ —

'Look at that, Bhagirath,' said Ganesh. He handed the prince a note from Meluha that had been recovered from a bird brought down by his archers. It was coded, but Bhagirath had broken the encryption weeks before.

Bhagirath read aloud: '"Prime Minister Siamantak, has Lord Bhrigu returned to Ayodhya? It's been months since he left Prayag but he still hasn't reached Meluha. We would also like to be informed of the location of Lord Shiva and General Parvateshwar, if you have that information."'

'It's been signed by Prime Minister Kanakhala,' he added. 'Interesting.'

'Interesting indeed,' said Ganesh. 'So where's Lord Bhrigu? And why is the Meluhan prime minister enquiring about General Parvateshwar? Doesn't she know he's defected to their side?'

'Where do you think they are?' asked Bhagirath.

'They're certainly not in Meluha,' said Ganesh, 'which makes things easier for my father.'

'Do you think Lord Shiva's reached Meluha by now?'

'I think he's probably still a few weeks away.'

'And the Ayodhyan army's still under siege,' said Bhagirath. 'The news just keeps getting better—'

They both looked round as Kartik rushed in, crying, '*Dada!* Magadh's mobilising!'

'Who told you? The Vasudev pandit?' asked Bhagirath.

'Yes,' said Kartik. 'Armaments are being loaded and the soldiers have been ordered to stand by for departure.'

Ganesh smiled. 'How many soldiers?'

'Seventy-five thousand.'

'Seventy-five thousand?' Bhagirath looked surprised. 'Is Surapadman committing everything? Magadh'll be left defenceless . . .'

'When are they expected to set sail?' asked Ganesh.

'In two weeks' time – at least, that's what the Vasudev pandit surmised.'

'You should leave in the next few days,' said Ganesh. 'Take a hundred thousand men.'

'Don't you need more men here with you?'

'I need enough to be able to sail the ships and shoot fire-arrows,' said Ganesh. 'If you don't manage to hold Surapadman off at the Bal-Atibal Kund, he'll just ram us with his larger ships and drown us all. Our soldiers will be put to better use under your command, not mine.'

'I'll prepare to leave at once,' said Kartik.

— ⚹ ⊚ ⋃ ⚐ ⊛ —

A hundred thousand well-motivated soldiers reached the forests near the Bal-Atibal Kund in the early afternoon. The Ayodhyan prince had accompanied the army as Kartik's chief advisor, while

King Chandraketu remained with Ganesh to ensure that the Branga soldiers in Kartik's army wouldn't be confused about the chain of command.

As soon as they arrived, Kartik ordered a thousand of his soldiers to construct coracles to use as devil boats to set the Magadh fleet on fire. The boats were hidden on the eastern bank, on the opposite side of the river from the Kund. Kartik planned to attack the enemy ships while the battle was being fought on the western bank.

Hidden platforms were built in the trees for the signal corps, who relayed information back and forth across the river using a clever but simple system: small metallic pipes had been fitted to earthenware pots so they could burn anthracite; by opening and closing the caps, the low, smokeless flame would shine out in a controlled manner. From a distance the light looked like a cloud of fireflies, but for Kartik's soldiers, the lights were signals conveying coded messages.

Kartik wanted the area around the Bal-Atibal Kund to be left undisturbed and instructed his army to stay strictly within the forested area.

'I don't understand,' said Bhagirath. 'Surely we want our men on the beach if they're to serve as bait, don't we? Isn't that what Ganesh had in mind?'

'It would be unwise to underestimate Surapadman, Prince Bhagirath, and I doubt he'll underestimate us, either. If he sees a small number of our soldiers casually stationed in an area visible from the river, he's likely to smell a trap – after all, if we're deserting our army, we wouldn't be stupid enough to camp where we could be seen, would we?'

'Fair enough. So what do you suggest?'

'We're on the west bank. Magadh is further south, also on the west bank of the Sarayu. If we were to march along the river, where the forest isn't too dense, Magadh wouldn't be more than two or three weeks' journey from here.'

Bhagirath smiled. 'You want Surapadman to guess our actual strategy: that the siege of Ayodhya was just a feint to try to draw him out. He'll realise that by conquering Magadh, we'll have much more effective control over any Ayodhyan ships sailing along the Surayu than we would by besieging Ayodhya itself.'

'Exactly. And if he's smart enough to suspect that – as I'm sure he is – he'll have lookouts checking the forest edge along the river. And when he receives reports of our massive army marching through the trees, he'll draw the obvious conclusion: that we're on our way to conquer Magadh while he's wasting his time sailing to Ayodhya.'

'Leave your home defenceless to conquer another land and you may return to find your own home conquered instead.'

'You've got it,' said Kartik. 'That's exactly what he'd expect a smart enemy to do and, as I said, I don't think Surapadman will underestimate us.'

'But what's to stop him from just turning around and sailing back to Magadh?'

'Turning a large fleet of ships around in a river is easier said than done, especially if you're short of time. But even if Surapadman manages that feat and speeds down the river to get to Magadh before us, he'd know that our army is likely to simply stop and never arrive at the gates of his city – and then his own Magadhans could well believe that Surapadman ran away from the battle at Ayodhya using the false pretext of Magadh itself being in danger. A crown prince can't afford to be seen as a coward, so he'll have no choice but to attack us here, exactly where we want him to. What do you think?'

'I like the plan,' said Bhagirath. 'It should work well with a good general like Surapadman. He'll have scouts riding along the riverbanks to keep him informed of what's going on, so we have to be sure to attack those scouts, but allow some of them to escape with information about the size of our army. Also, our camp in the forest stretches for a mile; so when their ships pass our position, we should have soldiers disturb the birds on top of the trees at one end of our camp and "carelessly" leave some fires burning at the other end; Surapadman will assume that there's a massive enemy army marching south along the riverbank and he'd be forced to attack.'

'My thinking exactly.'

'Let's station some devil boats on the western bank as well.'

'But the battle will be fought here on the western bank,' said Kartik, frowning. 'When their men engage us in battle here, any fire coracles on this side of the river would be clearly visible. Devil boats are only effective when they have an element of surprise. If they're visible, they can be easily sunk, which is why I've positioned them on the eastern bank.'

'Think about it for a moment,' said Bhagirath. 'Surapadman will be forced to put his men ashore on the sands of the Bal-Atibal Kund – the forest's far too dense further north on the western bank. So if we keep our coracles up north, they'll still remain hidden from enemy eyes. As soon as his ships anchor to investigate our position, we'll use them to attack the northern end of his convoy.'

'Good point. I'll issue those orders immediately.'

— ⵣ ⴱ Ს ⵜ ⴲ —

Kartik's army was ready and poised for action when they heard the first sounds of a massive navy rowing up the Sarayu. Judging by the dull drumbeats of the timekeepers and the faint sound of the oars moving through the water, Kartik estimated that the Magadhan ships would reach the Bal-Atibal Kund within the next hour or two. The soldiers were ordered to battle stations. Weapons were checked, defences tested.

Kartik walked to the edge of the forest and surveyed the sands of the Bal-Atibal Kund and the river beyond. A crescent moon did little to brighten the darkness and a light seasonal fog had begun to spread along the river, both of which suited his strategy perfectly. With a practised eye, he checked whether the communication pots were still visible in the fog and was pleased with what he saw.

Turning to face Bhagirath, Divodas and the other commanders of the Branga army, Kartik said, 'My friends, unlike my father, I'm not good with words so I'll keep this short. The Magadhans will be fighting only for conquest and glory. Those are weak motivations. You are fighting for vengeance and retribution, for your families and for the soul of your nation. You are fighting to destroy the *Somras* that's killed your children and crippled your people. You are fighting to stop the scourge of this Evil. You have to fight to the bitter end; until they are finished. I don't want prisoners. I want them dead. Anyone who takes the side of Evil forfeits their right to live. Remember the suffering of your children!'

As one, the Branga commanders roared, 'Death to the Magadhans!'

'This land we stand upon,' continued Kartik, 'has been blessed by the feet of Lord Ram. We shall honour him today with blood. *Jai Shri Ram!*'

'*Jai Shri Ram!*'

'To your positions!' ordered Kartik.

The Branga commanders hurried away. As soon as the men were out of earshot, Bhagirath asked Kartik, 'Why do you want them all dead?'

'If we take too many prisoners we'll have to leave behind a large force to guard them. Our eventual purpose is to get as many soldiers as possible to Meluha. If the Magadhan army's decimated, a few thousand of our soldiers will be enough to control the city. Also, by killing all the Magadhans, we send a powerful message to Ayodhya; it might make them reconsider their alliance with Meluha.'

Bhagirath was forced to accept Kartik's brutal but effective logic.

CHAPTER 23

Battle of Bal-Atibal Kund

Kartik's army had heard the low, monotonous drumbeats long before they sighted the Magadhan ships passing the Bal-Atibal Kund.

Kartik motioned for the signal to be relayed from man to man all the way to the southern end of the camp, more than a mile away. A group of soldiers waiting there quietly pulled a rope, releasing a net that had been secured over a flock of birds, which took flight in a great flurry, startled by their unexpected freedom. Kartik detected some movement aboard the Magadhan ships – they'd clearly heard the birds. Straining his eyes in the darkness, he could just make out Magadhan soldiers on deck staring towards the top of their ships' mainmasts.

'Shit!' whispered Bhagirath as he realised the implications, and a small, wry smile of appreciation for a worthy enemy flickered over Kartik's face.

He turned to Divodas, who was standing right behind him,

and whispered, 'Divodas, let our treetop soldiers know that the Magadhans have lookouts stationed in their crows' nests: our men should remain low to avoid detection.'

As Divodas left quietly to carry out his commander's orders, Kartik reflected once again on how cautious Surapadman was, for river vessels rarely had crows' nests.

'Look! They're slowing,' said Bhagirath, pointing towards the ships that had already passed the Kund, although they'd been moving fast enough that at least ten ships passed them before the fleet came to a standstill.

'Now we wait,' said Kartik as Surapadman's men stared hard into the dense forests on the western banks.

— ⁂ —

Bhagirath leaned towards Kartik and whispered, 'Their scout's a short distance behind us, close to the water's edge.'

Kartik stretched his arms and then said out loud to Divodas, 'Check whether their ships have started moving up ahead.'

As Divodas headed towards the river, the scout fell back silently, and Divodas returned mere moments later to report, 'Lord Kartik, their scout's swimming back to one of the ships.'

Kartik rose immediately and crept silently to the bank.

'The attack will begin soon,' said Bhagirath. 'We should fall back to our positions.'

'Let's wait a few moments,' said Kartik. 'I want to see which ship he boards – it'll tell us where Surapadman is.'

'It's been almost half an hour,' said Bhagirath. 'What's he waiting for?'

Kartik and his army remained within the forest, hoping to give Surapadman the impression that the Brangas didn't wish to engage in a battle in the hope he'd be lulled into believing he could launch a surprise attack.

Kartik suddenly exclaimed, 'Son of a bitch!'

'Lord Kartik?' asked Divodas.

'Message the lookouts, quickly,' said Kartik. 'Tell them to find out what's happening on the other side of the river.'

Bhagirath slapped his forehead. 'Oh my God – we told our lookouts to stay low!'

Divodas rushed off, but he was back in no time with worrying news. 'They're mobilising on the other side! Their soldiers are boarding rowing boats even as we speak—'

'That cunning son of a flea-ridden dog!' said Bhagirath. 'He's going to row downriver, hidden by his own ships, and attack us from the south.'

'What do we do, Lord Kartik?' asked Divodas.

'Find out whether the Magadhans are disembarking from their tenth ship – that's where Surapadman is. I suspect he's going to launch a two-pronged attack: he'll want to keep us busy here at the Bal-Atibal Kund, while another contingent comes from the south to flank us, trapping us between two sections of his army.'

'Which means we need to split up,' said Bhagirath. 'One of us will stay here at the Kund, while the other rides out to meet their southern force.'

Divodas ran up and said urgently, 'Lord Kartik, they're disembarking from Surapadman's ship.'

'Prince Bhagirath,' said Kartik, 'you'll lead our main force here. Make sure the Magadhans don't get past Bal-Atibal – I want you to make this a death-trap for them.'

'It will be, Kartik, I promise – but don't leave too many men with me. You'll need a strong force to deal with Surapadman's southern contingent.'

'Trust me, I won't,' said Kartik, 'and remember: he won't have any horses. I will.'

Bhagirath understood immediately what Kartik was thinking: a single mounted cavalry warrior was generally equal to ten foot soldiers, with not only the advantage of height but his horse's fearsome hooves and teeth as well.

As he rose, Kartik ordered Divodas to ride south, to let their men know the Magadhans would be charging soon. 'You'll be leading them,' he said, clapping him on the shoulder. 'I'm going to ride west with two thousand cavalrymen in a giant arc – I intend to attack Surapadman's forces from behind. We'll crush them between my horses and your troops.'

'That we will!' said Divodas with a fierce grin.

'*Har Har Mahadev!*' said Kartik.

'*Har Har Mahadev!*' echoed Divodas, before running to his horse, swinging into the saddle and riding away at speed.

Bhagirath watched Kartik for a moment. The young warrior appeared to be running over all their plans in his mind, not wanting to miss a single detail.

'I've fought many battles, Kartik,' said Bhagirath with an amused look. 'Go and fight yours. Let me take care of mine.'

Kartik smiled. 'We'll gift my father a famous victory.'

'That we shall,' replied Bhagirath, looking at the same steely look in the boy's eyes that he'd seen many times while they'd been hunting, and a familiar combination of fear and fascination entered the prince's heart. He whispered, 'God have mercy on Surapadman . . .'

Kartik chuckled softly. 'He'll have to, because I won't.' Then the young son of the Neelkanth turned his horse and galloped away into the dark.

The slender moon was cloaked in cloud, its faint light hidden in the mist. Bhagirath could barely make out the lines of men amongst the trees, but he could hear the sound of their breath rasping in the darkness and the metallic tang of sweat hung heavy in the air. He felt perspiration beading on his upper lip and trickling into the corner of his mouth. Whispers like a prayer floated back to his ears from up and down the line – '*Har Har Mahadev . . . Har Har Mahadev*' – as the men braced themselves to face Surapadman's army.

Suddenly the moon burst through the clouds and Bhagirath

could see men running up and down the decks of the enemy ships carrying torches, lighting arrows for the archers.

'Shields up!' he shouted and his soldiers, mainly Brangas, jumped to obey as the sky lit up as the archers shot a great volley of fire-arrows into the jungle. Bhagirath had kept his men behind the treeline, which worked well as their first line of defence; the few arrows that got through were easily blocked by the raised shields.

The Magadhans had probably hoped their fire-arrows would set the forest aflame, thought Bhagirath. But instead of sowing chaos and confusion amongst the Brangas, the mist and the night's chill had dampened the whole place and the flames soon fizzled out.

As the last few arrows fell, Bhagirath roared, '*Har Har Mahadev!*' and his soldiers' echoing cry rent the air.

The Magadhans quickly fired another volley, but once again the trees and the Brangas' shields ensured that Bhagirath's men suffered no casualties, and the Brangas let out their war cry once more, taunting their enemies: '*Har Har Mahadev!*'

Then, as the archers drew their bows a third time, Bhagirath spotted rowing boats being lowered from the ships: the attack was about to begin in earnest. He beckoned his aide and said, 'Send a message to launch the devil boats – now!' And, as his aide rushed away, he turned back and watched his enemies rowing towards the Kund as yet another wave of burning arrows arched into the night sky.

'Don't move!' shouted Bhagirath, steadying his men, who were anxious to join battle with their enemies. 'Let them get here first.' He wanted a large contingent of enemy soldiers to land before launching his three-pronged attack from the adjoining forest; that way he'd inflict maximum casualties. An impregnable phalanx of his infantry, standing shoulder to shoulder behind their shields, would advance and push back the frontline Magadhan soldiers, forcing those bringing up the rear into the water, where they'd be weighed down by their weapons and armour and drown, even as the now outnumbered frontline would be decimated.

'Shields!' he ordered once again as he saw more arrows being lit. His gut told him this would be the last volley: enemy soldiers were already jumping off their boats onto the sands of Bal-Atibal and Bhagirath could feel the adrenalin rushing through his veins. He could almost smell the blood that was about to be shed.

'Charge!' he bellowed.

— ☥ ◍ ⋃ ⚶ ✺ ◉ —

'Faster!' Kartik roared as he rode furiously in front of his two-thousand-strong cavalry brigade. He could see the waves of fire-arrows being shot from the Magadhan ships even through the dense foliage; that must mean that the southern contingent of the Magadhan army was in position.

He took a moment to glance back towards the river and saw that the ships at the centre of the Magadhan fleet had already caught fire: the devil boats had struck. Bhagirath's tactics were obviously hurting the Magadhan navy. He was surprised, though, to see the southern end of the fleet also aflame: the Vaishali forces must have arrived and begun to attack the Magadhan navy from the rear.

He could hear a great din up ahead, the sound of fierce battle. The southern contingent of the Magadhans had come up against Divodas' Brangas.

'Ride harder!' he cried as they twisted and turned through the great trees. Parts of the camp were on fire now, but this served as a beacon for Kartik's horsemen as they spurred their steeds onwards. The Brangas at the southern end of Kartik's brigade were hard at work holding almost twenty thousand enemy soldiers at bay, but the Magadhans had expected to decimate an unprepared enemy and they were obviously shocked by the fierce resistance they were facing.

Things are about to get a lot worse for them, Kartik thought with a fierce grin. *They're not expecting danger from behind as well as in front!*

'*Har Har Mahadev!*' he yelled as he drew his long sword.

'*Har Har Mahadev!*' roared the Branga horsemen as they charged.

The last rows of the Magadhan foot soldiers, completely unprepared for a cavalry charge from the rear, were ruthlessly butchered as Kartik's brigade cut a wide swathe through them, horses trampling helpless soldiers underfoot, and chopping down any who tried to stand in their path.

The massive sizes of the rival armies and the brutal din and clamour of a battle well joined meant the cavalry's rear attack initially went unnoticed by the Magadhans further forward. As they overcame their surprise, many brave soldiers leapt at the horsemen, stabbing the beasts and even fearlessly holding on to the stirrups, hoping to bring them down. A clutch of infantrymen targeted Kartik as the leader and tripped his steed, bringing them both down in a crash.

Kartik sprang to his feet with cat-like reflexes, drawing his second sword and slashing at the first of the soldiers pressing towards him. The Magadhan crumpled in mid step and fell silently to the ground, his windpipe severed. A gush of air whistled from his slit throat and splattered blood on those around him. A second soldier charged and was cut down before he'd taken two steps, as a single stroke of Kartik's blade sliced through his torso almost to his spine.

The remaining soldiers, now cautious of this boy who could kill with such ease, spread out around him in a circle, their own swords at the ready. Kartik, expecting them to rush him together, waited for them to make their move.

The charge came, two from the front, one from the back and a fourth from the left, but Kartik crouched and then, with near-inhuman speed, sidestepped to the left and swung fiercely, with all his strength, brutally slicing through limb, sinew, head and trunk. Blood and entrails flew and the swords in his hands were bathed in blood. Without giving the men time to regroup, he selected his next opponent and charged again: Kartik had become Death, the Destroyer of Worlds.

The fighting raged for half an hour as the tide of the battle tipped more and more against the Magadhans, but still they fought on, for Kartik and his men gave no quarter.

Slowly the screams of the dying lessened and finally were silenced as Surapadman's army perished. Soldiers stopped their slaughter and stood quietly amongst the dead, leaning exhausted on their swords and panting. But Kartik never slackened, pressing attack after attack on any who remained standing.

Divodas tried to force himself to run as he approached Kartik, but his legs were weak and trembling and he could scarcely manage more than a stumbling trot. He was covered with blood from a dozen smaller cuts, and a deep gash on his shoulder had left his right arm dangling limply at his side. 'My Lord,' he called out, breathless and hoarse, 'my Lord!'

Kartik was lost in the red mist of battle. He swung viciously, the speed of his movement building formidable momentum in his curved blade, but Divodas managed to get his shield up in time to take the blow, though his hand reverberated with the shock, numbing his left arm to the shoulder.

'*My Lord!*' he pleaded desperately. '*It's me! It's Divodas!*'

Kartik suddenly stopped, his long sword held high in his right hand, his curved blade held low in his left, his breathing laboured, his eyes bulging with bloodlust.

'My Lord!' shrieked Divodas, his fear palpable. 'You've killed them all! Please, stop!'

As Kartik's breathing slowed, he allowed his gaze to take in the scene of destruction all around him. Hacked bodies littered the battlefield. Surapadman's once-proud Magadhan army had been utterly destroyed.

Kartik could feel the adrenalin coursing furiously through his veins.

Divodas, still afraid of Kartik, whispered. 'You've won, my Lord.'

Kartik raised his curved blade high to join his long sword and shouted, '*Har Har Mahadev!*'

All around him, the Brangas roared, '*Har Har Mahadev!*'

Kartik bent down and flipped a Magadhan's decapitated head face-up with his sword, then turned to Divodas. 'Find Surapadman. If there's life left in him, I want him brought to me alive.'

'Yes, my Lord,' said Divodas, still shaking, and rushed to obey.

Kartik wiped both of his swords on the clothing of a fallen Magadhan soldier and carefully re-sheathed the blades in the scabbards tied across his back. The Branga soldiers maintained a respectful distance from him, terrified of the brutal violence they'd just witnessed. He walked slowly towards the river, bent down to scoop some water in his palms and splashed it on his face. The river had turned red with the blood of his enemies. He was covered with gore from head to foot, but his eyes had cleared. The bloodlust had left him.

Later in the day, when the dead would be counted, it would emerge that seventy thousand of the seventy-five-thousand-strong Magadhan army had been butchered, burned or drowned.

Kartik had lost only five thousand of his hundred thousand men. This was no battle. It was a massacre.

Kartik looked up at the sky. The first rays of the sun were breaking on the horizon, heralding a new day, and the birth of a new legend: Kartik, the Lord of War!

CHAPTER 24

The Age of Violence

The golden orb of the rising sun peeked from behind the mainland as a strong southerly wind filled their sails, speeding them towards the port of Lothal. Shiva, with Sati at his side, stood poised on the foredeck, eyes transfixed northwards, wishing their ship would move faster.

'I wonder how the war's going in Swadweep,' said Sati.

Shiva turned to her with a smile. 'We don't know if there's been a war at all, Sati. Maybe Ganesh's tactics have worked.'

'I hope so.'

Shiva held Sati's hand. 'Our sons are warriors. They're doing what they're meant to do – you don't need to worry about them.'

'I'm not worried about Ganesh. I know he'll avoid bloodshed if he can – not that he's a coward, but he understands the ultimate futility of war. But Kartik . . . He loves the art of war. I fear he'll go out of his way to court danger.'

'You're probably right,' said Shiva, 'but you can't change his essential character – and isn't that what being a warrior is all about?'

'But every other warrior goes into battle reluctantly. Kartik's not like that – he fights because he *has* to, because his *swadharma* is war, and that worries me,' said Sati.

Shiva drew Sati into his arms and kissed her lips reassuringly. 'Everything will be all right.'

Sati smiled and rested her head against Shiva's chest. 'I must admit, that helped a bit . . .'

Shiva laughed softly. 'Let me help you some more, then.' He raised her face with his fingertips and kissed her again.

'Ahem!'

Shiva and Sati turned around to find Veerbhadra and Krittika approaching. 'Get a room,' said Veerbhadra, teasingly.

Krittika hit Veerbhadra lightly on his stomach, embarrassed. 'Shut up!'

Shiva smiled. 'How are you, Krittika?'

'Very well, my Lord.'

'Krittika,' said Shiva, 'how many times do I have to tell you? You're my best friend's wife. Please, call me Shiva.'

Krittika smiled shyly. 'I'm sorry. I keep forgetting.'

Shiva rested his hand on Veerbhadra's shoulder. 'What did the captain say, Bhadra? How far do we still have to go?'

'At the rate we're sailing, just a few more days. The winds have been kind.'

'Have you ever been to Lothal or Maika, Krittika?' Shiva asked.

Krittika shook her head. 'It's been difficult for me to get pregnant – and that's the only way an outsider can enter Maika.'

Shiva winced at Krittika's crestfallen expression. He'd unintentionally touched a raw nerve. Veerbhadra didn't care that Krittika couldn't conceive, but it still distressed her.

'I'm sorry,' he started, but Krittika waved his apology away.

'No, no,' she said with a brave smile. 'Veerbhadra's convinced me that we're enough for each other, just the two of us. We don't need a child to complete us.'

Shiva patted Veerbhadra's back. 'Sometimes we barbarians surprise even ourselves with our good sense.'

Krittika laughed softly. 'But I have visited Old Lothal.'

'Old Lothal?'

'Didn't I tell you?' asked Sati. 'The seaport of Lothal is actually a new city. Old Lothal was a river port on the Saraswati, but when the Saraswati stopped reaching the sea, there was no water left around the old city, ending its usefulness as a port. The locals decided to recreate their hometown next to the sea, so the new Lothal is exactly like the old city, except that it's a seaport rather than a river port.'

'Interesting,' said Shiva. 'So what happened to Old Lothal?'

'It's practically abandoned, but a few people continue to live there.'

'So why didn't they give the new city a different name? Why call it Lothal?'

'The old citizens were very attached to their city. It was one of the greatest cities of the empire, and they didn't want the name to disappear in the sands of time. They also assumed most people would quickly forget Old Lothal.'

Shiva looked towards the sea. 'New Lothal, here we come!'

By the third hour of the second *prahar* the sun had risen high over the Bal-Atibal Kund. The bodies of the fallen Magadhans and Brangas were being removed to a cleared area in the forest for cremation, accompanied by the drone of ritual chanting. The massive number of Magadhan dead made this back-breaking work, but Kartik had been insistent: valour begot respect, whether in life or in the aftermath of death.

'Has Surapadman not been found yet?' asked Bhagirath, his eyes scanning the sands of the Kund. Yesterday they'd been pristine white. Today they were a pale shade of pink, discoloured by the massive quantities of blood.

'Not yet,' said Kartik. 'At first I thought he was fighting on the southern front, but when we didn't find him there, I assumed he'd be here.' He turned to the Vaishali king and asked, 'How far off is my brother's fleet, King Maatali?'

Maatali had proved his naval acumen by destroying the rearguard of the Magadhan fleet. Tales of Kartik's valour and ferocity made him look at the boy with newfound respect. Gone were the last traces of indulgence for the Neelkanth's son.

'I've sent some of my rowing boats upriver to find out, but the water's clogged with the debris of the Magadhan ships. Our boats are trying to clear up the mess, but in the meantime

Lord Ganesh is moving carefully so our fleet doesn't sustain any damage. It'll be a while before they get here.'

Kartik nodded his approval of Ganesh's caution.

'But he's been informed of your great victory, Lord Kartik,' said Maatali. 'He's very proud of you.'

Kartik frowned. 'It's not *my* victory, your Majesty: it's *our* victory. And it wouldn't have been possible without my elder brother, who destroyed the northern end of the Magadhan navy.'

'That he did,' said Maatali.

'My Lord!' Divodas called as he crossed the sands of the Bal-Atibal Kund from the dense forest. He was still weak from his injuries and his shoulder was heavily bandaged. Five men were helping him to drag something.

It took Kartik a moment to realise what was trussed up in the ropes. 'Divodas! Treat him with respect!'

Divodas stopped immediately as Kartik ran towards him, closely followed by Bhagirath and Maatali. The corpse they'd been dragging was that of a tall, well-built, swarthy man. His clothes and armour were soaked dark with blood and his body was covered with wounds, some dried and black, others still fresh, red and wet. His skull had been split open near his temple, obviously the killing blow. His injuries were too numerous to be counted, clearly indicating this combatant's valour. All the wounds were on his front, not a single one on his back. His had been an honourable death.

'Surapadman . . .' whispered Bhagirath.

'He was on the southern front, my Lord,' said Divodas.

Kartik pulled out his knife, bent down to cut the ropes tied around Surapadman's shoulders and then gently lowered the fallen prince back onto the ground. He noticed Surapadman's right hand was still tightly gripping his blood-caked sword.

Divodas started trying to prise open Surapadman's fingers, but Kartik stopped him. 'Prince Surapadman will carry his sword into the other world,' he commanded, and Divodas immediately withdrew his hand and fell back.

The Magadh prince's mouth was half open and Kartik gently closed it, lest an evil spirit enter the soulless body.

'Find the chief Brahmin,' said Kartik, 'and prepare Surapadman's body for the funeral pyre. He shall be cremated like the prince he was.' As Divodas left to do his bidding, Kartik turned to Bhagirath. 'We'll wait until my brother returns, then Surapadman will be cremated with full state honours.'

— ⚶ Ꝋ Ư ⚷ ✴ —

Ganesh stood on the ramparts of the Magadhan fort, watching the great Sarayu merge into the mighty Ganga. The setting sun had tinged the waters a brilliant orange. King Mahendra and the citizens of Magadh, stunned by the complete annihilation of their huge army and the death of Prince Surapadman, had surrendered meekly when Ganesh's forces entered the city. He hadn't expected much resistance, for there were almost no soldiers left in Magadh. The war in Swadweep had gone exactly according to Ganesh's plan and he could now blockade the Ayodhyan army's movements with far fewer soldiers than would have been required to besiege Ayodhya itself. He planned to leave a small force of ten thousand men to man the fort and stop any Ayodhyan ships attempting to pass by while he took the rest to meet up with Shiva's army in Meluha. They would leave the next day.

'What are you thinking, *dada*?' asked Kartik.

Ganesh smiled at his brother as he pointed towards the confluence of the two rivers. 'Look at the *sangam*, where the Sarayu meets the Ganga.'

Kartik could hear the swirling waters even before he turned to watch the young, impetuous Sarayu crashing into the mature, tranquil Ganga, jostling for space between her banks. The Ganga's mighty current easily pushed aside the waters of the Sarayu, creating eddies and currents in its wake. And then Ganga, the eternal mother, drew the ebullient tributary into her bosom and the two rivers flowed on peacefully as one.

'There's always unity at the end,' said Ganesh, 'and it brings a new tranquillity. But the meeting of two worlds causes a lot of temporary chaos.'

Kartik smiled, but Ganesh could see he was bemused by this notion.

'This confrontation couldn't have been avoided,' said Ganesh, 'but King Mahendra's stricken visage was heartbreaking. Every single house in Magadh has lost a son or a daughter in the Battle of Bal-Atibal.'

'But King Mahendra was the one who forced Prince Surapadman to attack, so he only has himself to blame,' said Kartik. 'People are saying Prince Surapadman would have preferred to remain neutral—'

'That may be true, Kartik, but it still doesn't change the fact that we've killed half the adult population of Magadh.'

'We had no choice, *dada*,' said Kartik.

'I know that,' said Ganesh, turning back to look at the *sangam* of the Ganga and the Sarayu. 'The rivers fight with each other using the only currency they know: water. We humans fight using the only currency we know in this age: violence.'

'But how else does one fight for one's beliefs?' asked Kartik. 'There are times when reason doesn't work, when peaceful efforts don't work. Violence is the last resort. This is the way it's always been. Perhaps the world will never be any different.'

Ganesh shook his head. 'It will be, one day. We live in the age of the Kshatriya and that's why we think the only way to effect change is with violence.'

'The age of the Kshatriya? I've never heard of that.'

'Have you heard of the four *yugs*? Time travels through the cyclical eras – the *Sat yug*, the *Treta yug*, the *Dwapar yug* and the *Kali yug* – in a never-ending loop.' At Kartik's nod, he went on, 'Within each of these *yugs* are smaller cycles dominated by different caste-professions: the age of the Brahmin, of the Kshatriya, of the Vaishya and of the Shudra.'

'The age of the Brahmin, *dada*? I haven't heard of that, either.'

'Sure you have – all of us have been told stories of the Prajapati, of a time of magic.'

Kartik smiled. 'Of course! Knowledge seems like magic to the ignorant.'

'Absolutely. So the main currency of the age of the Brahmin was knowledge. And in our age – the age of the Kshatrya – it's violence. Some philosophers believe that our epoch will be followed by the age of the Vaishya.'

'And the people of that age won't use violence to establish their way of life?'

'Violence will never die, Kartik, and neither will knowledge. But they won't be the determining factors in an age dominated by the way of the Vaishya, which is governed by profit. They'll use money.'

'I can't imagine a world like that!'

'It will come, and I pray it comes soon – not that I'm afraid of violence, but it leaves too many grieving hearts in its wake.'

'*Dada*, even if I can believe that such a time will come, are you saying that money will cause less devastation than violence? Won't there be winners and losers even then? Will sadness disappear?'

Ganesh raised his eyebrows, surprised. He smiled and patted his brother's back. 'You're right. There will always be winners and losers, for that's the way of the world. But that still doesn't lessen the grief of knowing that we've caused others to suffer.'

'This may sound strange to you,' said Shiva, reclining in the comfort of the Lothal governor's residence, 'but I feel as if I've come home. Meluha's where my journey began.'

Just as Kali had expected, Chenardhwaj, Governor of Lothal, had broken ranks with the Meluhan nobility and opened the gates of his city for Shiva's army, pledging loyalty to the Neelkanth.

'And this is where it'll end,' said Sati. 'Then we can all go and live in Kailash.'

Shiva smiled. 'Kailash isn't as idyllic as you imagine. It's a difficult, barren land.'

'But you'll be there, which will make it heaven for me.'

Shiva laughed and kissed his wife lovingly, holding her close.

Sati savoured the kiss, then pulled back a little and said, 'But first, we need to deal with those who defend the evil *Somras*.'

'That's already begun with the defeat of the Magadhans.'

'That's true. Now that Magadh's firmly under our control we can easily blockade the Ayodhyan navy. Ganesh and Kartik have left for Meluha – when do we leave for Mrittikavati?'

'In a few days.'

Sati had learned to recognise the resolute expression Shiva now wore and couldn't help feeling a twinge of anxiety for her homeland. 'For their own sake, I hope they surrender.'

'I hope so, too.'

CHAPTER 25

God or Country?

'By the great Lord Brahma!' growled Bhrigu as he finally reached Devagiri. He'd been delayed on the recently built road between Dharmakhet in Swadweep and Meluha by the floodwaters of the overflowing Yamuna, which had submerged the pathway and transformed what should have been a quick journey of a few weeks into an exhausting trek of many months. While he was stuck in this no-man's-land between the Chandravanshi and Suryavanshi Empires, Bhrigu availed himself of the facilities of the travellers' guest-house built alongside the road by the Meluhans – though its comforts did little to calm him, for he needed to be in Devagiri as soon as possible.

What did alleviate his stress a little was the arrival of General Parvateshwar and Anandmayi, and as the three of them travelled onwards together the maharishi used the opportunity to discuss battle strategy with the general.

Now Bhrigu, Daksha, Parvateshwar and Kanakhala gathered

in the private royal office of Devagiri to debate the ramifications of the Neelkanth's proclamation.

'May I see the notice, Maharishiji?' asked Parvateshwar.

Bhrigu handed over the stone tablet, then asked, 'When were they put up?'

'A few months ago, my Lord,' said Daksha.

'At every major temple in practically every city within the empire,' added the prime minister.

'And was this a simultaneous event?' asked Parvateshwar, impressed by the logistical feat.

'Yes,' said Kanakhala. 'Only the Neelkanth could have organised this. But why would he do it? He loves Meluha and we worship him, so we assumed that someone who wanted to slander our Lord's reputation must have done it. Sadly, we still haven't made any headway in our investigation. We have yet to discover who the real perpetrators are.'

'Do you have traitors in your administration, your Majesty?' asked Bhrigu.

The emperor bristled, but didn't dare make his anger apparent. 'Certainly not, my Lord. You can trust the Meluhans like you trust me.'

Bhrigu's ironic smile pulled no punches. 'What do you make of it, Lord Parvateshwar?'

'I'd have expected nothing less from the Neelkanth,' said Parvateshwar.

Kanakhala was stunned by this revelation, but prudently decided to remain silent.

'But I must tell you that we responded efficiently, my Lord Bhrigu,' said Daksha. 'They were all removed within a few days and replaced with official notices stating that the others had been posted by a fraud and shouldn't be believed.'

Kanakhala reeled in shock, realising she'd inadvertently sinned; when she put up Daksha's new notices she'd become party to a lie. For a moment she considered resigning, but of course she could not. It was obvious that a war was imminent, and her wartime duties were clear: complete and unquestioning loyalty to king and country. But she'd never before faced a situation where her duties conflicted with her *dharma* . . .

'So you see, my Lord,' Daksha continued, 'this particular problem has been handled. Now we need to focus on how to repel Shiva's forces.'

'Not now, your Majesty,' said Bhrigu, gesturing for Daksha to leave his presence. 'Let me first confer with General Parvateshwar in private.'

'The proclamation *was* made by the Lord Neelkanth,' said Kanakhala. 'How can we go against his word? This is wrong. If the Lord says that the *Somras* isn't to be used, then I don't see how we can disobey him.'

Parvateshwar, realising Kanakhala was profoundly disturbed by the morning's events, had gone to her office after his meeting with Bhrigu.

'I've already stopped using the *Somras*, Kanakhala,' he said.

'As will I, from this moment on – but that's not what's troubling me. The Neelkanth wants the whole of Meluha to stop using the *Somras*, and the consequences of ignoring his ruling are made very clear in his message: if we keep using the *Somras*, we become his enemies.'

'I'm aware of that. For all practical purposes, war's already been declared. His army is mobilising even as we speak.'

'Meluha must stop using the *Somras*.'

'Does the law allow either of us to issue an order banning the *Somras*?'

'No – only the emperor can do that.'

'And he hasn't, has he? And the emperor's orders are never to be questioned in times of war.'

'Is there no way to avoid a war? Why don't you speak to Maharishi Bhrigu? He respects you.'

'The maharishi isn't convinced that the *Somras* has become evil.'

'Then we should approach the people directly.'

'Kanakhala, you know better than that. That would mean breaking your oath as prime minister, since you'd be going directly against your emperor's order.'

'But why should I follow his orders? He made me lie to our own people!'

'I assure you that nothing like that will happen again for as long as I'm alive and in Meluha.'

Kanakhala looked away as she struggled to get a grip on her raging emotions.

'Kanakhala, say we do approach the Meluhans directly,' said Parvateshwar. 'We'll have to convince our countrymen to voluntarily choose to cut their lives short, and we have nothing to give them in return. Convincing people to do this will be no easy task, even people as duty-bound and honourable as the Meluhans. It'll take time. But the Neelkanth has no patience when it comes to the *Somras*. He wants its use to end right now and the only way he can do that is by attacking the place where it's manufactured.'

'Which is Meluha . . .'

'Exactly. So right now our task is to protect our country. Lord Ram's laws are very clear: our primary duty is towards our country – he himself said that, even if it comes to choosing between Lord Ram and Meluha, we should choose Meluha.'

'Who would have imagined that it'd *actually* come down to such a choice, Parvateshwar? That we would need to choose between our god and our country?'

Parvateshwar smiled sadly. 'My duty to my country is above all others, Kanakhala.'

Kanakhala ran her hand over her bald pate and touched the knotted tuft of hair at the back of her head, trying to draw strength from it. 'What kind of challenge is fate throwing at us?'

— ♈ ⦿U♈⊛ —

'It's a stupid idea, your Majesty,' said Bhrigu. 'Your problem is that you never look beyond the next three months when you dream up your strategies.'

Daksha had been sitting expectantly at the maharishi's feet, eagerly awaiting his praise for the 'brilliant' scheme he'd come up with to avoid the war altogether.

Unmoved by the look of horror on Daksha's face, Bhrigu leaned towards him from his stone bed. 'We're not fighting the Neelkanth but, rather, the devotion he inspires in your people. Making him a martyr will turn your people against you and the *Somras*.'

Daksha acknowledged Bhrigu's logic with a resigned nod. 'You're right, my Lord. Had we succeeded in killing him in Panchavati, the people would have blamed the Nagas. The failure of that enterprise was most unfortunate.'

'You should also bear in mind, your Majesty, that while it's not considered unethical to attack an unprepared enemy, some codes simply can't be broken, like killing a peace ambassador or a messenger, not even in times of war.'

'Of course, my Lord.' In spite of the maharishi's criticism, his mind was already working on refinements to his plan.

'Are you listening to me, your Majesty?' asked Bhrigu, irritated by Daksha's distracted demeanour.

Chastened, the emperor looked up immediately. 'Of course I am, my Lord.'

Bhrigu sighed and waved his hand, dismissing the tiresome man from his chamber.

Parvateshwar strode into his house and nodded at the attendant as he ran up the steps that skirted the central courtyard. As he headed across the first floor, he suddenly remembered something. He leaned over the balustrade to look into the central courtyard below and called, 'Rati!'

'Yes, my Lord?' replied the attendant.

'Isn't this the day Lady Anandmayi bathes in milk and rose petals?' he asked.

'Yes, my Lord, the day of the sun, and warm water every other day.'

Parvateshwar smiled. 'So is her bath ready?'

Rati smiled indulgently. She'd served Parvateshwar her entire life, but she had never seen him as happy as he'd been the last few days, ever since he'd returned with the new mistress. 'It'll be ready any moment now, my Lord.'

'Be sure to inform the lady as soon as it's ready.'

'Yes, my Lord.'

Parvateshwar turned and ran up the remaining two flights of stairs to his private chamber on the top floor, where he found Anandmayi relaxing on the balcony in a comfortable chair, observing the goings-on in the street below. A cloth canopy screened her from the evening sun.

She turned around when she heard Parvateshwar rush in. 'What's the hurry?' she asked, with a warm smile.

Parvateshwar stopped and gazed at her. 'I'm just keen to know how you're doing.'

Anandmayi beckoned him to her and he sat down on the

armrest of her chair. She rested her head on his arm as she continued to study the street below. The markets were still open, but unlike the loud and garrulous Chandravanshis, the citizens of Devagiri were achingly polite. The road, the houses, the people – everything reflected the prized Suryavanshi values of sobriety, dignity and uniformity.

'What do you think of our capital?' asked Parvateshwar. 'Isn't it astonishingly well planned and orderly?'

Anandmayi tapped his arm playfully and said, 'It's heartbreakingly lacklustre and colourless.'

Parvateshwar laughed. 'You're perfectly capable of adding more colour to this city than it can handle!'

Anandmayi placed her hand on Parvateshwar's as she remarked, 'So, this is the land where I will die . . .'

Parvateshwar turned his hand and held hers, palm to palm, in reply.

'Any news?' she asked. 'Has the Lord entered Meluhan territory?'

'No reports as yet,' said Parvateshwar. 'What's truly worrying is the absence of bird couriers from Ayodhya.'

Anandmayi straightened up, frowning with concern. 'Has Ayodhya been conquered?'

'I don't know, darling. But I don't think the Lord has enough men to conquer the city: it has seven circular walls, although they're not well designed, but that's a formidable defence, even if the soldiers are inadequately trained.'

Anandmayi narrowed her eyes in irritation. 'They may be

poorly led, Parvateshwar, but the soldiers are brave men. My country's generals might be idiots, but the commoners will fight for their homeland to their dying breath.'

'Which only strengthens my argument that the Lord Neelkanth couldn't have conquered Ayodhya with only a hundred and fifty thousand Brangan and Vaishali soldiers.'

'So what do you think has happened?'

'Clearly, Meluhan interests aren't being served in Ayodhya. One possibility is that King Dilipa has allied with the Neelkanth.'

'Impossible! My father's too much in love with himself. Lord Bhrigu's medicines are keeping him alive – he won't risk losing his supply for anything.'

'The people of Ayodhya may have rebelled against their king and thrown in their lot with the Neelkanth.'

'Hmmm. That's possible. My people are certainly more devoted to the Neelkanth than to my father.'

'And if the Neelkanth has Ayodhya under his control, he'll soon turn his attention to his main objective: Meluha.'

'His aim is to destroy the *Somras*, Parva – he won't indulge in wanton destruction. Why would he do that? It would turn your people against him. He'll only go after the *Somras*.'

Parvateshwar's eyes flashed wide. 'Of course! He'll target the secret *Somras*-manufacturing facility and its scientists – that will end the supply of the *Somras* and people will have no choice but to learn to live without it.'

'There you are, then – that's his target. So where *is* this secret *Somras*-manufacturing facility?'

'I don't know. But I'll find out.'

'Yes, you should.'

'In any case,' said Parvateshwar, 'I've told Kanakhala not to send any more messages to Ayodhya. We could just be passing on information to the enemy.'

'If Ayodhya's already taken and they leave now, they could be in Meluha soon.'

'In as little as six months. With Ayodhya on his side, the Lord will have a massive army indeed.'

'Then you must redouble your preparations.'

'Yes . . . I'll also order Vidyunmali to leave for Lothal with twenty thousand soldiers.'

'Lothal? Just because they didn't send you their monthly report? Isn't that a bit of an overreaction?'

'I don't have a good feeling,' Parvateshwar admitted, slowly shaking his head. 'They didn't respond to my bird courier.'

'Can you afford to send twenty thousand soldiers away based on a hunch?'

'Lothal isn't too far away. It's also a border town – it's the closest Meluhan city to Panchavati. It might not be such a bad idea to reinforce it.'

CHAPTER 26

Battle of Mrittikavati

The exhausted scout stumbled into the tent, barely able to conceal his anxiety. Shiva jerked his head up from the map he'd been poring over as the soldier managed a hasty salute. 'What?'

His sharp tone made Kali, Sati, Gopal and Chenardhwaj look up too, and worry creased their faces. Shiva's army had marched in quickly from Lothal and was now just a day away from Mrittikavati.

'My Lord, I have bad news.'

'Just give me the facts. Don't jump to conclusions.'

'Mrittikavati is much better defended now than it was earlier. Brigadier Vidyunmali sailed into the city a few days back — apparently, he was on his way to Lothal to strengthen Meluha's defences at the border, but instead he's remained in Mrittikavati. Clearly Emperor Daksha has no idea yet that Lothal's pledged loyalty to you, my Lord.'

'How many men does Vidyunmali have?' asked Chenardhwaj.

'Around twenty thousand, my Lord, in addition to the five thousand soldiers already stationed there.'

'We still have a substantial advantage in terms of numbers, my Lord,' said Chenardhwaj, 'but Mrittikavati's defences might enable even twenty-five thousand men to mount a significant challenge.'

Shiva thought for a moment, then said, 'I don't think that should be a problem. It doesn't matter how many soldiers they have – we only want to commandeer their ships, not conquer their city. And if Vidyunmali's just arrived with twenty thousand soldiers, his transport ships will also be in the port, right? So there are even more ships for us to capture now.'

Kali smiled. 'That's true!'

'Prepare to march,' said Shiva. 'We attack in two days.'

— ⟨ symbols ⟩ —

Shiva watched the panic-stricken people rush back into Mrittikavati as the warning conches were blown repeatedly from the ramparts. The unexpected appearance of a massive enemy force had – understandably – shocked the Meluhans.

From horseback atop a nearby hill, he had a clear view over Mrittikavati. Like most Meluhan cities, it had been built on a massive platform half a mile away from the Saraswati as a protection against floods. But it was the port that fascinated him.

The circular harbour was vast, with only a single narrow opening to the great river. A pool of water separated the semi-circular dock from the outer ring of the port, while a dome-covered inner dock protected the shipyards. There were mooring points along the outer side of the inner dock and the inner side of the outer pier, an ingenious design that could accommodate some fifty vessels in a relatively small space. The expanse of water between the two semicircles of boats allowed for free movement of the vessels, which could move fairly quickly in single file within the harbour.

The harbour had been designed for effective defence from river attacks: not only would the gate allow only one vessel in or out at a time, but Shiva could also see the numerous fortified positions around the walls. *Typically foolproof Meluhan planning,* he thought with a smile.

Kali leaned across and said, 'The pathway between the city and the port may be a weakness.'

'I agree,' said Sati. 'Let's attack there. If the pathway's walls are breached, they'll be forced to choose between securing the port or the city. I suspect they'll withdraw their soldiers into the city and sacrifice the port.'

Shiva looked at Sati speculatively. 'Vidyunmali's aggressive – he doesn't like to make compromises. Once he realises we're after their ships rather than the city, he may take a gamble and mount a rearguard assault on our attacking forces in the hope that he can rout us on the pathway and thus save both the port and the city. I hope he does make that mistake!'

— ☥ ⺽U☥⟡ —

Shiva rode up and down, surveying the battalions of Brangas, Vasudevs, Nagas and a squadron of Suryavanshis from Lothal. Sati and Kali were also on horseback, leading their sections of the army. The soldiers were ready, but they knew that the Meluhans were well fortified.

'Soldiers!' roared Shiva. 'Mahadevs! *Hear me!*'

Silence descended on the men as Shiva cried, 'We're told that a great man walked this earth a thousand years ago: Lord Ram, Maryada Purushottam, the most celebrated king amongst kings. But we know the truth! He was more than a man! He was a god!'

The soldiers listened in pin-drop silence.

'These people,' said Shiva, pointing to the Meluhans stationed on Mrittikavati's walls, 'only remember his name. They don't remember his *words*. But I remember the words of Lord Ram. I remember that he said, "If you have to choose between my people and *dharma*, choose *dharma*! If you have to choose between my family and *dharma*, choose *dharma*! Even if you have to choose between me and *dharma*, always choose *dharma*!"'

'*Dharma!*' bellowed the army with a single voice.

'The Meluhans have chosen Evil,' bellowed Shiva. 'We choose *dharma*!'

'*Dharma!*'

'They have chosen death! We choose victory!'

'Victory!'

'They have chosen the *Somras*!' roared Shiva. 'We choose Lord Ram!'

'*Jai Shri Ram!*' shouted Sati.

'*Jai Shri Ram!*' Kali joined the war cry.

'*Jai Shri Ram!*' shouted the soldiers.

'*Jai Shri Ram!*'

'*Jai Shri Ram!*'

The familiar cry from the Neelkanth's army reverberated within the walls of Mrittikavati. The cry that had once rallied the Meluhans for battle this time filled them with fear.

Surrounded by his shouting warriors, Shiva turned to Kali and nodded at her. A small, cold smile curved her lips and she nodded back, her eyes glittering, and swung her sword so it flashed in the sun. Then she raised a single hand to the soldiers behind her and a wave of silence rolled out across the army until all that could be heard was the wind snapping the banners flying above their heads. She signalled again and the men tensed and readied their weapons. Then she raised one sword and pointed towards the sky. With a blood-curdling scream she brought her blade forwards to unleash a roaring tide of men at the walls.

Shiva observed the battle raging on the fortified pathway. Kali had concentrated the Vasudev elephants and makeshift catapults in one place with the aim of breaching a small section of the wall. A few exceptionally brave Naga soldiers fought against daunting odds as the Meluhans fired arrows at them and poured boiling oil from the battlements lining the pathway. The Nagas, famed for their superhuman courage, were ideal for this battle of attrition and small breaches began to open up along the pathway's walls. Shiva's soldiers would soon be able to flood through and block the city's access to its port.

This triggered exactly the reaction Shiva had expected from Vidyunmali: the main gates of Mrittikavati were thrown open and the Meluhans marched out, arranged in the tortoise formation they'd learned from Shiva himself: squares of twenty by twenty men, each covering the left half of his own body and the right half of the soldier to the left of him with his shield while the soldier behind used his shield as a lid to cover himself and the soldier in front. Each warrior extended his spear through the space between his own shield and the one next to him.

The tortoise formation had been created by Shiva, and he knew the one weakness: if they were attacked from behind, there was little the soldiers could do to defend themselves. There was no protection of any kind at the back, and being weighed down by their shields and armour and with their heavy spears pointing forwards made it difficult for them to turn around quickly.

Shiva turned towards Sati with a smile. 'Vidyunmali is so predictable.'

Sati grinned back. 'To formation?'

'To formation,' he agreed and she immediately turned and rode out to the right, quickly leading her unit towards the pathway wall, where she started deploying her troops between the Meluhan tortoises emerging from the city gates and Kali's brave Nagas, who were attacking the fortified pathway behind her. Her task was to first fight hard and then begin to retreat slowly, giving the Meluhans a false sense of imminent victory that would keep them marching forwards.

She knew her men were in for a tough battle, one that would result in heavy casualties, as they would be right in front of the unstoppable tortoise formations. But as the Meluhans moved ahead, space would open up behind them, allowing Shiva's cavalry to get in and attack them from the rear.

'Steady,' called Shiva to the Vasudev brigadier as he rode towards the elephant corps and the cavalry. They would have to move quickly once the gap had opened, but it had to be at the right time. If he charged too early, Vidyunmali would smell the trap.

As Veerbhadra saw the Meluhan tortoises charge into Sati's troops, he turned to Shiva, a worried expression clouding his face. 'The task is too difficult for Sati. We should—'

'Stay focused, Bhadra,' said Shiva. 'She knows what she's doing.'

The Meluhans were bearing down hard on Sati's soldiers. In the best traditions of Suryavanshi warfare, Sati was leading from the front and she could see the wall of shields moving steadily towards her at a slow, jostling run, a forest of spears bristling out of every crevice. The sun bounced off the polished metal with every thudding step they took. She breathed out slowly and urged her horse from a smooth canter into a gallop, holding herself ready for her moment.

As she came closer and closer, her eyes were searching for a gap. For a moment a shield shifted slightly out of alignment as the Meluhans ran, exposing a soldier's neck, and without shifting in her seat, Sati drew a knife and flung it with deadly accuracy, striking home and felling the soldier mid step.

The tortoise was almost upon her and she pulled hard on the reins. Her horse reared up as she tried to turn and she felt a sharp pain in her shoulder. She heard her horse neighing desperately as it faltered beneath her and, though she herself was gasping in pain from the spear thrust, Sati tried to kick free from her dying mount as it collapsed to its knees. She looked up to see which soldier had stabbed her, but she couldn't make out which pair of eyes, peering over the shields, belonged to the soldier whose spear was now buried in her shoulder. As the spear pierced deeper, she couldn't stop herself from crying out, as much in anger as in pain. With tears springing to her eyes, she swung her sword violently, hacking off the spear shaft, as she rolled off the horse and onto her feet.

A few arrows flew past her, striking more soldiers in the tortoise through the gap she'd just created, and for a moment the Meluhan charge slowed and faltered, the shield line crumbling slightly until replacement soldiers had struggled forward and sealed the breach with admirable swiftness. As the Meluhans quickly re-formed and resumed their charge, Sati stepped back a pace and so did her troops, almost as if they were in lockstep with her, then they fought on bravely, continuing to withdraw gradually, almost imperceptibly, as though they were being forced back by the unstoppable tortoise corps.

Just a few more minutes of slow retreat, Sati thought, *and the Meluhans will have marched forward far enough for Shiva to ride out behind them and destroy them!*

— ⚹ ⍉⎍⏚ ⊕ —

Shiva was paying close attention to the Meluhan chariots on either side of the tortoise formations which were protecting their flanks. Each vehicle carried a charioteer to steer the horses and a warrior to engage in combat. The two-man teams combined frightening speed and brutal force – and they might just succeed in stalling Shiva's cavalry.

'I want your elephants to take out those chariots – *now*,' he ordered the Vasudev brigadier, who quickly relayed the orders to his *mahouts*.

As the elephants charged out at a fearsome pace, the ground rumbling beneath them, the Meluhan warriors aboard the chariots confidently observed their approach. They took the reins from the charioteers, who in turn pulled out drums – the Meluhans well remembered former battles against Chandravanshi elephants and knew that loud drums always disturbed the giant animals, making them run amok and often crushing their own army.

But much to the shock of the Meluhan charioteers, the elephants continued their charge, completely unperturbed by the frantic drumming.

Seeing their normal tactic fail, the charioteers immediately abandoned the drums and took up the reins again while the warriors pulled out their spears and readied themselves for battle. The Meluhan chariots moved quickly as the Vasudev elephants drew near, weaving around the pachyderms as they charged, throwing their spears at the giant beasts, hoping to injure or at least slow them down – but the elephants were prepared, and, expertly swinging their massive metal balls, they smashed through horses, chariots and soldiers with ease. Some of the Meluhans were fortunate enough to die instantly, but others were left suffering in agony.

And the Vasudevs had a second surprise in store for the Meluhan charioteers. All of a sudden, fire spewed out of the elephants' *howdahs* as the mahouts deployed the fearsome flame-throwers. Any Meluhan chariots that escaped the conflagration were stamped out of existence under massive elephant feet: they were no match for the Vasudev elephants.

Shiva drew his sword and held it high. Turning to his cavalry, he shouted over the din, 'Ride hard into the rear of those formations! Charge them! *Destroy them!*'

Even as Shiva's cavalry thundered out, Sati was still playing her part perfectly. Her soldiers had been moving back, step by step, drawing the Meluhans further and further into the open, exposing a massive breach between the rear of their tortoise formations and the fort walls. In order to keep the Meluhans engaged in battle, Sati's soldiers weren't running away in haste but continuing to fight, taking many casualties in the process.

Sati herself now had serious injuries to both shoulder and thigh, but she battled on. She knew she couldn't afford to fail; her troops' success in their task was crucial to their overall victory.

Shiva's cavalry rode hard in a great arc around the main battle lines. The Vasudev elephants had decimated the Meluhan chariots on his right, leaving them with no defence against the new threat from his cavalry. As he reached the unprotected rear of the Meluhan tortoise formations, he thundered, '*Jai Shri Ram!*'

'*Har Har Mahadev!*' bellowed his cavalry, kicking their horses hard, and the three thousand soldiers charged into the Meluhans. Locked into their tortoise formations and weighed down, they were unable to turn and, within moments of this brutal attack, the Meluhan formations started to disintegrate, some surrendering, others simply running away. By the time Vidyunmali, fighting at the head of his army, received the news of the decimation of his troops at his rear, it was already too late: the Meluhans had been outflanked and defeated.

CHAPTER 27

The Neelkanth Speaks

The survivors had been disarmed and chained together in groups, and the chains fixed to stakes buried deep in the ground. The prisoners were surrounded by four divisions of Shiva's finest, and escape was impossible. Ayurvati had commandeered the outer port area and created a temporary hospital where the injured, Meluhans and those from Shiva's armies alike, were being treated.

Shiva squatted next to a low bed where Sati was recovering after field-surgery. The wound on her shoulder would soon heal, but the thigh injury would take some time. Kali and Gopal stood at a distance.

'I'm all right,' said Sati, pushing Shiva away. 'Go to Mritti-kavati. You need to take control of the city quickly. They need to see you — you need to calm them down. We don't want skirmishes breaking out between the citizens of Mrittikavati and our army.'

'I know, I know – I'm going,' said Shiva. 'I just needed to check on you first.'

Sati smiled and pushed him again. 'I'm fine! I won't die that easily. Now go!'

'*Didi*'s right,' said Kali, 'we need to stage a flag march through the city to let them know who's in charge now.'

Shiva, surprised, turned around. 'We're not taking our army into the city.'

Kali threw up her hands in exasperation. 'Then why did we conquer it?'

'We haven't conquered the city – we've only defeated their army. We need to get the citizens of Mrittikavati on our side so we'll be free to sail out of here with our entire army. We have ten thousand Meluhan prisoners of war – do you want to commit our soldiers to guarding them? If Mrittikavati comes over to our side, we can keep the Meluhan army imprisoned in the city itself.'

'They're not going to do that, Shiva. If they see any weakness in us, they'll sense an opportunity to rebel.'

'It's not weakness, Kali, but compassion. People usually know the difference.'

'You've got to be joking! How in God's name are you going to convince them of your compassion after massacring their army?'

'I'll do it by not marching into the city with my troops – I'll take only Bhadra, Nandi and Parshuram. And I'll speak to the citizens myself.'

'How will that help?'

'Believe me, it will.'

'You've just destroyed their army, Shiva! I don't think they'll be interested in listening to anything you have to say.'

'They will – I'm their Neelkanth.'

Kali could barely contain her irritation. 'At least let me accompany you with some Naga soldiers. You may need protection—'

'No.'

'Shiva—'

'Do you trust me?'

'What does that have to—?'

'Kali, do you trust me?'

'Of course I do.'

'Then let me handle this,' he said firmly before turning to Sati. 'I'll be back soon, darling.'

Sati smiled and touched Shiva's hand.

'Go with Lord Ram, my friend,' said Gopal as Shiva rose and turned to leave.

Shiva smiled. 'He's always with me.'

— ⭥ ◎ Ⓤ ⭧ ◉ —

The collective buzz of a thousand voices hovered over the central square as the citizens of Mrittikavati came in droves for a glimpse of their Neelkanth. News of his presence in the city had spread like wildfire.

Was it the Neelkanth *who attacked us?*

Why would he attack us?

We're his people! He's our god!

Was it really him who banned the Somras and not a fraud Neelkanth after all? Did our emperor lie to us? No, that can't be true . . .

Shiva stood tall on the stone podium, surveying the milling, excitable crowd, his blue throat – the *neel kanth* – uncovered and clearly visible to all. Nandi, Veerbhadra and Parshuram, unarmed as ordered, stood apprehensively behind him.

'Citizens of Mrittikavati,' thundered Shiva, 'I am your Neelkanth!'

As whispers hummed through the square, Nandi raised his hand and cried, 'Silence!' and the audience quietened immediately.

'I come from a faraway land deep in the Himalayas. My life was changed by what I believed was a wondrous elixir – but I was wrong,' Shiva started. 'This mark I bear on my throat isn't a blessing from the gods but a curse of Evil, a mark of poison. I carry this mark,' he said, pointing to his blue throat, 'but, my fellow Meluhans, you bear this scourge as well – and you don't even know it!'

The audience listened in silence, spellbound.

'The *Somras* gives you a long life and you're grateful for that. But these years it gifts to you aren't free! The *Somras* takes more from you than it gives, and its hunger for your souls has no limit!'

A sinister breeze rustled the leaves of the trees lining the square.

'For a few additional years of life, you pay an eternal price. It's no coincidence that so many women in Meluha can't bear children – that's the curse of the *Somras*!'

Shiva's words resonated in the Meluhans' hearts, many of which had been broken by the long, lonely wait for children from the Maika adoption system. They all knew the misery of growing old without a child.

'It's no coincidence that the revered Saraswati – mother of your country, mother of Indian civilisation itself – is slowly drying to extinction. The thirsty *Somras* continues to consume her waters, and her death will come at the hands of the evil *Somras*!'

No river was just a body of water to most Indians. All rivers were holy, and the Saraswati, their spiritual mother, was the holiest of them all.

'Thousands of children are born in Maika with painful cancers that consume their bodies. Millions of Swadweepans are dying of a plague brought on by the waste generated during the production of the *Somras*. These people curse those who use the *Somras*. They're cursing you, and your souls will bear this burden for many births – *that* is the evil of the *Somras*!' Shiva touched his blue throat and smiled sadly. 'It may look as though the *Somras* has my throat, but in fact, it has all of Meluha by the throat! And it's slowly squeezing the life out of you, so slowly that you don't even realise it. And by the time you do, it'll be too late. All of Meluha, all of India, will have been destroyed!'

The citizens of Mrittikavati remained silent, engrossed in his speech.

'I tried to stop this peacefully. I sent out a notice to every city in every kingdom, all across our fair land of India. But in Meluha, my message was replaced by another put up by your emperor. He told you that it wasn't I who had banned the *Somras* but some fraud Neelkanth.'

Nandi could sense the tide of the crowd's emotions turning.

'Your emperor *lied* to you! Emperor Daksha occupies the position that was Lord Ram's more than a thousand years ago. He represents the legacy of the great seventh Vishnu. He's supposed to be your protector – but he *lied* to you.'

Parshuram looked at Shiva with reverence. He could tell the Neelkanth had already swayed the Meluhans firmly to his side.

'As if that wasn't bad enough, he sent his army to drive a wedge between you and me – but I know that *nothing* can tear us apart. I know that you'll listen to me because I'm fighting for Meluha. I'm fighting for the future of your children!'

A collective wave of understanding swept through the crowd: the Neelkanth was fighting *for* them, not *against* them.

'Every Meluhan has heard of the mythic tribe of Vasudevs left behind by our great lord, Shri Ram – but the tribe is no legend! Lord Ram's own tribe *does* exist, and its members carry Lord Ram's legacy. And they are with me, sharing my mission. They also want to save India from the *Somras*.'

Shiva's revelation that the Vasudevs not only existed in flesh and blood but were also on the Neelkanth's side drove the issue beyond debate in their minds.

'I'm going to save Meluha! I'm going to stop the *Somras*!' roared Shiva. 'Who is with me?'

'I am!' screamed Nandi.

'I am!' shouted every citizen of Mrittikavati.

'I love Meluha more than the *Somras*,' said Shiva, 'so I sent out a proclamation banning the *Somras*. Your emperor loves the *Somras* more than Meluha, so he decided to oppose me. Whose side are you on? Meluha or the *Somras*?'

'Meluha!'

'Then what do we do with the army that fights for your emperor, the army that fights for the *Somras*?'

'Kill them!'

'Kill them?'

'Yes!'

'No!' shouted Shiva.

The people fell silent, dumbfounded.

'Your army was only following orders, and the soldiers have surrendered. It would be against Lord Ram's principles to kill prisoners of war. So I ask you again – what should we do with them?'

The audience remained quiet.

'I want the soldiers to be imprisoned in Mrittikavati,' said Shiva. 'Will you ensure that they don't escape? If they do, they'll follow your emperor's orders and fight me again. Will you keep them captive in your city?'

reasonojré

'Yes!'

'Will you ensure that not one of them escapes?'

'Yes!'

Shiva allowed a smile to curve his lips. 'I see gods standing before me: gods who are willing to fight Evil! Gods who are willing to give up their attachment to Evil!' Shiva raised his balled fist high in the air. '*Har Har Mahadev!*'

'*Har Har Mahadev!*' roared the people.

Nandi, Veerbhadra and Parshuram raised their hands and repeated the stirring cry of those loyal to the Neelkanth. '*Har Har Mahadev!*'

'*Har Har Mahadev!*'

— ⸻ —

The governor's palace in Mrittikavati was soon modified to serve as a prison for the surviving Meluhan soldiers, and Shiva's troops escorted them into the palace in small groups. Shiva, Kali, Sati, Gopal and Chenardhwaj were standing near the entrance when Vidyunmali was led in. He tried to break free and lunge at Shiva, but a soldier kicked him hard and tried to push him back in line.

'It's all right,' said Shiva. 'Let him approach.'

Vidyunmali was allowed to walk through the soldiers' wall of bamboo shields to stand before Shiva.

'You were doing your duty, Vidyunmali,' said Shiva, 'and I understand that: you were following the orders of your emperor. I have nothing against you personally, but you'll have to stay imprisoned until the *Somras* has been destroyed. Then you'll be free to do whatever you want to do.'

Vidyunmali stared at Shiva with barely concealed disgust. 'You were a barbarian when we found you and you're still a barbarian. We Meluhans don't take orders from barbarians!'

Chenardhwaj drew his sword. 'Speak to the Neelkanth with respect.'

He spat at the governor. 'I don't speak to traitors!'

Kali drew her knife and moved towards Vidyunmali. 'Perhaps you shouldn't speak at all, Brigadier—'

'Kali,' whispered Shiva, before turning towards Vidyunmali. 'Your country isn't my enemy. I tried to achieve my purpose through peaceful means. I sent out a proclamation asking all of you to stop using the *Somras*, but—'

'We are a sovereign country! We will decide what we can and cannot use!'

'Not when it comes to Evil,' said Shiva firmly. 'When it comes to the *Somras*, you'll do what's in the best interests of the people and the future of Meluha.'

'Who are you to tell us what's in our best interests?'

Shiva had had enough and waved his hand dismissively. 'Take him away.'

Nandi and Veerbhadra immediately dragged Vidyunmali, kicking and screaming, towards the makeshift prison.

'You will lose, you *fraud*,' he shouted. 'Meluha will not fall!'

'Shiva, I'd like you to meet someone,' said Brahaspati, entering Shiva's private chamber and gesturing towards the Brahmin accompanying him. 'This is Panini. He was my assistant at Mount Mandar.'

'Of course; I remember him,' said Shiva. 'How are you, Panini?'

'I'm well, great Neelkanth,' the Brahmin said, clasping his hands in a formal namaste, first to Shiva, then to Sati, Gopal and Kali.

'I found Panini in Mrittikavati,' said Brahaspati, 'leading a scientific project being conducted at the Saraswati delta. He's asked me if he can join us in our battle against the *Somras*.'

Shiva frowned, wondering why Brahaspati was disturbing him with such an inconsequential request at this time. 'He was your assistant. I completely trust your judgement. You don't have to check with me about—'

'He has some news that may be useful,' interrupted Brahaspati.

'What is it, Panini?' asked Shiva politely.

'My Lord,' said Panini, 'I was recruited by Maharishi Bhrigu to conduct some secret work at Mount Mandar.'

Shiva's interest was immediately piqued. 'I thought the *Somras* factory at Mount Mandar hadn't been rebuilt yet.'

'My mission had nothing to do with the *Somras*, my Lord. I was asked to lead a small team of Meluhan scientists, personally chosen by the Maharishi, to make *daivi astras* from materials he'd provided.'

'*What?* Was it you who made the *daivi astras*?'

'Yes, my Lord—'

'Did the Vayuputras come and help you?'

'We were trained by Maharishi Bhrigu himself. I already knew a bit about the technology of *daivi astras*, but not enough to make any usable weapons. Perhaps I was selected because even my little knowledge is more than most have.'

'But weren't any Vayuputras present to assist you?' asked Shiva once again. 'Did you see them with Maharishi Bhrigu, perhaps?'

'I don't think the materials the maharishi gave us came from the Vayuputras.'

Surprised, Shiva glanced at Gopal, then asked, 'What makes you say that?'

'The little I know of the *daivi astra* technology is based on Vayuputra knowledge. Maharishi Bhrigu's processes and the materials he gave us were completely different.'

'Did he supply his own materials to make the *daivi astras*, then?'

'It appeared so.'

The implications were obvious and portentous. Shiva turned to Gopal and started to speak when Panini said, 'There's something else. I think Maharishi Bhrigu may have used the last of his *daivi astra* ingredients when he asked me to prepare the weapons. He was always exhorting me to be careful with the materials, to waste nothing, and when we accidentally spoilt a minuscule amount of it he was livid – he told me this was all the *daivi astra* core material he possessed and that we should be more careful.'

Shiva took a deep breath before saying to Gopal, 'He may be an even more formidable opponent if he can make the core materials himself – but he has no more *daivi astras*.'

'It appears so,' answered Gopal.

'And the Vayuputras aren't with him.'

'That would be a fair assumption.'

'Shiva,' said Brahaspati, 'there's even more.'

Shiva turned back to Panini.

'My Lord,' said Panini, 'I also believe that the secret *Somras* factory is in Devagiri. I'm sure you're aware that production of the *Somras* requires large quantities of the Sanjeevani tree – I was brought to Devagiri on a regular basis – but only ever at night – to check the quality of the Sanjeevani logs coming into the city.'

'I don't understand,' said Shiva. 'Isn't it part of your normal duties to check the consignment before it's sent off to the *Somras* factory?'

'That's true, my Lord, but I have a friend in the customs department, and he told me the Sanjeevani logs never actually left the city. If such huge quantities of Sanjeevani logs are being brought into Devagiri and not shipped on elsewhere, then the most logical assumption is that this is where the *Somras* is being manufactured.'

Shiva's expression reflected his gratitude to the Brahmin. 'Panini, *thank you*. You have no idea how useful your information is.'

CHAPTER 28

Meluha Stunned

'Magadh has fallen?' Parvateshwar repeated Kanakhala's words. She'd finally received a bird courier from Ayodhya, after many months of silence.

'There's more,' said the prime minister. 'The entire Magadhan army has been routed. Prince Surapadman is dead and King Mahendra has gone into deep mourning. The Brangas are now in control of Magadh.'

Parvateshwar pinched the bridge of his nose as he absorbed the implications. 'If they control Magadh, they control the chokepoint on the Ganga. They'd only have to keep a few thousand soldiers at Magadh Fort to be able to attack any Ayodhyan ship that tries to sail past.'

'Exactly!' said Kanakhala. 'Which means that Ayodhya won't be able to come to our aid quickly enough. They'll have to march through the forests north-west of Magadh instead.'

'If Magadh's been conquered, the Lord Neelkanth can leave a

small force in that city while he sails up the Ganga with the rest of his forces and marches into Meluha from Swadweep. We can expect an attack within as little as the next three or four months. We should ask our Ayodhyan allies to leave for Meluha at once. I'll speak to Lord Bhrigu.'

'There's more.' Kanakhala sounded as worried as she looked. 'The courier said the army that besieged Ayodhya and attacked Magadh was led by Ganesh, Kartik, Bhagirath and Chandraketu.'

'Then where's the Lord Neelkanth?'

'Exactly!' said Kanakhala. 'Where *is* the Lord Neelkanth?'

Just then, an aide rushed into Kanakhala's office. 'My Lord, my Lady, Lord Bhrigu has requested your presence immediately.'

As Kanakhala and Parvateshwar left the office, another aide approached them with a message for the Meluhan general. From the stamp, it was clear that the message was from Brigadier Vidyunmali. Parvateshwar broke the seal, intending to read the letter on the way to the emperor's office.

'What is it, Parvateshwar?' asked Kanakhala, watching his face turn white as he read Vidyunmali's message. But before Parvateshwar could answer, they had reached Daksha's office.

No sooner had they entered the emperor's chamber than Daksha unleashed his fury. 'Parvateshwar! Are you in control of the army or not? What in Lord Ram's name have you been up to?'

Parvateshwar was afraid he knew exactly what the emperor

was talking about – but he also knew that discussing the situation with the emperor would be a waste of time, so he kept silent and saluted Daksha with a short bow of his head and his hands folded in a namaste.

'Bad news, General,' said Bhrigu. 'Mrittikavati's been attacked and conquered by Shiva.'

'*What?*' Kanakhala was stunned. 'How did they even reach Mrittikavati? How could they get through Lothal's defences?'

Bhrigu raised a sheaf of papyrus. 'This is from the Governor of Mrittikavati. Apparently Chenardhwaj has pledged loyalty to Shiva. The traitor!'

'That swine,' growled Daksha. 'I knew I should never have trusted him!'

'Then why did you appoint him Governor of Lothal, your Majesty?' asked Bhrigu.

Daksha lapsed into a sulk.

Bhrigu turned to Parvateshwar. 'Your suspicions about Lothal were correct, Lord Parvateshwar. I should apologise for not having listened to you earlier. Had we perhaps sent Vidyunmali to Lothal promptly with a strong force, we'd still be in control of that city.'

'We can't undo what's happened, my Lord,' said Parvateshwar. 'Let's concentrate on what we can do now. I've received a message from the brigadier.'

Bhrigu glanced at the letter in Parvateshwar's hand. 'And what does he have to say?'

'It sounds like an intelligence failure to me,' said Parvateshwar.

'He says Lord Shiva took them by surprise, appearing at the gates of Mrittikavati with a hundred thousand soldiers. Vidyunmali mounted a brave defence with his mere twenty-five thousand, but was eventually routed.'

Kanakhala understood Mrittikavati's strategic significance. 'Mrittikavati houses the headquarters of the Saraswati fleet, and Vidyunmali took the remainder of our warships there as well. If the Lord controls Mrittikavati, he now controls the Saraswati River.'

'Shiva is *not* a lord!' screamed Daksha. 'How dare you? Who are you loyal to, Kanakhala?'

'Your Majesty,' said Bhrigu, his calm tone belying the menace beneath.

Daksha recoiled as the maharishi said silkily, 'Your Majesty, perhaps it would be better if you retired to your personal chambers.'

'But—'

'Your Majesty,' said Bhrigu, 'that was *not* a request.'

Daksha closed his eyes, shocked at the immense disrespect being shown to him, nevertheless, he got up and left his office, muttering under his breath about what was due to the Emperor of India.

Bhrigu turned to Parvateshwar unperturbed, and continued as if nothing had happened. 'General, what else does Vidyunmali say?'

'The entire Saraswati fleet is under the Lord Neelkanth's control now. But it gets worse.'

'How can it be worse?'

'The people of Mrittikavati have now pledged loyalty to him, and they are holding the survivors of Vidyunmali's army. Fortunately for us, Vidyunmali managed to escape with five hundred soldiers and sent this message.'

'So the Neelkanth's stationed himself in Mrittikavati for now?' asked Bhrigu, careful not to use the term 'fraud Neelkanth' in Parvateshwar's presence. 'He'll have to commit his own soldiers to guard ours, right?'

'No,' said Parvateshwar, 'our army's being held prisoner by the citizens of Mrittikavati.'

'The *citizens*?'

'Yes – so the Lord Neelkanth doesn't have to commit any of his own soldiers to the task. He's managed to take twenty-five thousand of our soldiers out of the equation, but he still has practically his whole army with him and he's commandeered our entire Saraswati fleet. I'm sure he's making plans to sail north even as we speak. Vidyunmali also describes a fearsome corps of exceptionally well-trained elephants in the Lord's army, which were almost impossible to defeat.'

'Lord Ram, be merciful!' Kanakhala whispered.

'This is worse than we ever imagined,' said Bhrigu.

'But there's one thing I don't understand,' said Kanakhala. 'How does the Lord have an army of a hundred thousand in Meluha when a hundred and fifty thousand of his soldiers were in Ayodhya a few weeks back?'

'Ayodhya?' Bhrigu looked surprised.

'Yes,' said Kanakhala, and proceeded to relate the message she'd just received from Ayodhya about the siege and the destruction of the Magadhan forces.

'By the great Lord Brahma!' said Bhrigu. 'This means the Ayodhyan army can't sail past Magadh – they'll have to march through the forest, which means it'll take them forever to come to our aid.'

'But I still don't understand how the Lord Neelkanth has so many soldiers in Meluha,' persisted Kanakhala. 'The Branga and Naga armies together don't add up to this number.'

The truth finally dawned on Bhrigu. 'The Vasudevs have joined forces with Shiva. They're the only ones other than the Suryavanshis and the Chandravanshis who could bring so many soldiers. This also explains the presence of the exceptionally well-trained elephants Shiva used in the Battle of Mrittikavati. I've heard stories about the prowess of the Vasudev elephants.'

He had not worked out that the Vasudevs' strongest strategic benefit wasn't their elephant corps but rather their secretive Vasudev pandits hidden in temples across the Sapt Sindhu, the eyes and ears of the Neelkanth, providing him with that most crucial advantage in war: timely and accurate information.

'Lord Shiva will be here soon, with a large army,' said Parvateshwar, 'and Ayodhya's three hundred thousand soldiers won't reach us in time. He's played his cards well.'

'I don't have a military mind, General,' said Bhrigu, 'but even I can see that we're in deep trouble. What do you advise?'

Parvateshwar brought his hands together and rubbed his chin with his index fingers. After a few moments, he looked up at Bhrigu. 'If Ganesh decides to enter Meluha from the north, we're finished. There's no way we can defend ourselves against a two-pronged attack. Our engineers have been working hard to repair the road ruined by the Yamuna floods. I'll send them instructions immediately to leave the road as it is. If Ganesh chooses to cross from there, we must make the journey difficult for him. Marching a hundred-and-fifty-thousand-strong army along a washed-out road won't be easy.'

'Good idea.'

'The Lord Neelkanth could be in Devagiri in a matter of weeks.'

'It's a good thing you've engaged the army in training exercises and simulations,' said Bhrigu.

'I will do everything in my power to ensure the Lord does not win here,' said Parvateshwar. 'That's my word to you, Maharishiji.'

'I believe you, General. But what do we do about the Vasudev elephants? We can't defeat Shiva's army unless we stop his elephants.'

— ☥ ⓪Ⓤ☥✹ —

'What do you think, Shiva?' asked Gopal as they re-evaluated their strategy in the light of Panini's revelations.

Kali's mind was clear. 'Shiva, I suggest you leave Mrittikavati and sail to Pariha. If you can convince the Vayuputras to give you a lethal *daivi astra*, say the *Brahmastra*, this war will be as good as over.'

'We can't use these *daivi astras*, your Majesty,' said Gopal, horrified by the suggestion. 'It would go against every law of humanity. We can only use such weapons as deterrents, to make the other side see sense.'

'Yes, yes,' said Kali dismissively, 'I agree.'

'How long will the journey to Pariha take, Panditji?' asked Shiva.

'At least six months,' said Gopal, 'and up to twelve months if the winds don't favour us.'

'Then I don't think it makes any sense to go to Pariha at this stage.'

'Why not?' Kali asked.

'We have momentum and time on our side at the moment,' Shiva said. 'Ayodhya's army won't reach Meluha for another six to eight months, at least. Ganesh and Kartik can travel to the northern frontiers of Meluha in a few weeks. We'll have a six-month window with two hundred and fifty thousand soldiers on our side against just seventy-five thousand on Meluha's. I like those odds. I say we finish the war here and now. The situation might be very different in the time it would take me to go to Pariha and back. Also, all we know for sure is that the Vayu-putras aren't with Maharishi Bhrigu – that doesn't necessarily mean they'll choose our side instead. They may well decide to remain neutral.'

'That makes sense,' Sati added. 'If we conquer Devagiri and

destroy the *Somras* factory, the war will be over, regardless of what the Vayuputras choose to believe.'

'So what do you suggest, Shiva?' asked Gopal.

'We should divide our navy into two parts,' said Shiva. 'I'll sail up the Saraswati and then head north up the Yamuna with a small sailing force of twenty-five ships. I'll meet Ganesh and Kartik as they march down the Yamuna Road and we'll board their soldiers onto my ships. We can get to Devagiri much quicker by sailing rather than waiting for them to march to the Meluhan capital. In the meantime, Sati will lead the rest of the navy and our entire army from Mrittikavati up the Saraswati to Devagiri. If she leaves three weeks after me, we'll reach Devagiri around the same time. With two hundred and fifty thousand soldiers besieging Devagiri, they might actually see some sense.'

'Sounds good in theory,' said Kali, 'but coordination may prove to be a problem in practice. If there are delays and one of our armies reaches Devagiri before the other, it might be too weak to defeat the Meluhans.'

'But Shiva's not suggesting that we mount an attack and conquer Devagiri as soon as either one of our forces arrives there,' said Sati. 'Whoever arrives first will just fortify themselves and wait for the rest to arrive. We only attack once we've joined forces.'

'But what if the Meluhans decide to attack while our army's still divided?' Kali looked around the room. 'Remember, anchored ships are sitting ducks for devil boats.'

'I don't see them stepping outside the safety of their fort,' said Shiva. 'I'll be leading an army of a hundred and fifty thousand soldiers who've just destroyed the mighty Magadhans. The Meluhans won't attack us with only seventy-five thousand soldiers. Sati's army will have a hundred thousand, and she'll also have the Vasudev elephants. So, even divided, our armies are capable of taking on the Meluhans on an open field. General Parvateshwar has a calm head on his strong shoulders. He'll know that it's better for them to remain safely inside their fort rather than marching out and attacking us.'

'But I take your point, Kali,' said Sati. 'If I arrive early, I'll encamp five miles south of Devagiri – there's a large hill on the banks of the Saraswati which will be a superb defensive position since it'll give us the advantage of height. I'll set up a *Chakravyuh* formation with our Vasudev elephants as the first line of defence. It'll be almost impossible for the enemy to break through.'

'I know that hill,' said Shiva, 'and that's exactly where I'll camp if I happen to arrive there before you.'

— ⚕ ◍Ʊ⚷ ◉ —

'There's no chance we could slow down for a bit, is there, my Lord?' Parshuram asked Shiva as they battled to keep their eyes open against the onslaught of the wind.

While none of the cities on the Saraswati was prepared for naval warfare since the Meluhans never expected an attack from that quarter, Shiva had decided not to tempt fate by travelling at a more leisurely pace, for the Meluhans weren't lacking in honour and courage. As an additional precaution, though he had just two thousand men with him, he'd included many of the courageous Naga soldiers in his navy. He was in the lead ship; Kali was travelling in the rearmost vessel.

'No, Parshuram, we must press on,' he said now. 'Speed is of the essence.'

Four teams of rowers kept the convoy going day and night, working in gruelling six-hour shifts. The timekeepers beat their drums to set the rhythm for the rowers, for Shiva didn't want the unpredictable winds to determine how fast they moved. He had added his own name to the roster for rowing duties and his six-hour shift would begin soon.

'It's a beautiful river, my Lord,' said Parshuram. 'It's sad that we may have to kill it.'

'What do you mean?'

'My Lord, I've been researching the *Somras*, and Lord Gopal has explained many things to me. An idea has struck me—'

'And what would that be?'

'The *Somras* can't be made without this,' said Parshuram, pointing to the Saraswati.

'Brahaspati tried to find some way to make the Saraswati waters unusable, but that didn't work, remember?'

'That's not what I meant, my Lord. If the Saraswati didn't exist, neither would the *Somras*, would it?'

Parshuram continued to explain as Shiva observed him closely. 'My Lord, there was a time when the Saraswati as we know it today had ceased to exist: the Yamuna began flowing east towards the Ganga, and the Saraswati can't exist without the confluence of the Yamuna and the Sutlej.'

'We can't kill the Saraswati,' said Shiva, almost to himself.

'My Lord, for all you know, maybe that's what Nature was trying to do more than a hundred years ago, when an earthquake changed the course of the Yamuna and it flowed into the Ganga. If Lord Brahmanayak, the father of the present emperor, hadn't changed the Yamuna's course to flow back into the Sutlej and restore the Saraswati, history would've been very different. Maybe Nature was trying to stop the *Somras*.'

Shiva listened silently.

'The Saraswati wouldn't actually be dead: its waters would disappear, but its soul would still flow in the form of the Yamuna and the Sutlej.'

Shiva stared into the Saraswati's depths. Parshuram had a point, but Shiva didn't want to admit it, not even to himself. Not yet, anyway.

CHAPTER 29

Every Army Has a Traitor

'Any news?' asked Bhagirath as he and Chandraketu joined Ganesh and Kartik on the lead ship. The massive navy sailing up the Ganga en route to Meluha was approaching from the north. Soon they would disembark and take the Ganga–Yamuna Road, but they'd slowed down for a few hours to allow a boat to rendezvous with them. The boatman brought a message from a Vasudev pandit.

'I've just received word that my father's army has conquered Mrittikavati,' said Ganesh.

Chandraketu was thrilled. 'That's great news!'

'It is indeed,' answered Ganesh. 'And it gets even better: the citizens of Mrittikavati have been won over to my father's side and they've imprisoned what was left of the Meluhan army inside the city.'

'Have they discovered the location of the *Somras* factory yet?' asked Bhagirath.

'Yes,' said Kartik. 'It's in Devagiri.'

'Devagiri? That's ridiculous – it's their capital. Surely they'd have built the factory in some secure, secret location.'

'But if they wanted to build the factory inside a city, it would have to be one with a large population, right? In that case, which city would be a better choice than Devagiri? They'll assume they can keep their capital safe, at least.'

'So what are our orders now?' asked Chandraketu. He listened closely as Ganesh explained, then grinned.

'So we'll have two hundred and fifty thousand soldiers, all fired up with the fervour of recent victories, against seventy-five thousand Meluhans holed up on their platforms,' he said.

'I like those odds,' Bhagirath added.

'That's exactly what *baba* must have said!' said Kartik with a grin.

'You are going to give me the answers I want to hear,' growled Vidyunmali, 'whether you like it or not.'

A Vasudev major captured from Shiva's army was bound to a moveable wooden rack with thick leather ropes. The stale air in the dark dungeon was putrid. The captured Vasudev was already drenched in his own sweat, but he was unafraid.

The Meluhan soldiers present looked at Vidyunmali warily. What their brigadier was asking them to do was against the laws of Lord Ram. Meluhan military training demanded unquestioning obedience to their commanding officer, and this training had forced the soldiers to suppress their misgivings and carry out Vidyunmali's orders – until now. But their moral code was about to be challenged even more strongly.

Vidyunmali heard the Vasudev whispering something again and again and he bent close. 'Do you have something to say?'

The Vasudev soldier kept mumbling softly, drawing strength from his words: '*Jai Guru Vishwamitra. Jai Guru Vashishta. Jai Guru Vishwamitra. Jai Guru Vashishta . . .*'

Vidyunmali sniggered. 'They aren't coming to help you, my friend.'

He turned and beckoned a startled Meluhan soldier, then pointed at a metal hammer and a large nail.

'My Lord?' whispered the nervous soldier, knowing full well that to attack an unarmed and bound man was against Lord Ram's principles. 'I'm not sure if we should—'

'It's not your job to be sure,' growled Vidyunmali. 'That's *my* job. Your job is to do what I order you to do.'

'Yes, my Lord,' said the Meluhan, saluting slowly. He picked up the hammer and nail, then walked slowly to the Vasudev and placed the tip of the nail on the captive's right arm, a few inches above the wrist. He raised the hammer and flexed his shoulders, ready to strike.

Vidyunmali turned to the Vasudev. 'You'd better start talking . . .'

'*Jai Guru Vishwamitra. Jai Guru Vashishta . . .*'

Vidyunmali nodded to the soldier.

'*Jai Guru Vishwamitra. Jai Guru*— AAAAHHHHHHH-HHHH!'

The Vasudev's ear-splitting scream resounded loudly in the confines of the dungeon, but there was no one to hear his howls in this hellhole deep underground somewhere between Mritti-kavati and Devagiri, for it had been abandoned for centuries — no one except the nervous Meluhan soldiers at the back of the room praying to Lord Ram, begging for his forgiveness.

The soldier hammered away mechanically, driving the nail deep into the Vasudev's right arm. The Vasudev screamed until his brain simply blocked the pain. He couldn't feel his arm any more. His heart was pumping madly and blood was spurting through the gaping injury with every beat.

Vidyunmali approached the Vasudev, who was breathing heavily, trying to focus on his tribe, on his gods, on his vows, on anything except his right arm.

'Do you need some more persuasion?' Vidyunmali whispered in the poor man's ear.

The Vasudev looked away, focusing his mind on his chant.

Vidyunmali yanked the nail out, took a wet cloth and wiped the Vasudev's arm. Then he picked up a small bottle and poured its contents into the wound. It burned horribly, but the Vas-udev's blood clotted almost immediately.

'I don't want you to die,' whispered Vidyunmali. 'At least, not yet . . .'

Vidyunmali turned towards his soldier and nodded.

'My Lord,' whispered the soldier, with tears in his eyes. He'd

lost count of the number of sins he was taking upon his soul.
'Please—'

Vidyunmali glared at him and the soldier picked up another
bottle, approached the Vasudev and poured some of the viscous
liquid into the wound he'd inflicted.

Vidyunmali stepped back and returned with a long knife, its
edge glowing red-hot. 'I hope you see the light after this.'

The Vasudev's eyes opened wide in terror, but still he refused
to talk. He couldn't reveal the secret. It would be devastating
for his tribe.

'Jai . . . Gu . . . ru . . . Vishwa . . .'

'Fire will purify you,' whispered Vidyunmali softly, 'and you
will speak.'

'. . . Mitra . . . Jai . . . Gu . . . ru . . . Vash . . .'

The dungeon resonated once again with the desperate screams
of the Vasudev as the smell of burning flesh defiled the room.

— ☥ ◍Ụ⚡⊛ —

'Are you sure?' asked Parvateshwar.

'As sure as I can ever be,' Vidyunmali said with a smile.

Parvateshwar took a deep breath. He knew that Shiva was
leading the massive fleet of ships that had sped past Devagiri
two weeks earlier; he suspected he was sailing north to pick
up Ganesh's army and bring the soldiers back to Devagiri. He
had also received reports about the delays faced by Ganesh's
army as they marched along the washed-out Ganga–Yamuna
Road. It would probably take a month for Shiva to return to

Devagiri along with the hundred and fifty thousand soldiers in Ganesh's army.

He also knew that a a hundred-thousand-strong contingent of the Neelkanth's army under Sati's command had just sailed out of Mrittikavati and would reach Devagiri in a week or two, ahead of Ganesh's men, so once Shiva and Ganesh's men sailed in, the enemy's strength would increase to two hundred and fifty thousand against his own seventy-five thousand.

His best chance was to attack Sati's army before Shiva and Ganesh arrived, and the only problem that he had no answer for was the unstoppable Vasudev elephant corps under Sati's command – until now.

'Chilli powder and dung?' asked Parvateshwar. 'It sounds so simple.'

'Apparently the elephants don't like the smell of chilli, my Lord. It makes them run amok. If we keep bricks of dung mixed with chilli at the ready, then set fire to them and catapult them towards the elephants, the acrid smoke will drive them crazy – and, hopefully, into their own army.'

'There are no elephants to test this on, Vidyunmali. We'd be testing this in battle. What if this doesn't work?'

'My apologies, General, but do we have any other options?'

'No.'

'Then what's the harm in trying?'

Parvateshwar nodded and turned to stare at his soldiers training in the distance. 'How did you get this information?'

Vidyunmali didn't reply.

Parvateshwar returned his gaze to Vidyunmali, eyes boring into him. 'Brigadier, I asked you a question.'

'There are traitors in every army, my Lord.'

Parvateshwar was stunned. The famous Vasudev discipline was legendary. 'You found a Vasudev traitor?'

'Like I said, there are traitors in every army. How do you think I escaped?'

Parvateshwar returned his attention to his soldiers. There was no harm in trying this tactic, and it just might work.

Devagiri, the abode of the gods, had become the city of the thoroughly bewildered. None of its two hundred thousand citizens could recall a time in living memory when an enemy army had marched upon their city, and yet here they were, witnesses to just such an unbelievable occurrence.

A few weeks earlier, a large fleet of warships had raced past their city, rowing up the Saraswati at a furious speed. It was clear that these ships were part of the Mrittikavati-based Meluhan fleet, and now in the enemy's control – but why they simply sailed by without attacking Devagiri was a mystery.

News had also filtered in about a massive army garrisoning itself next to the Saraswati, about five miles south of the city. The normally secure Devagiri citizens now confined themselves within the walls of their city, not venturing out unless absolutely necessary. Merchants halted all trading activities and their ships remained anchored at the port.

Rumours ran rife in the city. Some whispered that the enemy army south of Devagiri was led by the Neelkanth himself, while others swore they had seen the Neelkanth on one of the warships that had sailed past, although they couldn't hazard a guess as to where Lord Shiva could be heading in such a hurry. Facts had also filtered in from other cities: with the exception of Mrittikavati, this mammoth army hadn't engaged any other Meluhan city along the Saraswati; they hadn't looted or plundered any villages, nor had they committed any acts of wanton destruction. Instead, they had marched through Meluha with almost hermit-like restraint.

Some citizens were beginning to believe that perhaps the rumours were true – that the Neelkanth wasn't against Meluha, only the *Somras*; that the proclamation they'd read many months ago was actually from their Lord and not a lie as their emperor had said – and that maybe the Neelkanth's army was waiting on the banks of the Saraswati without attacking because the Lord himself was negotiating possible terms of surrender with the emperor.

But there were others, still loyal to Meluha, who refused to believe that their government could have lied to them. They'd heard that Shiva's armies comprised the Chandravanshis and the Nagas; that the Naga queen herself was a senior commander in the Neelkanth's army and the Neelkanth had been led astray by the evil combination of Chandravanshis and Nagas. They were willing to lay down their lives for Meluha.

What they couldn't understand was why their army hadn't engaged in battle yet.

— ♀ ◍U♀⊛ —

'Are you sure, General?' Bhrigu asked Parvateshwar.

'I am. It's a gamble, but we have to take it. If we wait too long, the Lord will arrive with Ganesh's army; combined with Sati's army, they'll then have a vast numerical advantage and it'll be impossible for us to win. Right now, our only opponents are Sati's soldiers. They have garrisoned themselves close to the river so they're obviously not looking for a fight. I plan to draw them out and then try to cause some chaos amongst their elephants. If it works, the elephants might charge back into their own army, who will have no room to retreat, not with the river right behind them. If everything goes according to plan, we might just win the day.'

'Isn't Sati your goddaughter?' asked Bhrigu, looking deeply into Parvateshwar's eyes.

Parvateshwar held his breath, then let it out on a long sigh. 'At this point in time, she's only an enemy of Meluha to me.'

Bhrigu continued to look at him, increasingly satisfied with what he saw there. 'If you're convinced, General, then so am I. In the name of Lord Ram, attack.'

— ♀ ◍U♀⊛ —

Sati knew her soldiers couldn't remain aboard the anchored ships – anchored, they were sitting ducks, susceptible to catapult bombardment and devil-boat assaults – so she decided to garrison herself on land. That would also protect her ships by deterring the Meluhans from coming too close to the riverbanks.

The location was perfect for her needs: a large, gently rolling hill right next to the river. The trees between the hill and the city had been felled, giving her a clear line of sight to the main gates some five miles away. The height of the hill gave her other advantages too: charging downhill was far easier than advancing uphill, which her enemies would have to do, and the elevation significantly increased her archers' range.

After occupying the high ground, Sati deployed her troops in the most effective defensive military formation she knew. The core of the *Chakravyuh* comprised columns of infantrymen in the tortoise formation, protected at the rear by the Saraswati fleet at anchor in the middle of the river, in case Meluhan forces attacked from behind. Rowing boats had been moored in the shallows as a contingency, should retreat become necessary. Rows of cavalry three layers deep reinforced the front lines of the core formation, while two rows of war elephants formed an impregnable semicircular outer shell, protecting the formations within. The giant *Chakravyuh* left adequate space between the lines for inner manoeuvrability and fortification of the outer shell by the cavalry in case of a breach. All the animals had been outfitted with flexible metal armour and the soldiers carried broad bronze shields to protect them from any long-range arrows.

It was a near-perfect defensive formation, designed to avoid battle and allow a quick retreat if necessary, and she intended to remain in this formation until she heard from Shiva.

CHAPTER 30

Battle of Devagiri

Sati sat atop a tall wooden platform constructed behind the cavalry line, which gave her a panoramic view of the entire potential battlefield and the city of Devagiri in the distance. She watched the city where she'd spent most of her life, which she'd once called home. A nostalgic corner of her heart still longed to revel in its quiet, sober efficiency and understated culture, to worship at the temple of Lord Agni, the purifying Fire God, performing the ritual required of her as a *vikarma*, an ostracised carrier of bad fate. Despite being so close, she couldn't even enter the city to meet her mother. She shook her head, banishing sentimentality. She had to focus.

She checked on her horse, which had been tethered to the platform's base. Nandi and Veerbhadra, her designated personal bodyguards, were waiting next to it.

This was going to be a difficult period, the time before Shiva returned with Ganesh's army. She had to keep her soldiers battle-ready whilst avoiding starting a war, and she knew as well as any general that constant vigilance sometimes bred restless irritability amongst the troops.

Her attention was drawn to some movement in the far distance and she blinked, not believing what she was seeing. The main gate of the city's bronze, or Tamra, platform was opening.

What are they doing? Why would the Meluhans step into the open? They're outnumbered!

'Steady!' she ordered. 'Everyone remain in position – we won't be provoked into launching an attack!'

Messengers waiting below immediately relayed her orders to all the brigade commanders. As long as Sati's soldiers remained in formation it would be almost impossible to beat them. The elephant line, at the periphery of Sati's formation, was especially crucial, for they were the bulwark of her defences.

Sati continued to watch the small contingent of Meluhan soldiers – no more than a single brigade – marching out of Devagiri. The gates closed behind them as soon as they were through.

Is it a suicide squad? she wondered. *For what purpose?*

The Meluhan soldiers continued their slow march towards Sati's position and she soon observed that the soldiers were being followed by carts laboriously pulled along by oxen.

What do these thousand foot-soldiers hope to achieve? And what's in those carts?

As the Meluhans drew close to the hill, she saw that many of the soldiers were carrying long weapons of some kind in their left hands.

Archers.

The moment they halted, she instantly knew what was about to happen. They'd clearly planned this excursion for a time when the prevailing wind would work in their favour, so her archers would not have the pleasure of giving as much as receiving.

'Shields!' shouted Sati. 'Incoming arrows!'

But the archers had overestimated the wind's strength, and the first wave of arrows barely reached Sati's forces. Even so, the strong oncoming wind meant that her archers couldn't respond to the Meluhan volley with their own. She watched the Meluhans creeping closer in front of the ox-drawn carts. In all her years, Sati had never seen ox-carts being used in warfare.

She frowned. *What in Lord Ram's name can oxen do against elephants? What's* Pitratulya *doing?*

She didn't want to test General Parvateshwar's strategy today – admittedly, it was tempting, for her elephants would wipe out this small contingent in minutes – but she smelled a trap, and she didn't want to leave the high ground. She knew what had to be done: hold position until Shiva returned. She didn't want to fight, not today.

The Meluhan archers moved closer and drew their bows again.

'Shields!' ordered Sati.

This time the arrows hit the shields on the right-hand side of Sati's formation. Having tested the range, the Meluhan archers moved again.

They probably have some secret weapon they're not absolutely sure about, she speculated. *The ox-drawn carts must have a role to play. They want to provoke some of my men into charging at them so they can test their weapon.*

The upshot was obvious. If her army refused to be provoked, no battle would take place. All her animals were well armoured and the soldiers had massive shields to defend themselves against the very arrow attack the Meluhans were attempting right now. Despite two volleys, her army hadn't yet suffered a single casualty. There was nothing to gain by breaking formation – and nothing to lose by staying in formation.

Now that the enemy had come so close, ordering her own archers to return fire might prove counter-productive. The ox-drawn carts weren't manned and a volley of arrows might drive the animals crazy, making them charge in any direction – perhaps even at her own army, along with whatever evil they carried in the carts. No, she had a better idea. She ordered a cavalry squad to ride out from behind the hill, thus hiding their movements, and head to an adjoining hill towards the west so they could launch a flanking attack from behind the crest of that hill, which would surprise and decimate the Meluhan archers and drive the oxen away. All she had to do was wait for the Meluhans to move a little closer to her position. Then she could blindside them with her cavalry charge.

Sati repeated her orders: 'Be calm! Hold the line! They can't hurt us if we remain in formation.'

The Meluhan archers came closer, drew their bows and fired again.

Sati's army was ready, and though the arrows reached the centre of their formations, not one soldier was injured.

The Meluhans held their bows at their sides and prepared to move nearer still, this time a little tentatively, Sati thought.

They're nervous now. They know their plan isn't working.

'What the hell!' growled an angry Vasudev elephant-rider to his partner. 'They're a puny brigade with oxen against our entire army. Why doesn't General Sati allow us to attack?'

'Because she's not a Vasudev,' spat his partner. 'She doesn't know how to fight.'

'My Lords,' said the *mahout* to the riders, 'our orders are to follow the general's orders.'

The Vasudev turned angrily on the *mahout*. 'Did I ask for your opinion? Your order is to follow *my* orders!'

The *mahout* immediately fell silent as the distant shout of the herald blew in with the breeze. 'Shields!'

Another volley of arrows. Again, no casualties.

'Enough of this nonsense!' barked one of the elephant-riders. 'We're Kshatriyas. We're not supposed to cower like cowardly Brahmins – we're supposed to fight!'

Sati saw a few elephants on the far right of her formation, the ones closest to the Meluhan brigade, begin to rumble out.

'Hold the line!' shouted Sati. 'Nobody will break formation!'

The messengers carried the orders to the other end of the field immediately and the elephants were pulled back into formation by their *mahouts*.

'Nandi,' said Sati, looking down, 'ride out and tell those idiots to do as they're told and stay put!'

'Yes, my Lady,' said Nandi, saluting as he prepared to gallop off to do her bidding.

'Wait!' said Sati as she saw the Meluhan archers loading another round of arrows. 'Wait out this volley and then go.'

The order of, 'Shields!' was relayed again and the arrows clanged harmlessly against the raised barriers. Still none of Sati's soldiers was injured.

But when she lowered her own shield and looked up, she was horrified by the sight of twenty elephants on the right recklessly charging out.

'Fools!' yelled Sati as she jumped from the platform and onto her horse and, followed by Veerbhadra and Nandi, she galloped forward to cover the breach opened up by the elephants. As she passed the cavalry line, she ordered the reserve troops to follow her, and within a few minutes, she had stationed herself in the position left open by the Vasudev elephants that had charged out of formation.

'Stay here!' she ordered the soldiers behind her as she raised her hand.

She could see her elephants sprinting forward in the distance, bellowing loudly as they were goaded on by their *mahouts*. The Meluhan archers stood their ground bravely and fired another round.

The Vasudev elephant-riders screamed loudly as they crashed into the archers, *'Jai Shri Ram!'* and the elephants started swinging the metal balls, flinging Meluhan soldiers far and wide. The few who remained standing were soon crushed under giant feet and, within a few moments of the start of this butchery, the archers began retreating.

It looked as if the twenty Vasudev elephants were smashing the Meluhan archers to bits, but Sati shuddered with foreboding as she felt a chill run down her spine. She screamed loudly, even though she knew the elephant-riders couldn't hear her, 'Come back, you fools!'

But the Vasudev elephant-riders were on a roll and oblivious to her orders. Encouraged by the easy victory, they goaded their *mahouts* to keep the elephants moving forward. They primed their weapons and long, spear-like flames burst forth from the *howdahs*. The riders aimed the weapons for maximum effect as they crashed into the next line of Meluhans. Seeing the ox-drawn carts a little further ahead, the elephants continued their mad dash forward.

And then the tide turned: the Meluhan archers paused in their retreat to loose a volley of fire-arrows towards their own carts and their volatile cargoes of chilli-laced dung cakes caught fire immediately. Smelling the blaze somewhere behind them, the startled oxen ran forward in panic, straight towards the advancing elephants.

It was the *mahouts* who had the first inkling that something was badly wrong. They were deeply attuned to their beasts and they began to sense their innate distress, but goaded on by the fire-throwing elephant-riders behind them, they continued to press their elephants forward. Soon the contents of the carts were completely aflame, releasing a thick, acrid smoke, but the Vasudevs, too committed to the charge, rode straight into the blinding smoke.

As soon as the smoke hit them, the elephants shrieked desperately. The *mahouts* recognised the smell of chilli and one screamed, 'Retreat!'

'No!' snapped a belligerent elephant-rider. 'We have them! Crush the oxen – keep moving forward!'

But the elephants, already in a state of frenzied panic, turned from the source of their discomfort and fled blindly, even as the hysterical oxen continued their own frantic sprint forwards, dragging the burning carts behind them as they sought to elude the blaze.

Sati watched the developing situation unfold from the distance. Whatever the oxen were carrying was making the pachyderms hysterical – and the oxen would reach her remaining outer elephant line within minutes and spread the panic deep into her troops. Then she saw a fire-arrow rising high above Devagiri as the city gates opened once again: the Meluhans, seeing their strategy was working, were committing themselves to a full-on attack. Her worst fears were confirmed as she watched the Meluhan cavalry thunder out through the gates. The city was five miles away, so she knew she had the luxury of a little time before they reached her. Her immediate concern was the oncoming oxen, which could make all the Vasudev elephants charge madly back into her own troops and destroy her army.

She turned to her herald and shouted, 'Tell the lines at the rear to retreat to the boats. *Now!*' Then she ordered the remainder of the elephant line to disband and escape southwards immediately.

Finally, she ordered her own cavalry forward.

'Charge these beasts moving towards us – we must divert them – and our own elephants – onto a different path! We need to give our soldiers time to retreat!'

Her cavalry drew their swords, roaring, '*Har Har Mahadev!*' and she repeated the cry as she drew her sword and charged. Her troops kept up a steady volley of arrows as they drew near the frantic beasts, but though it succeeded in deflecting many of the oxen away from the main army, the elephants continued their headlong charge. The elephant-riders had lost control of their flame-throwers, and many of the *howdahs* were now emitting fire continuously.

The only way to bring the elephants down was by riding close behind the beasts and slashing their hamstrings so their rear legs would collapse, but this was easier said than done with the malfunctioning flame-throwers spewing continuous streams of fire in every direction. Sati led her fearless cavalry headlong into the fray, dodging both flames and the wildly swinging metal balls. The twenty elephants were quickly brought down, but not before many of the cavalrymen had lost their lives, some crushed, many burned alive by the flame-throwers. Sati herself was wounded, one side of her face scorched in the melee.

But the rest of her cavalry had managed to redirect all the

charging oxen through the skilled use of spears and arrows and now the panic-stricken bulls were charging westwards with the burning carts still tethered to them, safely away from the rest of Sati's elephant corps.

Sati looked eastwards, where many of her foot soldiers were already sailing out to the safety of the ships aboard the rowing boats she'd kept ready for just such an eventuality.

But this minor victory was soon swallowed by absolute disaster. The Meluhan cavalry, riding hard towards the battle-field, had made good time and, as the oxen stampeded away, the Meluhan riders charged straight into Sati's cavalry in a great crash of clashing swords.

Sati's three thousand riders had been evenly matched with the Meluhans at the outset, but her men had just emerged from a bruising encounter with the panic-stricken animals, which had reduced their numbers and sapped their strength. But retreat wasn't an option, not now. She had to fight on a little longer until all her foot soldiers had returned to the safety of the ships.

Then Sati heard the sounds of the elephants once again. She quickly despatched the Meluhan in front of her and glanced behind.

'Lord Ram, be merciful!'

Some of the elephants she'd ordered south were now thundering back towards her cavalry, trumpeting desperately as fire spewed in all directions from the abandoned *howdahs* secured to their backs. The *mahouts* had long since fallen off, leaving the animals totally out of control. Behind the elephants charged the oxen, the burning carts still tethered to them.

In a brilliant strategic move, the Meluhans had stationed another corps of carts south of Sati's position. As the terrified elephants charged away from Sati's men, the reserve carts were set on fire and, just as Parvateshwar had expected, the elephants immediately turned in alarm and charged back onto the battlefield.

Sati had the Meluhan cavalry in front of her and a huge horde of charging, panic-stricken elephants spewing fire behind.

'Retreat!' she yelled, and her cavalry disengaged immediately and galloped towards the river. Fortunately for them, the Meluhans, alarmed by the sight of the maddened elephants speeding towards them, turned and rode towards the safety of their city's walls.

Many of Sati's horsemen were trampled or burned to death by the rampaging elephants, but some of the riders managed to reach the river. They rode into the waters without a second's hesitation and the exhausted horses swam desperately towards the ships, trying to carry themselves and their riders to safety – but too many sank into the Saraswati under the weight of their light armour, dragging their riders with them into the depths. Sati, Veerbhadra and Nandi were amongst the lucky few who managed to reach the vessels.

While most of the foot-soldiers had been saved, the elephant and cavalry corps had been decimated. Jubilant memories of the elephants' killer blows in the Battle of Mrittikavati were quickly forgotten as the magnitude of the disaster sank in.

Chenardhwaj was in command of the ships and he quickly ordered a retreat as soon as the last of the survivors were aboard. Without the protection of the land army, their stationary navy would be a sitting duck for further attacks.

CHAPTER 31

Stalemate

'Absolute decimation,' crowed Vidyunmali. 'We should chase those imbeciles and finish off what's left of the fraud's army. That'll teach them that nobody invades our fair motherland and survives.'

Vidyunmali had joined Daksha, Bhrigu, Parvateshwar and Kanakhala in the emperor's private office. Though brigadiers didn't normally participate in strategy meetings, Daksha had insisted that he be allowed to attend, given his sterling role in providing the information about the elephants.

Parvateshwar raised his hand to silence Vidyunmali. 'Let's not get ahead of ourselves, Brigadier. Sati's tactics under pressure were exceptional: she managed to save most of her army. We still won't have a decisive numerical advantage if we chase them now.'

Vidyunmali fumed silently, keeping his gaze pinned on the floor. *Praise for a rival general? What's wrong with Lord Parvateshwar?*

She might have been a Meluhan princess once, but now she's a sworn enemy of our motherland.

'Nor should we forget,' added Kanakhala, 'that the Neel-kanth's sailing from the north with another large force. The safest place for our army right now is within these walls.'

Neelkanth? fumed Vidyunmali silently, unwilling to argue openly with the empire's senior officers but outraged all the same. *He's not the Neelkanth, he's our enemy. And our army should be out there fighting, not keeping itself safe behind high walls!*

'Kanakhala's right,' said Daksha. 'We should keep our army here and attack that fraud Neelkanth the moment his ships dock. That coward left my daughter to fight alone while he went gallivanting up the Yamuna – he should pay for his craven behaviour!'

Vidyunmali couldn't believe what he was hearing. *Does anyone here put Meluha's interests above all else?*

'Let's worry about Meluha instead of Princess Sati and her husband's duties towards her,' said Bhrigu, exchoing Vidyun-mali's thoughts. 'Lord Parvateshwar's right: we've won a great victory, but we should measure our next steps carefully. What do you suggest, General?'

'My Lord, we've taken out their elephant corps and cavalry,' said Parvateshwar. 'Sati's army is in retreat, so I'm not expecting the Neelkanth to stop and attack us here.'

'Of course he won't,' quipped Daksha. 'He's a coward.'

'Your Majesty,' said Bhrigu, barely hiding his irritation before addressing Parvateshwar. 'Why won't he stop here, General?'

'My scouts have sent back confirmation of our earlier esti-
mates of Ganesh's army,' said Parvateshwar, 'and they do indeed
have a hundred and fifty thousand soldiers. That's a big army,
but it's not big enough to defeat our forces if we remain within
our walls, given that Sati's troops are no longer available to aug-
ment Shiva's. We could slowly but surely wear his army down
from our defensive positions, so the Neelkanth won't want to
commit to a long siege here. He'll gain nothing and will lose
men unnecessarily.'

'So what do you think he'll do?'

'He'll sail past Devagiri and join up with Sati's army, perhaps
in Mrittikavati or Lothal.'

'Then we should attack their ships as they pass,' interrupted
Daksha.

'That will be difficult, your Majesty,' said Parvateshwar, 'as
we have no warships on the Saraswati under our control. That
means they'll be sailing downriver while our troops will have to
march alongside. There's no way we could keep pace with them.'

'So where should we attack them, then?' asked Bhrigu.

'If we *have* to attack them, I'd prefer to do so at Mrittikavati.'

'Why?'

'Lothal's not a good idea. I designed Lothal's defences myself,
and, sacrificing false modesty, those defences are solid. We'd
need a ten-to-one advantage in numbers to conquer Lothal. We
don't have that. We'd be pitting seventy thousand of our men
against more than two hundred thousand of theirs. Attacking
Lothal would be disastrous for us – we'd lose too many. Mrit-

tikavati's defences, on the other hand, don't require that kind of numerical advantage. Also, we have twenty thousand of our own troops already within Mrittikavati — admittedly, they're currently imprisoned, but if they find out that their fellow soldiers are besieging the city, they could create a lot of trouble for the Lord from within. Having said that, I'd expect the Lord to retreat to Lothal and not Mrittikavati for this very reason.'

Bhrigu had an inkling that Parvateshwar would prefer an altogether different strategy. 'I sense that, left to your own devices, General, you'd choose not to attack at all.'

'Not attack at all?' Daksha sounded surprised. 'Why not? Our army's tasted victory. Parvateshwar, you should—'

'Your Majesty,' interrupted Bhrigu, 'perhaps we should leave it to an expert like Lord Parvateshwar to suggest what we should do. Go on, General.'

'The reason I'd suggest avoiding aggression right now is that the Lord Neelkanth will be hoping that we'll attack,' said Parvateshwar. 'He knows as well as I do that one can't attack a well-defended fort without the advantage of numbers. We don't have that, so by attacking his army, we'll gain nothing and lose too many men. So I say we should stay safely within Devagiri's walls for the time being. If we wait six more months, Ayodhya's army will get here. Their three hundred thousand soldiers combined with ours will give us a huge numerical advantage over the Lord's army.'

'So you are suggesting that we just sit around like cowards?' asked Daksha.

'It's not cowardly to refrain from attacking when the situation isn't in our favour,' said Bhrigu, before turning back to Parvateshwar. 'Go on, General.'

'Once Ayodhya's troops arrive, we should march to Karachapa,' said Parvateshwar. 'We still have control over our navy in the Indus. Our soldiers and Ayodhya's combined will give us an army of four hundred thousand men, and when you add to that the vastly superior naval fleet we have in the Indus, we could mount a very solid attack on Lothal.'

'What you're saying makes sense,' said Bhrigu, before turning to Daksha. 'I suggest we follow Lord Parvateshwar's strategy. Your Majesty?'

Daksha immediately nodded his assent, but Vidyunmali sensed that the emperor's heart wasn't in this decision and began to wonder if this might be an opportunity for him to convince the emperor of a more aggressive course of action.

Ganesh's stunned army was transfixed by the devastation on the hilly battlefield south of Devagiri as they sailed past along the Saraswati. The bloated, rotting carcases of elephants, oxen and horses littered the hill. Great hordes of flies buzzed around them and jackals, crows and vultures fought viciously over the entrails, even though there were corpses enough to feed them all.

But there were no human bodies on the battlefield. The Meluhans, true to their honourable traditions, had in all likelihood conducted funeral ceremonies for all their enemy warriors, Shiva guessed. But there was no debris in the Saraswati, which meant Sati's ships must have escaped the devastation – hopefully with most of her army intact.

Shiva stood on the deck of the lead ship alongside his sons and sister-in-law, surveying the battlefield. He knew he couldn't stop now and engage in a battle at Devagiri; he no longer had the strength of numbers. He would have to retreat further south and find what was left of Sati's army. His scouts told him that the devastation looked worse than it must have been; most of the infantrymen had survived and her ships were sailing south to safety. If much of Sati's army was intact, he would still have a fighting chance to win this the war, but he would have to reformulate his strategy.

All that was for later, though. For now, a single thought ran through his mind: was his Sati hurt? Was she *alive*?

'Neelkanth,' said Gopal, rushing up to Shiva. 'I've just received word from a Vasudev pandit – he's been hiding on the eastern bank of the Saraswati, waiting for our ships to arrive. Lady Sati was still alive when she was pulled aboard one of the retreating ships.'

Shiva's voice was very quiet. 'What exactly does "still alive" mean?'

'She was badly injured, Shiva. She personally led the cavalry against rampaging elephants and Meluha's horsemen – Nandi and Veerbhadra managed to pull her to safety, but she was unconscious by the time she was aboard. Unfortunately, the man I talked to didn't have any further information.'

Shiva's convoy would be able to sail only as quickly as the slowest vessel and he couldn't wait that long.

'Ganesh, I'm taking our fastest ship and sailing south immediately. I have to find your mother. Kali, you and Kartik will remain with the fleet – avoid all battles, sail as quickly as you can and meet me at Mrittikavati.'

Ganesh and Kartik stood mute, both sick with worry about their mother.

'She's alive,' said Shiva, holding his sons' shoulders. 'I know she's alive. She can't die without me.'

— ⚓ ⵉ ⵔⵓ ⵀ ◉ —

Shiva's ship had raced down the Saraswati and soon caught up with Sati's retreating fleet, and with huge relief he discovered that his Sati was out of danger now, although still bedridden. But his relief was tempered by terrible news received from a Vasudev pandit. Reports of the devastation of Sati's army in Devagiri had given the Meluhan prisoners of war in Mrittikavati the courage to challenge their citizen captors. They'd broken out of their prison and taken control of the city, and three thousand citizens loyal to the Neelkanth had died in the process. Shiva had no choice but to avoid Mrittikavati for now, for the city was no longer safe for his army. He ordered his army to retreat to Lothal, and passed on the command to Ganesh's army via another Vasudev pandit.

Shiva remained on Sati's ship as it sailed down the Saraswati. He descended below decks to his wife's cabin, where he found Ayurvati seated by her bedside, applying soothing herbs to her burned face. She quickly and efficiently secured a compress of neem leaves over the wounded flesh. 'This will ensure that your wound doesn't get infected,' she said.

'Thank you, Ayurvatiji,' Sati whispered.

Suspecting that Sati would be concerned about the burn covering nearly a quarter of her face, the doctor added, 'Please don't worry about the scar. Whenever you're ready, I'll perform a cosmetic surgery to smooth out your skin.'

Sati nodded, her lips pursed tight.

Ayurvati looked at Shiva and then back at Sati. 'Take care, my child,' she said, and quietly left the cabin as Shiva was going down on his knees.

He held his beloved's hand as she murmured, 'I'm sorry, Shiva. I failed you.'

'Please stop saying that,' said Shiva. 'I've been told what happened – it's a miracle you managed to save as many of our people as you did.'

'You're just being kind because I'm your wife. We've lost our elephant corps and most of our cavalry. This is a disaster.'

'Why are you so hard on yourself? What happened at Devagiri wasn't your fault: we'd lost our elephant corps the moment the Meluhans discovered that burning chillies would send them into a state of panic.'

'But I should have withdrawn earlier—'

'You withdrew as soon as you saw the effect of the smoke on the elephants. You had no choice but to go in with the cavalry – our soldiers would have been massacred otherwise. Practically our entire army is still intact. Your quick thinking ensured that we didn't suffer even higher casualties.'

Sati looked away unhappily, still feeling terribly guilty.

Shiva touched her forehead gently. 'Sweetheart, listen to me—'

'Leave me alone for a while, Shiva.'

'Sati—'

'Shiva, please . . . please leave me alone.'

Shiva kissed her gently. 'This wasn't your fault,' he repeated. 'There are enough tragedies in life for which we're genuinely responsible. Feel guilty about them, but there's no point burdening your heart with guilt over events that aren't your fault.'

Sati turned to Shiva with a tortured expression. 'And what about you, Shiva? Do you really think a six-year-old child could have done anything to save that woman at Kailash?'

It was Shiva's turn to be silent.

'The honest answer is no,' said Sati, 'and yet you still carry that guilt, don't you? Why? Because you expected more from yourself.'

Shiva's eyes welled up with the agony of that childhood memory. There wasn't a day when he didn't silently apologise to that woman he hadn't been able to save; the woman he hadn't even *tried* to save.

'I expected more from myself as well,' said Sati, her eyes moist.

They empathised with each other in a silent embrace.

Shiva had avoided the tributary which led to Mrittikavati, but his convoy had now reached the last navigable point on this particular tributary of the Saraswati; from here on, the river would be too shallow for the ships to pass. Further on, the Saraswati itself ran dry, no longer reaching the sea.

His army would have to march to the frontier stronghold of Lothal from here, though leaving the empty ships behind was fraught with risk. It would be only a matter of time before the Meluhans learned what he'd done; in effect he would be handing twenty-five well-fitted military ships back to the Meluhans, which would allow them to move their army up and down the Saraswati with frightening speed. He had no choice: the ships had to be destroyed.

Once his entire army had disembarked and readied themselves to march to Lothal, Shiva gave the order, and they watched as the flames made short work of the ships. Lost in thought, he didn't hear Gopal and Chenardhwaj as they approached.

'Lord Agni consumes things rapidly,' said Gopal.

Shiva glanced at him before turning back to the burning vessels. 'We have no choice, Panditji.'

'No, we don't.'

'What do you suggest we do now, Panditji?' asked Shiva.

'The rainy season is here,' said Gopal, 'and it'll be difficult to mount a campaign to attack Devagiri any time soon. Even if we could, without the advantage of our cavalry, it's unlikely that we'll be able to conquer such a well-designed citadel.'

'But it'll be equally difficult for them to attack us in Lothal,' said Shiva. 'Lothal is even better designed for defence than Devagiri.'

'True,' said Gopal, 'so it's a stalemate, and that suits the Meluhans just fine since all they have to do is wait for the Ayodhyan army to reach Meluha – and they could be here in as little as six months.'

Shiva gazed in silence at the burning ships, contemplating this unhappy turn of events.

Chenardhwaj spoke up. 'I have a suggestion, my Lord.' As Shiva turned to him, he explained, 'We can form a crack force of Nagas and the best men from amongst my troops and these commandos will attack the *Somras* factory stealthily. It'll be a suicide mission, but we will destroy it.'

'No,' said Shiva.

'Why not, my Lord?'

'Because Parvateshwar will certainly be prepared for that. He's not an idiot. It'll be a suicide mission all right, but not a successful one.'

'There is one other way,' whispered Gopal.

'The Vayuputras?' asked Shiva.

'Yes.'

Shiva looked back at the burning ships, his expression inscrutable. The Vayuputras appeared to be their only recourse now.

CHAPTER 32

The Last Resort

Shiva rode alongside the covered ox-drawn cart that carried his injured wife. She was strong enough to walk now, but Ayurvati had insisted on caution. It was a grey, drizzly day and Shiva had wrapped a light cloth around his head and face, leaving his eyes uncovered. His *angvastram*, draped across his muscular torso, afforded some protection from the fine rain. He parted the curtains on the cart and looked at his sleeping wife, smiled and drew the curtain shut again, then kicked his horse into a canter.

'Panditji,' he said, slowing his horse to a walk as he approached Gopal, 'About the Vayuputras . . .'

'Yes?'

'What's that terrible weapon of theirs that Kali mentioned?'

'The *Brahmastra*?' asked Gopal. 'The fearsome "weapon of Brahma" is different from other *daivi astras*. Though most of them kill large numbers of men, there are a few, like the *Brahmastra*, that can destroy entire cities – kingdoms, even.'

'By the Holy Lake! How can a single weapon do that?'

'The *Brahmastra*'s a weapon of absolute destruction, my friend. It's a destroyer of cities and a mass-killer of men. When it detonates, a giant mushroom cloud rises high enough to touch the heavens, and everyone and everything in the blast-zone is instantly vaporised. Those beyond this inner circle of destruction might survive, but they'll suffer for generations. The water in the land will be poisoned for decades – centuries, even – and the land will be unusable for even longer, for no crops will grow on it. This weapon doesn't just kill once; it kills again and again, for hundreds of years after it's been used.'

'And people actually contemplate using a weapon such as this?' Shiva was horrified. 'Panditji, using such a dreadful weapon would surely be a crime against humanity.'

'Precisely, great Neelkanth. A weapon like this can never actually be used, but it can be an effective deterrent. One cannot win against the *Brahmastra*, so the mere threat of it is enough to persuade people to surrender.'

'Do you think the Vayuputras will give this weapon to me? Or am I being too presumptuous? After all, I'm not one of them – they think I'm a fraud, don't they?'

'I can think of two reasons why they may help us. First, they haven't tried to assassinate you, which they would have, had a majority of them truly believed you to be a fraud. Perhaps some amongst them still remember and respect your uncle, Lord Manobhu.'

'And the second reason?'

'Lord Bhrigu used *daivi astras* in his attack on Panchavati – not the *Brahmastra*, admittedly, but he broke Lord Rudra's laws by using any of them. That, I suspect, will have turned the Vayuputras against him. And an enemy's enemy—'

'—is a friend,' said Shiva, completing Gopal's statement. 'But I'm not sure these are reasons enough for them to help us.'

'We have no other choice, my friend.'

'Perhaps . . . How do we get to the land of the Vayuputras?'

'Pariha is a long way west of where we are. We can march there overland, through the great mountains, but that route's risky and it'll be time-consuming. The other option is the sea route, but we'll have to wait for the north-easterly winds to favour us.'

'The north-easterlies? But they don't begin until the rains stop, and that won't be for another couple of months.'

'Then we'll have to wait a while, my friend.'

'I have an idea,' said Shiva. 'I'm sure the Meluhans will place spies and scouts in and around Lothal once they know we've retreated into the city. If we take the conventional route to Pariha, they'll know I've sailed west and Lord Bhrigu may guess that I've gone to the Vayuputras to seek help, and that might in turn encourage him to send assassins in pursuit. How about sailing south with a small convoy of military ships?'

Gopal understood immediately. 'Which will make them think we're heading to the Narmada – to either Ujjain or Panchavati.'

'Exactly,' said Shiva. 'We'll disembark somewhere out of sight and head for Pariha aboard a merchant ship.'

'Brilliant! The Meluhans will be busy searching for you along the Narmada while we're on our way to Pariha.'

'Right.'

'And if we use just one merchant ship instead of an entire convoy, we'd have a much better chance of keeping the voyage a secret and travelling quickly.'

Shiva smiled.

— ⚘ ⓌＵ⚘⬡ —

Sati stood at a window in a lookout shelter on the southern edge of Lothal's fort, staring at the vast expanse of sea beyond its walls. The monsoon had arrived in earnest and heavy rain was pelting the city. The army was well fortified within the city walls, and Ganesh was expected to arrive within a week or two, along with his soldiers.

Ayurvati rushed into the shelter and, after propping her cane and cloth umbrella beside the entrance, announced with a loud whoop, 'Lord Indra and Lord Varun be praised! They've decided to deliver the entire quota of this year's rain in a single day!'

Sati turned with a distracted look as Ayurvati sat next to her and squeezed water from her drenched *angvastram*. 'I love the rain. It seems to wash away sorrows and bring new life with renewed hope, doesn't it?'

Sati nodded politely, not really interested. 'Yes, Ayurvatiji.'

Ayurvati was not one to give up easily. Determined to lighten Sati's mood, she went on, 'I'm not too busy at the moment

– there aren't many injured and the monsoon diseases have, surprisingly, infected few this year.'

'That's good news, Ayurvatiji,' said Sati.

'Yes, it is. So, I was thinking this would be a good time to perform your surgery.'

There was an ugly blemish on her left cheek, where scar tissue had formed over the burns she'd suffered during the Battle of Devagiri.

'There's nothing wrong with me,' said Sati politely, but her tone had a warning edge.

'Of course there isn't. I'm only talking about the scar on your face. It can be removed very easily with cosmetic surgery.'

'No. I don't want surgery.'

Ayurvati assumed Sati was worried about the long recovery time and the possible impact on her ability to participate in the next battle. 'It's a very simple procedure, Sati – you'll be fully recovered in a couple of weeks. It looks as though the monsoon rains are going to be particularly heavy this year, so there'll be no warfare for a few months. You won't miss any battles.'

'*Nothing* would keep me away from the next battle.'

'Then why don't you want this surgery, my child? I'm sure it would make the Lord Neelkanth happy.'

A hint of a smile broke through her solemn demeanour. 'Shiva keeps telling me I'm as beautiful as ever, scar or no scar. I know I look horrendous. He's lying because he loves me, but I choose to believe it.'

'Why are you doing this to yourself?' asked an anguished Ayurvati. 'It won't hurt a bit – not that you're scared of pain—'

'No, Ayurvatiji.'

'Why not? You have to give me a reason.'

'Because I need this scar,' said Sati grimly. 'It's a constant reminder of my failure. I won't rest till I've set it right and recovered the ground I lost for my army.'

'Sati! It wasn't your fault that—'

'Ayurvatiji,' said Sati, firmly interrupting the former chief surgeon of Meluha, 'you of all people shouldn't tell me a white lie. I was the commanding officer and my army was defeated. It was my fault.'

'Sati—'

'This scar stays with me. Every time I look at my reflection, it'll remind me that I have work to do. Let me win a battle for my army, and then we can do the surgery.'

— 🜨 —

Ganesh's army had just arrived at Lothal. They too had avoided Mrittikavati on the advice of a Vasudev pandit and, just like Shiva, Ganesh had ensured that all his ships were destroyed on the Saraswati before his army marched south to Lothal.

They were received at the city gates by Governor Chenardhwaj himself. Ganesh and Kartik wanted to see their parents immediately, but Chenardhwaj informed them that Shiva had asked to meet with them by himself first. He wanted to prepare them for their first encounter with Sati so they wouldn't inadvertently upset her with their reactions to her scarred face.

Meanwhile, the Neelkanth's allies – Prince Bhagirath of Ayodhya, King Chandraketu of Branga and King Maatali of Vaishali – were escorted to their respective chambers in the Lothal governor's residence. The Chandravanshi royalty, used to the pomp and pageantry of their own land, were distinctly underwhelmed by the austere Meluhan accommodations. It was difficult to believe that the governor of one of the richest provinces of the richest empire in the world lived in such simplicity. However, they accepted their housing with good grace, knowing it was Shiva's will.

It was a tribute to Meluha's robust urban planning that such a massive army – now totalling nearly two hundred and fifty thousand soldiers – could be so quickly accommodated in reasonable comfort in guest houses and temporary shelters erected throughout the city.

As soon as Shiva had prepared them for Sati's injuries, Ganesh and Kartik rushed to see their mother. While Kartik was able to control his anger and shock, as Shiva had requested, Ganesh's obsessive love for his mother overwhelmed him.

'*Dada*,' whispered Kartik, gently placing his hand on his angry brother's arm.

Ganesh clenched his fists, gritted his teeth and breathed rapidly, his normally calm eyes blazing, as he stared at his mother's disfigured face. His long nose was stretched out, trembling with anger, and his big floppy ears were rigid. He growled, 'I will kill every single one of those b—'

'Ganesh,' said Sati calmly, interrupting her son, 'the Meluhan soldiers were only doing their duty, as was I. They've done nothing wrong.'

'*Dada, maa*'s right,' said Kartik.

Their words did not calm Ganesh's fury.

'Ganesh, these things happen in a war,' she went on. 'You know that.' She stepped close and embraced her elder son, then pulled his face down and kissed his forehead, smiling lovingly. 'Calm down, Ganesh.'

Kartik hugged them both. '*Dada*, battle scars are a mark of pride for a warrior.'

Ganesh held his mother tight, tears streaming down his face. 'You're not entering a battlefield again, *maa*. Not unless I'm standing in front of you.'

— ⚛ ⚝ U ⚡ ⊕ —

Shiva entered his room to find that Sati had moved some of the furniture to create a training circle and was practising her sword-work. He leaned against a wall and watched his wife quietly, not wanting to disturb her. He admired every perfect warrior move: the sway of her hips as she transferred her weight; the quick thrusts and swings of her sword; the rapid movement of her shield, which she used as an independent weapon. Shiva was overcome; this was yet another reminder of why he loved her so much.

Sati swung around with her shield held high and her eyes fell on Shiva. 'How long have you been watching me?' she asked, surprised.

'Long enough to know that I should never challenge you to a duel!'

Sati smiled slightly but said nothing. She quickly sheathed her sword and put down her shield. Shiva stepped over and helped unbuckle her scabbard.

'Thank you,' she whispered as she took the scabbard from Shiva, then returned her shield and sheathed sword to the mini-armoury on the wall.

'We won't be able to go to Pariha together,' said Shiva.

'I know. Gopalji told me the Parihans allow only Vayuputras and Vasudevs to enter their domain and I am neither.'

'Well, technically, nor am I.'

Sati pulled her *angvastram* over her head to cover the scar on her left cheek. 'But you're the Neelkanth – rules can be broken for you.'

Shiva pulled her close, then raised a hand to the *angvastram* covering her face and gently tried to pull it back. Even though she knew he didn't care, she still preferred to hide her scar from Shiva. It didn't matter to her if others saw it, but not Shiva.

'Shiva . . .' she whispered, holding her *angvastram* firmly against her cheek.

He tugged hard and pulled the *angvastram* free. Upset, Sati tried to yank it back, but he overpowered her and held her close. 'I wish you could see your ethereal beauty through my eyes,' he whispered.

Sati rolled her eyes and, still struggling in Shiva's arms, turned away. 'I'm ugly, and I know it! Don't use your love to insult me.'

'Love?' asked Shiva, wiggling his eyebrows in mock surprise. 'Who said anything about love? It's lust, pure and simple!'

Sati stared at Shiva for a moment, then she burst out laughing.

Shiva pulled her to him again, grinning. 'This is no laughing matter, my princess. I'm your husband. I have rights, you know.'

Sati hit Shiva playfully on his chest, still laughing.

Shiva kissed her tenderly. 'I love you.'

'You're mad!'

'That I am. But I still love you.'

CHAPTER 33

The Conspiracy Deepens

'Brilliant idea, your Majesty,' said Vidyunmali, the emperor's new confidant. The Meluhan brigadier's increasing frustration with Parvateshwar's cautious approach – he believed the general's wait-and-watch strategy was giving Shiva's army time to recover from its defeat at Devagiri – had forged a new alliance between them. He was spending more and more time with the emperor, who had him reassigned to lead the thousand-strong brigade tasked with guarding the royal family and palace and with carrying out any missions he had personally mandated.

Feeling increasingly comfortable with this new relationship, Daksha finally confided in Vidyunmali his idea to end the war, and, much to his delight, the brigadier's reaction had been very different from Bhrigu's.

'Exactly!' he exclaimed happily. 'Why can't the others understand?'

'Your Majesty, you are the emperor,' said Vidyunmali. 'It

doesn't matter if others don't agree with you: whatever you decide is the will of Meluha.'

'You really think we should go ahead—?'

'It doesn't matter what *I* think, your Majesty. What do *you* think?'

'I think it's a brilliant idea!'

'Then that's what Meluha thinks as well, your Majesty.'

'I think we should implement it.'

'What are your orders, your Majesty?'

'I haven't worked out all the details, Brigadier,' said Daksha. 'That's your responsibility. My job is to look at the big picture.'

'Of course, your Majesty,' said Vidyunmali. 'But I don't think we can execute our plan until the maharishi and General Parvateshwar have left the city – they'll try to stop us if they find out what we're doing.'

'They're going to Karachapa – or that's Parvateshwar's latest plan, at least. I wasn't supportive of the idea earlier, but now I think I'll encourage it and hasten their departure.'

'An inspired move, your Majesty. We must also choose the right assassins.'

'I agree, but where will we find them?'

'They must be foreigners, your Majesty – we don't want anyone to recognise them. They'll have to wear cloaks and masks if they're to look like Nagas, right?'

'Yes, of course.'

'I know some people, the best in the business.'

'Where are they from?'

'Egypt.'

'By the great Lord Varun, that's too far away – it'll take too much time to bring them here.'

'Not if I leave immediately, your Majesty – if I have your permission, that is.'

'Of course you have it. Accomplish this, Vidyunmali, and Meluha will sing your praises for centuries.'

'Lord Gopal and I will leave within a week,' said Shiva, looking around the governor's office at Sati, Kali, Ganesh, Kartik, Bhagirath, Chenardhwaj, Chandraketu and Maatali. The monsoons were drawing to an end, the once-constant rain now just occasional light showers. Shiva and Gopal's small convoy of military ships would rendezvous with a merchant ship at a secret location north of the Narmada delta that would set sail westwards towards Pariha, taking advantage of the dry season's northeasterly winds. With luck, the Meluhans woud not realise where Shiva was really going.

'Our destination *must* be kept secret,' Shiva said, 'for victory is assured if our mission succeeds. In my absence, Sati will be in command.'

Everyone nodded their agreement, unaware that Sati had fought this decision. After Devagiri, she didn't think she deserved this command. But Shiva had insisted; he trusted her with his life.

'Pray to Lord Ram and Lord Rudra that our mission is a success,' said Gopal.

Shiva stood on the shores of the Mansarovar Lake, watching the slow descent of the sun in the evening sky. There was no breeze and everything was eerily still. A sudden chill enveloped him and he looked down, surprised to see that he was standing in knee-deep water. He turned around and began wading out of the lake. Thick fog had blanketed the banks and he could no longer see his village. As he stepped out of the lake, the mist magically cleared.

'Sati?'

Sati was sitting calmly atop a thick pile of wood, armed and armoured. Engraved armbands glinted in the dusk light; her sword lay by her side and her shield was fastened on her back. She was prepared for war. But why was she wearing a saffron angvastram, *the colour of the final journey?*

'Sati,' said Shiva, walking towards her.

She opened her eyes and smiled serenely. She looked as though she was speaking, but Shiva couldn't hear the words at first. The sound reached his ears only after a few moments' delay. 'I'll be waiting for you—'

'What? Where are you going?'

Suddenly a hazy figure appeared bearing a burning torch. Without a moment's hesitation, he rammed it into the pile of wood upon which Sati was perched. It caught fire instantly.

'Sati!' screamed Shiva as he raced towards her.

Sati continued to sit upon the burning pyre, at peace with herself, her beatific smile an eerie contrast to the flames now leaping up around her.

'*Sati!*' *shouted Shiva.* '*Jump off!*'

But Sati remained where she was. Shiva was just a few yards away from her when a platoon of soldiers jumped in front of him. Shiva drew his sword in a flash and tried to push the soldiers aside, but they fought him relentlessly. The soldiers were huge and unnaturally hairy, like the monster from his nightmare. Shiva battled tirelessly but couldn't push through. Meanwhile, the flames had almost hidden Sati from his sight. And yet she continued to sit on the pyre, making no attempt to escape.

'*Sati!*'

— ⅄ ⑩∪⚡ ⊛ —

Shiva woke up in a sweat, reaching out desperately for his wife. It took a moment for his eyes to adjust to the darkness. Sati was asleep, her scarred cheek clearly visible in the moonlight. Shiva gathered her into a tight embrace.

'Shiva . . . ?' whispered Sati groggily.

Shiva didn't reply, just held her against his chest as tears streamed down his face.

'Shiva?' asked Sati, fully awake now. 'What's the matter, darling?'

But Shiva was so choked with emotion that he couldn't utter a word.

Sati pulled her head back to get a better look at him in the dim light. She reached up and touched his cheeks. They were moist.

'Shiva? Sweetheart? What's wrong? Did you have a bad dream?'

'Sati, promise me that you won't go into battle until I return.'

'Shiva, you've made me the leader. If the army has to go into battle, I'll have to lead them. You know that.'

Shiva kept quiet.

'What did you see?'

He shook his head.

'It was only a dream, Shiva. It doesn't mean anything. You need to focus your attention on your journey. You're leaving tomorrow. You must succeed in your mission with the Vayu-putras — that will bring an end to this war. Don't let worries about me distract you.'

Shiva remained silent, refusing to let her go.

'Shiva, you carry the future on your shoulders. I'll say it again — don't let your love for me distract you. It was just a dream, that's all.'

'I can't live without you.'

'You won't have to. I'll be waiting for you when you return. I promise.'

Shiva pulled back a bit and stared deep into Sati's eyes. 'Stay away from fires.'

'Shiva, seriously, what—'

'Sati, promise me you'll stay away from fires.'

'Yes, Shiva, I promise.'

CHAPTER 34

With the Help of Umbergaon

Shiva was ready to leave. His bags had already been sent to his ship and he'd ordered all his aides out of his chamber. He wanted a few minutes alone with Sati.

'Goodbye, my love,' whispered Shiva.

She smiled and embraced him. 'I'll be waiting for you. Nothing's going to happen to me – you won't get rid of me that easily.'

Shiva laughed softly, for Sati had used his own line on him. 'I know. It was just an overreaction to a stupid nightmare.' He cupped her face and kissed her deeply. 'I love you.'

A couple of weeks later, the small convoy sneaked into a hidden lagoon a short distance north of the Narmada delta. Shiva and Gopal disembarked into rowing boats, along with a skeleton crew, and stole onto the beach, ready for the merchant ship that was due to arrive early next morning to take them to Pariha.

'Hmmm . . . good workmanship,' Shiva said, admiring the vessel as it pulled in.

It was bulky, obviously designed to carry a large cargo, but any sailor could see that it was also built for speed, with its double masts, high stern and low bow. In addition, the ship had been outfitted with two banks of oars for human propulsion if it was needed.

'We won't really need the rowers,' said Gopal, as if reading Shiva's mind. 'We'll have the north-easterly winds in our sails.'

'Where's this beauty from?' asked Shiva.

'A small shipping village called Umbergaon, south of the Narmada River delta. That region's not part of any empire, Swadweepan or Meluhan, which makes it a perfect place to build ships one doesn't want tracked. The local ruler, Jadav Rana, is a pragmatic man. The Nagas have helped him many times and he values their friendship. Just as importantly, his people are expert shipbuilders. This vessel will get us to Pariha as fast as is humanly possible.'

'How can I express our gratitude for their invaluable help?'

'No need,' said Gopal, with a smile. 'It's Pariha that should be grateful to Umbergaon, for the Umbergaonis have ensured that the gift of the Neelkanth will reach Pariha.'

Shiva looked discomfited. 'I'm no gift,' he muttered.

'Yes, you are, for you will help the Vayuputras achieve their purpose. You will help them fulfil their vow to Lord Rudra: to not let Evil win.'

Shiva remained silent, embarrassed by his words.

'I have no doubt,' continued Gopal, 'that, one day, Pariha will send a gift to Umbergaon in return.'

'How are you feeling now, my friend?' asked Gopal as soon as he entered Shiva's cabin.

The merchant ship bearing Shiva's small party had been sailing the open seas for a little more than a week. They were far from the coastline and unlikely to encounter the Meluhan navy, but they'd run into choppy waters during the last few days. The sailors were not troubled by it, and nor was Gopal, who had travelled these waters many times, but Shiva had only undertaken one sea voyage before, from the Narmada delta to Lothal, and the ship had stayed close to the coast. It was no surprise to anyone else that the rough weather had given the Neelkanth a severe bout of seasickness.

Shiva looked up from his bed and cursed, his eyes half shut. 'I have no stomach left! It's all been vomited out! A plague on these wretched waters!'

Gopal laughed softly. 'It's time for your medicine, Neelkanth.'

'What's the point, Panditji? Nothing stays in my stomach!'

'For whatever little time it remains there, it will serve its purpose. Take it.'

Gopal poured his herbal infusion into a wooden spoon and offered it to Shiva, who swallowed it quickly and fell back on the bed.

'Holy Lake, help me,' whispered Shiva. 'Let this medicine stay within me for a few minutes, at least.'

But the prayer was probably still winging its way to Mansarovar Lake when Shiva lurched to one side and retched into the large pot that had been placed there for just that purpose.

Gopal handed Shiva a damp towel and he slowly wiped his clammy face. He shook his head and looked up at the ceiling of his cabin in disgust. 'Crap!'

Bhrigu and Parvateshwar rode on horseback at the head of a massive army that had marched out of Devagiri towards the Beas River, where they would board ships and sail down to Karachapa.

'It occurs to me that having the powerful fleet harboured in Karachapa isn't the only advantage we'll gain from our decision to shift our command headquarters,' said Bhrigu.

Parvateshwar frowned. 'What other benefit does it offer, my Lord?'

'Well, you won't have to suffer any more idiotic orders from your emperor – you'll be free to conduct the war however you deem fit.'

Parvateshwar knew that Bhrigu held Daksha in contempt, but he was far too disciplined a Meluhan to speak out openly against his emperor. He remained stoic in his silence.

Bhrigu smiled. 'You really are a rare man, General, a man of the old code. Lord Ram would have been proud of you.'

Aided by the north-easterly winds filling its sails, the merchant ship cut rapidly through the waters. After a few days, Shiva had finally adapted to the sea and was at last able to enjoy the stiff morning breeze. He stood on the main deck, at the bow, with Gopal for company.

'We're now leaving our Western Sea via a very narrow strait,' said Gopal. 'It's only a little over twenty-five miles across.'

'What's on the other side?' asked Shiva.

'The Jam Zrayangh.'

'Sounds scary. What in Lord Ram's name does *that* mean?'

Gopal laughed. 'Something absolutely benign, I assure you. "Zrayangh" simply means "sea" in the local language.'

'And what does "Jam" mean?'

'It means "to come to".'

'So this is "the sea that you come to"?'

'Indeed. This is the sea you must come to if you want to travel to Elam or Mesopotamia or any of the lands further west – but most importantly, this is the sea you must come to if you need to go to Pariha.'

'I've heard of Mesopotamia – it has strong trade relations with Meluha, doesn't it?'

'Yes, it's a very rich and powerful empire established between two great rivers in the region, the Tigris and the Euphrates.'

'Is this empire bigger than Meluha and Swadweep?'

'No,' said Gopal, 'it's not even as big as Meluha. But they believe human civilisation began in their region.'

'Really? Didn't human civilisation began here?'

'We believe that, yes.'

'So who's right?'

Gopal shrugged. 'I don't know. These claims have been made for many thousands of years – but, frankly, does it matter who became civilised first so long as all of us eventually became civilised?'

Shiva smiled. 'True. And where's Elam?'

'Elam is a much smaller kingdom to the south-east of Mesopotamia.'

'So Elam's closer to Pariha?' asked Shiva.

'Yes – it acts as a buffer state between Pariha and Mesopotamia, which is why the Parihans have occasionally helped the Elamites, unofficially, of course.'

'But I thought Pariha never got involved in local politics?'

'They try to avoid it. And most people in the region haven't even heard of the Vayuputras. But they were concerned that an expanding Mesopotamia would encroach into their land.'

'Expanding Mesopotamia?' Shiva asked, hoping Gopal might share more stories of strange lands.

'A gifted gardener once conquered the whole of Mesopotamia,' the Chief Vasudev started.

'A gardener? How did a gardener become a warrior? Did he train in secret?'

Gopal smiled. 'From what I've heard, he wasn't trained at all.

He was very talented, but not in gardening! Nobody knows his original name, but he called himself Sargon and he conquered the whole of Mesopotamia – and surprisingly quickly too. But that didn't satiate his ambition, and so he went on to conquer the neighbouring kingdoms as well, including Elam.'

'Which would have brought him to the borders of Pariha.'

'Uncomfortably close,' Gopal admitted, 'and the Vayuputras were troubled enough to offer anonymous assistance to Elam, which enabled the Elamites to rebel, and the conquest of the Mesopotamians didn't stay conquered for too long either.'

'King Sargon sounds like a very interesting man,' Shiva said, musing on this ambitious king.

'He was: he challenged the entire world, and even Fate itself. He was so feisty that he dared to name his empire the Empire of the Akkadians, after his adoptive father, a water-carrier named Akki.'

'And does this empire still exist?' And when Gopal shook his head, Shiva added, 'That's sad. I would have loved to meet these remarkable Akkadians.'

'The people of Elam would have a very different opinion, Lord Neelkanth,' the Vasudev said with a wry smile.

Kartik and Ganesh were happy to find Kali with their mother. Ganesh immediately voiced his concern. 'The soldiers are bored and restless with no action, nothing to do,' he started.

'I was just discussing exactly that with *didi*,' said Kali. 'The men are spending their time gambling and drinking to keep themselves occupied. Training's suffering because they don't see the point of it when there's virtually no chance of combat in the near future.'

'It's at times like this when stupid incidents occur which can blow up into serious problems,' said Sati.

'Let's find ways to keep them busy, then,' suggested Kartik. 'How about organising some hunting in the forests around the city? We know the Meluhan army hasn't left Karachapa yet, so there's no real risk, even sending our men out in large groups. Hunting will give them some action to make up for the lapsed training, and help alleviate the boredom.'

'Good idea,' agreed Kali. 'We can also use the meat to organise feasts for the citizens of Lothal – that'll help assuage some of their irritation at having to host such a large army for so long.'

'I agree,' said Sati. 'I'll issue the orders immediately.'

Shiva and his companions had been on board the merchant ship for nearly a month and a half. They were currently anchored off a desolate coast on the Jam Sea. Shiva gazed out over the blasted landscape. There didn't appear to be any habitation of any kind – in fact, it looked as though this land had never been disturbed by humans. Shiva wasn't surprised. Like the Vasudevs, the Vayuputras were secretive about their existence. But while he hadn't expected a major port, he had assumed there'd be some secret symbol, like the emblematic Vasudev flame on the banks of the Chambal near Ujjain.

Then he looked more closely. He thought he detected something: a thick row of tall bushes, maybe twelve or fifteen feet high, that ran along the edge of the coast appeared to have an abundance of reddish-orange fruit hanging from them. They were covered with small dark-green leaves except at the top, where the foliage was bright red, and these vermilion leaves combined with the glowing fruit to give the impression that the bushes were on fire.

A burning bush . . .

Shiva turned and began climbing the mainmast to the crow's nest. From that vantage point, the symbol was instantly recognisable: the bushes, white sand and brownish rocks came together to form the symbol of *Fravashi*, the holy flame, the feminine spirit.

Shiva came down to find Gopal waiting for him.

'Did you see something, my friend?' asked Gopal.

'I saw the holy flame, the pure being – I saw the *Fravashi*.'

For a moment Gopal was astonished, but then he chuckled. 'Of course! Lord Manobhu would have told you about the *Fravashi*. It's a symbol of the faith of Lord Rudra's people. The *Fravashi* represents pure spirits, the angels. The scriptures tell us there are tens of thousands of them; they send forth human souls into this world and support them in the eternal battle between Good and Evil. They're also believed to have assisted God in the creation of the universe.'

Shiva nodded. 'The Vasudevs believe in the *Fravashi* as well, I assume.'

'We respect the *Fravashi*, but it's a Parihan symbol.'

'Then why do you have a *Fravashi* on the border of your land?'

Gopal frowned. 'A *Fravashi* symbol? Where?'

'In the clearing on the Chambal, where we contacted you through the clapping code—'

'Oh!' said Gopal with a smile as understanding dawned upon him. 'My friend, we do indeed have a symbolic flame, but we don't call it *Fravashi*. We call it *Agni*, the God of Fire.'

'But the symbol's almost exactly the same as the *Fravashi*.'

'Yes, it is. The Parihans give enormous importance to fire rituals, as do we Indians. The first hymn of the first chapter in the *Rig Veda* is dedicated to Agni. The importance of the element of fire is, I believe, common to all the world's religions.'

'Fire is the beginning of human civilisation.'

'It's the beginning of all life, my friend, the source of all energy. One way of looking at the stars is to see them as great balls of fire.'

Shiva smiled at the pandit as a sailor approached them.

'My Lords, the rowing boat has been lowered. We're ready to disembark.'

The rowing boat was still a hundred yards from the coast when a tall man appeared from behind the bushes. He wore a long brownish-black cloak and held what looked like a staff, or perhaps a spear. Shiva couldn't be sure and instinctively reached for his sword.

Gopal reached out to stay Shiva's hand. 'It's all right, my friend.'

Shiva spoke without taking his eyes off the stranger. 'Are you sure?'

'Yes. He's a Parihan, come to guide us.'

Shiva relaxed his grip but kept his hand close to the hilt. He watched the stranger reach into the bushes and tug at something that looked like ropes and he reached for his sword again – but to his surprise, four horses emerged from behind the foliage. Three of them had nothing but saddles on their backs and were clearly intended for riders. The fourth beast bore a massive sack on its back. Perhaps it was carrying provisions, Shiva speculated. He moved his hand away from his sword again and let it relax.

The stranger was a friend.

CHAPTER 35

Journey to Pariha

'I'm glad the Vayuputras have sent someone to meet us,' said Gopal, watching the sailors offloading their provisions from the rowing boat. Shiva, Gopal and the Parihan would carry some on their horses, while the rest would have to be loaded onto the already overburdened fourth beast.

'How could the Vayuputras ignore the Chief Vasudev, my Lord?' asked the Parihan, bowing low towards Gopal. 'We received your message from the Vasudev pandit of Lothal in good time. You are our honoured guest. My name is Kurush and I will be your guide to our city, Pariha.'

Shiva studied Kurush intently. His cloak couldn't hide the fact that he was armed and he wondered whether Kurush would manage to draw his sword quickly in an emergency. The man was unnaturally fair-skinned, a colouring not often seen on the hot plains of India, but surprisingly he was neither pale nor unattractive. His long, sharp nose and full beard somehow enhanced the man's beauty, though he still looked like a warrior. He wore his hair long, in common with the Indians, and on his head was perched a square white hat made of cotton. Shiva was most interested in his distinctive beard, which was curled into tufts just like the one gracing Lord Rudra's visage in the holy Vishwanath Temple at Kashi.

'Thank you, Kurush,' said Gopal. 'Please allow me the pleasure of introducing the long-awaited Neelkanth himself, Lord Shiva.'

Kurush turned towards Shiva and nodded curtly. Clearly he was one of the Vayuputras who considered Shiva a usurper: a Neelkanth who hadn't been authorised by his tribe. Shiva kept his thoughts to himself. He knew the only opinion that mattered was that of their chief, the Mithra.

— ⚐ ◍Ս⯑◉ —

Shiva mounted his horse, then turned and waved to the sailors as they rowed back to their ship. They intended to sail on a little further and anchor in a hidden cove. After two months had passed, the captain would send out a rowing boat once every two days to this spot, to check if they had returned.

Kurush had already ridden ahead, leading the horse bearing most of the provisions, so Gopal and Shiva kicked their horses into a trot. While the Parihan was safely out of earshot, Shiva said, 'Why does the name Kurush sound familiar?'

'Kurush is sometimes shortened to Kuru,' said Gopal, 'and Kuru was a great Indian emperor in ancient times.'

'So which name came first – Kuru or Kurush?'

'Do you mean who influenced whom?' asked Gopal. 'Did India influence Pariha or was it the other way around?'

'Yes, that's a better way of putting it.'

'I don't know. It was probably a bit of both. We learned from their noble culture and they learned from ours. Of course, we argue endlessly about who learned how much and from whom, but that's nothing but our egos trying desperately to prove that our culture's superior to others. It's a foolish quest,' the Chief Vasudev said firmly. 'It's best to learn from everyone, regardless of the cultural source of that knowledge.'

— ⁂ ◍Ü⚑⦿ —

The Parihan rode ahead of the others in solitary splendour. They'd been travelling for a week now, and Kurush had determinedly remained uncommunicative, giving only monosyllabic answers to Shiva's companionable queries. The Neelkanth had finally stopped talking to him.

'Did Lord Rudra grow up here?' Shiva asked Gopal.

'Yes, he was born in this region. He came to India when we needed him.'

'So he was from the land of fairies – that would make him our guardian spirit as well.'

'Actually, I don't believe he was born in Pariha, but somewhere close by called Anshan.'

'Doesn't "*anshan*" mean "hunger"?' When Gopal nodded, he

asked, 'They named their land "hunger"? Was it really such a bad place to live?'

'Look around you: this is a harsh, mountainous desert. Life is perennially difficult here, although once in a while a great man comes along who has the ability to tame this land.'

'And Lord Rudra and his tribe proved to be such men?'

'Yes. They established the kingdom of Elam.'

'Elam? The same Elam that the Mesopotamians conquered? So that would explain why the Vayuputras supported them, wouldn't it? The Elamites were Lord Rudra's people.'

'No, that's not the reason. The Vayuputras supported the Elamites because they genuinely felt the need for a buffer state between them and the Mesopotamians. In fact, Lord Rudra gave his fellow Elamites an ultimatum: they could either join the Vayuputra tribe, giving up all links with any other identity they'd previously cherished, or they could choose to remain Elamites. Those who chose to follow Lord Rudra became the Vayuputras we know today.'

'So Pariha's not where Anshan used to be.'

'No. Anshan is the capital of the Elamite kingdom. Pariha's further east.'

'Am I right in thinking that the Vayuputras accepted other outsiders, and not just the Elamites? My uncle was a Tibetan.'

'Yes, the Vayuputras accept members solely on merit, not by virtue of birth. Many Elamites try to become Vayuputras but don't succeed. The only people accepted in large numbers was a tribe of refugees from our country.'

'From India?'

'Yes – Lord Rudra felt personally guilty about what he'd done to them, so he took them under his protection and gave them refuge in his land, amongst the Vayuputras.'

'Who were these people?'

'The Asuras.'

Before Shiva could react to this astonishing piece of information, Kurush turned and addressed Gopal. 'My Lord, the path ahead leads through a narrow mountain pass with few resting places. Shall we take a break here?'

Lunch was an entirely unappetising and cold affair, with the harsh mountain winds adding to the discomfort, but the dry fruit Kurush had brought along provided a boost of energy, much needed for the back-breaking ride that lay ahead.

As soon as they were back on the road, Shiva continued his conversation with Gopal. 'The Asuras took refuge here?' He was still shocked at the revelation.

'They did,' replied Gopal. 'Lord Rudra himself brought the few surviving Asura leaders to Pariha. Others, who were in hiding, were rescued from India by the Vayuputras. Some Asuras went further west, beyond Elam, even – I'm not sure what happened to them – but many of them remained in Pariha.'

'And these Asuras assimilated into the Vayuputra tribe?'

'Not all of them. Lord Rudra found that a few of the Asuras couldn't detach from their former allegiances sufficiently to become members of the tribe so they were allowed to live in Pariha as refugees. But most became Vayuputras.'

'Many of them would have been Asura royalty,' he mused. 'Didn't they want to attack India and take revenge on the Devas who'd defeated them?'

'No, my friend: once they joined the Vayuputra brotherhood they ceased to be Asuras. They gave up their old identities and embraced the primary task Lord Rudra had set the Vayuputras: to protect the holy land of India from Evil.'

Shiva rode on in silence for a while as he absorbed this. The Asuras had been able to move beyond their hatred of their former enemies and work for the mission to protect them mandated by Lord Rudra.

Gopal echoed Shiva's thoughts. 'In a strange twist of fate, the Asuras, who were regarded as demons by the Devas, were in fact actively working behind the scenes to protect them from the effects of Evil.'

'But Panditji, surely the Asuras didn't forget their old culture entirely? They must have influenced the Parihan way of life somehow. Cultural heritage doesn't die easily — unless, of course, one becomes as detached as the ascetics.'

'You're right. The Asura culture did impact the Parihans. For instance, do you know the Parihan term for gods?'

Shiva shook his head.

Gopal glanced at him conspiratorially. 'Go on – take a guess. But I should tell you that in the old Parihan language, there was no "s" sound. It was pronounced either "sh" or "h" instead. So what do you think they called their gods?'

Shiva frowned, then grinned. 'Ahuras?'

'Exactly.'

'Good Lord! What were their demons called, then?'

'Daevas.'

'By the great Lord Brahma! It's the exact opposite of the Indian pantheon. We call our gods Devas and our demons Asuras.'

Gopal smiled slightly. 'They're different, but they're not evil.'

CHAPTER 36

The Land of Fairies

Shiva, Gopal and Kurush had been on the road for a little over a month, and the late winter was making the journey through the harsh terrain a real test of will. Shiva had lived most of his life in the highlands of Tibet and was coping well, but the Chief Vasudev was used to the moist heat of the plains and he found the cold and the rarefied atmosphere challenging.

'We're here,' said Kurush out of the blue one day, raising his hand to signal a stop on the narrow pathway, no more than twelve feet wide. Shiva dismounted, tied the reins to a rocky outcrop and went to assist Gopal, tethering his horse before helping him to dismount. When he'd made the Chief Vasudev as comfortable as he could, he passed over his water flask and Gopal sipped the life-nurturing fluid slowly.

Only then did Shiva take a look around. To the left, the sheer mountain extended upwards for several hundred feet. To the right was a precipitous drop to a dry valley far below. There wasn't a sign of any life anywhere as far as the eye could see: no human habitation, no animals, not even the few valiant plants and twisted trees they'd seen at lower heights.

Shiva looked at Gopal and whispered, 'We're here?'

Gopal gestured towards Kurush, who was carefully running his hands over the mountain wall, his eyes shut, as if trying to locate something. Shiva moved towards him and, when Kurush's hand stopped moving, he saw the faint indentation of a symbol carved into the mountainside: a *Fravashi*.

Kurush pressed the ring on his index finger into the centre of the symbol and a block of rock the size of a human head emerged to his right. Kurush quickly placed both his hands on the block, stepped back to get some leverage and pushed hard.

Shiva watched in wonder as the mountain appeared to come to life. A substantial section, nearly twelve feet across and nine feet wide, receded inwards and then slid aside, revealing a pathway leading deep into the heart of the mountain.

Kurush turned to Shiva and indicated that they should start moving and Shiva helped Gopal back onto his horse. As he walked towards his own beast he noticed that the rocky outcrop where he'd tethered the horses looked natural at first glance, but it was in fact man-made. He mounted his horse and quickly joined Gopal and Kurush, and the concealed entrance closed behind them as smoothly as it had opened.

A flaming torch on one of the walls threw its light ahead of them for a few yards, but beyond that it soon lost its struggle against the omnipresent darkness. Kurush pulled three unlit torches from a recess in the wall, lit them and handed one each to Gopal and Shiva. Then, holding his own torch aloft, he swiftly rode ahead. Shiva and Gopal kicked their horses and made haste after him.

Soon the pathway forked, but Kurush chose one of the paths without hesitation. Shiva recalled the Nagas' multiple pathways threading through Dandak Forest. Only a Vayuputra guide would be able to find the secret pathway here; unauthorised visitors would inevitably get lost deep within the mountain.

Shiva expected many more such misleading paths along the way. He wasn't disappointed.

— ⁂ ⑩Ʊ⇪❀ —

Half an hour later, after a monotonous ride, the travellers emerged on the other side of the mountain and were almost blinded by the sudden onslaught of bright sunlight. Even as his eyes adjusted, Shiva's jaw dropped in amazement as he took in what lay ahead.

This side of the mountain was dramatically different from the one they'd left behind. A broad, winding road had been cut into the mountainside – the Parihans called it the Rudra Avenue, Kurush informed them – and it snaked gently downwards into the valley below. A beautifully carved railing ran along the edge to prevent horses or carriages from falling to what would be certain death in the sheer-sided ravine below. The splendour of nature notwithstanding, Shiva was most impressed with the man-made creation of Pariha: here, hidden away from prying eyes in this secluded spot, protected by steep, unconquerable mountains, the Vayuputras had truly created a land fit for fairies.

The Rudra Avenue ended at a terrace, but, unlike the Meluhans' city platforms, this one hadn't been constructed as protection against floods but to create a smooth base on which Pariha had been built.

The three men approached at the valley's lowest point, where the platform was at its tallest, standing nearly sixty feet high. A massive ceremonial gate was the only way in. The road, which had high walls on both sides here in the valley, narrowed as it approached the gate. Shiva saw at once that any attacking force would be funnelled into a narrow choke point, a great defensive move by the Parihans.

The massive gates had been hewn from the local brown stone and they were flanked on either side by large pillars on which crouched imposing creatures, poised as if ready to pounce in defence of their city. These unfamiliar creatures had the head of a man on the body of a lion, and the broad wings of an eagle sprouted from their backs. Parihan pride was unmistakable in the facial features: a high forehead above a sharp, hooked nose; a drooping moustache and neatly beaded beard, with lengthy locks emerging from beneath a square hat. The aggressive, warrior-like visages were tempered somewhat by calm, almost friendly eyes.

Kurush conversed with the gatekeeper for a few moments, then walked back and spoke respectfully to Gopal. 'My Lord, the formalities have been completed. Please accept my apologies that it took us so long to get here. Shall we?'

'There's no need for an apology, Kurush,' said Gopal politely. 'Let's go.'

Shiva quietly followed Kurush and Gopal, keenly aware of the gatekeeper's quizzical, perhaps even judgemental eyes as they crossed a vast tiled courtyard and guided their horses onto the cobbled pathway leading to the top of the platform. The gentle gradient made it easy for the beasts to negotiate the single hairpin bend they encountered. A few pedestrians sauntered up and down the accompanying steps, which had long treads to facilitate the climb. All along the pathway, the rocky face of the platform had been carved and painted. Against a background of glazed tiles, sculpted Parihans with distinguished features in long coats and square hats gazed at passers-by. Water rippled down the centre of the rock face, leaving a lilting musical sound in its wake, and Shiva made a mental note to ask Gopal the secret of this water source in the harsh alpine desert.

But his questions were quickly forgotten when he reached the top and exclaimed in wonder at the sheer beauty of the city laid out before him. 'By the Holy Lake!' he cried as he caught his first glimpse of the exquisite symmetrical gardens of Pariha. This extraordinary creation was called 'Paradaeza' by the Parihans, 'the walled place of harmony'.

The Paradaeza, situated along the rectangular city's central axis, was surrounded by magnificent buildings and, like the city, extended all the way to the base of a great mountain at the upper end of the valley, which Gopal said the Asuras had named the Mountain of Mercy. Water emerged from the heart of the mountain and was channelled through the garden in an unerringly straight line and fed large square ponds with flamboyant fountains that spewed water high into the air. The left and right halves of the gardens were perfect mirror-images of each other and the entire expanse was covered with a carpet of lush manicured grass, with flowerbeds and trees arranged in perfect harmony. The flora had obviously been imported from all around the world; roses, narcissus, tulips, lilacs, jasmine, orange and lemon trees and many more varieties dotted the landscape in poetic profusion.

Shiva was so lost in the beauty of the garden that he didn't hear his friend call his name.

'Lord Neelkanth?' repeated Gopal, and Shiva turned apologetically as the Chief Vasudev said, 'We can always come back here later, my friend, but for now, we need to retire to our guest house.'

— ⚘ ⑩Ⓤ⚶⊕ —

Shiva and Gopal were given rooms in the state guest-house, reserved for elite visitors to the land, and here too they encountered the Parihan obsession with beauty and elegance. The building's entrance led to a wide, comfortable verandah lined with neat rows of perfectly circular columns, supporting a magnificent stone ceiling. The columns were coloured a vivid pink up to a point near the ceiling, above which they were carved with animal figures. Shiva squinted to get a better look.

'Bulls,' Gopal confirmed. 'Bulls and cows are sacred to us

Indians, central to the spiritual experience of life, but the Parihans also revere bulls – they symbolise strength and virility.'

As they reached the other end of the verandah they encountered three elegantly dressed Parihans. One proffered a tray of warm moistened and scented towels and Gopal immediately picked one up and began to wipe the accumulated dust and grime from his face and hands. Shiva followed his example.

A Parihan woman bowed low to Gopal and said softly, 'Welcome, honoured Chief Vasudev Gopal. We can hardly believe our good fortune in hosting the representative of the great Lord Ram.'

'Thank you, my Lady,' said Gopal. 'But you have me at a disadvantage – you know my name, but I don't know yours.'

'My name is Bahmandokht.'

'The daughter of Bahman?' said Gopal, for he was familiar with Avesta, their ancient language.

Bahmandokht smiled. 'That's one of the meanings, yes, but I prefer the other: a maiden with a good mind.'

Gopal smiled and folded his hands into a respectful namaste. 'I'm sure you live up to that name, my Lady.'

'I try my best, Lord Gopal.'

Unlike the Parihans Shiva had met so far, who had studiously ignored him for the most part, Bahmandokht addressed the Neelkanth with a polite bow. 'Welcome, Lord Shiva. I do hope we've given you no cause for complaint.'

'None at all,' said Shiva graciously.

'I know you're here on a mission,' said Bahmandokht. 'I

wouldn't be so bold as to speak for my entire tribe, but personally, I hope you succeed. India and Pariha are connected by ancient bonds. If something needs to be done in the best interests of your country, I believe it's our duty to help – that's the dictate Lord Rudra laid down for us, after all.'

Shiva acknowledged the courtesy and held his hands together in a namaste. 'That spirit is returned in full measure by my country, Lady Bahmandokht.'

Bahmandokht glanced at a tall woman standing behind her, towards the end of the lobby, and Shiva followed her gaze. The woman was dressed in what he guessed was traditional Parihan garb, but despite the attire, it was obvious that she wasn't a native: she was bronze-complexioned with jet-black hair. Her large, beautiful doe-eyes and voluptuous body stood out amongst the slender locals. She was a gorgeous woman indeed, Shiva reflected.

'Lord Shiva,' said Bahmandokht, and the Neelkanth returned his attention to her. 'My aide will show you to your chamber.'

'Thank you,' said Shiva.

As Gopal and Shiva were escorted away, the Neelkanth looked back. The mystery woman had disappeared.

Shiva and Gopal were led into a lavish suite of rooms with two separate bedchambers furnished with every luxury imaginable. Glass doors at the far end opened onto a huge balcony equipped with large recliners and a couple of low cloth-covered seats that could double up as tables. The living room contained a miniature fountain on one side, its cascading waters creating a soothing tinkle. Thick woven carpets covered the entire floor and bolsters and cushions of various sizes were strewn around. An ornately carved oak table surrounded by cushioned chairs occupied one corner, and a selection of musical instruments was artfully arranged in another corner. Lavish gold- and silver-plated ornaments decorated the mantelpiece and shelves, and Shiva reflected that the chamber was ostentatious even by the standards of Swadweepan royalty.

The two bedrooms contained comfortable soft beds made up with soft linens. Bowls of fruit had been placed on the low tables next to each bed and the cupboards were filled with clothes, including traditional Parihan cloaks, for the two guests.

Shiva looked at Gopal with a twinkle in his eye. 'I guess these miserable quarters will just have to suffice!'

CHAPTER 37

Unexpected Help

After a sumptuous dinner, Gopal and Shiva returned to their chambers, welcoming the opportunity for some much-needed relaxation. The fountain attracted Shiva's attention again and he asked, 'Panditji, where do they get their water from?'

'For this fountain?' asked Gopal.

'For all the fountains, ponds and channels we've seen. This is a desert land with almost no natural rivers and I was told they don't even have regular rains – so where does all this water come from?'

'It's all down to the brilliance of their engineers: there are massive natural springs and aquifers north of Pariha.'

'But surely a spring can't be as bountiful as a river?'

'Ah, scarcity engenders ingenuity. When you don't have enough water, you learn to use it judiciously. All the water in the fountains and canals here is recycled waste-water.'

Shiva had dipped his hand into one of the fountains. As he

immediately recoiled, Gopal laughed and said, 'Don't worry, my friend – the water's been filtered and treated. It's safe enough to drink!'

'I'll take your word for it.' He wiped his hands on a napkin and asked, 'How far away are these springs?'

'The ones that supply this city? Between thirty and fifty miles,' Gopal said.

Shiva whistled softly. 'That's a long way. How do they get the water here in such large quantities? You mentioned canals, but I haven't seen any yet.'

'That's because they're underground.'

'That must have been a colossal undertaking,' said Shiva, stunned.

'They're narrower than the canals we have back home – about the size of our underground drains.'

'But fifty miles is still a long way to transport water. How do they do that? Do they have underground pumps powered by animals?'

'No, they use one of nature's most powerful forces instead: gravity. The underground channels slope all the way from the springs to the city.'

'That's brilliant,' said Shiva, then added, 'Building something like that must need precision engineering skills of a very high order.'

'Absolutely. The angle of the descent would have to be precise over very long distances. If the gradient's even slightly steeper than required, the water would begin to erode the bottom of the channel and over time that would destroy it.'

'And if the slope's too gentle, the water would simply stop flowing.'

'Exactly,' said Gopal. 'A project like that required flawless design and execution.'

'But when did they—?'

Shiva was interrupted by a soft knock on the door. He immediately lowered his voice to an urgent whisper. 'Panditji, are you expecting someone?'

Gopal shook his head. 'No. And where's our guard? Isn't he supposed to announce visitors?'

Shiva drew his sword and gestured for Gopal to follow him as he tiptoed to the door. The Vasudev chief was a Brahmin, not a warrior; the safest place for him was behind Shiva. Shiva waited near the door and as the soft knock came again he whispered, 'As soon as I pull the intruder in, shut the door and lock it.'

Holding his sword to one side, Shiva pulled the door open and yanked the intruder into the room. As he pushed the Parihan to the ground, Gopal shut the door and bolted it.

'I'm a friend!' said a feminine voice as the sprawled figure raised her hands in surrender.

Shiva and Gopal stared at the veiled woman on the ground.

She slowly got to her feet, her eyes fixed on Shiva's sword. 'You don't need that. Parihans don't kill their guests – it's one of Lord Rudra's laws.'

Shiva refused to lower his blade. 'Reveal yourself,' he commanded.

The woman removed her veil. 'You saw me earlier, great Neelkanth.'

Shiva recognised the intruder immediately – it was the dark-haired mystery woman he'd seen in the lobby while he was talking to Bahmandokht.

Shiva smiled. 'I was wondering who you were.'

'I've come to help you,' said the woman, still unable to tear her eyes away from Shiva's sword. 'Please, sheathe your blade, my Lord – we Parihans would never break Lord Rudra's laws.'

Shiva did as she asked, but remained alert for any trickery. 'What makes you think we need your help?'

'For the same reason you don't need your sword here – we Vayuputras never break Lord Rudra's laws. I've come to help you get what you came for.'

Shiva glanced at Gopal, who gestured for her to make herself comfortable on the soft cushions.

'What's your name?' asked Shiva. 'And why do you want to help us?'

'My name is Scheherazade.'

'That's an ancient Parihan name, my Lord,' said Gopal. 'It means "person who gives freedom to cities".'

Shiva narrowed his eyes. 'But you're not a native of this land. What's your real name?'

'I am Parihan, my Lord, and my name is Scheherazade.'

'How can we trust you if you won't even tell us your real name?'

'My name has nothing to do with your mission. The only thing that truly matters is what the Amartya Shpand, the Vayuputra Council, thinks of your mission.'

'And you can tell us what they think?' asked Gopal.

'That's why I'm here – to tell you what you need to do to fulfil your mission.'

The Mithra, the chief of the Vayuputra tribe, was resting in the antechamber of his office when he heard a soft noise from the verandah. The nascent moon was too faint for him to see but he knew who it was as soon as he heard the voice and he smiled.

'Great Mithra, I've sent her to them.'

'Thank you, Bahmandokht. The Vayuputras will be indebted to you in perpetuity, for you have helped our tribe fulfil our mission and our vow to Lord Rudra.'

Bahmandokht bowed low. There had been a time when she had loved the man who had become the Mithra, but once he had assumed that office, the only feelings she allowed herself were devotion and respect. Rising to her feet, she walked away quietly.

The Mithra stared at Bahmandokht's retreating form for a moment, then returned to the antechamber and sat down, leaned back and closed his eyes. The ancient memory of that fateful conversation with Manobhu, his close friend and brother-in-law, was still as fresh in his mind as if it had happened yesterday.

'Are you sure?' asked the Parihan who would one day become the Mithra.

The Tibetan feigned outrage as he looked at his friend and fellow Vayuputra.

'I mean no disrespect, Manobhu, but I hope you realise that what we're doing is illegal,' the Parihan went on.

Manobhu allowed himself a slight smile as he scratched his shaggy beard. His matted hair had been tied up in a bun with a string of beads in the style favoured by his tribe, the fierce Gunas. His body was covered with deep scars acquired during a lifetime of battle. He was tall, with a muscular physique, and he was always alert, ever ready for war. His demeanour, his clothes and his hair all conveyed the impression of a ruthless warrior, but his eyes told a different story, for they were a window into to his calm mind, a mind that had found its purpose and was at peace. Manobhu's eyes had always intrigued the Parihan.

'If you're unsure, my friend,' said Manobhu, 'you don't have to do this.'

The Parihan looked away.

'Don't feel pressured to do this just because my brother married your sister.'

The Parihan returned his gaze. 'The reason doesn't matter. What matters is the result. What matters is whether Lord Rudra's commandment is being obeyed.'

Manobhu's mirthful gaze remained locked with the Parihan's. 'You should know Lord Rudra's commandments better than I do — after all, he was a Parihan, like you.'

The Parihan stole a nervous glance towards the back of the room, *where a diabolical concoction was boiling inside a copper vessel set atop a steady flame.*

Manobhu stepped forwards and put his hand on the Parihan's shoulder. 'Trust me, the Somras is turning evil. Lord Rudra would have wanted us to do this. If the council doesn't agree, then to hell with them. We'll ensure that Lord Rudra's commandments are followed ourselves.'

The Parihan looked at Manobhu and sighed. 'Are you sure your nephew has the potential to fulfil this mission? That he can one day be Lord Rudra's successor?'

Manobhu smiled. 'He's your nephew, too, you know. Your sister's his mother.'

'I know, but the boy doesn't live with me and I've never met him — I don't even know if I ever will. And you won't even tell me his name, so I ask again: are you sure he's the one?'

'Yes,' Manobhu said confidently. 'He's the one who will grow up to be the Neelkanth and carry out Lord Rudra's commandment. He's the one who'll take Evil out of the equation.'

'But he needs to be educated — he needs to be prepared.*'*

'I'll prepare him.'

'But what's the point? The Vayuputra Council controls the emergence of the Neelkanth. How will our nephew be discovered?'

'I'll arrange it at the right time,' said Manobhu.

The Parihan frowned. 'But how will you—?'

'Leave that to me,' interrupted Manobhu. 'If he isn't discovered, it'll mean that the time for Evil is not yet upon us. On the other hand, if I'm able to ensure that he is discovered—'

'Then we'll know that Evil has risen,' the Parihan finished.

'To be more precise,' said Manobhu, gently correcting his brother-in-law, 'we'll know that Good has turned into Evil.'

The conversation was interrupted by a soft hissing sound from the far corner of the room: the medicine was ready. The two friends walked over to the fire and peered into the vessel. A thick reddish-brown paste had formed and small bubbles were bursting through to the surface.

'It only needs to cool down now,' said the Parihan. 'The task is done.'

Manobhu looked at his brother-in-law. 'No, my friend. The task has just begun.'

The Mithra inhaled deeply as he brought himself back to the present moment. 'I never thought our rebellion would succeed, Manobhu,' he whispered.

He rose from his chair, walked over to the verandah and looked up at the sky. In the old days, his people had believed that when great men surrendered their mortal flesh, they went up to live amongst the stars and kept watch over their tribe. The Mithra focused on one particular star and smiled. 'Manobhu, it was a good idea to name our nephew Shiva – it definitely helped me guess that he's the one!'

'First I must tell you that most of the Vayuputras are against you,' said Scheherazade.

'That's not much of a secret,' said Shiva wryly.

'You can't really blame them. Our laws state very clearly that only one of our own tribe can become the Neelkanth, and you've emerged out of nowhere – our laws don't permit us to recognise or help someone like you.'

'Yet here you are,' said Shiva. 'And I don't think you're working alone. I saw you in the lobby earlier, even though you were hiding right at the back. I bet you're not fully accepted by the Parihans yourself, and I can't see someone having the courage to do something like this all by themselves. That means some powerful Parihans must be putting you up to it, and that makes me believe that some Vayuputras realise what I'm saying is true: that Evil has risen.'

Scheherazade's lips curved in a small smile. 'You're right: there are some very powerful Vayuputras on your side – but they can't help you openly. Unlike most of the earlier Neel-kanth pretenders, your blue throat is genuine, and this leads to one inescapable conclusion: a Vayuputra must have helped you many decades ago. Can you imagine the chaos this has caused? Parihans are accusing each other of having broken Lord Rudra's laws and helping you clandestinely when you were young and the discord has been tearing the Vayuputras apart – then Lord Mithra put an end to it when he confirmed that no one from our tribe authorised you as Neelkanth. He suggested it was someone from your own country.'

'So if any Vayuputra does help me, they'll be seen as the traitor who started it all many years ago.'

'Exactly,' Scheherazade said.

'What's the way around this?' asked Gopal.

'You, my Lord Chief Vasudev, must request aid,' said Scheherazade. 'Lord Shiva must stay in the background. Don't ask for assistance to be provided for the Neelkanth, but rather to *you* as a member of the Vasudev tribe, seeking justice. They can't deny a just demand from the representative of Lord Ram.'

'Forgive me for being slow, but I don't understand.'

'What does the Neelkanth need, Lord Gopal?' asked Scheherazade. 'He needs the *Brahmastra* to threaten Meluha—'

'How did you—?'

'With all due respect, please don't ask unnecessary questions, Lord Gopal. What Lord Shiva needs is obvious, and we have to devise the best way for him to get it. If you ask for the *Brahmastra* so that you can fight Evil, there will be questions regarding Lord Shiva's legitimacy in deciding what Evil is, for he has been neither authorised nor trained by the Vayuputras. Instead, seek redress for a crime committed on Indian soil – the unauthorised use of *daivi astras* – by a person the Vayuputras have supported in the past—'

'—Lord Bhrigu.' Gopal competed her sentence.

'Exactly. Lord Rudra's laws are very clear on the punishments for unauthorised use of *daivi astras*. For the first offence it's a fourteen-year exile in the forests. The second is punishable by death. Many in the council agree that Lord Bhrigu has got off lightly, despite having used *daivi astras*.'

'So you're suggesting that Gopal, as Chief Vasudev, should present himself as demanding Lord Rudra's justice?'

'Exactly. It'll be impossible for a Vayuputra to say no to such a request. All you have to do,' she said to Gopal, 'is say that the law regarding the *daivi astra* ban was broken by Lord Bhrigu, the Emperor of Meluha and the King of Ayodhya, that they need to be punished, and that the Vasudevs will see justice done.'

'We tell the Vayuputras that Bhrigu and the others may well have more reserves of *daivi astras*, so we need the *Brahmastra* to threaten them with, to encourage them to do the right thing,' Shiva finished.

Scheherazade smiled. 'Exactly. Evil must be stopped, we're all agreed on that – but I've been asked to tell you that you shouldn't—'

'We will *never* use the *Brahmastra*,' Gopal broke in with a shudder.

'Deploying a weapon of such horrifying power doesn't just defy Lord Rudra's laws,' added Shiva. 'It goes against the fundamental laws of humanity.'

Scheherazade smiled. 'Once you've told the council that the Vasudevs are determined to punish those who broke Lord Rudra's law for using the *daivi astras*, insist on meeting with Lord Mithra in private. You'll get what you came here for.'

Shiva smiled as he realised who amongst the Vayuputras was helping him. But he was still intrigued by Scheherazade, or whatever her real name was.

'Why are you helping us?' asked Shiva.

'Because I've been told to do so.'

'I don't believe that's the only reason. Something else is driving you. Why are you helping us?'

Scheherazade looked down at the carpet, and then she turned

towards the balcony and stared into the dark night beyond. She turned back to Shiva after a moment, blinking tears from her eyes. 'Because a man I once loved told me that the *Somras* was turning evil, but I didn't believe him.'

'Who is this man?' asked Gopal.

'It doesn't matter any more,' said Scheherazade. 'He's dead – he was killed, perhaps by those who wanted to stop him. Ending the reign of the *Somras* is my way of apologising—'

Shiva leaned towards her and looked straight into her eyes. 'Tara?' he whispered, and the woman, shocked, jerked back – she had not been called by that name in years. Shiva continued to hold her gaze. 'By the Holy Lake,' he whispered, 'it *is* you.'

Scheherazade had taken a new name and kept her relationship with Brahaspati secret because too many Parihans believed that the *Somras* was still a force for Good and that the former chief scientist of Meluha was wrong. She had never wanted to live in Pariha, but her presence there had served a purpose for her guru, Lord Bhrigu. Believing her love was dead, she had no reason to return to her homeland.

'But you're Lord Bhrigu's student,' said Shiva. 'Why are you going against his wishes?'

'I'm not Tara,' she said firmly.

'I know you are,' said Shiva. 'Why are you betraying your guru? Do you believe Lord Bhrigu got Brahaspati killed at Mount Mandar?'

Scheherazade stood up and turned to leave, but Shiva rose quickly and grasped her hand. 'Brahaspati isn't dead.'

Dumbstruck, Scheherazade stopped dead in her tracks.

'Brahaspati's alive,' said Shiva. 'He's with me.'

Scheherazade started to weep as Shiva repeated softly, 'He's with me, Tara. Your Brahaspati is alive. We'll take you back with us when we're done here, I promise. I'll take you back to your Brahaspati.'

Her tears now of joy, Scheherazade collapsed into Shiva's arms. She would be Tara once again.

CHAPTER 38

The Friend of God

The strategy Tara had suggested worked like a charm. The Amartya Shpand was genuinely surprised when Gopal entered their audience chamber alone. When he raised the issue of Maharishi Bhrigu's misuse of the *daivi astras*, they knew they had no choice but to grant Gopal an audience with the Mithra. That was the law.

The following day, Gopal, this time accompanied by Shiva, was led into the audience hall within the Mithra's official residence, the most modest structure in Pariha. It was built at one end of the city, abutting the Mountain of Mercy, on a simple stone base constructed over the water channel that emerged from the mountain. Twelve-foot-high plain pillars supported a simple wooden roof. Immediately inside the doors was a simple audience hall furnished with functional chairs and sombre carpets. The Mithra's personal quarters were further back, behind stone walls and a wooden door. Shiva thought the structure looked like a stylised stone replica of a large ceremonial tent, with stone pillars instead of tent-poles and a wooden roof in place of the cloth canopy. It was a symbolic link to the nomadic past of Lord Rudra's people. Like a tribal leader of the old code, the Mithra lived in penurious simplicity while his people lived in luxury. The only indulgence the Mithra had allowed himself was the beautiful garden that surrounded his abode. It was bountiful in its design, precise in its symmetry and extravagant in its colourful flora.

Shiva and Gopal were settled comfortably in the audience hall and then left alone for a few moments. When the Mithra entered, the two men immediately stood up and greeted him with the ancient Parihan salute: left hand on the heart, fist open as a mark of admiration while the right arm was held rigidly to the side of the body and bent upwards at the elbow with the open palm held outwards in greeting.

The Mithra smiled genially and folded his hands together into the traditional Indian namaste.

Shiva grinned, but he remained silent, waiting for the Mithra to speak.

The Vayuputras' leader, a tall, fair-skinned man, was wearing a simple brown cloak. A white hat covered his long brownish hair, and tiny beads were wrapped around separated tufts of his beard, like the other Parihan men Shiva had seen so far. The sack-like cloak made it difficult to be sure, but Shiva thought he was strong and muscular, though his delicate hands had long, slender fingers, more like a surgeon's than a warrior's. But Shiva was most intrigued by the Mithra's nose, which was sharp and long. It reminded him of his beloved mother's.

The Mithra walked up to Shiva and grasped the Neelkanth warmly by his shoulders. 'What a delight it is to finally meet you.'

Shiva noted that the Mithra didn't even glance at his blue neck, something most people couldn't resist. The man's attention was focused on Shiva's eyes.

And then the Mithra said something even more intriguing. 'You have your father's eyes – and your mother's nose.'

He knew my father – and my mother?

Before Shiva could say anything, the Mithra gently touched his back and smiled at Gopal. 'Come, let's sit.'

As soon as they were seated, he said to Shiva, 'I can see the questions that are running through your mind: how do I know your father and mother? Who am I? What was my name before I became the Mithra?'

Shiva smiled. 'This eye-reading business is very dangerous – it doesn't allow one to have any secrets.'

'Sometimes it's important that there be no secrets,' said the Mithra, 'especially when such big decisions are being made. How else can we be sure that we're taking the right step?'

'You don't have to answer if you don't wish to,' Shiva said. 'The questions running through my mind right now aren't important to our mission in any way.'

'You're right – and you've been trained well: these questions may trouble your mind, but they're not important. But then again, can one really carry out such a mission with a troubled mind?'

'A troubled mind does sometimes makes one lose sight of things,' admitted Shiva.

'And the world can't afford to have you lose sight of your mission, great Neelkanth. You're too important to us. So let me answer your personal questions first.'

Shiva noticed that the Mithra had called him the Neelkanth; Tara was the only other Parihan to have used his title.

'My original name isn't important,' said the Mithra, 'because it's not mine any more. My only identity is my title: the Mithra.'

Shiva nodded politely, but the Mithra kept talking. 'And how do I know your mother? That one's simple: I grew up with her. She was my sister.'

Shiva's eyes opened wide in surprise. 'So you're my uncle?'

'I was your uncle before I became the Mithra.'

'Why haven't I met you before now?'

'It's complicated – but I was good friends with your father's brother, Lord Manobhu. I held him in deep regard and we decided to seal our friendship with a marriage between our two families. My sister went to live with Lord Manobhu's brother in Tibet after their wedding, and you were born from that union.'

'But my uncle had rebellious ideas . . .' said Shiva, trying to guess why the Mithra had been forced to keep his distance from their family.

The Mithra shook his head. 'Manobhu didn't have rebellious

ideas, he had inspiring ones. But an inspiration before its time often looks like a rebellion.'

'So the Vayuputras didn't force you to stay away from my family?'

'Oh, I was forced all right, but not by the Vayuputras.' Shiva smiled. 'Uncle Manobhu could be very stubborn at times.'

The Mithra returned Shiva's smile, remembering his brother-in-law's intractable commitment to an idea once he decided something had to be done in a certain way.

'When did you learn that I was your long-lost relative?' asked Shiva. 'Did you have spies following me?'

'I recognised you the moment I first heard your name.'

'Didn't you know my name already?'

'No – your uncle always refused to tell me, but now I understand why. It was a clue he left for me. If you ever emerged, he knew I'd recognise you by your name.'

'How so?' asked Shiva, intrigued.

'Very few people – not even the majority of the Vayuputras – know that Lord Rudra's mother had a special personal name for her son. She called him *Shiva*. Lord Rudra's name means "the one who roars" and he was called that because when he was born, he cried so loudly that he drove the midwife away!'

Shiva was nodding agreement; he'd heard that story.

The Mithra went on, 'This is a secret known to only a very few Vayuputras: legend has it that Lord Rudra was actually stillborn.'

'What?' Gopal looked shocked as he took in the Vayuputra's words.

'Yes,' said the Mithra, 'and the midwife and Lord Rudra's mother tried everything they could think of to revive him. Finally, in desperation, the midwife tried something very unorthodox: she put the stillborn Lord Rudra to his mother's breast, trying to get him to suckle, and much to his mother's surprise, the baby started breathing and roaring loudly with his very first breaths.'

'By the Holy Lake,' whispered Shiva.

'Amazing,' Gopal added in in awe.

'It is. The midwife left soon thereafter and was never heard of again. Lord Rudra's mother was an immigrant; she was a believer in the Mother Goddess, Shakti, and she was convinced that the midwife had been sent by the goddess to save her son. She believed her son was born a *shava*, a "body without life", whom Goddess Shakti then infused with life, and in so doing, the goddess transformed a *Shava* to *Shiva* – "the auspicious one". His mother named him Shiva in honour of the Mother Goddess for saving her son's life. Consequently, the moment I heard your name, I knew that was the clue Manobhu had left for me to identify the one he'd trained.'

'So you knew Lord Manobhu was planning all this?'

The Mithra smiled. 'Your uncle and I made the medicine together.'

'You mean the medicine that made my throat turn blue? But didn't that have to be given to me at a specific time in my life?'

'I'm assuming that's what Manobhu did, for here you are.'

'But Lord Mithra, this isn't the way the system was supposed to work – as an unfolding series of implausible coincidences. So many things could have gone wrong – I might not have been trained well enough, or the medicine might not have been given to me at the right time, or I might never have been invited to Meluha. And worst of all, I might not have recognised the *Somras* as the true Evil.'

'You're absolutely right: this isn't the way our Vayuputra system was designed to work. But Manobhu and I had faith that this is the way the *universe's* system is supposed to work. And we were right, weren't we?'

'But is it a good idea to leave such significant outcomes to a roll of the universe's dice?'

'You make it sound as if it was all left to dumb luck. We didn't abandon everything to chance, Shiva. The Vayuputras were sure the *Somras* hadn't turned evil, but Manobhu and I felt otherwise. Had Manobhu still been alive, he'd have guided you through this period, but in spite of his untimely death, Good has prevailed. Manobhu always said we should allow the universe to make the decision, and it did. We set in motion a chain of events that would work out as they have only if the universe so willed it. Frankly, I wasn't sure we were doing the right thing, but I didn't stop him because I assumed his plan simply wouldn't succeed if that wasn't the universe's will. I did help him to make the medicine, though, and when I saw his plan coming to fruition, I knew it was my duty to do whatever I could to help you.'

'But what if I'd failed – what if I hadn't identified the *Somras* as Evil? Then Evil would have won, right?'

'Sometimes the universe decides that Evil is supposed to win. Perhaps a race or species becomes so harmful that it's better to allow Evil to triumph and destroy that species. It's happened before. But this obviously isn't one of those times.'

Shiva was clearly overwhelmed by the number of things that could have gone wrong.

'Something's still troubling you,' said the Mithra.

'I've discussed this with Panditji, too,' said Shiva, pointing to Gopal. 'So much of what I've achieved can be attributed to pure luck – just random turns of the universe.'

The Mithra leaned towards Shiva and whispered, 'One makes one's own luck, but you have to give the universe the opportunity to help you.'

Shiva still didn't look convinced by the Mithra's words.

'You had every reason to run away when you first arrived in Meluha. You were in a strange new land where peculiar people who were evidently so much more advanced than you insisted on calling you a god. You were tasked with a mission, the enormity of which would have intimidated practically anyone in the world. I'm sure you thought you couldn't possibly succeed. And yet you didn't run away. You stood up and accepted a responsibility that was thrust upon you. That decision was the turning point in your journey against Evil, and it had nothing to do with the twists and blessings of fate.'

Shiva looked at Gopal, who looked as if he was in complete

agreement with the Mithra. At last Shiva said, 'You're giving me too much credit, Lord Mithra.'

'I'm not,' said the Mithra. 'You're on course to fulfil *my* mission without any help from me. But I can't allow you to do that! You must allow me the privilege of helping you in some way, otherwise how will I face the Ahura Mazda and Lord Rudra when I meet with them?' Then he looked directly into Shiva's eyes once again and said, 'But there are some things I must still be sure of before we go any further. What are you planning to do with the *daivi astra*?'

'I plan to use it to threaten—' Shiva stopped speaking as the Mithra raised his hand.

'I've seen enough,' said the Mithra.

Shiva frowned.

'Thoughts move faster than the tongue, great Neelkanth. I know you won't use these terrible weapons of destruction. I can also see that the reason you won't use them isn't just because of the Vayuputra ban but because you believe these weapons are too horrifying ever to be used.'

'I believe that with all my heart.'

'I'm glad to hear it. But I still can't give you the *Brahmastra*.'

This was unexpected. Shiva had thought the discussion had been going his way.

'I can't give you the *Brahmastra* because its effects are uncontrollable. It destroys everything in its path, incinerating every living thing at the epicentre of the blast and unleashing deadly radiation over a wide area around it. Lord Bhrigu will work out that you're only using the weapon as a threat because you wouldn't want to hurt your own army, which would be right in the exposure zone if the *Brahmastra* were to be detonated.'

'So what can you give us instead?'

'The *Pashupatiastra* is a weapon designed by Lord Rudra; it has all the power of the *Brahmastra*, but with much greater control. Its destruction is limited to the area immediately around the epicentre of the explosion, and life outside this zone won't be impacted at all. In fact, you can even focus the effects of the *Pashupatiastra* in one direction only. If you threaten to use this weapon, Lord Bhrigu will know you can destroy Devagiri without endangering your own people or those in adjoining areas. Such a threat will be credible.'

That made sense to Shiva, and he nodded in agreement.

'But you can't use this weapon either, Neelkanth,' the Mithra said firmly. 'The devastation is unimaginable, and the after-effects would poison the region for centuries to come.'

'I give you my solemn word, Lord Mithra,' said Shiva. 'I will never use these weapons.'

The Mithra smiled. 'Then I have no problem giving you the *Pashupatiastra*. I'll issue the orders immediately.'

Shiva raised his chin as a faint smile played on his lips. 'I think you'd already made your decision about this before you even met me, Uncle.'

The Mithra laughed softly. 'I'm just the Mithra. I bet you didn't expect this to be so easy, right?'

'No, I didn't.'

'I've heard stories about you, especially about the way you've fought your battles. So far, you've behaved in an exemplary manner. Even when you could have gained by doing something wrong, you refrained. You didn't fall prey to the logic of doing a small wrong for the sake of the greater good, of the ends justifying the means, and that takes moral courage. So yes, I had already made up my mind – but I wanted to meet you in any case. You'll be remembered as the greatest man of our age, and generations will revere you as their god. How could I not want to meet you?'

'I'm no god, Lord Mithra,' said an embarrassed Shiva.

'Wasn't it you who said "*Har Har Mahadev*"? That all of us are gods?'

Shiva laughed. 'You've got me there.'

'We don't become gods because we *think* we're gods,' said the Mithra. 'That's just ego. We become gods when we realise that a part of the universal divinity lives within us; when we understand our role in this great world and strive to fulfil it. No one is striving harder than you, Lord Neelkanth, and that makes you a god. And remember, gods don't fail. You *can't* fail. You must remember your duty: you have to take Evil out of the equation – but you shouldn't destroy every trace of the *Somras*, for it may become good again in the future. A time may come when it's required again, so you have to keep the knowledge of the *Somras* alive. You'll have to establish a tribe that will keep the secret of the *Somras* until it's required again. Once all this is done, your mission will be over.'

'I will not fail, Lord Mithra,' said Shiva, 'I promise.'

'I know you'll succeed,' said the Mithra, before turning to Gopal. 'Great Chief Vasudev, once the Neelkanth creates his own tribe, the Vayuputras won't be responsible for fighting Evil any more. That task will pass to the Neelkanth's tribe. The Vayuputras' relationship with the Vasudevs will become like one between distant relatives, rather than the closer bond that's entailed a joint duty towards a common cause.'

'Your relationship with the Vasudevs and with my country will exist forever, Lord Mithra,' said Gopal. 'You've helped us in our hour of need. I'm sure that we, in turn, will help Pariha if the need ever arises.'

'Thank you,' said the Mithra.

CHAPTER 39

He is One of Us

The following morning, the Mithra summoned all the city's residents to the town centre. Shiva and Gopal stood next to him as he addressed the crowd. 'My fellow Vayuputras, I'm sure your minds are teeming with many questions and doubts. But this isn't the time for talk; this is the time for action. We entrusted our secret knowledge to a man who worked closely with us, but he has betrayed us. Lord Bhrigu broke Lord Rudra's laws, and Lord Gopal, the chief of the Vasudevs and the representative of Lord Ram, has come here demanding justice. But this isn't just about retribution for Lord Bhrigu's treacherous actions. We must also do justice to India, and to Lord Rudra's principles. My fellow Parihans, we serve a common purpose that transcends laws: a purpose defined by Lord Rudra himself.'

The Mithra pointed at Shiva and continued, 'Behold this man. He may not be a Vayuputra, but he bears the blue throat. He may not be a Parihan, but he fights like one, with honour and integrity. We may not have recognised him yet, but the Vasudevs consider him the Neelkanth. He may not have lived amongst us for much of his life, but he respects and idolises Lord Rudra as much as we do. And, above all, he is fighting for Lord Rudra's cause.'

The Vayuputras were listening with rapt attention as the Mithra went on, 'This man is not a Vayuputra, and yet he is one of us, and so I am supporting him in his battle against Evil. And so shall you.'

Many of the Vayuputras were swayed by the Mithra's words, but even those who weren't persuaded knew that it was the Mithra's right to choose whom to support within India. And so, while their reasons might have differed, all the Vayuputras agreed with the Mithra's decision.

— ☥ ⓪Ʊ✦❂ —

Shiva and Gopal received a large crate the following evening, together with the news that an entire Parihan cavalry platoon would transport the incredibly heavy trunk safely back to the sea. Shiva had no idea what kind of material the *Pashupatiastra* might me made of, but from the size of the trunk he assumed it must be a huge quantity, enough to threaten an entire city. He was amazed when Gopal told him they were carrying only a tiny amount of the *Pashupatiastra* material, just enough to fill a cupped hand.

'Are you serious?'

'Entirely, Lord Neelkanth,' he said with a smile. 'A handful is enough to destroy a city. The trunk is insulated with lead, wet clay and leaves from bilva trees, which will protect us from exposure to the *Pashupatiastra* radiation.'

'By the Holy Lake!' said Shiva. 'The more I learn about these *daivi astras*, the more convinced I am that the weapons must have been created by demons.'

'They were, my friend – that's why Lord Rudra called them evil and banned their use. And that's also why we won't use the *Pashupatiastra*, only *threaten* to use it. But to make the threat credible to the Meluhans, we'll have to actually set the weapon up outside Devagiri.'

'Do you know how to do that?'

'No, I don't – only a select few Vayuputras are privy to that knowledge. I do know it's a complicated process combining engineering, mantras and other preparations, but we'll have to perform them properly to convince Lord Bhrigu that we mean business. Lord Mithra and his people will start our training tomorrow morning.'

— ꠹ ⑩Ｕ⍥⊛ —

Parvateshwar was sitting in the Governor of Karachapa's residence with Bhrigu and Dilipa, but his attention was focused on the view outside the window. The residence was on the *dwitiya*, the second platform of the city, and from this height the Western Sea was a vast expanse of blue stretching towards the distant horizon. Dilipa's Ayodhyan army had finally arrived in Meluha, many months after the Battle of Devagiri, and had sailed to Karachapa to join Parvateshwar's Suryavanshi forces.

'The sea's our only option,' Parvateshwar said as they debated their next move.

'But I thought that was the whole point of bringing our forces to Karachapa – to attack Lothal by sea,' said Dilipa. 'What's new about that idea?'

'I'm not talking about attacking the city, your Majesty.' Although he now had four hundred thousand men under his command, he knew that even those vast numbers were not sufficient to defeat a force of two hundred and fifty thousand if they were entrenched in the well-designed citadel of Lothal. And despite many attempts at provocation, Sati had resolutely refused to send troops out, thus denying the general any opportunity to bring his numerical superiority into play on an open battlefield. The war had, for all practical purposes, ground to a stalemate.

'Please explain, General,' said Bhrigu, hoping the Meluhan army chief had come up with some brilliant idea to end the frustrating détente. 'What's your new plan?'

'I think we should send a fleet towards the Narmada River and make very sure those ships are visible.'

Dilipa frowned. 'Have your spies discovered the route Lord Shiva took?'

'No,' answered Parvateshwar shortly.

'Then what's the point of sending our ships in that direction? The Neelkanth's scouts will know that our ships are sailing to the Narmada and we'll lose the element of surprise.'

'That's precisely what I want,' said Parvateshwar. 'We don't want to hide.'

'By the great Lord Brahma!' exclaimed an impressed Bhrigu. 'General Parvateshwar, have you discovered the Narmada route to Panchavati?'

'No, my Lord.'

'Then I don't understand . . . Oh, *right*—' Bhrigu stopped mid-sentence as he finally understood what Parvateshwar had in mind.

'I don't know the Narmada route to Panchavati,' said Parvateshwar, 'but the Lord Neelkanth's army doesn't know that. They might assume we've discovered this secret route and that the Lord's life is in danger. Furthermore, a significant number of the warriors in that army are Nagas – will they do nothing in the face of imminent danger to Panchavati, the city established by their Goddess Bhoomidevi herself?'

'No,' said Dilipa. 'They'll be forced to sail out of Lothal and pursue our ships.'

'Exactly,' said Parvateshwar, 'and since we will send out fifty ships, they'll have to match our numbers. Our convoy will wait in ambush in a lagoon far beyond the Narmada delta—'

'And once they've begun sailing up the Narmada, we'll charge in from behind and attack them,' said Dilipa.

'No,' said Parvateshwar.

'No?' Dilipa sounded surprised. He'd thought he had understood the general's plan.

'No, your Majesty. I intend to send out a crack team of commandos to the Narmada before we send our ships. They'll wait until the Naga ships have travelled a considerable distance away from the sea – naval movements in a river are constricted, no matter how large the river, and their ships will be sailing close to each other. Our commandos will have devil boats ready, tasked to simultaneously take out the first and last ships in the convoy.'

'Brilliant!' said Dilipa. 'Their fleet will be trapped, and our fleet can charge upriver from the hidden lagoon and cut their soldiers down.'

'No, your Majesty,' said Parvateshwar, reflecting that he wouldn't have to explain all this to someone with Shiva's strategic brilliance. 'Our fleet isn't going to engage in battle at all – it's just a decoy. Only the commandos will attack. If the first and last ships in the convoy are set on fire, there's a pretty good chance all the ships between them will eventually catch fire as well.'

'But won't that take too long?' asked Bhrigu. 'Many of their soldiers would be able to abandon ship and escape onto land.'

'True,' said Parvateshwar. 'But they'll be stranded far from their base with no ships. I discovered in Panchavati that there's no road between Maika-Lothal and the Narmada so it will take them at least six months to march back to Lothal through those dense forests. I'm hoping that when Sati sees the size of our decoy fleet, she'll commit at least a hundred thousand men to pursuing us – and with those hundred thousand enemy soldiers stuck in the jungles along the Narmada, our army will be vastly superior numerically, with a ratio of almost four to one. If we attack then, we'll have a good chance of taking Lothal.'

Dilipa still didn't understand the entire plan. 'But won't many of our own soldiers be aboard the decoy fleet? We'll have to wait for them to come back to Karachapa before—'

'Since I'm not planning to engage our decoy fleet in battle,' said Parvateshwar, 'I won't be loading them up with soldiers. Each ship will have a skeleton crew, just enough men to sail the vessels. We won't be committing more than five thousand men. Imagine what we can achieve then: only five thousand of our men, including the commandos, will leave Karachapa, but if our plan succeeds, we'll take nearly a hundred thousand enemy men out of the equation by stranding them in the jungles around the Narmada, at least a six-month march from Lothal. And not a single arrow will have been fired. We can then march on Lothal.'

'Brilliant!' said Bhrigu. 'So we'll march on Lothal as soon as our ships leave for the Narmada—'

'No, my Lord,' said Parvateshwar. 'I'm sure Sati has scouts lurking in and around Karachapa. If they see four hundred thousand of our troops marching out of the city, they'll know our ships are minimally manned and will see through our ruse. Our army will have to remain hidden within the walls of Karachapa to convince them that our attack on Panchavati is genuine.'

— ⚹ ⦿Ʊ♀⊕ —

The customs officer at Karachapa frowned at the merchant ship's manifest. 'Cotton from Egypt? Why would any Meluhan want cotton from Egypt? It's no match for ours.'

The customs procedure in Meluha was based on an honour system: ship manifests were accepted at face value and the relevant duty applied, on the understanding that a customs officer could check a random ship's cargo from time to time. This was shaping up to be one of those random occasions.

The officer turned to his assistant. 'Go down into the ship's hold and check what's in there.'

The ship's captain glanced nervously to his right, towards the closed door of the deck cabin, then turned back to the customs officer. 'Why's that necessary, sir? Do you think I'm lying about my cargo? You know that the amount of cotton I've declared matches the maximum carrying capacity of this ship. I'm already paying the highest customs duty. Your search will serve no purpose.'

The Meluhan customs officer looked at the door the captain had surreptitiously glanced at. The door suddenly swung open and a tall, well-built man stepped out and stretched his arms as he yawned lazily. 'What's the delay, Captain?'

The customs officer gasped when he recognised the man and instantly executed a smart Meluhan military salute. 'Brigadier Vidyunmali! I didn't know you were aboard this ship.'

'Now you know,' said Vidyunmali, yawning once more.

'I'm sorry, my Lord,' said the customs officer as he handed the manifest back to the captain and ordered his assistant to issue the receipt for the duty payment. The paperwork was done in no time.

The customs officer started to leave, but then turned back

and hesitatingly asked Vidyunmali, 'My Lord, you're one of our greatest warriors – why aren't you stationed with our army?'

Vidyunmali shook his head with a wry grin. 'I'm not a warrior now, officer. I'm a bodyguard. And also, apparently, a transporter of royal fashions.'

The customs officer smiled politely, then hurried off the ship.

'Why the delay?' the Egyptian asked the brigadier as he made his way into the lowest hold, deep in the ship's belly. The only porthole, high in one corner, had been shut tight and the space was unnaturally dark. As his eyes adjusted to the gloom, he began to make out the countenances of the three hundred or so assassins sitting with cat-like stillness.

'Nothing important, Lord Swuth,' said Vidyunmali to the Egyptian. 'A stupid customs officer got it in his head to check the ship's hold. It's been taken care of. We're sailing past Karachapa now and will soon be in the heart of Meluha. There's no turning back.'

Swuth nodded silently.

'My Lord,' said the captain as he entered the hold quietly. He handed over a shielded torch and stepped aside to allow in two men carrying large jute bags. At his gesture they dropped them next to the brigadier.

'Wait outside,' said Vidyunmali, and the captain and his men obeyed immediately.

Vidyunmali studied the Egyptian in the dim light of the

flickering torch. Swuth was the commander of the shadowy group of Egyptian assassins Vidyunmali was escorting back to Devagiri. He and his men had stripped down to their loincloths in the sweaty heat of the hold. Battle scars adorned Swuth's body, but it was his numerous tattoos that drew Vidyunmali's attention. The Meluhan brigadier was familiar with one of them: a black fireball on the bridge of the man's nose, with rays streaming out in all directions; he knew it was usually the last thing the assassin's hapless victims saw before he butchered them, and that the fireball represented the Sun God, to whom Swuth and his assassins were dedicated. But Swuth had called him Aten . . .

'I thought Ra was your sun god?' said Vidyunmali.

Swuth shook his head. 'No. Most people call him Ra, but they're wrong. Aten is the correct name. And this symbol,' he said, pointing to the fireball tattoo, 'is his mark.'

'What about the jackal tattoo on your arm?'

'It's not a jackal – it's an animal that *looks* like a jackal. We call it Sha. This is the mark of the god after whom I am named.'

Vidyunmali was about to move on to the other tattoos, but Swuth raised his hand. 'I have too many tattoos on my body and too little interest in small talk,' he said. 'You're paying me good money, Brigadier, so I'll do your job. You don't need to build a relationship with me to motivate me. Let's talk about what you really want.'

Vidyunmali smiled. It was always a pleasure to work with professionals. They focused all their attention on the work at hand. The mission Emperor Daksha had tasked him with was a difficult one. Any brute could kill, but to kill with so many conditions attached required professionals, artists dedicated to their dark art.

'My apologies,' said Vidyunmali. 'I'll get right to it, then.'

'That would be good,' said Swuth sarcastically.

'We don't want anybody to recognise you, for a start.'

Swuth narrowed his eyes as though he'd just been insulted. 'Nobody *ever* sees us killing, Brigadier Vidyunmali. More often than not, even our victims don't see us while they're being killed.'

Vidyunmali shook his head. 'Perhaps I'm not making myself clear. I want you to be seen, but not recognised.'

As Swuth frowned, Vidyunmali walked over to one of the jute bags, opened it and pulled out a large black cloak and a mask. 'I need all of you to wear these, and I want you to be seen when you kill.'

Swuth took the cloak from him. He recognised the style instantly – it was the garment the Nagas wore whenever they travelled abroad. The mask was the kind worn during Holi celebrations. He looked at the brigadier, his eyes two narrow slits. 'You want people to think the Nagas did it?'

As Vidyunmali nodded he added, 'These cloaks will hinder our movements, and the masks will restrict our vision. We're not trained with these accoutrements.'

'Are you telling me the warriors of Aten can't do this?'

Swuth took a deep breath. 'Please leave.'

Vidyunmali stared at Swuth, stunned by his insolence.

'Leave,' clarified Swuth, 'so that we can put on these cloaks and masks and practise. And please leave the torch here.'

'Of course,' said Vidyunmali, and he fixed the torch into a sconce on his way out of the foetid hold.

CHAPTER 40

Ambush on the Narmada

'They aren't coming here?' Sati exclaimed. She'd been enjoying a glass of sweet saffron milk with Kali, Ganesh and Kartik, but they'd been interrupted all too soon by Bhagirath, Chandraketu, Maatali, Brahaspati and Chenardhwaj, the party bringing fresh news. The information just received from the Vasudevs suggested that a fleet of nearly fifty ships had sailed out of Karachapa a few weeks ago. They'd been expected to head for Lothal, but the latest reports said that the ships had turned south.

'It looks like they're heading towards the Narmada,' said the Vasudev pandit who had brought the intelligence.

'That can't be!' Kali, panic-stricken, looked at Ganesh. She hadn't agreed with Shiva's tactic of misleading the Meluhans by pretending to travel up the Narmada but sailing to Pariha instead, for she'd been afraid this would lead the Meluhans to the secret route to Panchavati. Shiva had dismissed her concerns, saying that Bhrigu was well aware that the river near Panchavati flowed from west to east, whereas the Narmada flowed east to west; clearly Panchavati wasn't on the Narmada itself. Even if they sailed up the Narmada, the Meluhans knew they'd have to disembark and march through the dense Dandak Forest to Panchavati, and that journey would be fraught with danger without a Naga guide.

But the news that the Meluhan navy was sailing towards the Narmada left Kali with only one logical conclusion: they had discovered the route to Panchavati.

'How could they have discovered the Narmada path to Panchavati?' Ganesh was bewildered.

Kali turned on Sati. 'Your husband didn't listen to me and stupidly insisted on sailing towards the Narmada—'

'Kali, the Meluhans have long been aware of all our comings and goings on the Narmada,' said Sati calmly. 'It's no secret that we use that river from time to time – but that knowledge wouldn't give them any information about the route from the Narmada to Panchavati. Shiva hasn't given anything away.'

'Nonsense!' shouted Kali. 'And it's not just Shiva's fault – you're just as much to blame for this. I told you to kill that traitor, *didi*. You and your misplaced sense of honour will lead to the destruction of my people!'

'*Mausi*,' said Ganesh, immediately springing to Sati's defence, 'I don't think we should blame *maa* for this. It's entirely possible that it's not General Parvateshwar but Lord Bhrigu who's discovered the Narmada route – after all, he knew the Godavari route, didn't he?'

'Of course, Ganesh,' said Kali sarcastically. 'It's not General Parvateshwar's fault. And it obviously can't be your beloved mother's fault, either. Why would the most devoted son in the history of mankind think his mother could make a mistake?'

'Kali . . .' whispered Sati.

But Kali continued to rant, 'Have you forgotten that you're a Naga, Ganesh? That you're the Lord of the People, sworn to protect your tribe to the last drop of your blood?'

Bhagirath decided to step in before things got out of hand. 'Queen Kali, there's no point debating how the Meluhans discovered the Narmada route. What we should be discussing is what we're going to do next. How do we save Panchavati?'

Kali turned to Bhagirath and snapped, 'We don't need to be maharishis to know what needs to be done. Fifty ships will set sail tomorrow with all the Naga warriors aboard. The Meluhans will regret the day they decided to attack my people!'

Kali, Ganesh and Kartik had assembled a hundred thousand men – all of the Nagas and many Branga warriors – at Lothal's circular port and the troops were rapidly boarding their ships. They knew that time was of the essence.

Sati had come to the port to see her family off. She was going to stay in Lothal, for she suspected that the Meluhans might mount a siege on the city once the ships had sailed, to try to take advantage of her divided army.

'Kali,' Sati began softly, but her sister gave her a withering look and turned her back.

'Board faster!' she screamed to her soldiers. 'Hurry up!'

Ganesh and Kartik stepped forward and bent to touch Sati's feet, to take their mother's blessings with them.

'We'll be back soon, *maa*,' said Ganesh, smiling awkwardly.

'I'll be waiting,' Sati said quietly.

'Do you have any instructions for us, *maa*?' asked Kartik.

Sati looked at her sister, who still had her back turned stiffly towards her. 'Take care of your *mausi*.'

Kali heard what Sati said, but still she refused to respond.

Sati stepped up and lightly touched her sister's shoulder. 'I'm sorry about General Parvateshwar,' she said. 'I did what I thought was right.'

Kali stiffened under Sati's hand. '*Didi*, one who clings to moral arrogance even at the cost of the lives of others isn't necessarily the most moral of people.'

Sati said nothing, just stared sadly at Kali's back. She could see Kali's two extra arms on top of her shoulders quivering, a sure sign that the Naga queen was deeply agitated.

Kali turned and glared at her sister. 'My people will not suffer for your addiction to moral glory, *didi*.' And with that, she stormed off, tongue-lashing her tardy soldiers as she headed for her ship.

— ⫶ ◍ U � ⊕ —

Kanakhala couldn't believe what she was hearing. They had a real shot at peace!

'This is the best news I've heard in a long time, your Majesty,' said Kanakhala.

Daksha smiled genially. 'I hope you understand this has to be kept secret. There are many who don't want peace. They think the only way to end this is an all-out war.'

The prime minister glanced at Vidyunmali, who was standing next to Daksha. She'd always assumed he was a warmonger, and she was surprised to see him agreeing with the emperor.

Perhaps, she thought, *the emperor means Lord Bhrigu is the one who doesn't want peace with the Neelkanth.*

'We've seen the loss of life and devastation caused by the minor battle fought outside Devagiri,' said Daksha. 'It was only Sati's wisdom that prevented it from becoming a massacre that would have hurt both Meluha and the Lord Neelkanth.'

Maybe the emperor's love for Sati is forcing his hand. He'd never allow any harm to come to his daughter. Whatever the reason, I'll support his peace initiative.

'What are you thinking, Kanakhala?' asked Daksha.

'Nothing important, my Lord. I'm just happy you're willing to discuss a peaceful solution.'

'You will have your work cut out,' he said. 'An entire peace conference has to be organised at short notice – and, in keeping with tradition, we'll name it after our prime minister: it will be the *yagna* of Kanakhala.'

Kanakhala, embarrassed, smiled shyly. 'You're most kind, my Lord, but the name doesn't matter. What matters is peace.'

'Peace is indeed paramount, which is why you must handle this with the utmost discretion and secrecy. Under no circumstances should news of the peace conference reach Karachapa.'

Karachapa was where Lord Bhrigu had stationed himself, along with King Dilipa of Ayodhya and General Parvateshwar.

'Yes, my Lord,' said Kanakhala, before bowing and rushing to her office; she needed to get down to work immediately.

Daksha waited for the door of his private office to shut before turning to Vidyunmali. 'I hope Swuth and his people won't fail me.'

'They won't, my Lord,' said Vidyunmali. 'Have faith in me. This will be the end of that barbarian from Tibet and everyone will blame the Nagas – they're already perceived as bloodthirsty, irrational killers. No reasonable citizen here has been able to swallow that fraud Neelkanth's championing of the Nagas, just like they didn't accept the freeing of the *vikarmas*, regardless of how bravely Drapaku and the rest of them fought in battle. The people will readily believe that the Nagas killed him.'

'And my daughter will return to me,' said Daksha. 'She'll have no choice. We'll be a family again.'

— ⵣ ⵯⵡ ⵓ ⵣ ⵯ —

The Parihans had loaded their precious cargo aboard the merchant ship, and everyone had said their goodbyes. The

Neelkanth, standing next to Gopal and Tara on the foredeck, ordered his ship to set sail on the Jam Sea.

'Scheherazade,' said Gopal, 'how long—?'

'Tara, please,' she said, blushing.

'I'm sorry?'

'My name's Tara now, great Vasudev. Scheherazade was left behind in Pariha.'

Gopal smiled. 'Of course. My apologies, Tara.'

'So what was your question?'

'I was wondering how long you had lived in Pariha.'

'Too long,' said Tara. 'Initially, I travelled there on an assignment from Lord Bhrigu – I thought it would be a short visit. He commanded me to work on the *daivi astras* with the Vayuputras, and he said I couldn't return until he gave me permission to do so. But after I heard of Brahaspati's death, I saw no reason to return.'

'Well, he's not too far away now,' said Gopal kindly. 'Just a couple of weeks on the Jam Sea, and then we'll sail east across the Western Sea to Lothal – and to Brahaspati.'

'Yes,' said Shiva, his eyes sparkling mischievously, 'but this whole journey is very confusing. Jam is the sea you "come to", but now it'll be the sea we "go from"! And then we have to travel east on the Western Sea! Only the Holy Lake knows where we'll finally end up!'

Tara raised her eyes to the Neelkanth, unsure how to respond.

'I know,' said Shiva. 'It's a terrible joke. I guess the law of averages catches up with everyone.'

Tara burst out laughing. 'It's not your joke that astonished me – though I agree, it really was a terrible joke.'

'Thank you – I think!' said Shiva, laughing softly. 'But what surprised you?'

'I'm assuming you think "Jam" means to "come to".'

Shiva glanced at Gopal with a raised eyebrow, for it was the Chief Vasudev who'd told him the meaning.

'Doesn't "Jam" mean to "come to"?' asked Gopal.

'That's what everybody thinks,' said Tara. 'Except for the Parihans.'

'So what do they believe?' asked Shiva.

'Jam is the Lord of *Dharma*, so this sea is actually the Sea of the Lord of *Dharma*.'

Shiva smiled. 'But in India, the Lord of Dharma—'

'Is Yam,' said Tara, completing Shiva's statement, 'who is also the Lord of Death.'

CHAPTER 41

An Invitation for Peace

Sati, Bhagirath, Chandraketu, Maatali and Brahaspati, assembled in Governor Chenardhwaj's private office, looked stunned at the message from Kanakhala.

'A peace conference?' Bhagirath repeated. 'What deception are they planning now?'

'Prince Bhagirath,' said Chenardhwaj, 'this is Meluha. We don't break the rules here. And the rules regarding a peace conference are very clear – they were designed by Lord Ram himself. Deception is out of the question.'

'But what about the attack on Panchavati?' asked King Maatali of Vaishali. 'They've clearly found the Narmada route to the Naga capital and sent their ships on an attack mission, even though they're trying to trick us into thinking otherwise.'

'How is that subterfuge, King Maatali?' asked Chenardhwaj. 'We're at war. They found a weak spot and decided to attack. That's how wars are conducted.'

'I don't have a problem with the Meluhans choosing to attack Panchavati, Governor Chenardhwaj,' said King Chandraketu of Branga. 'What's worrying me is that they chose to attack Panchavati and call a peace conference at the same time. That sounds fishy to me.'

'I agree,' said Bhagirath. 'Maybe it's a ruse to draw us out of the city.'

'But Prince Bhagirath,' said Brahaspati, 'we've also received word that the Meluhan army still hasn't marched out of Karachapa. If their plan is to trick us out of Lothal, why wouldn't they mobilise their army at the same time?'

Chandraketu nodded. 'That is confusing.'

'Maybe Meluha's divided,' suggested Brahaspati. 'Maybe some people want peace while others want war?'

'We can't trust this invitation wholeheartedly,' said Sati, 'but we can't ignore it, either. If there's any possibility that the *Somras* can be stopped without any more killing, it's worth grabbing, right?'

'But the message is for Lord Shiva,' said Bhagirath. 'Shouldn't we await his return?'

Sati shook her head. 'He's not due back for months. We don't even know if he's succeeded in convincing the Vayuputras to help us. What if he hasn't? That would put us in a very weak position from which to negotiate banning the *Somras*. Right now, it's a stalemate – even the Meluhans know that. We might be able to negotiate good terms at the conference.'

'Maybe,' said Chandraketu. 'Or we might be marching straight into a trap.'

This was a difficult decision, and it couldn't be made in a hurry. 'I need to think about this some more,' Sati said, and ended the discussion.

Sati walked into the heavily guarded room. The messenger from Devagiri who had brought Kanakhala's invitation had been housed in comfortable quarters in the governor's office building. He had been treated well, but the windows of his room had been boarded up and the doors were kept locked at all times, just to be on the safe side. He'd been blindfolded while he was led through the city, and his men had been made to wait outside the city gates. Sati had no intention of allowing the peace envoy to observe any of their defensive arrangements.

'Your Highness.' The Meluhan rose and saluted Sati. She was still the Princess of Meluha to him.

'Brigadier Mayashrenik,' said Sati with a formal namaste. She'd always thought well of the Arishtanemi brigadier.

Mayashrenik looked towards the door with a frown. 'Isn't the Neelkanth joining us?'

Bhrigu had decided against sharing intelligence with Daksha. It would only cause Daksha's unwelcome interference in war strategies to continue, which Parvateshwar, being a disciplined Meluhan, would always find difficult to withstand. Consequently Mayashrenik, along with every other Meluhan in Devagiri, had no idea what Parvateshwar suspected: that Shiva might have sailed up the Narmada and then marched to Panchavati.

Sati didn't want to reveal to Mayashrenik that Shiva wasn't in Lothal, but she didn't want to lie, either. Best to keep it simple, then. 'No.'

'But—'

'When you speak with me,' said Sati firmly, 'it's as good as speaking with him.'

Mayashrenik frowned. 'But I don't understand why the Lord Neelkanth doesn't want to meet with me himself. Doesn't he want peace? Does he think that destroying Meluha is the only way forward?'

'Shiva doesn't think Meluha's evil – only the *Somras* is evil. He's all in favour of suing for peace if Meluha will meet just one simple demand: abandon the *Somras*.'

'Then he must come to Devagiri for the peace conference.'

'And that's the problem – what assurances do we have that Kanakhala's invitation is genuine?'

'Your Highness—' Mayashrenik sounded stunned. 'Surely you don't think Meluha would lie about a peace conference? How could we? Lord Ram's laws forbid it!'

'Meluhans may always follow the law, Brigadier, but my father doesn't.'

'Your Highness, the emperor's efforts are genuine.'

'And why should I believe that?'

'I'm sure your spies have already told you that Maharishi Bhrigu is in Karachapa.'

'So what?'

'Maharishi Bhrigu is the one who doesn't want any compromise, your Highness. Your father wants peace. He has an opportunity to negotiate for it while the Maharishi is away. You know that once your father signs a peace treaty, it'll be very difficult for Maharishi Bhrigu to overrule it. Meluha recognises only the emperor's orders. Even now, while Maharishi Bhrigu may be giving the orders, they're all issued in the emperor's name.'

'You want me to believe that my father's suddenly developed enough character to stand up for what he thinks is right?'

'You're being unfair—'

'Really? Don't you know that he killed my first husband? He has no respect for the law.'

'But he loves you.'

Sati rolled her eyes in disgust. 'Please, Mayashrenik. Do you really expect me to believe that he's pushing for peace because he loves me?'

'He saved your life, your Highness.'

'What utter nonsense! Have you fallen for that ridiculous explanation as well? Do you really believe that my father banished my Naga child and kept him hidden from me for nearly ninety years so he could "save my life"? He did nothing of the sort. He did what he did to protect his own name. He broke the law so no one would find out that Emperor Daksha has a Naga grandchild.'

'I'm not talking about what happened ninety years ago, your Highness, but about what happened just a few years ago.'

'What?'

'Who do you think raised the alarm at Panchavati?'

Sati remained silent, stunned by the revelation.

'The timely triggering of that alarm saved your life.'

'How do you know about that?'

'Lord Bhrigu sent the ships to destroy Panchavati, but your father ordered me to sabotage that operation. I raised the alarm that saved you all, and I did it on your father's orders. He damaged his empire and his own interests in order to protect you.'

Sati stared at Mayashrenik, flabbergasted. 'I don't believe you.'

'It's the truth, your Highness,' said Mayashrenik. 'You know I don't lie.'

Sati took a deep breath and looked away.

Mayashrenik pressed his point. 'Even if his Majesty is only suing for peace because of his love for you rather than his duty towards Meluha, wouldn't our country benefit all the same? Do we really want this war to continue until Meluha's destroyed?'

Sati returned her gaze to Mayashrenik, but kept her thoughts to herself.

'Please, speak to the Neelkanth, my Lady. I know he listens to you. The peace offer is genuine.'

Sati still said nothing.

'I beg you to grant me an audience with the Neelkanth, your Highness,' said Mayashrenik, still unsure whether Sati believed him, or that she had committed herself to peace.

'That's not possible,' said Sati. 'One of my guards will guide you to the city gates. Return to Devagiri. I'll give serious thought to what you've said.'

'We should seriously consider attending this peace conference,' said Sati after she returned to the governor's residence.

'That's not a wise idea, my Lady,' said Bhagirath. 'Lord Ram alone knows what traps they might have set for us.'

'On the contrary, I think it might be a very wise decision. How likely is it that the army in Karachapa doesn't know what my father's doing in Devagiri?'

'It's possible,' Brahaspati admitted, 'but do you really think your father's driving the peace conference? Does he have the strength to make it happen?'

'Perhaps he's not alone in this endeavour – Prime Minister Kanakhala's certainly involved, for one,' said Sati. 'The invitation's in her name.'

'Kanakhala has some influence over the emperor, no doubt,' agreed Chenardhwaj, 'and she's certainly no warmonger. Her instincts are usually towards peace – and she's a devoted follower of the Neelkanth.'

'Does she have the capability to enforce the peace accord?' asked Bhagirath.

'Yes, she does,' said Sati. 'The Meluhan system works on the principle of written orders. The supreme written orders come from the emperor. Lord Bhrigu doesn't issue orders himself – he makes proposals and asks my father to ratify them. If my father issues an order for peace before Lord Bhrigu finds out about it, all Meluhans will be forced to honour it. So if Prime Minister

Kanakhala can persuade my father to issue the order, she'll have the authority she needs to enforce the peace accord.'

'If we could eliminate the *Somras* without further bloodshed, it'll be a deed Lord Rudra would be proud of,' said Maatali.

'But we should respond carefully,' Bhagirath persisted. 'If it's true that only Emperor Daksha and Prime Minister Kanakhala are pursuing peace, we'll put our army at risk if we march out of Lothal – Karachapa's not very far away from here.'

'You're right,' said Sati, who had a healthy respect for General Parvateshwar's tactical brilliance. 'If *Pitratulya* hears about our army moving out, he'll assume we're attacking Devagiri. He'll race out of Karachapa to intercept us at the Saraswati River.'

'Damned if we respond and damned if we don't,' said Chandraketu.

'So what do we do?' asked Chenardhwaj.

'I'll go,' said Sati. 'The rest of you, including the army, should stay safe within Lothal's walls.'

'My Lady,' said Maatali, aghast, 'that would be most unwise. You'll need the army's protection in Devagiri.'

'The Meluhans might engage my army in battle outside Devagiri,' said Sati, 'but they won't attack me in my father's house if I go alone.'

Bhagirath shook his head. 'Apologies, my Lady, but your father hasn't exactly proved himself to be a paragon of virtue so far. I'd be unhappy about you travelling to Devagiri without protection. We can't discount the possibility, no matter how remote, that the peace conference is a ruse to draw our leaders to Devagiri and then assassinate them.'

Chenardhwaj was genuinely offended now. 'Prince Bhagirath, I'm saying this for the last time – such things do not happen in Meluha. Arms can't be deployed at a peace conference under any circumstances. Those are the rules of Lord Ram himself. No Meluhan will break the laws of the seventh Vishnu.'

Sati raised her hand, signalling for calm, then turned towards Bhagirath. 'Prince, trust me, please. My father will never harm me. He loves me – in his own twisted way, he really does care for me. I'm going to Devagiri. This is our best shot at peace, and it's my duty not to let it slip by.'

But Bhagirath couldn't shake off his sense of foreboding. 'Princess, I insist you allow me and an Ayodhyan brigade to travel with you.'

'Your men will be put to better use here, Prince Bhagirath,' said Sati. 'Also, you and your soldiers are Chandravanshis. Please don't misunderstand me, but I'd much rather take some Suryavanshis along. I'm going to the Suryavanshi capital, after all. I'll take Nandi and my personal bodyguards.'

'But my child,' said Brahaspati, 'that's only a hundred soldiers. Are you sure that'll be enough?'

'It's a peace conference, Brahaspatiji,' said Sati, 'not a battle.'

'But the invitation was for the Lord Neelkanth,' said Chandraketu.

'The Lord Neelkanth has appointed me as his representative,

your Majesty,' said Sati. 'I can negotiate on his behalf and I've made up my mind – I'm going to Devagiri.'

'I have a bad feeling about this, my Lady,' pleaded Veerbhadra. 'Please don't go.'

Parshuram and Nandi looked equally anguished as Sati said calmy, 'Veerbhadra, please don't worry. I'll return with a peace treaty that'll end the war as well as the reign of the *Somras*.'

'But why won't you let Veerbhadra and me come with you, my Lady?' asked Parshuram. 'Why is only Nandi being given the privilege of travelling with you?'

Sati smiled. 'I'd love to have both of you with me, but I'm only taking Suryavanshis – they're familiar with Meluhan customs. This is going to be a sensitive conference and I wouldn't want anything to go wrong inadvertently before it even begins.'

'But my Lady,' Parshuram tried again, 'we're sworn to protect you. How can we let you go without us?'

'I'll be with her, Parshuram,' said Nandi. 'Don't worry, I won't let anything happen to Lady Sati.'

'There's absolutely no reason why anything untoward should happen, Nandi. It's a peace conference and, if we don't arrive at a peace settlement, the Meluhans will have to allow us to return here unharmed. That's Lord Ram's law.'

Veerbhadra continued to brood silently, clearly unconvinced.

Sati reached out and patted Veerbhadra's shoulder. 'We must

at least try to find a peaceful solution; you know that. We could save so many lives. I have no choice. I must go.'

'You *do* have a choice,' argued Veerbhadra. 'Don't go yourself – you can nominate someone to attend the conference on your behalf.'

Sati shook her head. 'No. I must go. I must . . . because it was my fault.'

'What?'

'It was my fault that so many of our soldiers died in Devagiri and our elephant corps was destroyed. I'm to blame for the loss of almost our entire cavalry. It's because of my decisions that we're not strong enough to beat them in open battle now. Since it's my fault, it's now my responsibility to set it right.'

'The loss in Devagiri wasn't your fault, my Lady,' said Parshuram. 'Circumstances were aligned against us. In fact, you salvaged a lot from a terrible situation.'

Sati narrowed her eyes. 'If an army loses, it's *always* the result of the general's poor planning. Circumstance is just an excuse for the weak to rationalise their failures. However, I've been given another chance to make up for my blunder. I can't ignore it. I *won't*.'

'My Lady,' said Veerbhadra, 'please, listen to me—'

'Bhadra,' said Sati, calling him by the name her husband used for his best friend, 'I'm going and I'll return unharmed *and* with a peace treaty.'

CHAPTER 42

Kanakhala's Choice

Kanakhala rushed to Daksha's private office the minute she received the bird-courier from Lothal. The invitation to the peace conference had been accepted. The door attendant tried to stop her, saying the emperor had asked him not to let anyone enter, but Kanakhala brushed him aside.

'That order won't apply to me. He asked me to come to him as soon as I received this,' said Kanakhala, brandishing the folded letter.

The door attendant moved aside and as Kanakhala opened the door she heard whispering: Vidyunmali and Daksha were speaking softly with each other. She gently shut the door behind her.

'Are you sure they're ready?' asked Daksha.

'Yes, my Lord. Swuth's men have been practising in Naga attire. That fraud Neelkanth won't know what hit him,' said

Vidyunmali. 'The world will blame the terrorist Nagas for their beloved Neelkanth's assassination.'

Daksha silenced him with a hand gesture when he noticed Kanakhala rooted at the entrance. Vidyunmali drew his sword.

Daksha raised his hand. 'Vidyunmali! Calm down. Prime Minister Kanakhala knows where her loyalties lie.'

'Your Majesty—' whispered Kanakhala, her eyes wide with shock.

'Kanakhala,' said Daksha, sounding eerily calm. He walked up to her and placed his hands on her shoulders. 'Sometimes an emperor must do what must be done.'

'But we can't break Lord Ram's laws,' she said, her breathing quickening.

'Lord Ram's laws regarding peace conferences apply to a king, not to his prime minister,' said Daksha.

'But—'

'No buts,' said Daksha. 'Remember your oath. This is war-time and you have to do whatever your emperor asks of you. If you reveal his secrets without his permission, the punishment is death.'

'But, your Majesty . . . This is *wrong*.'

'What would be wrong, Kanakhala, would be for you to break your vow.'

'Your Majesty,' said Vidyunmali, 'this is too risky. I think the prime minister should be—'

Daksha interrupted him. 'We'll do no such thing, Vidyun-mali. If she's not here to organise the conference, Shiva's men will be suspicious the moment they arrive. It is, after all, the "Conference of Kanakhala".'

Kanakhala was speechless with horror.

'You've been loyal to me for decades, Kanakhala,' said Daksha. 'Remember your vows and you will live; you will continue to be prime minister. But if you break them, not only will you be given the death sentence, you'll also be damned by the Parmatma.'

The prime ministerial oath decreed that if she betrayed her emperor, not only would she be executed, but worse, no funeral ceremonies would be conducted for her. Without those rites, her soul wouldn't be able to cross the mythical Vaitarni River to *Pitralok*, the land of her ancestors, and her soul's onward journey, either towards liberation or back to earth to inhabit another body, would be interrupted and she would remain in the land of the living as a *Pishach*, a ghost.

'Remember your vows and do your duty,' said Daksha. 'Focus on the conference.'

— 太 ◍ U ⭧ ⊛ —

Kanakhala stood quietly on the terrace outside her home office, listening to the sound of water from the small fountain in the centre of the chamber. She loved that sound – it kept her mind focused and calm. Glancing up at the sky, she saw that the sun was already setting.

She took a deep breath and looked towards the street. The soldiers weren't even trying to hide. Kanakhala didn't feel any anger towards the men who were keeping watch outside her house. They were good soldiers, and they were simply following their commanding officer's orders.

It would be pointless trying to send a message to Lothal to warn the Neelkanth; Kanakhala was quite sure Vidyunmali had archers positioned along the route to bring down any bird-couriers. It was also likely that the Neelkanth's convoy had already left Lothal. Her only hope was General Parvateshwar: if he and Lord Bhrigu managed to reach Devagiri in time, this sin could be stopped. But getting a message to Karachapa wouldn't be easy.

Kanakhala looked at the small message in her hand. She had addressed it to the Neelkanth. She rolled the message tightly and slipped it into a small canister attached to a pigeon's leg. She sealed the canister, closed her eyes and whispered, 'Forgive me, noble bird. Your sacrifice will aid a greater cause. *Om Brahmaye Namah*.'

Then she threw the bird into the air.

The soldiers below reacted immediately and she saw an archer emerge from the rooftop of a building some distance away. He quickly nocked an arrow and released, hitting the pigeon with deadly accuracy and piercing the bird's body. The dead pigeon dropped like a stone and the soldiers quickly scattered to find it and retrieve the message. She knew it would immediately be taken to Vidyunmali, and they would believe it was genuine since it was in Kanakhala's handwriting and addressed to the Neelkanth.

Kanakhala looked towards the street once again and from the corner of her eye she saw her servant slip quietly out of the side door, using the soldiers' temporary distraction to leave the building unseen. He would release a second courier-bird outside the city walls, a homing pigeon bound for Karachapa. She prayed Bhrigu and Parvateshwar would be able to get to Devagiri in time to stop this madness, to prevent this terrible subversion of Lord Ram's laws. After releasing the bird, the servant had been instructed to ride hard southwards, towards Lothal, in an attempt to stop the Neelkanth and his peace negotiators from walking into the trap.

Kanakhala had done all she possibly could.

She sighed. She'd broken her vow of loyalty to her emperor, but she sought solace from an ancient scriptural verse: *Dharma matih udgritah* – *dharma* is that which your mind judges to be right; think deeply about *dharma* and your mind will tell you what is right.

In this case she was sure that breaking her vows was the right thing to do, for that was the only way to stop an even bigger crime from being committed. But she was no fool: she knew what her punishment would be – though she had no intention of giving Daksha that pleasure.

Kanakhala smiled sadly and walked back into her office. From her writing desk she picked up a bowl containing a clear greenish medicine which she quickly swallowed. It would numb her pain and make her feel drowsy, exactly what she needed. She walked calmy over to the fountain – the small pool at the base was perfect, deep enough to keep her hand submerged. The blood wouldn't clot if the wound was continually washed by flowing water.

She picked up the sharp ceremonial knife she carried with her. For one brief moment, she wondered whether she would roam the earth forever as a ghost, then she shook her head and dismissed her fears.

Dharma rakshati rakshitaha: *dharma* protects those who protect *dharma*.

She closed her eyes, balled her left hand into a fist and submerged it beneath the water. She then took a deep breath and whispered softly, '*Jai Shri Ram.*'

With one swift move, she slashed deep, slicing through skin, veins and arteries, and blood burst forth in a rapid flood. She rested her head on the side of the fountain and waited for death to take her away.

'It doesn't change the plans at all, your Majesty,' said Vidyunmali to the emperor, who looked stunned. They had just received word of Kanakhala's suicide.

'Your Majesty?' said Vidyunmali, when he didn't get a response.

'Yes . . . ?' Daksha was still reeling from the news.

'Listen to me,' said Vidyunmali firmly. 'We'll go ahead as planned. Swuth's men are ready.'

'Yes . . .'

'Your Majesty!' said Vidyunmali loudly, and this time Daksha's eyes focused on the brigadier as he asked again, 'Did you hear me, your Majesty?'

'Yes.'

'Everyone will be told that Kanakhala died in an accident. The peace conference will continue in her memory.'

'Yes.'

'And now I have to go.'

'What?' Daksha was approaching full-blown panic.

'I told you, your Majesty,' said Vidyunmali patiently, as if talking to a child, 'one of Kanakhala's servants is missing and I fear he may have set out to warn the fraud Neelkanth. He must be stopped. I'm going to take a platoon. I'll head south.'

'But how will I manage all this by myself?'

'You don't have to do anything, your Majesty. Everything's under control. My soldiers will find a way to bring Princess Sati safely into the palace – nobody else from her party will be allowed to accompany her. The moment she's with you, you'll signal my man, who will be waiting at your window. He'll shoot a fire-arrow in the air, and that will alert Swuth's assassins that the coast is clear. They'll quickly move in and kill the fraud Neelkanth. They've been instructed to leave a few of Shiva's people alive to testify that they were attacked by Nagas.'

Daksha still looked nervous, and the brigadier stepped closer and spoke gently. 'You don't have to worry, your Majesty. I've planned everything in meticulous detail and there'll be no mistakes. All you have to do is signal my man when Princess Sati enters your room. That's it.'

'That's it?'

'Yes, that's it. Now I really need to go, your Majesty. If Kanakhala's man manages to reach the fraud Neelkanth, it'll be the end of our plans.'

'Of course. Go.'

'Those sons of bitches!' Kali scowled at Jadav Rana, the ruler of Umbergaon, who had just reached the Naga fleet aboard a fast cutter. His small kingdom lay to the south of the Narmada and the Nagas had helped him on many occasions; he was not an ungrateful man.

When some fishermen from his kingdom told him of a large Meluhan fleet stationed in a hidden lagoon nearby, he'd gone personally to investigate. He had seen the massive fleet with his own eyes and immediately surmised that this must have something to do with the war raging in the north between the Neelkanth's forces and the Meluhans. When he'd received news that the Nagas were racing along the western coast towards the mouth of the Narmada he immediately set off to intercept the Nagas before they got to the river that marked the southern boundary of the Sapt Sindhu. He was convinced the Meluhans intended to take the Nagas by surprise and attack them from the rear.

'Your Majesty,' said Jadav Rana now, 'I believe the Meluhans are intending to enter the Narmada behind you to assault your rearguard – they could devastate your entire fleet before you even realised what had happened.'

'I wouldn't be surprised if they have a forward ambush planned for us as well,' said Kartik.

'We'll attack them in their hidden lagoon,' said Kali. 'We'll burn their ships down to the waterline and hang their rotten carcases on the trees.'

Ganesh had remained silent until now. Something was amiss, though he wasn't yet sure what. 'Your Majesty, how many Meluhans are there?'

'Fifty ships, Lord Ganesh,' said Jadav Rana, 'a reasonably large force. But you have more than enough ships to take them on.'

'I didn't ask you about the ships, your Majesty,' said Ganesh. 'I asked how many men were aboard them.'

Jadav Rana frowned. 'I don't know, Lord Ganesh.' Turning to his men, he asked, 'Do you have any idea?'

'It's difficult to be sure, my Lord, since they've mostly remained on board,' said one of Jadav Rana's lieutenants, 'but judging by the amount they've been foraging, I don't think there are more than five thousand in total. You have many more men, Lord Ganesh. You can win easily.'

Ganesh held his head and whispered, 'Bhoomidevi, be merciful.'

Kali stared at Jadav Rana's lieutenant. 'Are you *sure*? Just five thousand?'

Jadav Rana didn't understand why the Nagas looked so upset. They outnumbered the Meluhans dramatically, so, logically, they should have been happy.

'My men are well acquainted with these coasts, your Majesty,' said Jadav Rana. 'If they say the Meluhans number only five thousand, I believe them.'

'We've been taken for a ride,' said Ganesh. 'There's no attack planned on Panchavati. They were trying to divide our forces. And they succeeded.'

Kartik, worried, looked at his elder brother. 'They're probably attacking Lothal even as we speak.'

'And we took a hundred thousand men away from *maa*,' said Ganesh, distraught.

Kali turned and yelled to Prime Minister Karkotak, 'Turn around, *right now*! We're going back to Lothal! Double rowing till we get there! *Move!*'

CHAPTER 43

A Civil Revolt

Bhagirath and Brahaspati, warned that Shiva's ship would be arriving soon, had come to the harbour to meet him. From their position sitting on the wall they could see both Shiva's merchant vessel sailing in from the east and Kali's naval contingent racing in from the south. It was beginning to look like they would all dock at the same time.

As Shiva's ship came in to the harbour Brahaspati gasped and went white, then he jumped off the wall and went running wildly to the mooring posts. Bhagirath wondered at Brahaspati's strange reaction. He stared at Shiva's ship as it was being moored – he could see Shiva and Gopal now, and standing on the foredeck next to them was an Indian-looking woman he'd never seen before.

He caught up with Brahaspati and asked, 'Who is she, Brahaspatiji?'

The scientist was crying openly and repeating, 'Oh Lord Brahma! Oh Lord Brahma!'

'Who is she?' the Ayodhan prince asked again, examining his friend, who looked delirious – delirious but happy!

'They let her go!' he cried, and, 'Shiva freed her! Lord Ram be praised, he freed her!'

'Isn't that Shiva's ship?' said Kali. They had rushed back to Lothal at full speed, fully expecting to find the city under siege. Ganesh and Kartik turned to follow her pointing finger and saw a merchant ship moored at the circular port just ahead of them.

Kali's ship docked at a nearby berth in less than fifteen minutes and as soon as the gangplank hit the dockside they rushed off to find Shiva, who was standing with Bhagirath and Brahaspati. Brahaspati, looking stunned, was embracing a woman none of them recognised, and both of them were crying profusely.

'Shiva!' shouted Kali as she sprinted towards him.

Shiva turned and smiled at her. 'I saw the Naga ships arriving behind us. Where've you been?'

'On a wild goose chase,' said Kali. 'We were led to believe that Panchavati was under attack.'

'The Meluhan ships were a decoy?' asked Bhagirath.

'Yes, Prince Bhagirath,' said Kartik. 'The ships had only five thousand men aboard in total. They had no intention of attacking Panchavati.'

'That's good news,' said Bhagirath.

'Where's Sati?' asked Shiva, looking around.

'There's some good news there as well,' said Bhagirath.

'And what would that be?' asked Ganesh.

'We may have a solution to end the war,' Bhagirath said.

'We've come back with a solution as well,' said Gopal, pointing to the large trunk that was being carefully lowered onto the dock.

Shiva glanced at Brahaspati who was refusing to let go of Tara. She was still crying with joy, and her head was gently nestled against Brahaspati's chest. They looked like teenagers in the first heady flush of love.

'Looks like there's good news all around,' said Shiva with a smile.

'How in the Holy Lake's name can this be good news?'

Bhagirath, fearful of Shiva's wrath, kept silent, but King Chandraketu explained, 'My Lord, Lady Sati herself believed this was our best chance for peace, and it looks like Emperor Daksha himself wants it. If he signs a peace treaty, the war will be over. And we don't want to destroy Meluha, do we? All we want is the end of the *Somras*.'

'I don't trust that goat of a man,' said Kali. 'If he hurts my sister, I'll burn his entire city to a cinder, with him in it.'

'He won't hurt her, Kali,' said Shiva, 'but I'm afraid he may make her a prisoner and use that to negotiate with us.'

'But my Lord,' said Governor Chenardhwaj, 'that's impossible. The rules governing a peace conference are very clear:

both parties are free to leave, unharmed, if a solution or compromise can't be found.'

'What's to stop my grandfather from ignoring the rules?' asked Ganesh. 'It won't be the first time he's broken a law.'

'My Lord,' said a Vasudev pandit who had just entered the chamber and approached Gopal, 'I have urgent news.'

'I think we can talk later, Panditji,' said Gopal.

'No, my Lord,' insisted the pandit, who was in charge of the Lothal Temple, 'we must speak now.'

Gopal was surprised by the man's persistence, but his Vasudev pandits didn't panic unnecessarily so it had to be something important. He rose and walked off to one side while the others continued to discuss Sati's plan.

'Lord Ganesh,' said Chenardhwaj, 'the peace conference rules were laid down by Lord Ram himself. They are fundamental rules, part of the set that can never be amended. They must be rigorously followed, on pain of a punishment worse than death – not even a man like Emperor Daksha will ever break those rules.'

'I pray to the Parmatma that you're right, Chenardhwaj,' snarled Kali.

'I have no doubt, your Majesty,' he said. 'The worst that can happen is that no deal will be struck, and then Lady Sati will return unharmed to us.'

'Lord Ram, be merciful,' exclaimed Gopal loudly, and everyone turned quickly to look at the Chief Vasudev, who was still standing with the Lothal Vasudev pandit.

'What's happened, Panditji?' asked Shiva.

Gopal turned to Shiva. Ashen-faced, he said, 'Great Neel-kanth, the news is disturbing. General Parvateshwar's army finally mobilised and marched out of Karachapa three days ago.'

A loud murmur erupted in the chamber. *We must prepare for battle . . .*

'Silence,' snapped Shiva. 'There's more, isn't there? What else, Panditji?'

'They turned back within a few hours,' he said.

'Turned back? Why?'

'I don't know,' said Gopal. 'My pandit tells me the army's been sent back to the barracks, but Lord Parvateshwar and Lord Bhrigu have set sail up the Indus in a single fast ship, accompanied only by their personal bodyguards. I've been told they're rushing towards Devagiri.'

Shiva felt a chill run up his spine as Gopal added, 'And a flurry of birds have been flying out of Karachapa, all of them heading towards Devagiri. My pandit at Karachapa doesn't know the contents of those messages, but he says he's never seen so much communication between the two cities.'

There was deathly silence in the chamber. Everyone was well aware of Parvateshwar's spotless reputation for honourable conduct. If he was rushing to Devagiri without a large army to slow him down, it could only mean that something terrible was going on in the Meluhan capital, and he was rushing there to stop it.

Shiva was the first to recover. 'Mobilise the army immediately. We're leaving.'

'Yes, my Lord,' said Bhagirath, rising quickly.

'And Bhagirath – I want to leave within hours, not days,' said Shiva.

'Yes, my Lord,' said Bhagirath, hurrying out, closely followed by Chandraketu, Chenardhwaj, Maatali, Ganesh and Kartik. There was much to do to mobilise an army as large as Shiva's in so short a time.

— 𑀆𑀑𑀉𑀢𑀣 —

'*Maa* will be all right, *baba*,' said Kartik, allowing hope to triumph over reason.

Shiva, wracked with worry, couldn't wait for everyone else. He had taken his entourage – Kartik, Ganesh, Kali, Gopal, Veerbhadra, Parshuram, Ayurvati and an entire brigade of soldiers – and set off shortly after they'd heard the news, leaving the main army, led by Prince Bhagirath, to follow the next morning. Shiva had taken the *Pashupatiastra* with him, as insurance.

'Kartik's right, great Neelkanth,' said Gopal as they stopped to grab a quick meal. 'It's possible that Emperor Daksha might break the rules of a peace conference, but he won't hurt Princess Sati, though he might try to imprison her to improve his negotiating position. But we have the *Pashupatiastra* and that changes everything.'

Shiva nodded silently.

Kali listened intently to Gopal, but the Chief Vasudev's words didn't give her any solace. She didn't trust her father, she was deeply troubled about her sister's safety and she was consumed with guilt about the petulant way she'd parted from Sati. Her two extra arms were quivering constantly.

Shiva held Kali's hand and smiled faintly. 'Relax, Kali. Nothing will happen to her. The Parmatma won't allow such an injustice.'

But Kali was too anguished to respond.

'Finish your meal,' said Shiva. 'We will leave in a few minutes.' He turned to Ganesh, who was staring into the forest, his eyes moist. He hadn't touched the food in front of him and Shiva could see he was praying under his breath, his hands clasped tightly as he repeated chants in rapid succession.

'Ganesh,' said Shiva, 'eat.'

Ganesh emerged from his trance. 'I'm not hungry, *baba*.'

'Ganesh,' said Shiva firmly, 'we may have to engage in battle the moment we reach Devagiri. I need all of you to be strong, and for that you need food. So if you love your mother and want to protect her, keep yourself strong. Eat.'

Ganesh looked at his banana-leaf plate. His father was right: he had to eat, whether he could stomach it or not.

Shiva turned to Veerbhadra, who had already finished and was wiping his hands on the cloth Krittika had handed to him. 'Bhadra,' he said, 'get the heralds to announce our departure in ten minutes.'

'Yes, Shiva,' said Veerbhadra, rising immediately to do his bidding.

Shiva pushed his own empty banana-leaf plate aside and walked to the wooden drum where the water was stored.

He scooped some up with his hands and gargled to clean his mouth.

A chill ran up his spine again. He looked up at the sky, towards the north, about to speak a prayer to the Holy Lake, then he stopped. It wasn't necessary.

He won't hurt her. He can't hurt her. If there's one person in this world that fool loves, it's my Sati. He won't hurt her.

— ⚊ 𓀂 ⊙𝒰⬆ ⊛ —

General Parvateshwar had ordered Brigadier Vraka to mobilise the army quickly and head for Devagiri – he hadn't explained why they were required in the Meluhan capital, and he himself had rushed off earlier with Maharishi Bhrigu. It had taken Vraka two days to get his soldiers provisioned and boarded to begin their journey up the Indus and now they'd been waylaid at Mohan Jo Daro by a non-violent protest.

The governor of the city had remained loyal to the emperor, but his people worshipped the Neelkanth, and when they heard that the Meluhan army was sailing up the Indus to do battle with the Neelkanth, they had decided to rebel. Almost the entire population of Mohan Jo Daro had marched out of the city, boarded their own boats and anchored them in a half-mile-long line across the entire massive breadth of the Indus.

'You're behaving like traitors!' Brigadier Vraka shouted helplessly. It would be impossible for him to ram his ships through such an effective blockade.

'We'll be traitors to Emperor Daksha,' said the leader of the protestors, 'but we won't be traitors to the Neelkanth!'

Vraka drew his sword. 'I'll kill you all if you don't move your ships immediately,' he warned.

'Go ahead – kill us all. We won't raise a hand against our own army, but I swear by the great Lord Ram, we will not move!'

Vraka snorted in anger. By choosing not to fight with him, the citizens had removed the only legal reason he might have to attack them. He was effectively – and bloodlessly – stymied.

As Vidyunmali slowly regained consciousness, he saw that he was lying on a cart that was ambling along the riverside road. He raised his head. The fresh stitches in his stomach hurt.

'Lie back down, my Lord,' said a soldier. 'You need to rest.'

'Is that traitor dead?' the brigadier asked, and smiled when the soldier nodded.

Vidyunmali's platoon had managed to waylay Kanakhala's servant, who was riding along the riverside road from Devagiri to Lothal to warn Shiva of the planned perfidy. The man had been killed, but not before he'd managed to stab Vidyunmali viciously in the stomach.

'How far are we from Devagiri?' asked Vidyunmali.

'At the pace we're going, another five days, my Lord.'

'That's too long—'

'You can't ride a horse, my Lord – your stitches might burst open. You have to travel by cart.'

Vidyunmali cursed under his breath, but consigned himself to the infuriatingly slow journey. He had no other option.

CHAPTER 44

A Princess Returns

Sati surveyed the scene from the deck of their ship in Devagiri Harbour. The fast merchant ship they had commandeered had sailed up the Saraswati speedily and reached the city in good time for the peace conference.

Nandi, standing beside Sati, gestured at the sky. 'Look,' he said, pointing to a small bird winging its way overhead. 'Another homing pigeon.'

It wasn't the first they'd spotted; Sati's warriors had reported quite a few pigeons flying in the direction of Devagiri.

'Lord Ganesh believes that eavesdropping can give us good intelligence regarding the enemy's plan,' said Nandi. 'Shall we shoot one of them and find out what's being discussed?'

Sati shook her head. 'We'll obey the laws Lord Ram gave us and negotiate in good faith. Lord Ram said that there's no such thing as a small wrong. Discovering our opponent's strategy prior to peace negotiations through the use of subterfuge will give us only a minimal advantage, but to behave without honour is against Lord Ram's way.'

Nandi bowed his head in Sati's direction. 'I'm Lord Ram's servant, Princess.'

As Sati turned away, Nandi glanced one last time at the tiny speck of a bird disappearing into Devagiri.

The docks had been completely cleared out. There was no sign of commerce, or any other activity. From the vantage point of her ship's deck, Sati could see the walls of Devagiri in the distance. Some folk had tried calling the city Tripura, after its three platforms, called Gold, Silver and Bronze, but the nickname had never really caught on. The citizens of Devagiri couldn't imagine tampering with the name Lord Ram himself had given it.

With a loud thud, the gangplank was lowered onto the dock. 'Let's go,' Sati whispered to Nandi.

As she began leading her men ashore, a Meluhan protocol officer walked up to her, a broad smile plastered on his face. He noticed Sati's disfigured left cheek, but wisely refrained from commenting on it. 'My Lady, it's an honour to meet you once again.'

'It's a pleasure to be back in my city, Major, and in better circumstances this time.'

The Meluhan acknowledged the reference with a solemn nod.

'I hope you'll succeed in negotiating a lasting peace, my Lady,' said the Meluhan. 'You can imagine how distressed we Meluhans are that our country is at war with our living god.'

'With Lord Ram's blessing, the war will end and we shall have lasting peace,' she said, smiling.

The Meluhan joined his hands together and looked up at the sky. 'With Lord Ram's blessing.'

As they left the port, Sati saw the large circular building that had been quickly constructed for the peace conference, for the rules laid down stipulated that it couldn't take place within the host city itself. The new venue, a healthy distance from the city walls, had been constructed on a large three-foot-high rectangular base of Meluhan bricks, into which tall wooden columns had been hammered. The columns served as the structure's skeleton, around which smaller bamboo sticks had been tied to create a circular building that was surprisingly strong, despite no mortar having been used in its construction.

Sati looked up at the high ceiling as soon as she entered and spoke loudly to check the acoustics. The sound didn't reverberate and she smiled. The Meluhan engineers hadn't lost any of their talent.

Large idols of Lord Ram and Lady Sita had been placed near the entrance of the cavernous chamber. From the flowers and other oblations scattered around the idols, Sati saw that the chief priest of Devagiri had already conducted the *Pran Prathishtha* ceremony, infusing the life force of the two deities into the idols, so now Lord Ram and Lady Sita themselves were residing in the idols and supervising the proceedings. Nobody would dare to break the law in their presence. A separate enclosure had been partitioned off at one end with a single large wooden door.

The room behind it had been completely soundproofed; it was intended for private discussions that might be held by either party during the course of the conference.

Sati nodded. 'The arrangements are precisely in keeping with the ancient laws.'

'Thank you, my Lady,' said the Meluhan.

'Now take me to the armoury,' she said.

'Of course, my Lady,' he said, gesturing towards the horses, which were saddled up outside. 'We can leave immediately.' He added, 'You do understand that, according to the laws, your animals must be secured next to the armoury.'

'All except mine,' said Sati. Few were more well versed with Lord Ram's laws than she was; the leader of the visiting delegation was allowed to keep his or her horse. 'My horse remains with me.'

'Of course, my Lady. But the Neelkanth—'

Sati interrupted the major, saying, 'And the horses will be returned to us as soon as the conference is over.'

'That's the law, my Lady.'

'The animals within Devagiri also need to be locked up.'

'Of course, my Lady,' said the Meluhan. 'That's already been done.'

'All right,' said Sati with a satisfied nod. 'Let's go.'

The temporary armoury had been built outside the city walls under the connecting bridge between the Svarna and Tamra platforms. A massive door with a double lock had been installed at the entryway. It looked almost impossible to break into. One of the keys was handed over to Sati, who personally checked that the door was locked, then the major used his key to double-lock the door, allowed Sati to check it again, and then fixed a seal on top of the lock. All the weapons in Devagiri had effectively been put out of reach.

Sati handed her key to Nandi and said softy, 'Keep this safe for me.'

As the protocol officer bowed and turned to leave, he hesitated, as if remembering something. 'My Lady, your weapons—? Aren't they supposed to be locked in here as well?'

'No,' said Sati.

'Umm, my Lady, the rules state that—'

'What the rules say, Major,' interrupted Sati, 'is that both armies have to be disarmed, but the leaders and their personal bodyguards are allowed to retain their weapons. I'm sure my father's bodyguards haven't been disarmed, have they?'

'No, my Lady,' he replied, 'they still have their weapons.'

'As will the bodyguards here,' said Sati, pointing to Nandi and her soldiers.

'But my Lady—'

'Why don't you check with Prime Minister Kanakhala? I'm sure she'll know the law.'

The Meluhan said nothing further, for he knew Sati was legally correct – and he also knew that Prime Minister Kanakhala couldn't be called upon for any clarifications. Meanwhile, Sati was looking at the giant animal enclosure a few hundred yards away inside which her army's horses had been temporarily sequestered.

'Also, my Lady,' said the protocol officer, 'Emperor Daksha has requested your presence at his palace for lunch.'

Sati turned to Nandi. 'I'll ride ahead. You check the lock on the animal enclosures and then join me in—'

'My Lady,' said the officer, interrupting Sati, 'the emperor's instructions were very clear. He wants you to come alone.'

Sati frowned. This was a very unorthodox request. She was about to refuse when the officer spoke up again. 'My Lady, I don't think this has anything to do with the conference. You're his Majesty's daughter, after all, and surely a father has the right to expect to share a meal with his daughter.'

Sati took a deep breath. She was in no mood to break bread with her father, but she would dearly like to see her mother – and in any case, the conference was scheduled to begin the following day and most of the necessary tasks had already been completed.

'Nandi, once you've checked the animals' enclosure, return to the conference building and wait for me there,' she said. 'I'll be back soon.'

'As you command, my Lady,' said Nandi. 'But may I have a word with you before you leave?'

'Of course,' said Sati.

'In private, my Lady,' said Nandi.

Sati frowned, but handed her horse's reins to a soldier who

was standing discreetly behind her, then walked aside with Nandi.

When they were out of the major's earshot, Nandi whispered, 'If I may be so bold as to make a suggestion, my Lady, please don't think of this as a meeting with your father. Think instead that you're going to meet the emperor with whom you'll be negotiating tomorrow. Perhaps you could use this lunch as an opportunity to set the right atmosphere for the peace conference tomorrow.'

Sati smiled. 'You're right, Nandi. I'll keep that in mind.'

— 🜊 ⬯🜂 —

Sati tethered her horse near the palace steps, refusing the attendant's proffered assistance. As she approached the main door the guards executed a smart military salute. She saluted back politely and continued walking.

She'd grown up in this palace, played in its private gardens, run up and down these steps a million times and practised the fine art of swordsmanship in its grounds. Yet the building felt alien to her now – maybe it was because she'd been away for so many years. Or more likely, it was because she no longer felt any kinship with her father.

She didn't need the aid of the various soldiers who kept emerging to guide her onwards, but she was a little surprised that she didn't recognise any of them. Perhaps Vidyunmali had changed the troops after taking over her father's security. She waved them away repeatedly and walked unerringly towards her father's chamber.

'Her Highness, Princess Sati!' announced the chief doorman loudly as he opened the door to the royal chamber, and she walked in to find her parents, and a huge man she didn't recognise. He was standing at the far end of the chamber, and judging by his armband, he was a colonel in the Meluhan army.

As she approached her parents, the Meluhan colonel looked out of the window and almost imperceptibly nodded at someone standing outside.

'By the great Lord Ram, what happened to your face?' exclaimed Daksha.

Sati folded her hands together into a namaste and bowed low, showing the respect due to her father. 'It's nothing, Father. Just a mark of war.'

'A warrior bears her scars with pride,' said the Meluhan colonel congenially, his hands held together in a respectful namaste.

Sati looked at him quizzically as she returned his namaste. 'I'm afraid I don't know you, Colonel.'

'I've been newly assigned, my Lady,' he replied. 'I serve as Brigadier Vidyunmali's second-in-command. My name is Kamalaksh.'

Sati had never really liked Vidyunmali, but that was no reason to dislike his colonel. She nodded politely at him before turning to her mother with a warm smile. 'How are you, *maa*?'

Sati had never before used the affectionate term – she had

always used the more formal 'mother' – but Veerini liked this change. She embraced her daughter, whispering, 'My child . . .'

Sati held her mother tight. Years spent with Shiva had broken the mould and she could now freely express her formerly pent-up feelings.

'I've missed you, my child,' whispered Veerini.

'I've missed you too, *maa*,' said Sati, her eyes moist.

Veerini touched Sati's scar and bit her lip.

'It's all right,' said Sati, with a slight smile. 'It doesn't hurt.'

'Why don't you get Ayurvati to remove it?' asked Veerini.

'I will, *maa*,' said Sati, 'but the beauty of my face isn't important right now. What is important is to find a way towards peace.'

'I hope Lord Ram helps your father and the Neelkanth to do so,' said Veerini.

Daksha smiled broadly. 'I've already found a way, Sati – and then we'll all be together again, a happy family, like before. By the way, I hope the Neelkanth doesn't mind waiting in the camp outside – it wouldn't be considered a good omen for us to meet before the peace conference.'

Sati frowned at her father's strange idea that all of them would be living together 'as a family' once again. She was about to tell him that Shiva hadn't come with her to Devagiri, but Daksha had already turned to Kamalaksh.

'Order the attendants to bring in lunch,' said Daksha. 'I'm famished, as are my wife and daughter, I'm sure.'

'Of course, your Majesty.'

Veerini was still holding Sati's hand. 'It's sad that Ayurvati wasn't here last week.'

'Why?' asked Sati.

'Had she been here, she'd certainly have been able to save Kanakhala. Nobody else has the medical skills she possesses—'

From the corner of her eye, Sati saw Daksha stiffen and he interrupted, saying, 'Veerini, you talk too much. We need to eat and—'

'One moment, Father,' said Sati, turning back to her mother. 'What happened to Kanakhala?'

'Don't you know?' Veerini sounded surprised. 'She died suddenly. I believe there was some kind of accident in her house.'

'An accident?' asked Sati, immediately suspicious. Turning to face Daksha, she asked, 'What happened to her, Father?'

'It was an accident, Sati,' said Daksha. 'You don't need to make a mountain of every molehill—'

Hearing her husband's evasive reaction to Sati's question, Veerini began to feel suspicious as well. 'What's going on, Daksha?' she asked.

'Will you two please give it a rest? We've come together for a meal after a very long time apart, so let's just enjoy this moment.'

'Everything will be fine soon, Princess,' said Kamalaksh, his voice soft.

Sati didn't look at him, but there was something unsettling in his voice that made her instincts kick in.

'Father, what are you hiding?'

'Oh, for Lord Ram's sake!' said Daksha. 'If you're so worried about your husband, I'll have some special food sent out for him as well!'

'I didn't mention Shiva,' said Sati. 'You're avoiding my question. What happened to Kanakhala?'

Daksha cursed in frustration, and slammed his fist on a desk. 'Will you trust your father for once? My blood runs in your veins – would I ever do anything that's not in your best interests? If I say Kanakhala died in an accident, then that's what happened.'

Sati stared into her father's eyes. 'You're lying.'

'Kanakhala got what she deserved, Princess,' said Kamalaksh, who was now standing directly behind her. 'As will everyone who dares to oppose the true Lord of Meluha. But you don't need to worry. You're safe because your father adores you.'

Stunned, Sati looked back at Kamalaksh, and then at her father.

Daksha's eyes were moist as he said with a wry smile, 'If only you could understand how much I love you, my child. Just trust me. I'll make everything all right once again.'

Sati tensed her muscular frame and jabbed her right elbow into Kamalaksh's solar plexus and the colonel, taken by surprise, doubled over in pain and staggered back. As soon as his head was within her range Sati sprang onto her left foot and swung her right leg in a great arc, a potentially lethal strike she'd learned from the Nagas. Her right heel crashed into Kamalaksh's head with brutal force, right between his ear and temple, bursting his eardrum and rendering him unconscious.

The colonel's giant frame came crashing down onto the floor. Sati smoothly swung full circle and came back to face Daksha again. Quick as lightning, her sword was drawn and pointed at her father's heart.

It all happened so quickly that Daksha had no time to react.

'What have you done, Father?' shouted Sati, her anger at boiling point.

'It's for your own good!' the emperor shrieked. 'Your husband won't trouble us any more.'

Sati finally understood. 'Lord Ram, be merciful . . . Nandi and my soldiers—'

'My God!' cried Veerini, moving towards him. 'What have you done, Daksha?'

'Shut up, Veerini!' screamed Daksha as he shoved her aside and rushed towards Sati.

Veerini staggered in shock. 'How could you break the laws of a peace conference? You've damned your soul forever!'

'You can't leave!' shouted Daksha, trying to get hold of Sati, but she pushed him hard and he fell to the floor. Then she turned and ran towards the door, her sword held tightly in her hand, ready for battle.

'Stop her!' yelled Daksha. 'Guards! Stop her!'

The doorman was stunned to see the princess sprinting towards him as he opened the door. The guards standing next to him were immobilised by shock until Daksha bellowed again, 'Stop her!'

But before they could react, Sati had crashed into them and

pushed them aside. She burst through the door and as she raced down the main corridor she could still hear her father screaming repeatedly for his guards to stop her. She had to get to her horse – no one else in the city had one at the moment, so she could easily outpace the guards and get out of the city.

'Stop the princess!' bellowed a guard from behind her and she saw a platoon taking position up ahead. They held their spears out, blocking her way. She glanced behind her without slowing down to see another platoon of soldiers running towards her from the other end of the corridor.

She was trapped.

Lord Ram, give me strength!

Sati heard her father's distant voice crying, 'Don't hurt her!'

A window on the left of the corridor was open. She was on the third floor and it would be foolish to jump – but this palace had been her home once and she'd known every entrance and exit. She knew there was a narrow ledge above the window and a short jump from there would take her to the palace terrace – from there she could get to a side-entrance and get to the palace gate before anyone could catch up with her.

She sheathed her sword and raised her hands as if in surrender. The soldiers, thinking they had her, moved forward, slowing their gait to calm the princess – but Sati suddenly jumped to the side and was out through the window in a flash. The soldiers gasped, thinking the princess must have fallen to certain death in the courtyard below, but Sati had stretched her hands out as she leapt through the window, jumping up and grabbing the edge of the protruding ledge, then swinging herself upwards and finally landing safely on top of the ledge. She took a moment to balance herself, then, with a couple of quick steps and a leap, she was safely on the terrace.

'She's on the terrace!' shouted a soldier.

Sati knew the route the soldiers would take and she quickly ran the other way, towards the far end of the terrace, and jumped onto another ledge. She crept along it until she reached the next terrace, then she leapt onto it and sprinted towards the staircase on the far side. She charged down the stairs three steps at a time to the landing above the first floor, which led to the side entrance she planned to use. While this entrance wasn't usually guarded, she wasn't taking any chances. She jumped from the balcony into the small garden at the side and quickly clambered up the tree growing right next to the wall. When she reached the highest branch she pulled herself over the boundary wall, landing right next to her horse, and in an instant she was mounted and kicking the animal into motion.

'There she is!' shouted a guard, and twenty men rushed towards her, but she pushed by them without slowing and galloped through the palace enclosure. Within seconds she was out into the city beyond, though she could still hear the distant cries of the guards, swearing and screaming, 'Stop her!' and 'Stop the princess!' behind her.

Startled Meluhans scrambled out of the way of Sati's steed to escape the flying hooves as she rode hard. She pushed her horse to its limits, and was through the iron gates in no time, but as soon as she was through, she could hear loud noises of battle in the distance.

Sati, still on the Devagiri city platform, had a clear view of the peace conference building, right next to the Saraswati River, nearly two miles away, and it was clear her people were under attack. A large number of cloaked and hooded men were battling with Nandi and his vastly outnumbered soldiers, and many already lay on the ground, wounded or dead.

'Hyaaah!' Sati screamed and kicked her horse into a swift gallop. She raced down the central steps of the Svarna platform, straight towards the battling men, screaming the war cry of those loyal to the Neelkanth: '*Har Har Mahadev!*'

CHAPTER 45

The Final Kill

As she sped towards the battleground, Sati estimated that there were almost three hundred cloaked assassins. They wore masks, like the Nagas, but their fighting style was nothing like that of the warriors from Panchavati; they were obviously some other group disguised to look like Nagas. Nearly half of Sati's hundred bodyguards were already on the ground, either grievously injured or dead.

The assassins and her soldiers were locked in man-to-man combat, so there was no clear line of enemies she could ride into and mow down, so she'd have to dismount and fight. As she approached the melee, she spotted Nandi, who was combating three assassins simultaneously, and headed towards him.

She heard Nandi's loud scream as he drove his sword into his enemy's heart and turned to his left, easily lifting the diminutive warrior impaled on his sword and flinging the hapless man's body onto an oncoming attacker. But another had already moved up to Nandi and was preparing to strike him from behind.

Sati pulled her feet from the stirrups and jumped onto her saddle, drawing her sword as she repositioned herself into a crouch. As she neared the assassin who was about to slash Nandi from behind she flung herself from her horse, swinging her sword viciously as she flew through the air and decapitating the attacker with one mighty stroke.

Sati landed on her side and smoothly rolled upright to stand behind Nandi as the quivering body of the beheaded assassin collapsed to the ground, blood bursting furiously from his gaping neck.

'My Lady!' yelled Nandi over the din, slashing hard at another warrior in front. 'Run!'

Sati stood steadfast, positioned defensively back-to-back with Nandi so between them they were covering all angles. 'Not without the rest of you!'

A cloaked attacker leapt at Sati from the side as she pulled her shield forward and, as he reached into the folds of his robe and threw something at her eyes, she instinctively pulled her shield up. A black egg cracked against it, deflecting its contents – vicious shards of metal – safely away from her eyes, but some of the shrapnel cut through her left arm.

Sati had heard about this lethal weapon: it was used by Egyptian assassins. Eggs were drained of their contents through a small hole and then filled with tiny pieces of sharp metal which, when flung at the eyes of enemies, usually blinded them. Luckily for her, she'd caught it in time, but Sati suspected the man's next move would be a low sword-thrust. Her vision was still blocked by her shield, but she followed her instincts and swerved to one side to avoid the anticipated low blow.

Then Sati pressed a lever on her shield and extended a short blade which she rammed into her opponent's neck, driving it through his windpipe. As the assassin began to choke on his own blood, Sati ran her sword through his heart.

Nandi, meanwhile, was effortlessly killing all those in front of him. He was a big man, and he towered over the diminutive Egyptians like a giant. None of the assassins could come close and he hacked his way through anyone who dared to challenge him. They threw knives and more of the black eggs at him, but, even with a knife buried in his shoulder and shrapnel piercing his body in many places, Nandi fought relentlessly. But they could both see that the odds were stacked heavily against them. Most of their men had been overwhelmed by the sheer surprise of the attack, and they were badly outnumbered. Escape wasn't an option, either, for they were surrounded on all sides. Their only hope was that other Suryavanshis in Devagiri might come to their aid.

An assassin swung at Sati from a high angle to her right and she swung back with vicious force, blocking his blow. The man turned and swerved in from the left this time, hoping to push Sati onto her back foot, but she met his second strike with equal ferocity. Completely unaware of Sati's unique fighting technique, he then dropped low and attempted to stab her in the abdomen.

Most warriors could only swing their swords away from their bodies; few had the strength and skill to swing the weapon towards themselves – but Sati had long mastered this technique. And unusually, both edges of her sword were sharpened. Sati executed the almost impossible stroke masterfully, pulling her sword arm towards her own body with tremendous force, and the surprised assassin's throat was cleanly cut before he could respond. The Egyptian's head, the eyes still rolling, fell backwards, dangling tenuously from his body by a shred of tissue, and Sati kicked it away as his body collapsed.

She saw movement on her left and realised her mistake, but it was too late: she tried to block the sword stroke from the second assassin but it glanced off her blade and pierced her scarred left cheek, cutting through her eye and grating off her skull. Her left eye collapsed in its socket and blood poured from the wound, obscuring the vision in her other eye. Though blinded, she executed a desperate defensive block, hoping to ward off any blows while she wiped the blood from her face. She heard a woman panting, almost sobbing, and realised that it was herself.

She braced herself as the man moved forward for a second attack, then detected movement from the right. Through her blurred, pink-coloured vision she saw Nandi swing from his massive height and behead the assassin with one stroke.

'My Lady!' he screamed, pulling his shield forward to protect himself from another assassin's blow. 'Run!'

The world had slowed around her and his voice came to

her as if from a great distance. She could hear her own heart beating; she could hear her breath gasping as she gazed at the carnage. The bodies of her guards lay bloodied and broken at her feet. Some of the fallen still lived, and they were reaching and clawing at the legs of the attackers in desperation until they were kicked aside in annoyance, their lives finished with half-distracted sword-strokes of irritation.

My arrogance, a voice whispered in her head. *I have failed them. Again.*

Her brain had blocked out the throbbing in her mutilated eye. She spat out the blood streaking down her face and running into her mouth, then swung into battle once more. She stepped back to avoid another assassin's brutal stab and slashed her own sword from the right, slicing through his hand. As the Egyptian howled in pain, she rammed her shield into his head, cracking open his skull, then stabbed the staggering assassin in his eye before quickly pulling her sword back and turning to face the next.

The assassin flung a knife across the distance between them and it cut through Sati's upper left arm and stuck in her biceps, restricting the movement of her defensive arm. She snarled in fury and swung her sword viciously, cutting through the man's cloak and slashing deep into his chest. As he staggered backwards, she delivered the killing blow, a stab straight through his heart.

But the flow of assassins was unrelenting and even as the other man fell to the ground another one ran up to engage her.

Using sheer willpower to move her exhausted body, Sati raised her blood-drenched sword once more.

Swuth was observing the battle from a short distance away. His orders were to ensure the death of the one they called Neel-kanth, and surely he must be the big one, the powerful warrior who was cutting down all his opponents with such ease. Swuth moved into the fray and strode towards him.

The big man looked up and turned to face his new opponent, swinging his sword fiercely to meet Swuth's blade. The Egyptian stepped back, his hand stinging from the force of the blow, and dropped his sword, instead drawing out two curved, serrated blades, something he kept for special occasions.

Nandi had never seen swords like these: they were less than two-thirds the length of his own weapon, and they curved sharply, almost like hooks. The swords' hilts were peculiar too, made of uncovered metal instead of being enveloped in protective leather or wood as usual. A sword fighter would have to be very skilled not to cut himself while holding such swords, for the hilts looked almost as sharp as the blades. And this man was no amateur, Nandi realised at once as he skilfully swung both swords in a circular motion with frightening speed. He had never seen swords or a fighting style like this, so he was naturally cautious and kept his shield held high as he waited for the Egyptian to move in.

Seeing Nandi focused on Swuth and Sati distracted by

another assassin, a third Egyptian moved in suddenly and slashed viciously at Nandi's exposed back, and Nandi roared with fury as his body lurched forward in reaction to the excruciatingly painful wound.

Swuth used this moment to suddenly hook his left sword onto his right, extending its reach twofold, and swung hard from a low angle, aiming a little below the shield. The sharp edge of the metal hilt sliced effortlessly through the warrior's left arm, severing it cleanly a few inches above his wrist and the Suryavanshi bellowed in pain as blood burst from his stump. Swuth stepped closer and slashed this time at Nandi's sword-arm, hacking through the limb just below the elbow. The mighty Suryavanshi collapsed to the ground with blood bursting forth from both his severed limbs and Swuth spat contemptuously as he kicked both of the man's hacked-off hands away.

He cursed; some spittle had stuck to the unfamiliar Naga mask – but he was careful enough to curse in Sanskrit, for he had strictly forbidden his people from speaking their native Egyptian tongue. The charade that they were Nagas had to be strictly maintained.

'Nandi!' screamed Sati as she swirled around and thrust her sword at Swuth, but he moved aside, easily avoiding her attack. Another assassin swung from behind Sati, cutting through her upper back and left shoulder.

'Wait!' said Swuth as two of his men were about to plunge their swords into her heart, and instead they grabbed the woman's arms and awaited their leader's instructions. Swuth would not sully his tongue by speaking to a woman, for they were far beneath men, only a little better than animals.

'Ask her which one is the blue-throat.'

One of his assistants looked at Sati and repeated Swuth's question, but she didn't hear either of them for she was staring in shock at Nandi, who was lying prone on the ground and losing blood at an alarming rate from his severed limbs. But the unconscious Suryavanshi was still breathing – the wounds were only on his limbs so the blood loss probably wouldn't be severe enough to cause immediate death. If she managed to keep him alive a little longer, expert medical help could still save his life.

'Is this the blue-throat?' asked Swuth, pointing at the fallen Suryavanshi.

Swuth's assistant repeated his question to Sati, but Sati was looking towards the gates of Devagiri from the corner of her eye. She could see people running towards her – they would probably arrive in another ten or fifteen minutes, and she had to keep Nandi alive until they got there.

Swuth shook his head when he didn't get any response from Sati and growled, 'A curse of Aten on these stupid baby-producing machines!'

Sati stared at him. He was definitely Egyptian, then, an assassin of the cult of Aten – she had learned about their culture in her youth and now she knew what she had to do.

Swuth pointed at Nandi and turned to his men. 'Behead this fat giant. He must be the blue-throat. Leave the other injured alive. They will bear witness that they were attacked by the Nagas. And collect our dead. We'll leave immediately.'

'He's not the blue-throated one,' spat Sati. 'Can't you see his neck, you Egyptian idiot?'

The Egyptian holding Sati hit her hard across her face.

Swuth sniggered. 'Leave the giant alive,' he said before turning to one of his fighters. 'Qa'a, torture this hag before you kill her.'

'With pleasure, my Lord.' Qa'a smiled unpleasantly. He might not be the best of assassins, perhaps, but he was an expert in the fine art of torture.

Swuth turned to his other men. 'How many times do I have to repeat myself, you putrid slops of camel dung? Start gathering our dead. We leave in a few moments.'

As Swuth's assassins started implementing his order, Qa'a moved towards Sati, returning his blood-streaked sword to its scabbard and pulling out a knife. A smaller blade always made torture much easier.

Sati suddenly straightened up and shouted loudly, 'The Duel of Aten!'

Qa'a stopped in his tracks, stunned, as Swuth stared at Sati, surprised beyond measure. This was the Egyptian assassins' ancient code; they were honour-bound to engage anyone who challenged them to a duel. It could only be a one-on-one fight, for if others joined in the attack, they would suffer the wrath of their fiery Sun God, Aten's everlasting curse.

Qa'a turned towards Swuth, unsure what to do.

Swuth stared at the torturer. 'You know the law,' he growled.

Qa'a nodded and sheathed his knife. He drew his sword, pulled his shield forward and waited.

Sati wrenched herself free from the assassins holding her. She bent down and ripped a piece from a fallen assassin's cloak, then tied the strip across her face, covering her mutilated eye in an effort to stem the blood flowing down her cheek and keep it out of her good eye, so she could make the most of the vision she had left. Then she slowly pulled out the knife buried in her upper arm and tied another strip of cloth around the injury, using her teeth to tighten the makeshift bandage.

Then she drew her sword and held her shield high, ready. Waiting.

Qa'a suddenly threw his shield away and the assassins standing around burst out laughing and began to clap. Clearly, Qa'a was taunting Sati, suggesting that he didn't even need his shield to combat a stupid woman. Much to his surprise, the woman threw her shield away as well.

Qa'a bellowed loudly and charged, swinging his sword at a high angle, but smoothly she leaned back and swerved to the left to avoid the strike. Qa'a turned swiftly and swung his sword high again, catching her by surprise, and his blade cut through her left hand, slicing off four fingers. Much to his surprise, she didn't flinch from the injury but swung her sword at Qa'a from above. Qa'a swerved and deflected the blow with an elevated strike.

Sati had quicky worked out that the swinging strike was Qa'a's preferred form of attack and she played to that. Both kept changing the direction of their blows in an attempt to surprise the other, but they were pretty evenly matched and neither suffered any serious injury – until suddenly Sati dropped to one knee and swung hard, hacking brutally through Qa'a's abdomen, cutting deep. He collapsed as his intestines spilled onto the ground.

Sati stood up, towering over the kneeling Qa'a, who was paralysed by the intense pain. She held her sword high, vertically, and thrust it through his neck, straight down, deep into his body and impaling his heart, killing him instantly.

Swuth stared at the woman, dumbfounded. It wasn't just her skill with the sword that had surprised him; it was her honour in battle – she hadn't beheaded Qa'a when she could easily have done so; instead she let him keep his head and had given him an honourable death, a soldier's death. She had followed the rules of the Duel of Aten, even though those rules weren't her own.

Sati stepped away from the corpse and ran her bloodied sword into the soft, muddy ground. She bent over and ripped another piece of cloth from Qa'a's cloak and tied it around her left palm, covering the area where her fingers had been severed.

She stood tall, pulled her sword from the ground and held it aloft, careful not to look at Nandi. *Just a few minutes more.*

'Who's next?'

Another assassin stepped forward, reached for his sword and then hesitated. He'd seen Sati battle brilliantly with her long blade. He drew a knife from his shoulder-belt instead.

'I don't have a knife,' she said, sheathing her sword. She was a warrior; she would fight fair.

Swuth pulled out his own knife and flung it high in her direction and she reached out and effortlessly caught the beautifully balanced weapon. In the meantime, the assassin had removed his mask and pulled back his hood. He didn't want to suffer the disadvantage of restricted vision against such a skilled warrior.

Having lost four fingers of her left hand, Sati couldn't fight this assassin the way she had Tarak in Karachapa all those years ago, when she had hidden the knife behind her back so she could confuse her opponent about the direction of attack. So she held the knife in front, in her right hand – but she held the hilt forward with the blade pointing back towards herself, much to the surprise of the gathered assassins.

The Egyptian adopted the traditional fighting stance and pointed his knife directly at the woman. He moved forward and slashed hard, and she jumped back to avoid the blow, but the blade sliced her shoulder, drawing some blood, which emboldened him to move closer, swinging the knife left and then right as he charged. She kept stepping back, allowing the assassin to run right into the trap, but he suddenly changed tack and thrust forward with a jabbing motion. She swerved right to avoid the blow, raising her right hand to hold the knife high above her left shoulder. But she hadn't moved back far enough and the assassin's knife sliced through the left side of her abdomen, lodging deep within her, right up to the hilt.

Without even flinching at the horrifying pain, Sati brought her hand down hard from on high, stabbing at the Egyptian's neck. The blow was so forceful that the knife pierced all the way through until its point stuck out of the other side of his throat. Blood burst forth from the assassin's mouth and neck and Sati stepped back as the Egyptian drowned in his own blood.

Swuth was staring at this strange woman, the sneer wiped off his face. She'd killed two of his assassins one-on-one, in a free and fair fight. She was bleeding desperately, and yet she stood tall and proud.

Sati, meanwhile, was breathing slowly, trying to calm her heart. She'd been cut in so many places that a rapidly beating heart would work against her, pumping more blood out of her body. She needed to conserve her energy for the duels that were surely to come. She looked at the knife buried deep in her abdomen. It hadn't penetrated any vital organ; the only danger was the continuous bleeding. She spread her feet, took a deep breath, grasped the knife's handle and yanked it out. She didn't flinch or make any sound of pain as she did so.

'Who is this woman?' asked a stunned assassin standing next to Swuth.

Sati bent down and ripped off two more pieces of cloak. She made a pad, then bound it tightly to her abdomen, staunching the blood flow. As she did so, she glimpsed the Meluhans from the corner of her eye; they were probably a third of the way to the battleground. She knew that now she'd identified the killers, they couldn't leave her alive, so her only chance was to continue duelling and hope she'd still be breathing when the Meluhans reached her.

She stood straight and drew her sword. 'Who's next?'

Another assassin stepped forward.

'No!' said Swuth, and the assassin stepped back. 'She's my kill,' Swuth said, drawing one of his curved swords – approaching the woman with both curved blades drawn would have been unfair according to the rules of the Duel of Aten, since Sati had only one sword hand. He held the weapon before him in his right hand and as he neared her he started swinging the sword around, turning the blade into a stunning circle of death as he moved inexorably towards her.

As Swuth's sword whirred closer, Sati slowly began to step back – then she suddenly thrust her sword forward quickly, deep into the circle of Swuth's circling blade, cutting deeply into the Egyptian's shoulder. She pulled her sword back just as rapidly, before Swuth's circling blade could come around to deflect the blade.

The wound must have hurt, but Swuth didn't flinch. He smiled. He'd never met anyone with the ability to penetrate his sword's circle of death before.

This woman is truly talented.

He stopped circling his sword and moved into a more traditional stance, then stepped forward, swinging viciously from the right. She bent low to avoid the blow and thrust her blade at Swuth's arm, inflicting a superficial cut – but he suddenly reversed the direction of his blade, slashing hard across her shoulder.

Sati swerved back just in time from what could have been a devastating blow. As the Egyptian's sword grazed her right arm and shoulder she growled in fury and stabbed with such rapid force that, taken by surprise, he had to jump back.

Swuth stepped back a couple more paces. This woman was a very skilled warrior and his standard tactics wouldn't work. He kept his distance, his sword pointed forward, while he debated what might be a good move to make against her.

Sati remained stationary, conserving her strength, knowing she couldn't afford to move too much for fear of increasing the blood loss from her numerous wounds. She was playing for time; she didn't mind a few moments of reprieve.

Swuth suddenly realised the woman was primarily injured on her left side, which would impair her movements in that direction. Grinning, he quickly took a giant step forward and swung viciously from his right, forcing her to twist to the left and swing her blade up to block his strike. He could see that the movement had made blood spurt out of her wounded abdomen. As she stabbed at Swuth again, she stepped a little to the left, trying to improve her angle, but, anticipating her move, Swuth stepped further to his right and kept on swinging again and again from that awkward angle.

The intense pain of continuously turning leftwards forced Sati to take a gamble: she pirouetted suddenly and swung her sword in a great arc from her right, hoping to decapitate him

– but that was exactly what the assassin was expecting and he ducked low and quickly stepped forward, easily avoiding her strike. At the same time he brought his sword up in a low, brutal jab and the curved serrated blade went right into her abdomen, ripping through her intestines, stomach, kidneys and liver.

Paralysed, her face twisted in agony, Sati lay impaled on the Egyptian's curved sword. Her own blade fell from her hand and he bent backwards, using the leverage to ram his sword even deeper until its point burst through her shattered back.

'Not bad,' said Swuth, twisting his blade as he pulled it out, ripping what was left of her organs to ribbons. 'Not bad – for a woman.'

Sati collapsed to the ground, her body shivering as dark blood began to pool around her. She knew she was going to die; it was only a matter of time. The blood flow couldn't be staunched now, and she knew her vital internal organs had been mortally damaged. But she also knew something else: she wouldn't die lying on the ground, slowly bleeding to death.

She would die like a Meluhan. She would die with her head held high.

She lifted her quivering right hand and reached for her sword. Swuth stared at her in awe, transfixed, as he watched her struggling to reach her blade. He knew she must be aware that she was going to die soon, and yet her spirit hadn't been broken.

Could she be the final kill?

The cult of Aten believed that every assassin would one day meet a victim so magnificent, so worthy, that it would be impossible for the man ever to kill again. His duty would then be to give his victim an honourable death and leave his profession to spend the rest of his life worshipping that last victim.

As her arm flopped to her side after another vain attempt to reach her sword, Swuth shook his head in disbelief. *It can't be a woman – this can't be the moment. My final kill can't be a woman!*

Swuth turned around and screamed at his people, 'Move out, you filthy cockroaches! We're leaving!'

The man standing next to Swuth didn't move but continued to stare beyond his leader, stupefied by the awe-inspiring sight playing out.

Swuth whirled around, stunned to see the woman up on one knee. She was breathing rapidly and trying to force some strength into her debilitated body. She'd dug her sword into the ground and her right hand was on its hilt as she tried to use the leverage to push herself upright.

Sati failed and took some quick breaths to fire more energy into her body before she tried once more. She failed again – then she stopped. She could feel eyes boring into her. She looked up and locked her gaze with the Egyptian's.

Swuth stared at the woman, dumbstruck. She was completely soaked in her own blood, cavernous wounds pierced her entire body and her hands were shivering with the tremendous pain she was experiencing. Her soul must know that death was but minutes away – and yet her eyes didn't hold even the slightest hint of fear. She stared directly at him with an expression of pure, raw, unadulterated defiance.

Tears sprang to Swuth's eyes and his heart felt immeasurably heavy. His mind grasped his heart's message instantly: this was indeed his final kill. He would never, ever kill again.

He knew what he had to do. He drew both of his curved swords, held them high by their hilts and thrust them downwards. In a flash, the swords were buried in the ground. For the last time, he looked at the half-buried, bloodied swords that had served him so well. He would never use them again. He went down on one knee, pulled his shoulders back to give himself leverage and then slammed the hilts outwards with his palms, snapping both blades in two.

Then he stood, pulled back his hood and removed his mask.

Sati saw the tattoo of a black fireball with rays streaming out over the bridge of his nose: the symbol of the cult of Aten.

Swuth reached behind and drew a sword from a scabbard tied across his back. Unlike all his other weapons, this sword was marked with Aten, the name of his god, and below that was inscribed Swuth, the name of the devotee. This blade had never been used before. It had but one purpose: to taste the blood of the final victim. Thereafter, the sword would never be used again. It would be worshipped by Swuth and his descendants.

Swuth bowed low before the woman, pointed at the black tattoo on the bridge of his nose and repeated the ancient vow: 'The fire of Aten shall consume you. And the honour of putting out your fire shall purify me.'

Sati didn't move. She didn't flinch. She continued to stare silently at the Egyptian as he went down on one knee.

Swuth had to give Sati an honourable death; beheading her was out of the question. He pointed his sword at her heart, holding the hilt with his thumb facing up. He pressed his other hand into the back of the hilt to provide support. Ready in every way, he stared at the face he knew would haunt him for the rest of his life and whispered, 'Killing you shall be my life's honour, my Lady.'

'*Noooooooo!*' The loud scream came from the distance and an arrow whizzed past and pierced Swuth's hand. As his sword dropped to the ground, he turned to find another arrow flying straight into his shoulder.

'Run!' screamed the assassins, and one of them pulled Swuth up and started dragging him along.

'Noooo!' roared Swuth, struggling against the men who were bodily carrying him away. Failure to kill the final victim was one of the greatest sins a follower of Aten could commit. But his men wouldn't leave him behind.

Nearly a thousand Meluhans had reached Sati, led by the distraught emperor and his wife.

'*S-a-t-i-i-i-i-i!*' screamed Daksha, his face twisted in agony.

'Don't touch me!' bellowed Sati as she collapsed to the ground.

Daksha buckled, crying inconsolably, digging his nails into his face.

'Sati!' screamed Veerini as she lifted her daughter into her arms.

'*Maa . . .*' whispered Sati.

'Don't talk – relax,' cried Veerini, before frantically screaming, 'Get the doctors! *Now!*'

'*Maa* . . .'

'Be quiet, my child—'

'*Maa*, my time has come—'

'No! *No!* We'll save you! *We'll save you!*'

'*Maa*, listen to me!' said Sati.

'My child—'

'My body will be handed over to Shiva.'

'Nothing's going to happen to you,' sobbed Veerini. The Queen of Meluha turned around once more and cried again, 'Will someone get the doctors? *Now!*'

Sati held her mother's face with surprising strength. 'Promise me! Only to Shiva!'

'Sati—'

'*Promise me!*'

'Yes, my child, I promise.'

'And both Ganesh and Kartik will light my pyre.'

'You're not going to die!'

'Both Ganesh and Kartik! Promise me!'

'Yes, yes – I promise.'

Sati slowed her breathing. She had heard what she needed to. She blocked out the weeping she could hear all around her, rested her head in her mother's lap and looked towards the peace conference building. The doors were open and Lord Ram and Lady Sita's idols were clearly visible within. She could feel their kind and welcoming eyes upon her. She would be back with them soon.

A sudden wind picked up, swirling dust particles and leaves lying around her on the ground. As Sati gazed at them, the particles appeared to form a figure and she stared as Shiva's image seemed to emerge. She remembered the promise she had made to him: that she would see him when he returned.

I'm sorry. I'm so sorry.

The wind died down just as suddenly as it had arisen and Sati could feel her sight blurring. Blackness was taking over. Her vision receded into a slowly diminishing circle with darkness all around it. The wind burst into life once again and the dust particles and leaves rose in an encore and showed Sati the vision she wanted to die with: the love of her life, her Shiva.

I'll be waiting for you, my love.

Thinking of her Shiva, Sati let her last breath slip quietly out of her body.

CHAPTER 46

Lament of the Blue Lord

Shiva had commandeered a merchant ship to reach the Meluhan capital as quickly as possible, and it docked at Devagiri little more than a week later.

'That must be Sati's ship,' said Shiva, pointing towards an anchored empty vessel.

'It means she's still in Devagiri,' said Ganesh. 'Bhoomidevi be praised.'

Kali clenched her fist. 'If they've taken her hostage in the hope of manipulating us, I will personally destroy everything in this city that moves.'

'Let's not assume the worst, Kali,' said Shiva. 'We all know that, whatever his faults may be, the emperor won't harm Sati.'

'I agree,' said Kartik.

'And don't forget, Queen Kali,' said Gopal, 'we have the fearsome *Pashupatiastra*. Nobody can stand up to it – *nobody*.

The mere threat of this terrifying weapon should be enough to achieve our purpose.'

Their conversation came to a stop with the sound of the gangplank landing on the dock.

'Where is everyone?' asked Shiva, frowning as he disembarked.

'And why has the port been abandoned?' Ayurvati was surprised; she had never seen anything like this in all the years she'd lived in Meluha.

'Let's go and find out,' said Shiva, unease trickling down his spine.

The entire brigade followed the Neelkanth ashore. As they left the harbour, their eyes fell on the large peace conference building. For some unknown reason, a colony of tents had been pitched outside the building.

'This area's been thoroughly cleaned recently,' said Gopal. 'Even the grass has been dug up.'

'Of course it would be,' said Shiva, quieting his fears. 'They'd need a purified area for the conference.'

A phalanx of Brahmins was conducting a *puja* next to the closed door of the peace conference hall.

'What are they praying for, Panditji?' asked Shiva.

'They're praying for peace,' said Gopal.

Shiva found nothing amiss in that.

Gopal listened more closely and said, 'But . . . they're praying for peace for the souls . . . the souls of the dead . . .'

Shiva instinctively reached to his side and drew his sword, and his entire brigade did likewise.

As they approached, Parvateshwar and Anandmayi stepped out from one of the tents, followed by a short man dressed in a simple white *dhoti* and *angvastram*, his head clean-shaven except for his long, flowing white beard and a tuft of hair at the crown signifying his Brahmin lineage.

'Lord Bhrigu,' whispered Gopal, immediately folding his hands together in a namaste.

'Namaste, great Vasudev,' said Bhrigu politely as he approached Gopal.

Shiva held his breath as he stared at his real adversary.

'Great Neelkanth,' said Bhrigu.

'Great Maharishi,' returned Shiva, his grip tightening reflexively around the hilt of his sword.

Bhrigu opened his mouth to say something, then hesitated and looked at General Parvateshwar, who was now standing next to him. Parvateshwar and Anandmayi bowed low in respect to their living god, but as Parvateshwar rose, Shiva got his first close look at his friend-turned-foe's face. He was stunned. The Meluhan general's eyes were red and swollen, as if he hadn't slept in weeks.

'Isn't the emperor allowing you to enter the city?' asked Shiva.

'We've chosen not to enter, my Lord,' said Parvateshwar.

'Why?'

'We no longer recognise him as our emperor.'

'Is that because you disagree with the conference's aims?

Is that why you're waiting here for us, with your Brahmins chanting hymns to the dead?'

Parvateshwar couldn't speak.

'If you want a battle, Parvateshwar, you shall have it,' announced Shiva.

'The battle is over, my Lord.'

'The entire war is over, great Neelkanth,' added Bhrigu.

Shiva frowned, astonished, then turned to Gopal for assistance, not knowing what to say or do next.

'Has Princess Sati managed to convince the emperor that all we want is the end of the *Somras*?' asked Gopal. 'If Meluha agrees to those terms, the Neelkanth's happy to declare peace.'

'My Lord,' said Parvateshwar as he touched Shiva's elbow, his eyes brimming with tears. 'Come with me.'

'Where to?'

Parvateshwar glanced at Shiva briefly, then returned his gaze to the ground. 'Please, just come.'

Shiva sheathed his sword and accompanied Parvateshwar to the peace conference building. His companions followed – all except Anandmayi, who remained outside her tent. She couldn't bear to see what was about to happen.

The Brahmins continued droning the Sanskrit *shlokas* as Parvateshwar approached the building's entrance. He took a deep breath and pushed the large doors open.

Shiva was stunned by the sight that greeted him: twenty beds had been laid out in the massive hall, and each bed was occupied by an injured soldier tended by a Brahmin doctor. On the first bed lay one of Shiva's most ardent devotees, the man who had found him in Tibet.

'Nandi!' exclaimed Shiva, racing to the man's bedside in a few giant strides.

Shiva went down on his knees and touched Nandi's face. He was unconscious. Both his arms had been severed, the left one close to his wrist and the right close to the elbow. Numerous tiny scars peppered his body, perhaps the result of small projectiles, and his face was pockmarked with wounds. The bed had been specially designed to keep part of Nandi's back untouched, and Shiva guessed he must have suffered a serious injury to his back as well. Shiva could see that the wounds were healing, but it was equally obvious that the injuries were grave and the recovery process would be long.

'The wounds have been left open so they can breathe, great Neelkanth,' said the Brahmin doctor, avoiding his eyes. 'We'll put on fresh dressings soon. Major Nandi will make a full recovery, as will all the other soldiers here.'

Shiva continued to stare at Nandi, gently touching his face as anger rose within him. He suddenly jumped to his feet, drew his sword and pointed it straight at Parvateshwar. 'I should kill the emperor for this!' Shiva growled.

Parvateshwar stood paralysed, still staring at the ground.

'If the emperor thinks he can force my hand by attacking these men and capturing Sati,' said Shiva, 'he's living in a fool's paradise.'

'Once *didi* knows we're here,' hissed Kali, 'she'll escape. And believe me, our wrath will be terrible. Tell that goat who rules your empire to release my sister. *Now!*'

But Parvateshwar remained still, silent. Then he began to shake almost imperceptibly.

'General?' said Gopal, his tone reasonable. 'There doesn't have to be any violence. Just let the princess go.'

Bhrigu opened his mouth to speak, but he couldn't find the strength to say what he needed to.

'Lord Bhrigu,' said Gopal, keeping his voice low but stern, 'we have the *Pashupatiastra*. We won't hesitate to use it if our demands aren't met. Release Princess Sati at once. Destroy the *Somras* factory. Do those things now and we'll leave.'

Bhrigu looked stunned when he heard the word *Pashupatiastra*. He glanced briefly towards Parvateshwar, but the general hadn't even registered the danger of the terrible *daivi astra*. He was crying openly now, his whole body shaking with misery, as he grieved the loss of the woman he'd loved like the daughter he'd never had.

'Parvateshwar,' snarled Shiva, moving his sword even closer to the general's chest, 'don't test my patience. Where's Sati?'

Parvateshwar finally looked at Shiva, tears streaming down his face.

Shiva stared back at him, a horrific foreboding seizing his heart. The space between his brows began to throb frantically.

'My Lord,' sobbed Parvateshwar, 'I'm so sorry—'

Shiva's sword slipped from his weakened grip. With terror-struck eyes, he stepped towards the general and whispered, 'Parvateshwar, where is she?'

'My Lord . . . I didn't reach her in time—'

Shiva pulled Parvateshwar towards him by his *angvastram* and put his hand around the weeping man's throat. 'Parvateshwar! Where is she?'

But Parvateshwar couldn't speak. He just continued to cry helplessly.

Shiva noticed Bhrigu glance behind him. He released Parvateshwar instantly and spun around. He saw a large wooden door at the far end of the hall.

'Sati!' screamed Shiva as he ran towards the room, Brahmin doctors hastily stepping out of the raging man's way. '*Sati!*'

The door was locked and he banged on it, and when he received no response, he stepped back to give himself room, then rammed his shoulder into the door. It yielded slightly before the strong lock snapped it back into place.

Through the crack, before the door slammed back into place, Shiva glimpsed a tower made of massive blocks of ice. His brow was burning now with a pain most mortals would have found impossible to tolerate.

One of the Meluhans went running for the keys to the room.

'Sati!' cried Shiva and slammed into the door again, splinters piercing his shoulder, drawing blood.

The door held strong.

Shiva stepped back and kicked hard and it finally fell open with a thundering crash.

The sight he beheld sucked the very breath out of the Neelkanth.

At the centre of the room, within the tower of ice, lay the mutilated body of the finest person he had ever known: his Sati.

'*Satiiiii!*'

As Shiva stormed into the room, his brow felt as if something had exploded within his skull. Fire was consuming the area between his eyes.

He banged his fists repeatedly against the ice block covering Sati's body, desperately trying to push it away. Blood poured from his shattered knuckles as he pounded against the immovable block, but still he kept hammering against the ice, breaking bits of it off, trying to shove it away, trying to reach his Sati. His blood started seeping into the frozen water.

'*Satiiii!*'

Some Meluhans came running in from the other side of the room and sank hooks into the block of ice covering Sati. They pulled hard on the ropes attached to the hooks and the block began to slide back. Shiva continued his barrage of blows, desperately trying to make it move more quickly, and it had moved barely halfway when Shiva leapt onto the tower. A small depression had been carved into the ice beneath the topmost block, like a tomb, and within that icy coffin lay Sati's body, her hands folded across her chest.

Shiva jumped onto the ice and pulled her body up, holding it tight in his arms. She was frozen stiff, her skin dulled to a greyish-blue. There was a deep cut across her face, and her left eye had been gouged out. Her left hand had been partially sliced off and there were two gaping holes in her abdomen. Frozen blood, which had seeped out of her multiple injuries, had congealed all over her mutilated body.

Shiva pulled Sati close as he looked up, crying desperately, screaming incoherently, his heart inundated with grief, his soul shattered.

'Satiiii!' His wail would haunt the world for millennia.

CHAPTER 47

A Mother's Message

The setting sun infused the sky with a profusion of colours, casting a dull glow on the peace conference building. Parvateshwar's camp had been cleared out. After a raging Kartik had threatened to kill every single man present, Bhrigu ordered Parvateshwar's troops to find alternative barracks inside Devagiri, to avoid further exciting the justified fury of the Neelkanth, his sons and Kali.

Gopal was in the temporary camp set up for Shiva's brigade, discussing the best course of action with the brigade commander. Everyone wanted vengeance, but attacking Devagiri with so few men would be suicide. Even though most of the Meluhan army and its allies remained blockaded in faraway Mohan Jo Daro, Devagiri still had soldiers enough to beat off an attack, and overcoming the capital's defensive features would require a far larger force than the one Shiva currently commanded. There were calls for the *Pashupatiastra* to be deployed, but Gopal rejected them immediately: both he and Shiva had given their word that the *daivi astra* wouldn't be used under any circumstances.

Ayurvati was supervising the recovery of Sati's injured body-guards in the peace conference building. As she attended to a patient her eyes strayed towards the locked door of the inner room, where Sati's dead body lay, surrounded by her mourning family. Ayurvati wiped the tears from her cheeks and got back to work. Keeping herself busy was the only way she could cope with her grief.

The room in which Sati's body was lying had been modified by the Meluhans to fulfil the princess's dying wish that her body be preserved until Shiva arrived. Huge bellows pumped a constant stream of cold, fresh air into the inner chamber through tiny holes drilled through the walls. The mechanism operating the bellows was a marvel of Meluhan ingenuity: twenty bulls were harnessed to a massive circular wooden wheel outside the peace conference building. As the beasts turned the wheel, it moved a system of smaller gears and pulleys, which in turn squeezed and released the bellows. The air it pumped into the room was cooled by an equally ingenious method: a pipe over-head dripped cold water continuously onto a screen made from jute and cotton hanging in front of the bellows. But now the tower of ice had begun to melt, warmed by the heat emanating from Shiva's body and his rapid breathing, and as the ice melted, Sati's corpse began to thaw, oozing a pale fluid, as if her wounds were weeping.

Shiva sat there, immobile, shivering with cold and grief,

staring into nothingness and stunned into absolute silence as he held Sati's lifeless body in his arms. His tears had stopped flowing, but his forehead still throbbed as if a great fire raged within his skull, and an angry blackish-red blotch had formed between his brows. He hadn't moved for hours. He hadn't eaten. He was almost as lifeless as the love of his life.

Kali sat near the door, sobbing loudly and cursing herself out loud for her behaviour during her last meeting with Sati, a guilt she would carry for the rest of her life. Uncontrollable rage was rising within her, slowly but steadily, but for now it was still swamped by her grief.

Krittika sat next to the tower of ice, shaking uncontrollably, touching the ice every few seconds. She'd cried until she had no tears left. Veerbhadra, his eyes as red and swollen, sat quietly next to her with one arm around her shoulders, drawing her close and giving comfort. But his other arm was stiff, his hand clenched in a tight fist. He wanted vengeance. He wanted to torture and annihilate every single person who had done this to Sati and who had done this to his friend.

Brahaspati and Tara sat quietly in another corner of the room. The former Meluhan chief scientist's face was soaked with tears too. He had always respected Sati as an icon of the Meluhan way of life – and he knew better than most that Shiva would never be the same again. *Never.* Tara stared at Shiva, her heart going out to the unfortunate Neelkanth. He was already a mere shadow of the confident, friendly man she'd met in Pariha.

Kartik and Ganesh sat impassively next to each other on the

icy floor, their backs resting against the wall, their eyes, almost blinded by their tears, fixed on their father's paralysed figure sitting on top of the ice tower, holding their mother's mutilated body in his arms. The deluge of sorrow had broken their hearts. They sat quietly, holding hands, desperately trying to make sense of what had happened.

Ganesh thought he saw movement on top of the ice tower and looked up to see a bewildering sight: his mother's spirit appeared to have risen from her body and was floating high up in the air. He glanced at his father and saw his mother's earthly body still lying motionless in Shiva's arms. He looked at his mother's apparition again, his mouth agape.

Sati flew in a great arc and landed softly in front of Ganesh. She wore a garland of fresh flowers. Her feet didn't touch the ground, but remained suspended in the air, just like those of a mythical goddess – but mythical goddesses didn't bleed. Sati was bleeding profusely, and Ganesh could see every wound on her mutilated body. Her left eye had been gouged out and the deep cut across her face was still leaking blood. The burn scar on her cheek was flaming red, as though it was still on fire. Blood spurted in time with her heartbeat from the stumps of the four fingers severed from her left hand, and streamed from two massive wounds in her abdomen, pumping out with the ferocity of a young mountain river. Small serrations all across her body seeped yet more blood. Her right hand was clenched in a tight fist and her body shaking with fury. Her right eye was bloodshot, and it was focused directly on Ganesh. Her blood-soaked hair was loose, fluttering as if a great wind blew around her.

She was a fearsome sight.

Maa!

'Avenge me!' Sati hissed.

Maa!

'Avenge me!'

Ganesh pulled his hand from Kartik's and clenched it tight. He gritted his teeth and within the confines of his mind, he whispered, *I will, maa!*

'Remember how I died!' Sati snarled.

I will! I will!

'Promise me you'll remember how I died!'

I promise, maa! I will always remember!

Sati suddenly vanished and Ganesh reached out with his hand, once again weeping desperately and crying, 'Maa!'

At exactly the same time, Kartik also saw his mother's apparition.

Sati's spirit appeared to escape from her body and hovered for some time before landing in front of Kartik – but unlike the vision Ganesh had seen, the apparition that appeared to Kartik was whole and complete. She bore no wounds, and looked exactly the way Kartik had last seen her: tall and bronze-skinned, her beautiful smile dimpling both her cheeks, her bright blue eyes shining with a gentle radiance. Her black hair was tied demurely in a bun. Her erect posture and calm expression reminded Kartik of everything she'd always symbolised:

an uncompromising Meluhan who always put the law and the welfare of others before herself.

Kartik burst out crying. *Maa . . .*

'My son,' whispered Sati.

Maa, I will torture everyone responsible for this! I'll kill every single one of them! I'll drink their blood! I'll burn down this entire city! I will avenge you!

'No,' said Sati softly.

Dumbfounded, Kartik fell silent.

'Don't you remember anything?' she asked gently.

I will remember you forever, maa. And I'll make all of Devagiri pay for what they did to you.

Sati's face became stern. 'Don't you remember anything I've taught you?'

Kartik remained silent.

'Vengeance is a waste of time,' said Sati. 'I'm not important. The only thing that matters is *dharma*. If you want to prove your love for me, do so by doing the right thing. Don't surrender to anger. Surrender only to *dharma*.'

Maa . . .

'Forget how I died,' said Sati, 'and remember how I lived.'

Maa . . .

'Promise me you'll remember how I lived.'

I promise, maa . . . I will always remember . . .

CHAPTER 48

The Great Debate

The following morning those amongst Shiva's brigade who were intent on vengeance cheered until they were hoarse when Bhagirath sailed into the harbour at the head of the entire army of two hundred and fifty thousand troops. The Ayodhyan prince had been worried about what might happen to his Lord if the Meluhans tried some trickery at Devagiri, and he'd marched the troops along the broad Meluhan highways all the way from Lothal to the Saraswati River, taking only brief food and rest breaks.

When they reached the Saraswati, he commandeered as many merchant ships as he could lay his hands on and raced up the great river to Devagiri.

'Oh, Lord Ram!' he whispered when Gopal described the brutal manner in which Sati had been killed.

'Where's the princess's body?' asked Governor Chenardhwaj, tears welling up in his eyes.

'In the peace conference building,' said Gopal. 'The Lord Neelkanth is with her. He hasn't moved from her side in the last twenty-four hours. He hasn't eaten. He hasn't spoken. He's just sitting there, holding Princess Sati's body.'

King Chandraketu of Branga looked up at the sky, then turned around and wiped away a tear. Those pearls of emotion were signs of weakness in a Kshatriya.

'We'll kill every single one of those bastards!' growled Bhagirath, his knuckles whitening as he clenched his fists. 'We'll obliterate this entire city. There'll be no trace of this place left to show it ever existed. They've hurt our living god—'

'Prince Bhagirath,' said Gopal, his palms open in supplication, 'we can't punish the entire city. We must keep clear heads. We should punish only those responsible for this atrocity. We should destroy the *Somras* factory – but we must leave the rest unharmed. That's the right thing to do—'

'Forgive me, great Vasudev,' interrupted Chandraketu, 'but some crimes are so terrible that the entire community must be made to pay. They killed Lady Sati in such a brutal manner—'

'But not everyone came out to kill her,' argued Gopal. 'The vast majority had no idea what the emperor was up to.'

'But they could have rallied to stop the killing once it had begun, couldn't they?' asked Chandraketu. 'Standing by and watching a sin being committed is as bad as committing it oneself. Don't the Vasudevs say this?'

'This is an entirely different context, King Chandraketu,' said Gopal.

'I disagree, Panditji,' said King Maatali of Vaishali. 'Devagiri must pay.'

'I think Lord Gopal's right, King Maatali,' said Chenardhwaj. 'We can't punish everyone in Devagiri for the sins of a few.'

'Why am I not surprised to hear you say that?' asked Maatali.

'What's *that* supposed to mean?' asked Chenardhwaj, stung to the quick.

'You're a Meluhan,' said Maatali, 'so of course you'll stand up for your people. But *we* are Chandravanshis – we're the ones who are truly loyal to the Lord Neelkanth.'

Chenardhwaj stepped up close to Maatali and said threateningly, 'I rebelled against my own people, against my country's laws, against my vows of loyalty to Meluha because I'm a follower of the Neelkanth. I'm loyal to Lord Shiva and I don't need to prove anything to you.'

'Calm down, everyone,' said Chandraketu. 'Let's not forget who the real enemy is.'

'The real enemy is Devagiri,' said Maatali. 'They did this to Lady Sati. They must be punished. It's as simple as that.'

'I agree,' said Bhagirath. 'We should use the *Pashupatiastra*.'

Gopal's anger flared. 'The *Pashupatiastra* isn't some random arrow that can be fired without a thought, Prince Bhagirath. It will leave death and devastation behind in this area for centuries to come.'

'Maybe that's what this place deserves,' said Chandraketu.

'These are *daivi astras*,' Gopal said, getting agitated. 'They can't be used casually, to settle disputes amongst men.'

'Lord Shiva isn't just another man,' said Bhagirath. 'He's divine. We must use the weapon to—'

'We can't use the *Pashupatiastra* and that's final,' said Gopal.

'I don't think so, Panditji,' said Chandraketu. 'Lady Sati was a great leader, a warrior who held herself to the highest moral standards. The Lord Neelkanth loved Lady Sati more than I've seen any man love his wife. I'm sure Lord Shiva wants vengeance – and frankly, so do we.'

'It's not vengeance we need, King Chandraketu,' said Gopal, 'but justice. The people who did this to Lady Sati must face justice – but only those who were responsible for this perfidy. Nobody else should be punished for their crimes, for that would be an even bigger injustice.'

'Yours is the voice of reason, Panditji,' said Maatali, 'but this isn't the time for reason. This is the time for anger.'

'I don't think the Neelkanth will make a decision in anger,' said Gopal.

'So why don't we ask Lord Shiva?' asked Bhagirath. 'Let him decide.'

'Kill them all!' growled Kali. 'I want this entire city to burn, with every single one of its citizens locked inside it.'

Shiva's family were seated with all the commanders in a secluded area on the peace conference platform, just outside the main building. Brahaspati and Tara had also joined them, but remained mostly silent. The area had been cordoned off by

soldiers to prevent anyone from eavesdropping on the deliber-
ations. But Shiva was not with them. Gopal had tried to
persuade the Neelkanth to attend, but he didn't respond to any
entreaties, instead remaining alone within the freezing inner
chamber, still holding Sati.

'Queen Kali,' said Gopal, 'my apologies for disagreeing with
you, but we can't do that. It would be morally wrong.'

'Didn't the Meluhans give their word that this would be a
peace conference?' she snapped. 'Nobody's supposed to use arms
at a peace conference, right? They did something *very* morally
wrong – why are you ignoring that, Panditji?'

'Two wrongs don't make a right.'

'I don't care,' said Kali, waving a hand dismissively. 'Devagiri
will be destroyed. They will pay for what they did to my sister.'

'Queen Kali,' said Chenardhwaj carefully, 'I respect you
immensely. You're a great woman, and you've always fought
for justice. Does punishing an entire city for the crimes of a
few serve justice?'

Kali cast him a withering look. 'I saved your life, Chenardhwaj.'

'I know, your Majesty – how could I ever forget that? That's
why—'

'You will do what I tell you to do,' interrupted Kali. 'My
sister will be avenged.'

Chenardhwaj tried to argue. 'But—'

'My sister will be avenged!'

He fell silent.

Bhagirath was staying silent, running through plans in his head. Anandmayi was in Devagiri. He agreed that the city should be destroyed, but he had to save his sister first.

'I agree with Queen Kali,' said Chandraketu. 'Devagiri must be destroyed. We must use the *Pashupatiastra*.'

At the mention of the devastating *daivi astra*, Kartik spoke up for the first time. 'The *astra* can't be used.'

Gopal looked at Kartik, grateful to have at least one member of the Neelkanth's family on his side.

'Justice will be done,' said Kartik. '*Maa*'s blood will be avenged. But not with the *Pashupatiastra*. It can't be done with that terrible weapon.'

'You're right, my son,' agreed Gopal immediately. 'The Neelkanth has given his word to the Vayuputras that he will never use the *Pashupatiastra*, not under any circumstances.'

'If that's the case, then we can't use it,' said Bhagirath.

Gopal breathed a little easier, glad to have pulled at least some of them back from the brink. 'The question remains: how do we give justice to Princess Sati?'

'By killing them all!' roared Kali.

'But is it fair to kill children who had nothing to do with this?' asked Bhagirath.

'You are assuming, Prince Bhagirath,' said Kali, 'that Meluhans care for their children.'

'Your Majesty,' said Bhagirath, 'please try to understand. Children who had nothing to do with this crime shouldn't be punished for it.'

'Fine!' said Kali, 'we'll allow their children to leave.'

'And non-combatants, too,' said Kartik.

'Particularly the women,' said Bhagirath. 'We must let them go – but once they are out, we should destroy the entire city.'

'Is there anyone else you'd like to save?' asked Kali sarcastically. 'What about the dogs? Should we save the cockroaches, too?'

Bhagirath didn't respond, knowing that anything he said would only inflame Kali further.

Kali cursed. 'All right! Children and non-combatants will be allowed out. Everyone else will remain imprisoned in the city, and they'll all be killed.'

'Agreed,' said Bhagirath. 'All I'm saying is that we should be fair.'

'That's not all there is to it, Prince Bhagirath,' said Kartik. 'The *Somras* isn't to be totally destroyed. My father's been very clear about that. It's only supposed to be taken out of the equation. We do have to destroy the *Somras* factory, but we also have to ensure that the knowledge of how to make the *Somras* isn't lost. So we will have to save the scientists and take them to a secret location: they'll become members of the tribe my father will leave behind; these people will keep the knowledge of the *Somras* alive. Today it's evil, but there may come a time in the future when the *Somras* will be good again.'

Gopal nodded. 'Kartik has spoken wisely.'

'This means that even if some of these scientists were involved with my mother's death,' said Kartik, 'we have to set aside our pain and save them. We have to save them for the sake of India's future.'

Ganesh glared at Kartik with dagger eyes. '*Set aside our pain?*'

Kartik immediately fell silent in the face of his brother's wrath.

Ganesh was breathing heavily, barely able to keep his emotions under control. 'Don't you feel *any* anger about *maa*'s death? Any rage? Any *fury?*'

'*Dada*, all I'm trying to say—'

'You've always received *maa*'s love on a platter, from the day you were born. That's why you don't value it!'

'*Dada*—'

'Ask me about the value of a mother's love . . . Ask me how much you desire and long for it when you don't have it!'

'*Dada*, I loved her, too. You know I—'

'Did you see her body, Kartik?'

'*Dada*—'

'Did you? Have you looked at her body?'

'*Dada*, of course I have—'

'There are fifty-one wounds on her body! I counted them, Kartik! *Fifty-one!*'

'I know—'

Tears of fury were pouring down Ganesh's face. 'Those bastards must have kept hacking at her even after she was dead!'

'*Dada*, listen—'

Ganesh's body was shaking with anger now. 'Didn't you feel *any* rage when you saw your mother's mutilated body?'

'Of course I did, *dada*, but—'

'But? What "but" can there possibly be? She was attacked simultaneously by a mob of those *Somras*-worshipping demons and it's *our* duty to avenge her! Our *duty*! It's the least we can do for the best mother in the world!'

'*Dada*, she *was* the best mother – but she taught us to always put the world before ourselves.'

Ganesh fell silent then. His long floppy nose had stiffened, as it always did on the rare occasions he became enraged.

Kartik spoke softly. '*Dada*, if we were any other family, I'd give in to my rage – but we're not just any other family.'

Ganesh looked away, too livid even to respond.

'We're the Neelkanth's family,' Kartik pressed on. 'We have a responsibility to the entire world.'

'Responsibility to the *world*? My *parents* are my world!'

Kartik fell silent as Ganesh pointed his finger threateningly at his brother. 'Not a single one of those *Somras*-worshipping bastards will get out of Devagiri alive.'

'*Dada*—'

'Every single one of them will be killed – even if I have to kill every single one of them myself.'

Gopal sighed as he looked at Kali, Ganesh and Kartik. There was too much anger here. He couldn't figure out a way to save the *Somras* scientists from Ganesh and Kali's rage. But at least he'd managed to steer the conversation away from the dangerous talk of using the *Pashupatiastra*. And maybe there was still hope that over the next few hours he could convince the Neelkanth's family to save the *Somras* scientists.

— ༖ ꪞU⚶ ✦ —

Shiva was still sitting quietly in the icy tomb, holding Sati's body in his lap. His eyes were sunken and expressionless, with no glimmer of hope in them, for he felt as if he'd no reason to go on living. The blackish-red blotch on his brow was visibly throbbing and he was shivering from the cold. A single drop of fluid escaped from Sati's good eye, which was now closed, and ran down her face like a tear. The room was preternaturally silent, except for the soft hissing of the cold air being pumped in.

A sudden sharp noise startled Shiva – perhaps from the bulls harnessed to the Meluhan cooling system? – and he looked around with his cold, emotionless eyes. There was nobody else in the chamber. He looked down at his dead wife, pulled her body close and gently kissed her forehead. Then he carefully laid her back on the ice.

Caressing her face tenderly, he whispered, 'Stay here, Sati. I'll be back soon.'

He jumped off the ice tower and headed for the door leading to the main room. As soon as he opened it, Ayurvati stood up. She and her medical team had been tending to Nandi and the other soldiers for the last twenty-four hours and they were exhausted.

'My Lord,' she said, her eyes red and swollen from accumu-lated misery and lack of sleep, but Shiva ignored her and continued walking. She looked at him with foreboding and terror. She'd never seen the Neelkanth's eyes look so hard and remote. He looked as if he'd gone beyond rage, beyond ruthlessness, beyond insanity.

Shiva crossed the main room and stepped outside. He heard voices to his right and turned to see his commanders in deep discussion. Tara was the first to notice him.

'Lord Neelkanth,' she said, immediately rising to her feet.

Shiva stared at her blankly for a few seconds, then took a deep breath and spoke evenly. 'Tara, the *Pashupatiastra* trunk is in my ship. Have it brought here.'

Panic-stricken, Gopal rushed towards Shiva – he knew Shiva hadn't eaten in twenty-four hours, nor had he slept. He'd been sitting on top of a tower of ice and he must be frozen to the core. Grief had practically unhinged him. He knew the Neelkanth wasn't himself. 'My friend . . . Listen to me. Don't make a decision like this in haste.'

Shiva looked at Gopal, his face frozen, utterly emotionless.

'I know you're angry, Neelkanth, but please, don't do this. I know your good heart. You'll repent of it.'

Shiva turned to walk back into the conference building. Gopal reached out and held his arm, trying to pull him back. 'Shiva,' he pleaded, 'you gave your word to the Vayuputras. You gave your word to your uncle, Lord Mithra.'

Shiva gripped Gopal's hand tightly and removed it from his arm.

'Shiva, the power of this weapon is terrible and unpredictable.' Gopal grasped at any argument that might avert the tragedy unfolding before him. 'The *Pashupatiastra*'s destruction might be restricted to the area around the point of detonation, but any attempt to destroy all three of Devagiri's platforms will surely kill us all. We'd be too close to the blast to survive. Do you really want to kill your entire army, your family and your friends?'

'Tell them to leave.'

Shiva's voice was soft, barely audible. His eyes remained remote and unfocused, staring into space. Gopal paused for a moment, watching Shiva with a glimmer of hope. 'Should I tell our people to leave? With the *Pashupatiastra*?'

Shiva didn't move. There was no reaction on his face. 'No. Tell the people of this city to leave – all except those who have made or protected the *Somras*, and those directly responsible for Sati's death. When I'm done there will be no more Daksha. There will be no more *Somras*. There will be no more Evil. It will be as if this place, this Evil, never existed. Nothing will live here, nothing will grow here and no two stones will be left standing upon each other to show that there ever was a Devagiri. It all ends. Now.'

Gopal was grateful that at least the innocent people of Devagiri would be saved – but what about Lord Rudra's law banning the use of *daivi astras*? 'Shiva, the *Pashupatiastra* . . .' he whispered, hoping against hope that Shiva would see reason.

Shiva stared emotionlessly at Gopal, and when he spoke, his voice was eerily composed. 'I will burn down this entire world.'

Gopal stared at the Neelkanth with foreboding as he turned around and walked back into the building to his Sati.

Tara rose.

'Where are you going?' whispered Brahaspati.

'To fetch the *Pashupatiastra*,' answered Tara softly.

'You can't! It'll destroy us all!'

'No, it won't. These weapons can be triangulated in such a way that the devastation will be confined within the city. We'll be safe if we remain more than three miles away.'

As Tara began to walk away Brahaspati pulled her back and whispered urgently, 'What are you doing? You know this is wrong. I feel for Shiva, but the *Pashupatiastra* . . .'

Tara stared at Brahaspati without a hint of doubt in her eyes. 'Lord Ram's sacred laws have been shamelessly broken. The Neelkanth deserves his vengeance.'

'Of course he does,' said Brahaspati, meeting her gaze without flinching. 'But not by means of the *Pashupatiastra*.'

'Don't you feel his pain? What kind of friend are you?'

'Tara, there was a time when I considered doing something wrong: I wanted to assassinate a man Sati was to face in a duel. Shiva stopped me. He stopped me from taking a sin upon my soul. If I'm to be a true friend to him, I have to stop him from tarnishing his soul. I can't let him use the *Pashupatiastra*.'

'His soul is already dead, Brahaspati. It's lying on top of that ice tower,' said Tara.

'I know, but—'

She pulled away from him, saying, 'You expect him to fight in accordance with the laws when his enemies haven't. They've taken everything from him – his life, his soul, his entire reason for existence. He deserves his vengeance.'

CHAPTER 49

Debt to the Neelkanth

Shiva's army was divided into three groups, one for each of Devagiri's three platforms, under the command of Prince Bhagirath, King Chandraketu and King Maatali. Maatali's troops blocked the gates of the Svarna platform, Chandraketu's forces guarded the exit from Rajat, and Bhagirath's troops were stationed at the steps of Tamra. Ignoring Kali's protests, Shiva's forces obeyed their Neelkanth's command and informed those within the city that all of them would be allowed to leave except for the Kshatriyas who had fought to protect the *Somras* and the Brahmins who had created it. Daksha and his personal bodyguards, including Vidyunmali, had also been specifically excluded from the amnesty. The evacuation had begun, but the Chandravanshis amongst Shiva's troops were amazed by the number of citizens who chose to stay and die with Devagiri.

Many people approached the city gates in a disciplined line, said a dignified goodbye to their families and then walked silently back to their homes to await death. There was no acrimony, no fighting at the gates, no last-ditch attempts to save the city — there was not even one single melodramatic farewell.

Gopal and Kartik had stationed themselves at the Tamra platform with Bhagirath's troops, who were primarily Brangas. Bhagirath joined them, exhausted after having supervised the construction of the perimeter barricades.

The Ayodhyan prince gestured towards the odd behaviour of citizens at the gate, half of whom were leaving and half of whom were returning to the city. 'What's going on there?'

Kartik dropped his eyes and said nothing, while Gopal's eyes welled with tears. 'It's a movement amongst the Meluhans that's gathering strength,' said the chief of the Vasudevs. 'An honourable sacrifice — stay and die with your city, for your soul will be purified if you die at the hands of the Neelkanth . . .' He fell silent, obviously overcome with emotion.

Bhagirath raised his eyebrows. 'I'm not sure I understand.'

Gopal gestured towards the crowd, where yet another woman had said goodbye to a couple before calmly turning back towards the city. 'See for yourself,' he said. 'Ask one of them, if you like. Perhaps they can explain it better than I can.'

Bhagirath paused for a moment, brows knitted, studying Gopal's face before walking over to the woman.

'Excuse me, madam,' Bhagirath called out to her, and she stopped and turned to face him. 'Why aren't you evacuating the city with the others?'

The folds of her *angvastram* wafted in the gentle breeze around her. She had a kind face, with dark, quiet eyes, and a soft voice. She spoke calmly, as if she were discussing the weather. 'I'm a Meluhan, sir. Being Meluhan isn't about the country you live in – it's about *how* you live, what you believe in. What is the purpose of a long life if not to strive for something higher? Lord Ram's most sacred law has been broken. We have fallen. All that we are has already been destroyed. What can we hope to strive for now in this life, if this is our *karma*?'

Bhagirath couldn't believe his ears.

The Meluhan woman continued, 'I believe in the Neelkanth. I've waited for him for so many years, and worshipped him – and this is what Meluha's done to him, to our princess – the most exemplary Meluhan of all, who lived every breath of her life according to Lord Ram's code. This is what Meluha has done to the laws that make us who we are.' She was quiet for a moment, her eyes searching his. 'I am guilty. I took the *Somras*. I followed the emperor, and through my complacency and silence, I was party to everything that conspired to bring about these tragic events. If this is Meluha's evil, then it's my evil, too – my *karma*. I'll pay my debt to the Neelkanth this day, and pray that my sacrifice may allow me to be reborn with a little less sin upon my soul.'

Bhagirath was stunned at this logic. She inclined her head towards him, then, with perfect composure, resumed her walk back into the city.

Gopal's voice came from behind him. 'I know. They all say

the same thing: I'm Meluhan. The law has been broken. It's my *karma*.'

They stood together in silence and watched the woman go.

'Prince Bhagirath.' The two men started slightly as Kartik's voice pulled them out of their silent contemplation.

'Yes, Kartik?' said Bhagirath, turning to face him.

'I want you to summon General Parvateshwar.'

'I've already sent a messenger to find Anandmayi,' said Bhagirath, 'but neither she nor her husband has come as yet. She won't leave without Parvateshwar – I'm still hoping I can convince both of them to join us.'

Gopal said, 'Tell them that Lord Kartik and I have invited them here and that we need to discuss something important that will affect India's future.'

Bhagirath frowned. Gopal and Kartik's suggestion might just be the only way to tempt his sister and her husband out of Devagiri. 'I'll go into the city myself,' he said.

'And, Prince Bhagirath . . .' Gopal hesitated.

'I understand, Panditji. I won't breathe a word of this to anyone.'

They stood in silence once again, looking at a city that would no longer exist tomorrow.

'Excuse me,' said a voice behind them. They turned around to see a small group of Meluhans approaching them. The man continued, 'We left the city this morning but we have changed our minds – we'd like to stay, after all. May we go back in?'

Gopal stared at them in disbelief and Bhagirath dropped his eyes, praying that he'd be able to convince his sister to leave.

It was late into the third *prahar* and the sun was well on its way towards the horizon. This would be the last time the sun set on Devagiri. Veerini looked up at the sky as she walked out of the royal palace.

'Your Majesty.' A guard saluted smartly and fell in step behind her.

Veerini absently waved her hand and walked towards the gate.

'Your Majesty? Are you leaving?' asked the shocked guard, who appeared genuinely stunned that the Meluhan queen was abandoning them and taking up the Neelkanth's offer of amnesty.

Veerini didn't bother to reply. She continued walking down the road, towards the Svarna platform gate.

'Did the Neelkanth issue this order?' asked Anandmayi, before looking at her husband. She and Parvateshwar were in a secluded area outside the Tamra platform, along with Gopal, Kartik and Bhagirath.

'It's what he'd want,' said Gopal. 'He just doesn't know it right now.'

Parvateshwar frowned. 'If the Neelkanth's said no, then it means no.'

'General, I appreciate your loyalty,' said Gopal, 'but we must also consider the larger picture. The *Somras* is evil now, but it's not supposed to be completely destroyed. You know as well as I do that it's only supposed to be taken out of the equation. We have to keep the knowledge of the *Somras* alive, for it may well be required again. We're talking about India's future.'

'Are you suggesting that the Lord Neelkanth doesn't care about India?' asked Parvateshwar.

'I'm saying no such thing, General,' said Gopal, 'but—'

Kartik suddenly spoke up. 'I appreciate your loyalty to my father, and I'm sure you're aware of my love for him, too.'

Parvateshwar nodded, but kept silent.

'My father's distraught right now,' said Kartik. 'You know how devoted he was to my mother. His grief over her death has clouded his mind. He's furious – and rightly so – but you also know that his heart is pure. He wouldn't want to do anything that goes against his *dharma*. I'm only suggesting we preserve the knowledge of how the *Somras* is made until my father's rage subsides. If, after calm reflection, he still decides that everything associated with the *Somras* should be destroyed, I'll personally see it done.'

Parvateshwar stared into space, his eyes brooding and dark.

'And in order to do that,' Gopal said, 'you must ensure the survival of the Brahmins and their libraries.'

Parvateshwar sighed. 'Many of those *Somras*-worshipping intellectuals would grab the opportunity to live, but there are some amongst them who have heard the call of honour. Kartik, you can't coerce a man to forsake his honour. You can't force him to live, particularly if, by living, he keeps alive the *Somras* declared evil by his Neelkanth, which has caused the destruction of his homeland.'

Kartik took Parvateshwar's hand. 'General, my mother appeared to me in a dream. She told me to do the right thing. She told me to remember how she lived, not how she died. You know in your heart of hearts that she would have done exactly what I'm trying to do.'

Parvateshwar looked up at the sky and quickly wiped away a tear. He was quiet for a long time.

'All right, Kartik,' he said at last. 'I'll bring those people out. I'll talk them out where I can, and force them out where I can't – but remember, they're your responsibility. They can't be allowed to propagate Evil any longer. Only the Lord Neelkanth can decide the fate of the *Somras*. Not you, not Lord Gopal, nor anyone else.'

Veerini walked rapidly down the Svarna platform steps as the assembled people made way for their queen. Maatali's forces were in charge here, checking the papers of everyone who sought to leave the city. The soldiers saluted Veerini as she approached them and she acknowledged them distractedly, but kept walking towards the massive wooden tower being constructed two miles from the city. It was the base from which the *Pashupatiastra* would be launched.

As she neared the tower, Veerini saw Shiva issuing instructions, and she immediately recognised the woman standing next to him: Tara, the love of Brahaspati's life. Ganesh was working with Tara, using his brilliant engineering skills to construct the solid tower. Kali sat a little distance away on a rock, lost in her own dark thoughts.

Kali saw the queen first and cried out, '*Maa!*'

As Veerini approached Shiva, Kali and Ganesh joined them.

Shiva looked at Veerini with glazed eyes, the now-constant throbbing pain in his brow making it difficult for him to focus. Veerini had always been struck by Shiva's eyes, by the intelligence, focus and mirth that resided in them – she believed it was his eyes rather than his blue throat that were the foundation of his charisma. But now they reflected nothing but pain and grief, a glimpse into a soul that had lost its reason to live.

Shiva hadn't believed for a moment that Veerini had been involved in Sati's assassination in any way. He bowed his head and brought his hands together in a respectful namaste.

Veerini took Shiva's hand even as her eyes were drawn to the throbbing blackish-red blotch on his brow. 'My son,' she started, 'I can't begin to imagine the pain you're going through.'

Shiva was quiet, looking lost and broken.

'I gave my word to Sati, a promise she extracted from me just before her death. I'm here to fulfil it.'

Shiva's eyes suddenly focused on Veerini's as she took a breath and then said, 'She insisted that she be cremated by both her sons.'

Ganesh sucked in his breath as tears slipped from his eyes. Tradition held that the eldest child should cremate the father, while the youngest should conduct the mother's funeral – and it was inauspicious for Nagas to be involved in any funeral ceremony. Consequently, Ganesh hadn't expected the honour of lighting his mother's pyre. Kali got up and took him in her arms and held him close.

'Traditionally only the youngest child may perform the mother's last rites,' said Veerini to Shiva, 'but if there's anyone who can challenge that tradition, it's you.'

'I don't give a damn about tradition,' said Shiva. 'If Sati wanted it, then it will be done.'

'I'll tell Kartik as well,' said Veerini. 'I gather he's at the Tamra platform.'

Shiva nodded silently before looking back towards the building where Sati's body lay, still entombed in ice.

Veerini stepped forward to embrace Shiva, who held his mother-in-law lightly. 'Try to find some peace, Shiva,' she said. 'It's what Sati would have wanted.'

'Have *you* been able to find peace?'

Veerini smiled wanly.

'We'll only find peace when we meet Sati again,' said Shiva.

'She was a wonderful woman. Any mother would be proud to have a daughter like her.'

Shiva nodded and wiped a tear from his cheek.

Veerini squeezed his hand. 'I have to tell you this, Shiva. When Sati found out about the conspiracy, she was in Devagiri, inside our palace – she could have chosen not to get involved, but instead, she fought her way out of the city and rushed into the battle to save Nandi and her other bodyguards. And she did save many of them. She died a brave, honourable warrior's death, challenging and fighting her opponents until her final breath. It was the kind of death she always wished for herself: the death any warrior wishes for himself.'

Shiva's eyes welled up again. 'Sati set very high standards for herself,' he whispered.

Veerini smiled sadly.

Shiva took a deep breath. He needed to focus on the *Pashupatiastra*. He pulled his hand from Veerini's and offered her a polite namaste. 'I should . . .'

'Of course,' said Veerini. 'I understand.'

Shiva bent and touched his mother-in-law's feet and she gently laid her hand on his head and blessed him. Then he turned and walked back to supervise the work on the weapon. It was the only thing stopping his spirit from imploding.

Veerini turned and embraced her daughter, Kali, and grandson, Ganesh. 'I have been unfair to both of you,' she said.

'No, you haven't, *maa*,' said Kali. 'It was Father who committed the sins, not you.'

'But I failed in my duty as a mother. I should have abandoned my husband when he refused to accept you.'

Kali shook her head. 'You had your duty as a wife to think of as well.'

'It's not a wife's duty to support her husband's misdeeds – in fact, a good wife corrects her husband when he's wrong, even if she has to ram it down his throat.'

'I don't think he'd have listened, *naani*,' said Ganesh, 'no matter how hard you tried. That man is—'

Veerini stared at her grandson as Ganesh checked himself before insulting his grandfather to her face. She noticed his eyes. They weren't calm and detached, like the last time she'd met him. They were full of rage and barely repressed fury over his mother's death.

'*Naani*, if you'll excuse me, I need to work on the tower.'

'Of course, my child.'

Ganesh bent down, touched his grandmother's feet and then walked back to Tara.

'*Maa*, wait here for a little while and Ganesh will take you to our ship,' said Kali. 'You can stay aboard until all this is over and then return with us to Panchavati. It'd be so wonderful to have you in my home, even if it's a hundred years after it was meant to be. Having you with us will help us all cope with our grief and the vacuum left behind by Sati's absence.'

Veerini smiled and embraced Kali. 'I'll have to wait for my next birth to visit your home, my child.'

Kali was aghast. '*Maa!* You don't have to be punished for that old goat's crimes! You will *not* return to Devagiri!'

'Don't be ridiculous, Kali. I'm Queen of Meluha. When Devagiri dies, so shall I.'

'Of course you won't!' cried Kali. 'There's no reason—'

'Would you leave Panchavati on the day of its destruction?'

Kali was momentarily stumped, but the Naga queen was not one to give in easily. 'That's a hypothetical question, *maa*. What's important here is that—'

'What's important, my child,' interrupted Veerini, 'is the identity of the man who helped your father to execute this atrocity. Many of the conspirators have escaped, as have the assassins: they won't die here tomorrow.' Her voice hardened. 'You need to find them. You need to *punish* them.'

CHAPTER 50

Saving a Legacy

The sun had long since set beyond the western horizon. Kartik, Gopal and Bhagirath were stationed at the far corner of the Tamra platform, out of sight of the other two platforms and Shiva's army encampment. It was the best place for Kartik to carry out his mission.

Kartik was accompanied by twenty of the Branga soldiers from Divodas' command who had become fanatically loyal to him after the Battle of Bal-Atibal Kund. Divodas and the soldiers were gradually lowering a cage via a pulley that had been rigged on top of the Tamra platform wall. The wooden cage carried ten Brahmins at a time, together with their books and essential equipment. Secrecy was essential, for removing any knowledge of the *Somras* from the city was forbidden and punishable by death.

A second rope tied to the cage as a failsafe was the responsibility of a group of Suryavanshi soldiers under Parvateshwar's command and both teams worked in tandem, playing out their ropes at the same pace so that the cage could descend gently to the ground. The angle of the wall made it impossible for Parvateshwar to see how the cage was moving, or to judge its distance from the ground, so he was relying on Bhagirath, standing far enough away that he could watch both teams at the same time. The moon aided Bhagirath's vision. His task was to keep whistling like a bird, but in a steady rhythm, until the wooden cage touched the ground, his whistle setting the pace for the soldiers.

Kartik whirled around when Bhagirath went silent. He realised that Divodas and his team were still releasing their rope at the same pace, but the Suryavanshis, accustomed to following orders, had instantly halted when Bhagirath stopped whistling. The wooden cage quickly became unbalanced and tilted heavily to one side.

'Stop!' hissed Kartik, and Divodas' team obeyed immediately, but the cage remained precariously suspended in mid-air. To Gopal's admiration, the Brahmins inside the cage remained quiet, despite the possibility that they might be about to fall to their deaths. Any unexpected noise would have alerted others to what was going on.

Kartik rushed towards Bhagirath, who appeared to be lost in his own world. 'Prince Bhagirath?' he whispered, and the Ayodhan prince immediately snapped out of his stupor and began to whistle again. The Suryavanshis started releasing their rope at a steady pace and the wooden cage descended gently to the ground and the Brahmins exited quickly in an orderly fashion.

Bhagirath's whistling wasn't needed while the teams pulled the empty cage back up. That part of the operation required speed, not steadiness.

'Prince Bhagirath, please pay attention,' said Kartik. 'Many people's lives are at stake.'

He knew exactly why Bhagirath was distracted: General Parvateshwar had refused to leave Devagiri. The Meluhan general had decided he would perish along with his beloved city, and to Bhagirath's utter dismay, his sister Anandmayi had decided to stay with her husband.

Bhagirath had fought passionately with her over her decision, pleading with her, begging her to reconsider. 'Do you think Parvateshwar wants you to die? And what about me? Why are you trying to hurt me? Do you hate me so much? I'm your brother – what have I done to deserve this?'

Anandmayi had just smiled, her eyes glistening with love and tears. 'Bhagirath, you love me and you want me to live, with every fibre of your soul – so let me live. Let me live every last second of my life in the way I believe my life should be lived. If you love me, let me go.'

Bhagirath shook his head as if to clear his mind. 'My apologies, Kartik.'

Kartik placed a hand on Bhagirath's arm. 'Prince, your sister was right about you. You'll make a far better king than your father.'

Bhagirath snorted. He already knew that the Chandravanshi army ordered to march to Devagiri under the command of the Meluhan Brigadier Vraka had rebelled against his father. The soldiers believed that Emperor Dilipa had led them into an ill-conceived war where they were fighting *with* their former enemies, the Meluhans, *against* their Neelkanth. A contingent of soldiers was on its way to Devagiri to convince Bhagirath to ascend the throne – but he didn't care about that. He was tormented by the impending loss of his beloved sister.

'Do you know what the mark of a great king is?' asked Kartik, and Bhagirath looked blankly at him. 'It's the ability to remain focused, regardless of personal tragedy. You'll have time to mourn your sister and brother-in-law, Prince Bhagirath, but not right now. You're the only one here who can whistle like a night bird and make it sound natural. We need you focused on the task at hand.'

'Yes, Lord Kartik,' said Bhagirath, addressing the young man as his lord for the first time.

Kartik looked around for a moment, then beckoned for a Branga soldier to join them. 'Prince Bhagirath,' he said, 'this man will remain here to support you in your task.'

Bhagirath didn't object, and Kartik quickly returned to Gopal.

Seeing the Vasudev chief's pensive expression, Kartik asked, 'What's happened, Panditji?'

Gopal pointed to a Suryavanshi soldier who had just arrived. 'Lord Parvateshwar's sent a message. Maharishi Bhrigu has refused to leave the city.'

Kartik shook his head. 'Why are the Meluhans so bloody eager to die?'

'What do I do, Lord Kartik?' asked the Suryavanshi.

'Take me to Maharishi Bhrigu.'

A flickering sacrificial flame spread a little light in the darkness, aided by its reflection on the nearby Saraswati River. Ganesh sat quietly on a *patla*, a low stool, with his legs crossed and his fleshy hands resting on his knees, his long fingers extended delicately. He was wearing a white *dhoti*. A barber was shearing his hair while Ganesh softly chanted a *mantra* and dropped ghee into the sacrificial flame.

When the barber was done, he put his razor down and wiped Ganesh's head with a cloth. Then he picked up a small bottle Ayurvati had given him, poured some of the disinfectant into his palm and rubbed it into Ganesh's scalp.

'It's done, my Lord.'

Ganesh didn't reply. He looked directly at the sacrificial flame and spoke softly. 'She was the purest of them all, Lord Agni. Remember that as you consume her. Take care of her and carry her straight to heaven, for that's where she came from. She was, is, and forever will be a goddess. She will be the Mother Goddess.'

It was late when an exhausted Shiva trudged back to his Sati.

The *Pashupatiastra* would be ready to fire as soon as Tara had conducted the few final tests. The peace conference area was within what she called the *Pashupatiastra*'s 'blast radius', so Sati's body would be moved from her icy tomb the next morning.

Nobody dared to say that, without the Meluhan cooling mechanism, her body would begin to decompose and she would need to be cremated as soon as possible. That was something Shiva was refusing to contemplate.

He opened the door of the inner chamber, shivering at the sudden blast of cold air, and saw Ganesh, his head shaved clean, standing next to the ice tower, holding his dead mother's hand. The Lord of the Nagas was standing on tiptoe, his mouth close to his mother's ear as he followed ancient tradition and whispered hymns from the *Rig Veda* to her.

Shiva walked up to Ganesh and touched his shoulder lightly. Ganesh immediately pulled up his white *angvastram* and wiped his eyes before turning to face his father.

Shiva embraced his son.

'I miss her, *baba*.' Ganesh held Shiva tightly.

'I miss her, too.'

Ganesh began to cry in earnest. 'I abandoned her in her hour of need.'

'You weren't the only one, my son. I wasn't there, either. But we will avenge her.'

Ganesh sobbed helplessly. 'I want to kill them all. I want to kill every single one of those bastards!'

'We'll kill the evil that took her life.' Shiva held his son quietly while he cried. He closed his eyes and pulled Ganesh in tighter and whispered hoarsely, 'Whatever the cost.'

Veerbhadra and Krittika were visiting the Rajat platform. Krittika had lived in Devagiri for a long time and knew many people there and she was trying to convince those who had announced they were staying behind to leave.

'Veerbhadra, I need to talk to you,' said a voice, and he and Krittika turned to see Kali and Parshuram standing behind them.

'Yes, your Majesty,' said Veerbhadra.

'In private,' she said.

'Of course,' said Veerbhadra, and touched Krittika lightly on the shoulder before walking away.

'Vidyunmali?' spat Veerbhadra, his face hardening with fury.

'He's the main conspirator,' said Kali. 'He's hiding in the city – he was badly injured in some recent skirmish.'

'We have to lead a small group into the city and locate him,' Parshuram said.

Kali touched her knife, a serrated blade that delivered particularly painful wounds. 'We must encourage him to talk. We need to know the identities of the assassins who escaped.'

'That son of a bitch deserves a slow, painful death,' growled Veerbhadra.

'That he does,' said Kali, 'but not before we've made him talk.'

Parshuram stretched out his hand, palm facing the ground. 'For the Lord Neelkanth.'

Veerbhadra placed his hand on Parshuram's. 'For Shiva.'

Kali placed her hand on top. 'For Sati.'

CHAPTER 51

Live On, Do Your Karma

'You want to enter Devagiri?' Krittika cried. 'Are you mad?'

'I'll be back soon,' Veerbhadra promised. 'The city's quite safe – you've seen the way the Meluhans are behaving.'

'That may be so, but Vidyunmali's men will surely be prowling the streets. What do you think they're going to do if they see you? Welcome you with flowers?'

'They won't even notice me, Krittika.'

'Nonsense! Everyone in Devagiri recognises you as the Lord Neelkanth's friend.'

'They'll only recognise me if they see me. It's the middle of the night – no one will even notice me.'

'Why can't you send someone else?'

'Because this is the least I can do for my friend. We need to find out who Princess Sati's actual killers are. Vidyunmali knows: he's the one who organised and implemented this peace conference farce.'

'But we're about to destroy the entire city – all the conspirators will be dead soon!'

'Many of the actual assassins escaped,' he said. 'Except for Vidyunmali, nobody knows who they are. If we don't learn their identities now, we'll never know.'

Krittika looked away. She'd run out of arguments, but she was still deeply troubled. 'I'm as angry as you are about Princess Sati's death, but the killing has to stop sometime,' she said after a moment.

'I have to go, Krittika.' He tried to kiss her goodbye but she turned her face away. He could understand her anger. She'd just lost the woman she'd idolised all her life. Her home town, Devagiri, was about to be destroyed and she didn't want to risk losing her husband as well. But he had to do this. Sati's killers had to be punished.

— ⁂ 𝕆𝕌⬆⊕ —

'Panditji,' said Kartik, his hands folded in a namaste and his head bowed low.

Bhrigu opened his eyes. The maharishi had been meditating in the grand Indra Temple next to the public bathhouse.

'Lord Kartik,' said Bhrigu, surprised to see Kartik in Devagiri at that time of night.

'I'm too young for you to address me as lord, great Maharishi,' said Kartik.

'Noble deeds make a man a lord, not merely his age. I've heard about your efforts to ensure the *Somras* isn't completely destroyed. History will thank you for that. Your glory will be recounted for generations to come.'

'I'm not working for my own glory, Panditji. My task is to be true to my father's mission. My task is to do what my mother would have wanted me to do.'

Bhrigu smiled. 'I don't think your mother would have wanted you to come here. I don't think she'd want you to save me.'

'I disagree,' said Kartik. 'You're a good man. You just picked the wrong side.'

'I didn't just *pick* this side, I *led* it into battle, and my *dharma* demands that I perish with it.'

'Why?'

'If the side I led committed such crimes, I must pay for them. If Fate has determined that those who supported the *Somras* have sinned, then the *Somras* must be evil. I was wrong, and my punishment is death.'

'Isn't that taking the easy way out?'

Bhrigu stared at Kartik, angered by the implied insult.

'So you think you've done something wrong, Panditji,' said Kartik. 'What's the way out? Escaping through death? Or actually working to set things right by balancing your *karma*?'

'What can I do? I've conceded that the *Somras* is evil. There's nothing left for me to do now.'

'You have a vast storehouse of knowledge within you, Panditji,' said Kartik. 'The *Somras* isn't your only expertise. Should the world be deprived of Lord Bhrigu's *Samhita*?'

'I don't think anyone's interested in my knowledge.'

'That's for posterity to determine. You should just do your duty.'

Bhrigu fell silent.

'Panditji, your *karma* is to spread your knowledge throughout the world,' said Kartik. 'Whether others choose to listen or not is *their karma*.'

A wry smile softened his expression and he admitted, 'You speak well, son of the Neelkanth. But I chose to support something that turned out to be evil and for this sin, I must die. There's no *karma* left for me in this life. I'll have to wait to be reborn.'

'One cannot allow a bad deed to arrest the wheel of *karma*. Don't banish yourself from this world as a punishment for your sin. Instead, stay here and do some good, so that you can cleanse your *karma*.'

Kartik continued as Bhrigu stared at him silently, 'You can't undo what's happened, but the inexorable march of time offers the wise man opportunities for redemption. I entreat you, don't run away. Stay in this world and work out your *karma*.'

Bhrigu smiled. 'You're very intelligent for such a young boy.'

'I'm Shiva and Sati's son,' said Kartik with a smile. 'I'm Ganesh's younger brother. When the gardeners are good, the flower will bloom.'

Bhrigu turned towards the idol of Lord Indra within the *sanctum sanctorum*. The great god, the killer of the primal demon, Vritra, stood resplendent, holding his favourite weapon, *Vajra*, the thunderbolt. Bhrigu folded his hands into a namaste and bowed, praying for the god's blessing.

Then the maharishi turned back to Kartik and whispered, '*Samhita . . .*'

'The *Bhrigu Samhita*,' said Kartik. 'The world will benefit from your vast knowledge, Panditji. Come with me. Don't sit here and wait for death.'

The sun rose on Devagiri's last day. The *Pashupatiastra* was ready. After barring the gates, Shiva's soldiers had been ordered to retreat beyond the safety line, out of the weapon's expected reach. The relatives of those remaining within Devagiri were herded into a safe zone by Chandraketu's Brangas, where they waited patiently and prayed for the souls of their loved ones, left behind in the city.

Maharishi Bhrigu and another three hundred people who knew the secrets of the *Somras* had been successfully spirited out of Devagiri the previous night and were now imprisoned in a temporary stockade five miles north of Devagiri under the watchful eye of Divodas and his soldiers. Kartik intended to wait for his father's anger to subside before talking to him about Bhrigu and the others.

The peace conference building had been abandoned. Nandi and the other surviving bodyguards had been evacuated to Shiva's ship, where a medical team under Ayurvati's supervision maintained a constant vigil.

Ayurvati was worried about the blackish-red mark on Shiva's brow, though he had brushed aside her concerns. It had appeared many times before, especially when Shiva was angry, but it had never lasted for so long.

Now Shiva, Kali, Ganesh and Kartik carried Sati's body gently to a specially prepared cabin aboard the ship, where her corpse was laid with great care within another tomb of ice. Sati's family took one last look at her before heading out to the deck.

Shiva ran his hand gently across Sati's face and whispered, 'Devagiri will pay for its crimes, my love. And you will be avenged.'

As he stepped back, the soldiers sealed the temporary tomb with another block of ice, enveloping her body.

Then the captain bellowed commands and the rowers manoeuvred the vessel back down the Saraswati River, far away from the *Pashupatiastra*.

'The weapon is armed, Lord Neelkanth,' said Tara.

Shiva cast an expressionless look at an unhappy Gopal and then turned back towards Tara. 'Let's go,' he said.

At the fourth hour of the second *prahar*, just a couple of hours before Devagiri was to be destroyed, Veerini knocked on Parvateshwar's door. There was no answer; Parvateshwar and Anandmayi were probably alone at home after dismissing their servants to be with their own families at this difficult time, she thought.

She pushed open the door and walked through the lobby into the central courtyard, calling, 'General?' but there was no response. 'General!' she cried, a little louder this time. 'It's Veerini.'

'Your Majesty!'

She looked up to see Parvateshwar, peering down from the balcony on the top floor. His hair was dishevelled and an *angvastram* had been hastily thrown over his shoulders.

'My apologies if I've come at a bad time, General.'

'Not at all, your Majesty,' he said.

'It's just, we don't have much time left,' said Veerini, 'and there's something I need to tell you.'

'Please give me a moment, your Majesty. I'll be down shortly.'

'Of course.' Veerini walked into the large waiting room next to the courtyard, where she settled on a comfortable chair and waited. A few minutes later Parvateshwar entered the room, clad in a spotless white *dhoti* and *angvastram*, his hair neatly combed. Anandmayi was with him, also clad in white, the colour of purity.

Veerini rose. 'Please accept my apologies for disturbing you.'

'Not at all, your Majesty,' said Parvateshwar. 'Please, sit.' As Veerini resumed her seat, he and Anandmayi sat next to her. 'What do you want to talk about, your Majesty?' he asked.

The queen hesitated for a moment, then smiled at Anandmayi and Parvateshwar. 'I want to thank you,' she began.

'Thank us?' Parvateshwar looked surprised. 'Thank us for what, your Majesty?'

'For keeping Devagiri's legacy alive,' she said, and as Parvateshwar and Anandmayi remained silent, their expressions reflecting their confusion, she gestured around and explained, 'Devagiri isn't just a physical manifestation. Devagiri also exists in its knowledge, its philosophies and its ideologies. By saving our intellectuals, you've managed to keep that alive.'

Parvateshwar didn't know how to react – how could he openly acknowledge having broken the law to save the scientists who worked at the *Somras* factory? 'Your Majesty, I didn't—'

Veerini raised her hand. 'Your conduct has been exemplary your entire life, Lord Parvateshwar. Don't spoil it by lying on your last day.'

Parvateshwar smiled and bowed his head in acknowledgement.

'The people you've saved aren't merely the repositories of our knowledge of the *Somras*, but also of the accumulated knowledge of our great land. They're the custodians of our philosophies, of our ideologies. They will keep our legacy alive, and for that, Devagiri and Meluha will be forever grateful to you.'

'Thank you, your Majesty,' said Anandmayi, accepting the gratitude on behalf of her discomfited husband.

'It's bad enough that both of you are dying for my husband's sins,' said Veerini. 'It would have been unthinkable had Maharishi Bhrigu and our intellectuals suffered for it as well.'

'I think what's really unfair is that *you* will suffer for your husband's sins, your Majesty,' said Anandmayi. 'He might not have been a good emperor, but you've been an excellent queen.'

'Not really,' Veerini admitted. 'If that were true, I would have stood up to my husband, instead of standing by him.'

They sat quietly together for a moment, then Veerini straightened her shoulders and rose to leave. 'Time grows short,' she said, 'and there are preparations we still have to make for our final journey. Thank you – both of you – for everything. Let us say our final farewells.'

CHAPTER 52

The Banyan Tree

Daksha sat quietly in his chamber, staring out of the window, waiting for his death. He looked towards the door, wondering where Veerini had gone so early in the morning.

Has she abandoned me as well?

As death approached, he was honest enough, at least with himself, not to blame her if she had.

He took a deep breath, wiped the tears from his eyes and turned his gaze back towards the window, towards the banyan tree in the distance. It was a magnificent tree, centuries old, even older than Daksha himself, and he remembered how vast he'd thought it when he was young, and how he'd marvelled over the fact that it never stopped growing. Its branches spread out over vast distances, and when they extended too far to be sustained by the main trunk, they dropped thin, reed-like roots to the ground which then anchored themselves deep into the earth, drawing nourishment from the fertile soil and growing into secondary trunks to support further extension of the branch that gave them birth. After a few decades, so many new trunks had sprung up that it was impossible to tell which was the original. It had been a single tree when Daksha was born; now it resembled a jungle.

All Indians revered the grand banyan tree: it was considered holy, a tree that unselfishly gave of itself to others, growing into an ecosystem that sustained many birds and animals. Innumerable plants found succour and shade under the protective cover of its branches, and it stood strong in the face of the most severe storms. Indians believed that ancestral spirits – and sometimes even the gods – inhabited the banyan tree.

For most citizens of Devagiri, this massive tree represented their ideal of life and they worshipped it.

Daksha's perspective, though, was very different. At a very young age he had noted that no offspring of a banyan was able to flourish or even grow anywhere near its parent – the parent tree's roots were too strong for the sapling's tender shoots to penetrate, so, for a sapling to survive, it had to move far from its parent.

I should have run away.

To a neglected child's imagination, the banyan tree's munificence was reserved for others. It didn't care for its own – in fact, it went out of its way to harm them. So while everyone else looked upon the banyan tree with reverence, Daksha viewed it with fear and hatred.

He was fearful because it wasn't the only banyan tree in his life. He had another: his father. Daksha had hated his father with a venomous intensity, but at a deeper level, he had also loved the man, and admired his abilities. Just like the banyan's desperate offspring, Daksha had tried to prove he could be as great as his father, a burden he'd carried all his life. But there was one time when he'd unshackled himself from his father's grip, when he'd been free for a few magical moments — it might have been more than a hundred years ago, but he remembered it as clearly as if it had been yesterday.

Sati had just returned from the Maika *gurukul*, a headstrong, idealistic girl of sixteen. In keeping with her character, she'd jumped in without a second thought to save an immigrant woman from a vicious pack of wild dogs. Daksha remembered how he and Parvateshwar had rushed to her rescue, and despite not being an accomplished warrior, he had, with Parvateshwar's help, courageously fought back the dogs attacking his daughter.

He had been seriously injured in that terrible fight.

Fortunately, the medic arrived in good time. Parvateshwar and Sati's injuries were superficial and had been quickly dressed, but Daksha's injuries were the most serious, for he'd been in the thick of the battle. The medical officer had taken him to the *ayuralay* so that senior doctors could examine him, but he arrived unconscious as a result of massive blood loss.

When he'd come round, he'd found himself in the *ayuralay*. He remembered scolding Sati for risking her own life to save an insignificant immigrant woman, and later, when he was recuperating in his room, he'd asked Veerini to bring his daughter to him so he could make peace with her — but before Sati had arrived, his father, Brahmanayak, had stormed into the chamber, accompanied by his doctor.

Brahmanayak, one of Meluha's most accomplished warriors, had mocked Daksha for allowing himself to be so badly injured by a pack of mere dogs — and the doctor had pulled him out of the room, using the excuse of a private conversation, to save his patient from any further mental anguish.

As soon as Brahmanayak had left the room, Veerini repeated the plea she'd made many times before: that they should escape from Meluha and live in Panchavati with their daughters. 'Daksha, trust me,' she had said, 'we'll be happy in Panchavati. If there was any other place where we could live with both Kali and Sati I'd suggest it, but there isn't.'

Maybe Veerini's right, he thought. *If I can escape the old man, perhaps we can be happy. I must also think of Sati. She's the only pure member of my bloodline — Veerini's corrupt soul has led to Kali's birth. There's not much I can do to help them, but I have to protect Sati from the terrible fate of seeing her father being insulted every day. My elder daughter is the only one worthy of my love.*

He sighed deeply and asked, 'But how——?'

'You leave that to me. I'll make the arrangements. Just say yes. Your father's leaving tomorrow for Karachapa. You're not so badly injured that you can't travel — we'll be in Panchavati before he knows you're gone.'

Daksha stared at Veerini. 'But——'

'Trust me. Please, *trust me*. It'll be good for us. I know you love me. I know you love your daughters. Deep inside, I know you don't really care about anything else. Just trust me.'

Perhaps this is what we need.

Daksha nodded and Veerini smiled and kissed him. 'I'll make all the arrangements.'

In a moment of solitude after she'd left the room, he had stared at the ceiling, feeling light and relaxed; feeling *free*.

Everything happens for a reason, perhaps even this battle with the dogs. We can be happy in Panchavati. We'll be away from my father and free of that monster. To hell with Meluha. To hell with the throne. I don't want any of it. I just want to be happy. I just want to be with my Sati and be able to take care of her. I'll also look after Veerini and Kali, of course. Who do they have besides me?

He noticed Veerini's prayer-beads on the chair, and next to the prayer-beads was the tiger claw Sati wore as a pendant. It must have fallen off during the battle with the dogs, and Veerini had recovered it to return it to her. Daksha stared at the blood-stains on the tiger claw: his daughter's blood. His eyes became moist again and he promised himself, *I will be nothing like my father. I'll take care of Sati. I'll love her like every father should love his child. I won't ridicule her in public. I won't deride her for the qualities she doesn't possess. Instead, I'll cherish every talent she does have. She'll be free to live her own dreams. I won't force my dreams upon her. I'll love her for who she is, not for what I'd like her to be.*

Daksha had looked at his own injured body and shook his head. *All of this to save an immigrant woman! Sati can be so naïve at times. But she's still a child. I shouldn't have screamed at her — I should have explained things to her calmly. After all, who does she have to look up to besides me?*

Just then the door had opened and Sati walked in, looking grouchy, almost angry.

Daksha smiled at her. *She's only a child.* 'Come here, my daughter,' he'd said, and when Sati stepped forward hesitantly, he laughed and repeated, 'Come closer – I'm your father; I'm not going to eat you!'

Sati had approached, but her face was still reflecting the righteous anger she felt within.

Lord Ram, be merciful! This girl still thinks she did the right thing by risking all our lives to save an unimportant immigrant woman.

Daksha reached out and took Sati's hand, saying patiently, 'My child, listen to me. I care for you. I only have your best interests at heart. It was stupid of you to risk your life for that immigrant, but I admit I shouldn't have shouted at—'

He had fallen silent as the door swung open suddenly and Brahmanayak strode in.

Sati withdrew her hand from her father's and looked at Brahmanayak, whose face broke into a broad smile.

'Aah!' he said as he walked up to Sati and embraced her. 'At least one of my progeny has my blood coursing through her veins!'

Sati looked at Brahmanayak adoringly, pure hero-worship in her eyes while Daksha had stared at his father with impotent rage.

'I've heard what you did, Sati,' said Brahmanayak. 'You risked your own life to protect a woman you didn't even know, and a lowly immigrant woman at that.'

Sati smiled in embarrassment. 'It was nothing, your Majesty.'

Brahmanayak laughed softly and patted Sati's cheek. 'I'm not "your Majesty" to you, Sati. I'm your grandfather.'

Sati smiled as he went on, 'I'm proud of you, my child. I'm honoured to call you a Meluhan, and honoured to call you my granddaughter.'

Sati's smile broadened and she embraced her grandfather once again.

Brahmanayak bent down and kissed her forehead, then he turned to his son, the smile immediately disappearing from his face. With barely concealed contempt, he said, 'I'm leaving for Karachapa tomorrow morning and will be gone for many weeks. Perhaps you'll need that much time to recover from your so-called injuries. We'll talk about your future when I return.'

Seething, Daksha turned his face away, refusing to answer Brahmanayak, who rolled his eyes, then patted Sati's head and promised, 'I'll see you when I return, my child.'

'Yes, Grandfather.'

Brahmanayak strode to the door and was gone, and Daksha glared after him.

Thank God I'm going to be rid of you, you beast! Insulting me in front of my favourite daughter? How dare you! Take the throne away, take all the riches away, take the world away, if you wish — but don't you dare take my good daughter away from me! She's mine!

He looked at Sati, who was staring at the door, her body shaking.

Is she crying?

Daksha thought Sati might be angry with Brahmanayak for insulting her father – she was his daughter, after all. He smiled and reached for her hand. 'It's all right, my child. I'm not angry. Your grandfather doesn't matter any more because—'

'Father,' interrupted Sati as she spun around, tears streaming down her cheeks, 'why can't you be more like Grandfather?'

Daksha stared at his daughter, dumbstruck as she whispered again, 'Why can't you be more like Grandfather?'

He opened his mouth, but no words would come out.

Sati suddenly turned around and ran out of the room and he stared at the door as it slammed shut behind her; fierce tears pouring from his eyes.

More like Grandfather? More like that monster?

I'm so much better than him!

The gods know that – they know I'll make a far better king! I'll show you!

You will *love me! I'm your creator!*

You will love me, not him – not that monster!

The sound of the door opening broke Daksha's train of thought and brought him back from that ancient memory to the present moment. He watched Veerini walk into the bedchamber. She glanced at him for an instant, then wordlessly walked up to her private desk and rummaged through it, looking for something – her prayer-beads. She brought them to her forehead reverently, then touched them to her eyes and lips. Holding the beads tightly between her palms, she turned to take one last look at her husband. The disgust she felt couldn't be expressed in words. She had no intention of desecrating her ears by listening to his voice. She hadn't spoken to him since Sati's death.

Daksha's eyes followed Veerini's movements around the room. He couldn't muster the courage to speak, even if only to apologise for everything he'd done.

Veerini entered the private prayer room next to the bedchamber and shut the door behind her before bowing before the idol of Lord Ram, who was surrounded by the idols of his favourite people: his wife, Lady Sita; his brother, Lord Lakshman; and his loyal devotee, Lord Hanuman, the Vayuputra.

She sat down on the floor cross-legged holding the beads high in front of her eyes and began chanting as she waited for death: '*Shri Ram Jai Ram Jai Jai Ram; Shri Ram Jai Ram Jai Jai Ram . . .*'

The faint echo of her chanting reached Daksha's ears.

I should have listened to her. She was right all along.

'*Shri Ram Jai Ram Jai Jai Ram; Shri Ram Jai Ram Jai Jai Ram . . .*'

Those divinely serene words should have brought him peace, but there was no chance of that. He would die a frustrated and angry man.

Daksha clenched his jaw and looked out of the window. He

stared at the banyan tree in the distance, tears streaming down his face.

Damn you!

The banyan shook slightly and its leaves ruffled in the strong wind. It looked as if the giant tree was laughing at him.

Damn you!

CHAPTER 53

The Destroyer of Evil

'The wind's too strong,' Tara murmured as she looked worriedly at the windsock set up close to the *Pashupatiastra*'s tower.

She and Shiva were mounted on horses, stationed far from the *daivi astra*. It was almost the end of the second *prahar* and the sun would be directly overhead in a few moments. Shiva's entire army and the refugees from Devagiri had been corralled four miles from the tower, safely outside the range of the *Pashupatiastra*.

Shiva glanced at Tara and then up at the sky, trying to judge the wind's strength and direction from the movement of dust particles in the air. 'Not a problem,' he announced, and returned his attention to stringing his bow. Parshuram had been working on this composite bow for months. Its basic structure was made of wood, reinforced with horn on the inside and sinew on the outside. It was curved much more sharply than a normal bow, and its ends pointed away from the archer. It had exceptional draw strength for its small size and was ideal for shooting arrows from horseback or riding in a chariot. Parshuram had named the bow Pinaka, after Lord Rudra's fabled longbow.

Though Parshuram hadn't known this while he was designing the bow, the Pinaka would prove ideal for Shiva's purpose, for setting off the *Pashupatiastra* was not going to be easy.

The Vayuputras had intended the *daivi astras* to be mounted on launching towers packed with a mixture of sulphur, charcoal, saltpetre and several other materials which would generate the explosive energy required to propel the *astra* towards its intended target. Once the *astra* was close to its target, a second set of explosive devices would trigger the weapon itself.

But the launch material within the tower had to be triggered from a safe distance, otherwise whoever was firing the *astra* would be incinerated in the initial launch explosion – so it was usually triggered by archers of enormous skill, shooting flaming arrows at it using longbows with a range of more than eight hundred yards.

The *Brahmastra* and *Vaishnavastra* didn't need to be aimed precisely, and since accuracy wasn't of the essence, the launch towers that cradled these weapons had huge firing targets.

The *Pashupatiastra*, however, was a different matter: it had to be launched precisely if it was to hit its intended target – and this time it was further complicated by the need to fire three missiles so that they would hit the Svarna, Rajat and Tamra platforms at the same time, guaranteeing the complete and instantaneous destruction of Devagiri. The target area was small, and more than eight hundred yards away, and Shiva would have to fire the arrow from horseback if he was to escape after shooting.

'Remember, great Neelkanth,' said Tara, 'the moment your arrow hits the target, you'll have less than five minutes before the *Pashupatiastra* explodes. You must cover at least a mile and a half within that time to be out of range.'

Shiva nodded distractedly, still testing his bow's draw.

'Neelkanth?' Tara repeated. 'It's crucial you ride as fast as you can – the blast could be fatal if you're too close when the bombs detonate.'

Shiva didn't respond but pulled the arrows from his quiver. He smelled them and then rubbed the tip of one against the rough leather of the pommel and it ignited immediately. *Perfect*. Shiva threw the burning arrow away and returned the rest to his quiver.

'Did you hear me? You need to move away as soon as you've fired the arrows.'

Shiva wiped his hand on his *dhoti* and turned to Tara. 'You should get beyond the safety line now.'

'Shiva! Promise me you'll shoot the arrow and ride away.'

Shiva looked at Tara, his gaze glassy. Tara could see the blackish-red blotch on his brow throbbing frantically.

'Promise me!'

Shiva nodded.

'Promise me!'

'I've already promised. Now go.'

Tara stared at Shiva. 'Neelkanth—'

'Go, Tara. The sun's about to reach its zenith – I need to fire the missiles.'

Tara nodded curtly and turned her animal around.

'And Tara—'

Tara reined in and looked back over her shoulder.

'Thank you,' said Shiva.

Tara sat still, watching the Neelkanth's face with eyes clouded by tears. 'Ride back beyond the safety line as fast as you can,' she repeated. 'Remember: all those who love you are waiting for you.'

Shiva held his breath. *Yes, my love is waiting for me.*

Tara kicked her horse into a canter and rode away.

Shiva pressed his forehead, right above the blackish-red mark, and the pressure seemed to ease the horrendous burning sensation. The pain had been immense and continuous for the last few days, ever since he'd first seen Sati's body. Then he shook his head and focused his attention on the tower. He could see the bright-red target in the distance.

He took a deep breath and looked towards the ground. *Holy Lake, give me strength.*

He took another breath and looked up. *Lord Ram, be merciful!*

Arrayed in front of him was an army, blocking his view of the *Pashupatiastra* launch tower: each figure was the giant hairy monster who had tormented his nightmares since his childhood – but when Shiva looked more closely, he noticed that none of the monsters had faces; each had a smooth, white slate where the face should have been. All had their swords drawn, and blood was dripping from every single blade. He could hear their ghastly roar, and for a moment, he imagined he was that terrified little boy once again.

Shiva looked up at the sky and shook his head as if to clear it. *Help me!*

He heard his Uncle Manobhu's voice call out, 'Forgive them! Forget them! Your only true enemy is Evil!'

He brought his eyes down and locked his gaze on the launch tower. The monsters had disappeared. He stared directly at the red spot, right at the centre of the tower, then pulled his horse's reins and turned it to the right, leaning forward and singing softly in its ear to calm the beast. The horse stilled, offering Shiva the stable base he needed and he turned his head to his left, creating the natural angle for a right-handed archer to get a straight shot. He pulled his bow forward and tested the string once more; he liked the twang of the bowstring. He pulled and released; it was as taut as it could be. He bent forward and pulled an arrow from the quiver, then held it to his side and looked up, judging the wind.

The art of shooting arrows from such a huge distance was all about patience and judgement: waiting for the right wind conditions, the ability to predict the arrow's parabolic movement, determining the ideal angle of release, controlling the speed of the arrow at release, deciding how far to draw the bowstring . . .

Shiva fixed his eyes on the windsock, keeping his breathing steady, trying to ignore the burning sensation between his eyes.

The wind's changing direction.

With the bow pointing towards the ground, Shiva nocked an arrow, gripping the shaft firmly between his hooked index and middle fingers.

The wind's holding.

He ignited the tip by rubbing it against the saddle's leather pommel. With muscles taut, he raised the bow and drew the string in one fluid motion, even as his warrior's mind instinctively calculated the correct angle of flight. He kept his dominant eye focused on the target and his left hand held the bow rock-steady, ignoring the searing heat from the tip of the arrow.

The wind's perfect.

He released the arrow without hesitation and watched the arrow move in a parabola as if in slow motion. His eyes followed its path until it hit the red target and depressed it. The fire immediately spread to the waiting receptacle behind the target. The *Pashupatiastra*'s initial launch sequence had been triggered.

'Ride away!' screamed Tara from the distance.

'*Baba*, turn your horse around!' shouted Kartik.

But Shiva couldn't hear either of them. They were too far away. As he stared at the rapidly spreading fire behind the target, the pain within his brow started ratcheting up once again. He felt as if the insides of his forehead were on fire now, just like the launch tower. He pulled his horse's reins and turned it around.

He could see his troops in the distance, and beyond them he could see his ship, anchored on the Saraswati. Sati's body was inside it.

She's waiting for me.

Shiva kicked his horse's flanks, but the animal didn't need much coaxing; it quickly broke into a gallop as the fire within the launch tower triggered the initial explosion and the three *Pashupatiastras* shot out of their pods, the two directed at the Tamra and Svarna platforms launched just a few milliseconds after the first.

Shiva kept kicking his horse, and it galloped faster and faster until he was just a few moments away from the safety line.

The *Pashupatiastras* flew in a great arc, leaving a trail of fire behind them, and seconds later, they began their simultaneous descent into the city, giant harbingers of absolute destruction.

'*Shiva!*'

Shiva could have sworn he heard the voice he loved beyond all reason – but it couldn't have been real. He shook his aching head and kept riding.

The *Pashupatiastra* missiles were descending rapidly.

'*Shiva! Shiva!*'

Shiva looked back to see a bloodied and mutilated Sati running after him. Her left hand was spewing blood in bursts in time with each beat of her pounding heart. Two massive wounds on her abdomen gaped open and more blood streamed out from them in a torrent. Her left eye had been gouged out and her burn scar looked as if it was on fire again. She was struggling desperately to stay upright, but she kept running towards Shiva.

'Shiva! Help me! Don't leave me!'

An army of soldiers was chasing Sati, holding their bloodied swords aloft. Each warrior was the exact likeness of Daksha. The area between Shiva's brows began throbbing even more desperately, the fire within struggling to burst through.

'Sati!' screamed Shiva as he pulled hard on his horse's reins to slow the animal's headlong gallop. He wasn't going to lose her again.

The horse balked at Shiva's command and refused to slow down.

'*Sati!*'

He yanked desperately at the reins again, but the horse had a mind of its own: the beast could smell the stench of death behind it and it wasn't going to slow down or turn for anyone.

Shiva pulled his feet from the stirrups and jumped to the ground, the speed of his fall making him lurch dangerously as he hit the ground. He rolled quickly and was up on his feet in a flash, screaming, 'Sati!'

The horse kept galloping towards the safety line as Shiva turned around, drew his sword and ran to protect the mirage of his wife.

'*Baba!*' shouted Ganesh. 'Come back!'

The blackish-red mark at the centre of Shiva's forehead burst open and blood spewed out as he ran desperately towards his wife, roaring at the army of Dakshas chasing her, 'Leave her alone, you bastards! Fight me!'

The three *Pashupatiastras* exploded simultaneously, exactly as planned, some fifty yards above the three platforms, in a blinding burst of light. Shiva's army and the Devagiri refugees shielded their eyes, stunned to see their own bodies glowing and translucent, blood, muscle and even bone visible in the blinding light. An echo of the devastating blasts over Devagiri flashed within their own bodies and sheer terror entered their hearts.

Almost immediately thereafter, three bursts of demonic fire descended from the heights where the three *Pashupatiastras* had exploded and tore fiendishly into Devagiri, incinerating all three platforms instantaneously, reducing to nothing the great City of the Gods, built and nurtured over centuries, in a fraction of a second.

'Lord Ram, be merciful,' whispered Ayurvati in absolute horror as she saw the massive explosion from aboard the ship that was carrying Sati.

As the fire ripped through Devagiri, three giant pillars of smoke shot up, and just as Tara had predicted, the energy blasts of the three *daivi astras* attracted each other, crashing into each other with diabolical rage as thunder and lightning cracked around them. The unified pillar of smoke now shot higher, higher than anything any living creature watching the explosion had ever seen, rising like a giant, steeply inclined pyramid – and then it exploded into a massive cloud half a mile above the ground.

And just as suddenly as it had appeared, the pyramid of smoke collapsed into itself and fell within the ruins of Devagiri.

Shiva was heedless of the terrible devastation taking place in front of him. He kept running forward, his sword drawn, his brow spouting blood at an alarming rate.

As soon as the pyramid of smoke collapsed, another silent

blast occurred – and the sound of the initial explosion reached Shiva's army, cowering behind the safety line.

'*Baba!*' screamed Ganesh as he jumped from the platform he was on and raced towards his horse.

The second blast was invisible – Shiva couldn't see it, but he could feel a demonic surge rolling towards him. He had to save his wife – and so he kept running towards her, screaming desperately, '*Sati!*'

His body was lifted high by the blast wave and for a moment he felt weightless, and then the wave propelled him back brutally. His brow and throat were on fire and blood spewed from his mouth. He landed hard on the ground, flat on his back, his head jerking as he felt a sharp sensation on the crown of his head.

And yet he felt no pain. He just kept screaming, '*Sa . . . ti . . . ! Sa . . . ti . . . !*'

Suddenly, he saw Sati bending over him. There was no blood on her – no wounds, no scars. She looked just like she had the day he'd met her, all those years ago at the Brahma Temple. She bent forward and ran her hand along Shiva's cheek, her smiling face suffused with love and joy: the smile that always set the world right for him.

She touched the crown of Shiva's head and the sharp sensation receded and was replaced by an uncanny calm – he felt as if he'd been set free. Strangely, his blue throat wasn't cold any more – equally strange was the realisation that his brow had stopped burning from within.

Shiva opened his mouth, but no sound emerged. Instead, he

thought about the words he wanted to say: *Take me with you, Sati. There's nothing left for me to do. I'm done.*

Sati bent forward and kissed Shiva lightly on his lips. She smiled and whispered, 'No, you're not done yet. Not yet.'

Shiva kept staring at his wife. *I can't live without you . . .*

'You must,' said Sati's shimmering image.

Shiva couldn't keep his eyes open any more. Sati's beautiful, calm face began to blur and he collapsed into a peaceful dream-like state. As he was descending into the depths of unconsciousness, he thought he heard a voice, almost like a command: 'No more killing from now on. Spread life. *Spread life.*'

CHAPTER 54

By the Holy Lake

Thirty years later, Mansarovar Lake (at the foot of Mount Kailash, Tibet)

Shiva squatted on the rock that extended over the Mansarovar. Behind him was Kailash Mountain, its four sides perfectly aligned with the four cardinal directions. It stood sentinel over the great Mahadev, the one who had saved India from Evil.

The long years and the tough Tibetan terrain had taken its toll on his body. His matted hair had greyed considerably, although it was still long and wiry enough to be tied in a traditional beaded bun. His body, honed with regular exercise and yoga, was still taut and muscular, but the wrinkled skin had lost its tone. His *neel kanth*, the blue throat, was as blue as it had ever been, but it didn't feel cold any more – not since the day he was hit by the neutron blast from the *Pashupatiastras* that destroyed Devagiri. The area between his brows no longer burned or throbbed either, but the mark there had taken on a darker hue, almost black, which contrasted sharply with his fair skin. It wasn't an indistinct, indeterminate mark either. It looked like the tattoo of an eye: an eye with the lid shut. It stood vertically on his forehead, between his natural eyes. Kali had named it Shiva's third eye.

Shiva looked across the lake at the setting sun. In the distance he spotted a pair of swans gliding over the shimmering waters. To him, it looked as if the birds were beholding the sight together, and he reflected that the setting sun couldn't be truly enjoyed unless shared with the one you loved.

He sighed deeply and picked up a pebble. When he was young, he could make such a stone skip off the surface of the lake — his record had been seventeen bounces. He flung the pebble, but it sank immediately into the lake with a plop.

I miss you.

Not a day passed when he didn't think about his wife. He wiped a tear from his eye before turning back to look at the bonfires burning outside his village compound. A large crowd had gathered around the fires and they were eating, drinking and making merry.

Some members of his Guna tribe had followed him when he returned to Kailash Mountain many years ago, and nearly ten thousand people from across India had decided to leave their homes and migrate to their Mahadev's homeland too. Chief amongst them were Nandi, Brahaspati, Tara, Parshuram and Ayurvati. The deposed Ayodhyan ruler, Dilipa, who was still alive thanks to Ayurvati's medicines, had also migrated to the shores of the Mansarovar, along with former Maika-Lothal governor, Chenardhwaj, and former Naga prime minister, Karkotak. Shiva's followers had established new villages close to his. Seeing the massive contingent Shiva now commanded, even the Pakratis, the local Tibetans who had waged a longstanding blood feud with the Gunas, had made peace with the Neelkanth.

The fires reminded Shiva of one of the worst days of his life: the day he destroyed Devagiri. Sati had been cremated that same day, later in the evening – but Shiva had no memories of that event. He was unconscious, having been battered by the *Pashupatiastra*'s neutron blast, and fighting for his life under Ayurvati's care. Everything he knew about Sati's cremation he'd learned from Kali, Ganesh and Kartik later.

They told him that a calm breeze had blown across the land, picking up the ashes from the ruins of Devagiri and scattering them. It was almost as if the ashes were trying to reach the waters of the Saraswati, to give some closure to the souls of the departed. Hazy specks had coloured the entire landscape a pale shade of grey around the Saraswati.

Ganesh and Kartik lit the sandalwood pyre with blazing torches. It took some time for the timber to ignite, as if even Lord Agni, the God of Fire, needed some coaxing to consume Sati's body. But once the flames took, the pyre raged like an inferno. Perhaps the task was so painful for Lord Agni that he wanted to finish it as quickly as possible.

Shiva regained consciousness three days later to find Kali,

Ganesh and Kartik sitting next to him, anxiously waiting for him to open his eyes. After he'd regained his strength, a tearful Ganesh had handed him an urn containing Sati's ashes.

A few drops of water splashed on Shiva, churned up, perhaps, by a fish swimming vigorously below the surface. They pulled him back from the thirty-year-old memory to the present.

Shiva tarried a little longer, allowing his gaze to dwell on the lake waters. As always, he could have sworn he saw Sati's ashes swirling in it. It was a mirage, of course. Her ashes had been immersed in the holy Saraswati the day after Shiva had regained consciousness.

He remembered struggling weakly onto the boat, helped by Ganesh and Kartik. They rowed to the middle of the river, where he and Kali scattered some of Sati's ashes into the water. He had refused to scatter them all, tradition be damned; he needed to keep some small portion of Sati for himself.

Indians believe that the body is a temporary gift from Mother Earth. She lends it to a living being so that the soul has an instrument with which to carry out its *karma*. Once the soul's *karma* is done, the body must be returned, in a pure form, so that the Mother may use it for another purpose. The ashes represent a human body that has been purified by the greatest purifier of them all: Lord Agni, the God of Fire. By immersing the ashes into holy waters, the body is offered back, with respect, to Mother Earth.

He recalled the Brahmins in the adjacent boat, chanting Sanskrit hymns throughout the ceremony. One specific chant from the *Isha Vasya Upanishad* had caught Shiva's attention and he still remembered every word:

Vayur anilam amritam; Athedam bhasmantam shariram.

Let this temporary body be burned to ashes. But the breath of life belongs elsewhere. May it find its way back to the Immortal Breath.

'My Lord!' shouted Nandi loudly and Shiva turned from the lake to see his friend standing at a distance. He had two hooks where his arms used to be.

'My Lord, everyone's waiting,' said Nandi.

Shiva held his hand up, signalling for Nandi to wait. He needed some more time with his memories. They'd sent Nandi to fetch him as they knew he'd become Shiva's favourite; he'd lost both of his hands thirty years ago, fighting bravely alongside Sati in a doomed attempt to save her.

Shiva glanced beyond Nandi and saw Maharishi Bhrigu, sitting away from the others, talking to Ganesh and Kartik. The sage appeared to be explaining something from a palm-leaf book. Both his sons were listening attentively, as were King Chandraketu of Branga and King Maatali of Vaishali.

He looked back towards the lake and took another deep breath. *Kartik saved my honour.*

Kartik had wisely waited to tell Shiva how he'd saved the Devagiri scientists who knew the secret of the *Somras*. It was the right time, for the Neelkanth had received the news with equanimity. Shiva was also glad that Bhrigu had been saved, as the great maharishi had played no role in Sati's death. The India of the future would be the proud inheritor of the legacy of his immense knowledge.

Shiva had decreed that the *Somras* scientists be given lands in central Tibet, far beyond the expanse of the Indian empires – far beyond the reach of *any* empire – and, with the help of Suryavanshi and Chandravanshi troops, they established their new home. They named it *Devagiri*, the Abode of the Gods, after their city of origin; in the local Tibetan language, it was known as Lhasa. The knowledge of the *Somras*, the elixir of immortality, would be the sacred secret of the citizens of Lhasa until the time came when India needed that knowledge again.

Shiva had also decreed that his two sons would choose the tribe that would protect Lhasa and they selected an eclectic mix of Chandravanshis, Suryavanshis and Nagas, combined with most of the Gunas, Shiva's tribesmen, and people from many other local Tibetan tribes. Veerbhadra, Shiva's closest friend and loyal follower, was appointed chief of this tribe and given the title of Lama, the Tibetan word for guru or master. The people of Lhasa and the followers of the Lama would protect India's ancient knowledge, and their sworn duty was to rise up and save India whenever it faced the onslaught of Evil again.

The site in Tibet, on the Tsangpo River, where the *Somras'* waste had been dumped was dug up and the waste taken further north, to a remote, inhospitable and mostly uninhabited part of the Tibetan plateau where it was reburied deep in the ground, enclosed within cases made of wet clay and lined with bilva leaves, themselves encased within boxes of thick lead. The boxes were buried deep under vast quantities of earth, snow and permafrost in the hope that this poison would remain undisturbed forever. Fortunately, there would be no new toxic waste to be disposed of since the manufacturing of the *Somras* had ended with the destruction of Devagiri.

Removing the knowledge of the *Somras* would not be enough to eradicate the drink of the gods from India, Shiva believed. Its very foundation had to be uprooted. Parshuram's idea was sound: without the Saraswati, the *Somras* couldn't be manufactured – and as the river was picking up radioactive waste at Devagiri and poisoning the lands further downstream, he needed to do something. The Saraswati emerged from the confluence of the Sutlej and the Yamuna Rivers – if these two tributaries were separated, the Saraswati would no longer exist, and its waters would not be available for manufacturing the *Somras* or for carrying radioactive waste downstream.

Shiva had decided that the Sutlej and Yamuna Rivers would part company forever, with the Yamuna being redirected into the temporary course it had taken more than a century before, when it had merged into the Ganga. But the resultant flooding would cause havoc, so the change had to be controlled.

Bhagirath and the Meluhan engineers came up with a brilliant plan to avoid the chaos of an uncontrolled flood, and at Shiva's order, the banks of the Yamuna were dug up and giant sluice gates were built along them. The gates, named by Bhagirath as the Locks of Shiva, were opened slowly, releasing the water in a controlled fashion and guiding the Yamuna onto its new course.

Over the next months, the river was slowly diverted to unite with the Ganga at Prayag. The addition of the massive Yamuna, already strengthened by the waters of the Brahmaputra, swelled the mighty Ganga into the biggest river system in India. Because the Yamuna carried the soul of the Saraswati, that made the Ganga the holiest river in India.

The burst of fresh, clean water from the Yamuna soon cleansed the poisonous waters in Branga, freeing the great rivers in that land from the *Somras* poison, and the Brangas living at Gangasagar, where the resurgent Ganga met the sea, began to believe that the Ganga had purified their land.

The myth wasn't far from the truth.

Without the centralising presence of Devagiri, Meluha devolved into independent kingdoms. Rid of Daksha's incompetent rule and revived with the fresh breath of freedom, a burst of creativity birthed an efflorescence of varied but equally beautiful cultures.

Shiva recognised Bhagirath by his loud laugh. He turned and saw him standing near a bonfire, talking animatedly to Dilipa, Gopal and Kali. Dilipa had been deposed by his army before the destruction of Devagiri, and his son, Prince Bhagirath, had ruled Ayodhya wisely, bringing in a new era of peace and prosperity. Judging by the expression on Dilipa's face as he listened to his son, the former emperor appeared to have made peace with his fate.

Shiva turned his attention to the lanky figure – perhaps the great Vasudev sensed that somebody was looking at him, for he turned and smiled at Shiva, folded his hands into a namaste and bowed low. Shiva returned Gopal's greeting with a formal namaste. Gopal too had made his peace with with the Neelkanth.

The outcome at Devagiri was not what the Vasudev chief had desired, but Evil had been removed and the *Somras* saved and that knowedge had brought him peace, in time. Once the malevolent effects of Evil had been removed India had rejuvenated herself. The Neelkanth had succeeded in his mission, which meant the Vasudevs had too. Gopal had quickly established formal relations with Veerbhadra and the citizens of Lhasa, the new tribe of the Mahadev; together the Vasudevs and the Lhasans would maintain their watch over India, ensuring that this divine land continued to prosper and grow with balance.

Seeing his friend Gopal also reminded Shiva of the Vayuputras, who had never forgiven him for using the *Pashupatiastra*. It had been a source of particular embarrassment for the Mithra, since he'd personally backed the announcement of Shiva as the Neelkanth against some virulent opposition. The punishment for the unauthorised use of a *daivi astra* was a fourteen-year exile, but in atonement, not just for breaking his word to them, but for having caused the death of his mother-in-law, Veerini, and his friends, Parvateshwar and Anandmayi, Shiva had exiled himself from India, not just for fourteen years, but for the rest of his life.

'*Baba . . .*'

Shiva hadn't noticed Ganesh, Kartik and Kali sneak up on him.

'Yes, Ganesh?'

'*Baba*, it's the feast of the Night of the Mahadev,' said Ganesh, 'and the Mahadev needs to be a part of the celebration, not just brooding next to the lake.'

Shiva nodded slowly. His neck had begun to hurt a bit: the perils of old age. 'Help me up,' he said as he made an effort to rise.

Kartik and Ganesh immediately leaned forward and helped their father to his feet.

'Ganesh, you get fatter every time I see you.'

Ganesh laughed heartily. He had suffered intensely and taken a long time to recover from his mother's death, but ultimately he had reconciled himself with that loss, choosing to learn from her life instead. He had taken it upon himself to spread the word of Shiva and Sati throughout India and that sense of purpose in his life had helped him return to his usual calm state of being; he was even jovial at times.

'Thanks to your wisdom, peace prevails all over India, *baba*,' said Ganesh. 'There are no more wars, no conflicts, so I do very little physical activity and eat a lot. Ultimately, the way I see it, it's your fault that I'm getting fatter.'

Kali and Kartik laughed loudly. Shiva smiled faintly, but his eyes didn't lose their seriousness.

'You should smile sometimes, *baba*,' said Kartik. 'It would make us happy.'

Shiva stared at Kartik. It had been a long time since Sati's death, and even young Kartik was beginning to acquire a smattering of white hair. His son had travelled a very long distance to come to Kailash. After Shiva had returned to Kailash–Mansarovar, Kartik had travelled south of the Narmada, deep into the ancient heartland of India: the land of Lord Manu, a prince of the Pandya dynasty which had ruled the prehistoric land of Sangamtamil. That land and its fine Sangam culture had been destroyed as sea levels rose with the end of the last Ice Age – but Kartik had discovered that many people continued to live in India's ancient fatherland, breaking Lord Manu's law that prohibited people from travelling south of the Narmada. Kartik had established a new Sangam culture on the banks of the Kaveri, India's southernmost major river.

'I'll smile when the three of you reveal your secret,' said Shiva.

'What secret?' asked Kartik.

'You know exactly what I'm talking about.' He had discovered that, on the night before the destruction of Devagiri, Kali, Parshuram and Veerbhadra had found and kidnapped Brigadier Vidyunmali and tortured him until he had revealed the names of Sati's assassins. They had given Vidyunmali a slow and brutal death.

A few years after the destruction of Devagiri, Kali, Ganesh, Kartik, Parshuram and Veerbhadra had slipped out of India – nobody knew for sure where they'd gone, and they'd refused to tell Shiva, perhaps because he'd prohibited any further reprisals for Sati's death. Around the same time, there had been rumours in Egypt about the near-complete destruction of the secretive cult of Aten; it was said that the death of each of the tribe's leaders had been long, slow and painful, their blood-curdling screams echoing through their followers' hearts.

What Sati's avengers didn't know was that Swuth had exiled himself, going south to the source of the Nile River, where he spent the rest of his life bemoaning the fact that he'd been unable to complete his holy duty of executing the final kill. But Sati's magnificence had been branded upon his soul. He didn't know her name, so he worshipped her as a nameless goddess, and after his death, his descendants continued that tradition. The few remaining survivors would have to wait for centuries before a revolutionary pharaoh reformed and revived the cult of Aten. That pharaoh would be remembered as the great Akhenaten, the living spirit of Aten – but that's another story . . .

'*Baba*, we—'

Kali placed her hand over Kartik's lips. 'There's nothing to reveal, Shiva, except that the food is extremely delicious. You need to eat, so follow me.'

Shiva shook his head. 'You still haven't lost your regal airs.'

Kali no longer ruled a kingdom. Within a few years of her return from Egypt she renounced her throne and supported the election of Suparna as the new Queen of the Nagas. Leaving her kingdom in capable hands, Kali joined Shiva, Ganesh and Kartik and together they toured India. The Neelkanth's family had established fifty-one Shakti Temples across the length and breadth of the country, and Kali had at last convinced Shiva to part with the portion of Sati's ashes he'd kept for himself. As

Sati belonged to the whole of India and not just to Shiva, small quantities of her ashes were consecrated at each of the fifty-one temples, so that Indians would forever remember their great goddess, Lady Sati.

Kali had finally settled down in north-eastern Branga, close to the Kamakhya Temple, and devoted the remainder of her life to prayer. Her spiritual presence had made the Kamakhya Temple one of the foremost Shakti Temples in India, and many Surya-vanshis, Chandravanshis and Nagas were inspired by the former Naga queen to follow her to her new abode. Over time, they set up their own individual kingdoms. The Suryavanshis named their kingdom Tripura, the Land of the Three Cities, after the three platforms of their destroyed capital. The Chandravanshis, worshippers of the seventh Vishnu, Lord Ram, had called their land Manipur, the Land of the Jewel, for the seventh Vishnu was a crown jewel of India. Kali's Naga followers established their own empire further to the east. All these different peoples fol-lowed the path of Kali: proud warriors forged from the womb of Mother India. If treated with respect, they would be your greatest strength, but if you disrespected them, no power on Earth would be able to save you.

'I might not have a kingdom any more, Shiva,' said Kali, her eyes dancing with mirth, 'but I will always be a queen!'

Ganesh and Kartik smiled broadly, but Shiva just stared at Kali's face. It was identical to Sati's, and it reminded him of how happy he had once been.

'Come, let's eat,' he said at last.

As the Mahadev and his family walked back towards the bonfires, Ganesh and Kartik started describing to Shiva the brilliant composition Bhrigu had just shown them; it would come to be known over the millennia as the greatest classic on the ancient science of astrology, the *Bhrigu Samhita*.

As time went by, Shiva became increasingly ascetic. He began spending days, even months, in isolation within the claustrophobic confines of mountain caves, performing severe penance. Nandi was the only person allowed to visit him at these times, and people began to believe that he was the only way to reach Shiva's ears.

Shiva started to devote long hours to the study of yoga, and the knowledge that he developed helped create a powerful tool for finding physical, mental and spiritual peace through unity with the divine. He added many fresh thoughts and philosophies to the immense body of ancient Indian knowledge and wisdom, and many of his ideas were inscribed in the holy scriptures of the *Vedas*, *Upanishads* and *Puranas*, benefiting humanity for millennia to come.

Though Shiva continued to be prodigiously productive, his heart never found happiness again, and despite repeated attempts by his family, the legend was that nobody ever saw Shiva smile again after that terrible day in Devagiri. Nobody saw his virtuoso dances or heard his soulful singing or sublime music. He gave up everything that offered even a remote possibility of bringing him happiness.

But Shiva did smile once, just once more, a moment before he left his mortal body to merge once again with the god from whom he had emerged. He smiled then, for he knew that the love of his life, his Sati, was just one last breath away.

Kartik's wisdom and courage ensured that the Sangam culture in South India continued to flourish, and its power spread far and wide. While Kartik continued to be adored in northern India, especially in Kashi where he was born, his influence in southern India was beyond compare, and he is remembered to this day as the Warrior God, he who can solve any problem and defeat any enemy.

The adoration for Kartik's elder brother, the wise and kind-hearted Ganesh, grew to astronomical heights in India, where he was revered as a living god. The belief spread throughout the country that he should be the first god to be worshipped in all ceremonies; by this, Ganesh would remove all obstacles from one's path. And so he came to be known as the God of Auspicious Beginnings. His profound intellect also led to him becoming the God of Writers, and his name acquired immense significance for authors and poets and other troubled souls.

The *Somras* had had an especially strong effect on Ganesh, who lived for centuries, far beyond all his contemporaries. Ganesh didn't mind this, for he loved interacting with people from across India, helping them, guiding them. But there came a time when, enfeebled by old age, Ganesh began to think that perhaps he had lived in this mortal body for too long.

He had to suffer the mortification of seeing the ancient Vedic Indians turn on each other in a catastrophic civil war when a minor dispute within a dysfunctional royal family escalated into a mighty conflict which sucked in all the great powers of the day. The calamitous bloodletting of that war destroyed not just all the powerful empires of the time, but also the Vedic Indians' way of life, leaving utter devastation in its wake.

Civilisation did rise again from these ruins, for such is the way of the world, but this new culture had lost too much. The descendents remembered only snippets of their ancestors' greatness; they were, in many ways, unworthy of their heritage. They believed that the great men of the past could not possibly have existed in reality, and instead they turned them into mythical gods. They could not understand brilliant science but saw it as magic, their limited intellects unable to comprehend the knowedge. Deep philosophies became no more than shallow rituals, for it took courage and confidence to ask questions. True memories were forgotten in the chaos, devolving into myths and legends as the vast arrays of *daivi astras* used in the Great War ravaged the land.

That war destroyed almost everything and it took India centuries to regain anything of its former cultural vigour and intellectual depth.

When the recreated history of that Great War was written, cobbled together from fragments of surviving information, the treatise was initially called *Jaya* or *Victory*. But even the un-sophisticated minds of the descendants soon realised this name was inappropriate, for that dreadful war brought victory to no one; every single person lost – in fact, the whole of India lost.

Today, we know the inherited tale of that war as one of the world's greatest epics: *The Mahabharat*. If the Lord Neelkanth allows it, the unadulterated story of that terrible war shall also be told one day.

Om Namah Shivaiy.
The universe bows to Lord Shiva. I bow to Lord Shiva.

Glossary

Agni: God of Fire.

Agnipariksha: A trial by fire.

Angaharas: Movement of limbs or steps in a dance.

Ankush: Hook-shaped prods used to control elephants.

Annapurna: The Hindu Goddess of Food, Nourishment and
    Plenty; also believed to be a form of Goddess Parvati.

Anshan: Hunger; it also denotes voluntary fasting. In this book,
    Anshan is the capital of the kingdom of Elam.

Apsara: Celestial maidens from the court of Indra, the Lord of
    the Heavens, akin to Zeus/Jupiter.

Arya: Sir.

Ashwamedh Yagna: Literally, the Horse Sacrifice. In ancient
    times, an ambitious ruler who wished to expand his terri-
    tories and display his military prowess would release a sacri-
    ficial horse to roam freely through the length and breadth of
    any kingdom in India. If any king stopped or captured the
    horse, that would be seen as a challenge: the ambitious ruler

would declare war, defeat the king and annexe that territory.
If the king did not stop the horse, the kingdom would auto-
matically become a vassal state of the ambitious ruler.

Asura: Demon.

Ayuralay: Hospital.

Ayurvedic: Derived from *Ayurved*, an ancient Indian form of
medicine.

Ayushman bhav: May you have a long life.

Baba: Father.

Bhang: Traditional intoxicant in India: milk mixed with marijuana.

Bhiksha: Alms or donations.

Bhojan graham: Dining room.

Brahmacharya: The vow of celibacy.

Brahmastra: Literally, the weapon of Brahma; spoken of in
ancient Hindu scriptures. Many experts claim that the
description of a *Brahmastra* and its effects are eerily similar to
that of a nuclear weapon; I have assumed this to be true in
the context of the Shiva trilogy.

Branga: The ancient name for modern West Bengal, Assam and
Bangladesh; the term is coined from the conjoint of the two
rivers of this land: *Bra*hmaputra and Ga*nga*.

Brangaridai: The capital of the kingdom of Branga; literally,
the heart of Branga.

Chandravanshi: Descendants of the moon.

Chaturanga: Ancient Indian game that evolved into the modern
game of chess.

Chillum: Clay pipe, usually used to smoke marijuana.

Choti: Braid.

Construction of Devagiri royal court platform: The description in the book of the court platform is a possible explanation for the mysterious multiple column buildings made of baked brick discovered at Indus Valley sites, usually next to the public baths, which many historians suppose could have been granaries.

Dada: Elder brother.

Daivi Astra: *Daivi* means Divine; *Astra* is Weapon; *daivi astra* is a term used in ancient Hindu epics to describe weapons of mass destruction.

Dandakaranya: Dandak is the ancient name for modern Maharashtra and parts of Andhra Pradesh, Karnataka, Chhattisgarh and Madhya Pradesh. *Aranya* means forest. *Dandakaranya* means the forest of Dandak.

Deva: God.

Dharma: *Dharma* literally translates as religion, but in traditional Hindu belief, it means far more than that: it encompasses holy, right knowledge, right living, tradition, natural order of the universe and duty. Essentially, *dharma* refers to everything that can be classified as 'good' in the universe. It is the Law of Life.

Dharmayudh: The holy war.

Dhobi: Washerman.

Divyadrishti: Divine sight.

Dumru: A small hand-held hour-glass-shaped percussion instrument.

Egyptian women: Historians believe that ancient Egyptians, just like ancient Indians, treated their women with respect. The anti-women attitude attributed to Swuth and the assassins of Aten is fictional, but, like most societies, ancient Egyptians did also have some patriarchal segments in their society, which did, regrettably, have some appalling attitudes towards women.

Fire song: This is a song sung by Guna warriors to *agni* (fire). They also had songs dedicated to the other elements: *bhūmi* (earth), *jal* (water), *pavan* (air or wind), *vyom* or *shunya* or *akash* (ether or void or sky).

Fravashi: The guardian spirit mentioned in the *Avesta*, the sacred writings of the Zoroastrian religion. Although most researchers beileve there is no physical description of Fravashi, the language grammar of *Avesta* clearly shows it to be feminine. Considering the importance given to fire in ancient Hinduism and Zoroastrianism, I've assumed the Fravashi to be represented by fire. This is, of course, a fictional representation.

Ganesh–Kartik relationship: In Northern India, traditional myths hold Lord Kartik as older than Lord Ganesh; in large parts of Southern India, Lord Ganesh is considered the elder. In my story, Ganesh is older than Kartik, but what is the truth? Only Lord Shiva knows.

Guruji: Teacher; *-ji* is a term of respect, added to a name or title.

Gurukul: The family of the Guru or the family of the teacher. In ancient times, also used to denote school.

Har Har Mahadev: This is the rallying cry of Lord Shiva's devotees. I believe it means 'All of us are Mahadevs'.

Hariyupa: This city is presently known as Harappa.

Holi: Festival of colours.

Howdah: The carriage borne on top of an elephant.

Indra: The God of the Sky, believed to be the King of the Gods.

Jai Guru Vishwamitra: Glory to the teacher Vishwamitra.

Jai Guru Vashishta: Glory to the teacher Vashishta. Only two Suryavanshis, Lord Ram and Lord Lakshman, were privileged to have had both Guru Vashishta and Guru Vishwamitra as their gurus (teachers).

Jai Shri Brahma: Glory to Lord Brahma.

Jai Shri Ram: Glory to Lord Ram.

Janau: A ceremonial thread tied from the shoulders across the torso. It was one of the symbols of knowledge in ancient India, but later it was corrupted to become a caste symbol to denote those born as Brahmins, not those who'd acquired knowledge through their effort and deeds.

-ji: A suffix added to a name or title as a form of respect.

Kajal: Kohl or eyeliner.

Karma: Duty and deeds; also, the sum of a person's actions in this and previous births, considered to limit the options of future action and affect future fate.

Karmasaathi: Fellow traveller in *karma* or duty.

Kashi: The ancient name for modern Varanasi. Kashi means the city where the supreme light shines.

Kathak: A form of traditional Indian dance.

Kriyas: Actions.

Kulhads: Mud cups.

Maa: Mother.

Mandal: Sanskrit word meaning circle. *Mandals* are created in ancient Hindu and Buddhist tradition to make a sacred space and help focus the attention of the devotees.

Mahadev: *Maha* means Great and *Dev* means God: *Mahadev* means the Greatest God, or the God of Gods. I believe that there have been many 'destroyers of Evil', but a few of them were so great that they would be called 'Mahadev'. Amongst the *Mahadevs* were Lord Rudra and Lord Shiva.

Mahasagar: Great Ocean; *Hind Mahasagar* is the Indian Ocean.

Mahendra: Ancient Indian name meaning conqueror of the world.

Mahout: Human handler of elephants.

Manu's story: Those interested in finding out more about the historical validity of the South India origin theory of Manu should read Graham Hancock's ground-breaking book, *Underworld*.

Mausi: Mother's sister, literally translating as *maa si*, or 'like a mother'.

Maya: Illusion.

Mehragarh: Modern archaeologists believe that *Mehragarh* is the progenitor of the Indus Valley Civilisation. *Mehragarh* represents a sudden burst of civilised living, without any archaeological evidence of a gradual progression to that level.

Those who established *Mehragarh* were most likely either immigrants or refugees.

Meluha: The land of pure life. This is the land ruled by the Suryavanshi kings. It is the area that we in the modern world call the Indus Valley Civilisation. A note on the cities of Meluha (or, as we call it in modern times, the Indus Valley Civilisation): historians and researchers have consistently marvelled at their apparent fixation on water and hygiene. Historian M. Jansen used the term *wasserluxus*, or obsession with water, to describe their magnificent interest in the physical and symbolic aspects of water, a term Gregory Possehl builds upon in his brilliant book, *The Indus Civilisation – A Contemporary Perspective*. In *The Immortals of Meluha*, the obsession with water is explained as a result of the need to cleanse the toxic sweat and urine triggered by consuming the *Somras*. Historians have long marvelled at the level of sophisticated standardisation in the Indus Valley Civilisation, one example of which is the bricks, which all had similar proportions and specifications.

Meluhans: People of Meluha.

Mudras: Gestures.

Naga: Serpent people.

Namaste: An ancient Indian greeting. Spoken along with the hand gesture of open palms of both the hands joined together. Conjoin of three words: *Namah*, *Astu* and *Te*, meaning 'I bow to the godhood in you'. *Namaste* can be used as both hello and goodbye.

Nirvana: Enlightenment; freedom from the cycle of rebirths.

Oxygen/antioxidants theory: Modern research backs this theory. Interested readers can read the article 'Radical Proposal' by Kathryn Brown in *Scientific American*.

Panchavati: The land of the five banyan trees.

Pandit: Priest.

Paradaeza: An ancient Persian word which means 'the walled place of harmony'; the root of the English word, 'paradise'.

Pariha: The land of fairies, modern Persia/Iran. I believe Lord Rudra came from this land.

Parmatma: The ultimate soul or the sum of all souls.

Parsee immigration to India: Groups of Zoroastrian refugees immigrated to India, perhaps between the eighth and tenth century AD, to escape religious persecution. They landed in Gujarat, where the local ruler, Jadav Rana, gave them refuge.

Pashupatiastra: Literally, the weapon of the Lord of the Animals. The descriptions of the effects of the *Pashupatiastra* in Hindu scriptures are quite similar to that of nuclear weapons. In modern nuclear technology, weapons have been built primarily on the concept of nuclear fission. While fusion-boosted fission weapons have been invented, pure fusion weapons have not (as yet). Scientists believe that a pure fusion nuclear weapon has far less radioactive fallout and can theoretically serve as a more targeted weapon. In this trilogy, I have assumed that the *Pashupatiastra* is such a weapon.

Patallok: The underworld.

Pawan Dev: God of the Winds.

Pitratulya: The term for a man who is 'like a father'.

Prahar: The ancient Hindus divided the day into four slots of six hours each; the first prahar began at twelve midnight.

Prithvi: Earth.

Prakrati: Nature.

Puja: Prayer.

Puja Thali: Prayer tray.

Raj Dharma: Literally, the royal duties of a king or ruler. In ancient India, this term embodied pious and just administration of the king's royal duties.

Raj Guru: Royal Sage.

Rajat: Silver.

Rajya Sabha: The Royal Council.

Rakshabandhan: *Raksha* is protection; *Bandhan* is a thread or tie: in this ancient Indian festival a sister ties a sacred thread on her brother's wrist, seeking his protection.

Ram Chandra: The face of the moon: *Ram* is face; *Chandra* is moon.

Ram Rajya: The rule of Ram.

Rangbhoomi: Literally, the ground of colour. Stadia in ancient times where sports, performances and public functions would be staged.

Rangoli: Traditional colourful and geometric designs made with coloured powders or flowers as a sign of welcome.

Rishi: Man of knowledge.

Sankat Mochan: Literally, reliever from troubles. One of the names of Lord Hanuman.

Sangam: A confluence of two rivers.

Sanyas: When a person renounces all his worldly possessions and desires to retreat to remote locations and devote his time to the pursuit of God and spirituality. In ancient India, it was common for people to take *sanyas* at an old age, once they had completed all their life's duties.

Sapt Sindhu: The Land of the Seven Rivers – the Indus, Saraswati, Yamuna, Ganga, Sarayu, Brahmaputra and Narmada. This was the ancient name of North India.

Saptrishi: One of the 'Group of Seven Rishis'.

Saptrishi Uttradhikari: Successors of the Saptrishis.

Shakti Devi: Mother Goddess; also Goddess of Power and Energy.

Shamiana: Canopy.

Shloka: Couplet.

Shudhikaran: The purification ceremony.

Sindhu: The first river.

Somras: Drink of the gods.

Sundarban: Beautiful forest – *sundar* means beautiful; *ban* is a forest.

Svarna: Gold.

Swadweep: The Island of the individual. This is the land ruled by the Chandravanshi kings.

Swadweepans: People of Swadweep.

Swaha: Legend has it that Lord Agni's wife was named Swaha, and it pleases Lord Agni, the God of Fire, if a disciple takes his wife's name while worshipping the sacred fire. Another interpretation of Swaha is that it means 'offering of self'.

Tamra: Bronze.

Thali: Plate.

Varjish graha: The exercise hall.

Varun: God of the Water and the Seas.

Vijayibhav: May you be victorious.

Vikarma: Carrier of bad fate.

Vishnu: The protector of the world and propagator of Good. I believe that it is an ancient Hindu title for the greatest of leaders who would be remembered as the mightiest of gods.

Vishwanath: Literally, the Lord of the World. Usually refers to Lord Shiva, also known as Lord Rudra in his angry avatar. I believe Lord Rudra was a different individual from Lord Shiva. In this trilogy, I have used the term *Vishwanath* to refer to Lord Rudra.

Yagna: Sacrificial fire ceremony.

ACKNOWLEDGEMENTS

I never imagined I would become an author. The life I live now – a life spent in pursuits such as writing, praying, reading, debating and travelling – actually feels surreal at times. There are many who have made this dream possible and I'd like to thank them.

Lord Shiva, my God, for bringing me back to a spiritual life. It is the biggest high possible.

Neel, my son, a rejuvenating elixir who regularly came and asked me while I was obsessively writing this book, '*Dad, aapka ho gaya kya?*' (Dad, have you finished?)

Preeti, my wife; Bhavna, my sister; Himanshu, my brother-in-law; Anish and Ashish, my brothers; Donetta, my sister-in-law. They have worked so closely with me that many times I feel this isn't just my book but a joint project which happens to have my name on it.

The rest of my family: Usha, Vinay, Meeta, Shernaz, Smita, Anuj and Ruta, for always being there for me.

Jo Fletcher, my editor in the UK, and her fantastic team at Quercus for their commitment to my books and for their astonishing respect and understanding for another culture.

Sharvani Pandit, my editor in India. She has battled severe health troubles without asking for any sympathy, and despite the trying times she has gone through, she has helped me fulfil my *karma*. I'm lucky to have her.

Rashmi Pusalkar, the designer of this book's cover. She's been a partner from the first book and, in my humble opinion, she's one of the best book-cover designers in Indian publishing.

Anuj Bahri, my agent, a typically large-hearted, boisterous Punjabi, brought to me by Fate to help me achieve my dreams.

Sangram Surve, Shalini Iyer and the team at Think Why Not, the advertising and digital marketing agency for the book. I have worked with many advertising agencies in my career, including some of the biggest multinationals, and Think Why Not ranks right up there amongst the best.

Chandan Kowli, the photographer for the cover, did a brilliant job, as always. Also: Atul Pargaonkar, for fabricating the bow and arrow; Vinay Salunkhe, for the make-up; Ketan Karande, the model; Japheth Bautista, for the concept art for the background; the Little Red Zombies team and Shing Lei Chua, for support on 3D elements and scene set-up; Sagar Pusalkar and team, for the post-processing work on the images; and Julien Dubois, for coordinating production. I hope you like the cover they've created. I love it!

Omendu Prakash, Biju Gopal and Swapnil Patil, for the photograph of me printed in this book. Their composition was exceptional; the model, regrettably, left a lot to be desired!

Chandramauli Upadhyay, Shakuntala Upadhyay and Ved-shree Upadhyay from Benaras; Santanu Ghoshroy and Shweta Basu Ghoshroy from Singapore, for their hospitality while I wrote this book.

Mohan Vijayan, a friend whose advice on media matters is something I always treasure.

Dr Ramiyar Karanjia, for his immense help in understanding the philosophies of Zoroastrianism.

And last, but certainly not least, you, the reader. Thank you from the depths of my being for the support you've given the first two books of *The Shiva Trilogy*. I hope in return I can give you a sense of completion with this concluding book.

Amish Tripathi,
India, 2014